W9-BAG-411

Behind the Curve

Behind the Curve

Steven Chance

Copyright © 2005 by Steven Chance.

Library of Congress Number:		2004098088
ISBN:	Hardcover	1-4134-6995-7
	Softcover	1-4134-6994-9

All rights reserved. No part of this book may be reproduced or transmitted in any form or by any means, electronic or mechanical, including photocopying, recording, or by any information storage and retrieval system, without permission in writing from the copyright owner.

This is a work of fiction. Names, characters, places and incidents either are the product of the author's imagination or are used fictitiously, and any resemblance to any actual persons, living or dead, events, or locales is entirely coincidental.

This book was printed in the United States of America.

To order additional copies of this book, contact:
Xlibris Corporation
1-888-795-4274
www.Xlibris.com
Orders@Xlibris.com

26705

Acknowledgments

I would like to thank my wife, Colleen, for providing the inspiration for this book, and my friends Sally Bilodeau, for giving me the impetus to publish it, and Paula Morgan for the organizational skills to help me finish the job.

Remembering

The worst fear of a sailor who goes offshore is the fear of going overboard. You lose your grip on the boat and on life itself at the same terrible moment. It begins with the terrible shock of that cold water closing over your head. And then the struggle to the surface just in time to see the transom of your boat passing you by and slipping slowly and inexorably out of your reach. I often dream about these terrible moments now. In my dreams, I always go overboard at night. I can see the stern light of a boat shining brightly, high above my head as I regain the surface. Shining brightly for a brief moment, a beacon of safety and hope in the dark, but then, I lose sight of it as I go down into the trough of a wave. Then, there it is again, as I am helplessly carried to the next crest, but smaller now and less bright. In my dream, I can't cry out for some reason. I can only watch as the stern light grows smaller and dimmer, and the intervals of obscurity become longer and longer. Then it is gone, and I am truly alone in the water, drifting. At the top of each crest, I am battered by the spray that the wind is literally ripping off the top of each wave. In the troughs, I can hear the wind screaming eerily high above my head, while I am enveloped by the calm created by the shelter of the wave that is about to lift me again to the maelstrom of the next crest.

I often wonder if my dream resembles how it really was for Norman Hawkins. I wonder if he cried out. I expect not. He knew there would be no point to it. I later learned a great deal about how it was for Norman on the night he went overboard. I learned a lot of the facts, and my speculations filled in the gaps of people's remembrances.

Remembrances that were, of course, colored by the need that everyone has to rationalize their own actions and, for several, the need to lie outright about what happened that night. Finally, there is my imagination that now fills in the ultimate gaps of what Norman was thinking and feeling as he floated alone in the sea that night.

Norman Hawkins was a man whom I knew only slightly. I had never really talked to him until the afternoon of the day that he set out on his last sea voyage. We might have been friends, but there wasn't time enough for that. We had our fateful conversation, and then he was gone. I wonder if he had a premonition of his fate. I imagine him at the wheel of that magnificent boat of his, driving it south into the confused seas of a near gale, with the wind driving the spray over the bow and back into his face. I can feel his satisfaction at controlling the power of a sixty-foot sloop on a reach driving through the waves. In the dark, when the eyes are useless, the feel of the boat is transmitted from the straining sails to the driving hull and rudder right up through the wheel and into your very hands. It can make you feel that you and the boat are the same being. For Norman, it must have seemed that way, with his son finally safe and his plans to regain control of his company finally coming together. He must have thought he had finally gotten ahead of the curve, but it was only an illusion.

It would have started with the shock of the mast going over the side followed by the gut-wrenching labor of freeing the debris to save the boat as she lay helplessly, wallowing in the threatening rollers. Then his relief at the unexpected rescue followed swiftly by betrayal. I never found out exactly how he went into the water. Was it an unexpected push? Did they throw him in bodily? Did he plead for his life? I don't know. And I never dream about that part of it. I dream about the sudden shock as the water closes over his head. He tries to breathe but inhales only bitter salt water. As he surfaces, his only universe is the water around him and that white, bright stern light. A light that might signify rescue, but he knows not for him. So he doesn't cry out, there is no point to it. He just watches the light grow slowly smaller until it is gone, and then he is left in the darkness to make his peace with himself and maybe his God. He couldn't have lasted very long in that cold water, five minutes or maybe ten, struggling to stay afloat and getting weaker and weaker. Moments before, he had been on top of the world and back in control of his own destiny. But now he is getting tired. His arms are like leaden things. The water is slopping into his mouth as he tries to draw a breath. And finally, he just lets go. He lets himself go into the blackness that awaits him. But I don't know any of this for sure. I cannot follow him down into death even in my imagination or my dreams.

Chapter I

The wind beat against the windows of my office as a late October nor'easter roared into its third day. I looked out at the marina across the street and watched the few fishing boats that were still in their slips rolling ceaselessly in the wind. A gust rattled the window again and then increased to a shriek. I shivered involuntarily, wondering how badly the storm was cutting the beach. Already in October it seemed dangerously narrow, and the wind, that constant wind that seemed to blow in North Beach from October right on through to May or June, had barely begun its annual winter assault. It was late on a Friday afternoon. There were some things I should have been doing, but not much that I was interested in starting on before I went home for the weekend. There is not much that happens in a Jersey shore town from September until the following spring.

As I watched the rain, I wondered again why I was in North Beach at all. I felt like a refugee, a refugee from a bad marriage, a refugee from a comfortable living at a Philadelphia corporate law firm, maybe a refugee from life. And like a refugee, I had not yet assimilated where I had landed. Sure I had been coming to North Beach all my life in the summers. But my decision, taken just two months before, to stay in North Beach on a permanent basis did not yet seem real to me, or, I suspected, the actual permanent residents of the town. At the moment with the wind beating against my window, I was wondering if I had made the right decision. I had spent the first month in town just doing the networking that was necessary for a new lawyer in the County. All that was pretty new to me. When I had started out as an associate at my old firm, I had gotten ahead by staying in my office and doing the work assigned to me. Someone else made the rain, and it had trickled down predictably on my head. No one had expected me to bring in new business. Right now I was wondering whether I had made the right decision. Maybe no decision would have been the right one. Dave Stockard, my old friend and new law partner, had promised me that I wouldn't have to pull my own weight as far as my own clients were concerned for a year. Meanwhile, he had enough overflow business, and I would have some time for his other partner, Linda Stevens, to break me in on the litigation side. Now I was realizing that, even with my year's grace period, for the long term, I would have to make my own way. It didn't help that Dave had predicted that I would be having just these feelings. So it was a cold, rainy day in October, and I was thinking I was never going to be able to pull it off.

I thought that I might as well go home as wait by a phone that was not going to ring. But there was nothing for me to go home for either. Another weekend with nothing planned. I was sitting in my chair weighing two equally unpalatable options when Donna, our office manager, stuck her head into my office.

"Hey Pete. There's someone here to see you."

"Who is it?"

"Norman Hawkins."

I looked up in surprise. "Norman Hawkins?" I repeated stupidly.

"That's what I said."

"Ahhh, OK, I'll be right out."

All thoughts of self-pity at the prospect of another empty weekend promptly vanished. Norman Hawkins was a bit of a mystery man around town. He had bought the old Beekman place on the beach about ten years before, torn it down and put up in its place what the residents called the Wedding Cake. I never knew if the name derived from its resemblance to Victor Emmanuel's palace in Rome. At least Victor had been trying to imitate the majesty of what had gone before. Norman Hawkins had raised a storm of controversy when he had constructed his palace. When it was built, it stood a lonely sentinel among the shingled cottages that were its neighbors up and down the beach. Now a fair number of those old cottages had also gone under the bulldozer's blade as rich newcomers, forced to pay over a million dollars for a spot on the ocean, wanted a modern house from which to watch the waves hit the beach. But none of these matched the monument to bad taste that Norman had erected.

As for Norman himself, he had remained mostly aloof in his palace. He had joined the North Beach Yacht Club. After all, the Club was about the only center for social activities in the town, especially for the summer folk. But after the social mating dance of joining, a rather simple process, he never seemed to participate in any of the Club's activities. It was not because of any disdain for boats. His own boat had been tied up for the last month at Dalton's Pier, the marina that was my view when I looked out the window of my office. I turned in my chair to look at her now. "Far Cry," a sixty-foot blue sloop, was shoehorned in at the end of the dock, a little apart from the frowzy fishing boats, a swan among the seagulls. Someone was just getting aboard her, his yellow foul weather gear a splotch of color against the white deckhouse. The figure climbed into the cockpit and disappeared down below.

What could Norman Hawkins want with me? I wondered as I stared out at his boat, rocking restlessly in the confines of Rick Dalton's largest slip. I had only met Norman a handful of times, and most of them in the first few years of his summer residence in the town. I could not remember seeing him at all for over a year. Only the occasional car entering the gates that guarded the front of his beach palace and the infrequent visits of "Far Cry."

So, why was I hesitating about going out to bring him back to my office? Perhaps it was some foreboding about what was to come. No, it couldn't have been that. I don't believe in such things. It must have been my lethargy on a wet Friday afternoon. Whatever it was, I shook it off, rose and went out to meet my visitor. I found him in our reception area staring out the front window in the direction of Cranberry Inlet. From where he stood, I knew he could see past the marina and the inlet bridge to the open sea. I had the impression that he wished he was out there in this storm. As if both he and his boat, pulling at her dock lines across the street, longed to be gone to test themselves against some force that they understood. I shook off this feeling and strode across the room holding out my hand.

"Norman," I said. "It's been a long time."

He turned away from the window to take my hand. He looked older and thinner than I remembered. Perhaps it was just the too large overcoat that made him seem smaller. He took my hand in a strong grip and fixed me with the same ice-blue stare that I remembered.

"Peter," he said. "It's good of you to see me without an appointment."

I laughed as I beckoned him back to my office.

"There's not much need for an appointment at this time of year."

He did not say anything while I led him back to my office and indicated the couch across from my desk. I took the chair in front of my desk where I could see him and still look out the window at the driving rain. For a moment neither of us said anything. It was as if he didn't know where to start, a situation that I guessed was unusual for him. I started off before the silence could go on too long.

"I see you've had 'Far Cry' here for almost a month. Are you going to take her south soon?"

He nodded as if thankful for the diversion. "Yes. She'll be on her way to Florida before too long, and then the Bahamas."

"Why wait until the end of October? It'll be a mite cold starting out, don't you think?"

He shrugged. "Maybe. I usually have her on the Chesapeake until the first of November, so I'm not really behind my normal schedule."

He lapsed into silence again. He got up, walked to the window and looked out. At what? I wondered. At the rain? At his boat? I couldn't tell. He turned from the window and returned to his seat on the couch.

"I really came to see Dave," he said.

I deflated a little. "I guess Donna told you. Dave's on vacation for two weeks."

"Yes, she did."

I waited. If he wanted to wait for Dave, I was not going to suggest it.

"I didn't know you worked with Dave."

"I just started about two months ago."

"What's your background? You were with some big firm in Philadelphia, weren't you?"

I was surprised he remembered. I gave him my quick resume. Penn Law School. Joined Davis & Piersall after graduation. Corporate, financial and securities practice. Some mergers and acquisitions. Associate and then partner. My selling speech.

He nodded as if he had heard it before. "What made you leave a partnership with a well-known firm like that?"

"Personal reasons. I needed a change. The pay's not as good here as in the big city, but my expenses are considerably less."

He nodded again as if he understood. It seemed like he came to a decision.

"Pete, I need some help. And as it happens you appear to be just what I need."

My spirits rose again. I spread out my hands. "That's what I'm here for."

"I need you to help me get back my son."

I looked at him in surprise. "Are you involved in a custody battle?"

He shook his head and smiled bitterly. "No, it's nothing like that. The custody battles are long lost."

"Well, maybe you should start at the beginning."

He nodded. "You're right. But, it's hard to know where the beginning is."

"Start with your son. Which one are you talking about? Jerry?"

"No, Norman, Jr. The youngest one." He paused. "He's twenty-five. He's my son from my second marriage. You remember Melanie?"

I shook my head.

"No, of course not. Melanie died before I ever came to North Beach. Norman must have been ten. Jane and Jerry were in their twenties. Their mother got custody of them in the divorce battle. That's what the courts did then. Give the kids to their mother. It didn't matter that she didn't give a damn about them and only wanted them to spite me." He sighed. "I didn't fight for them either. I was too busy building my business to have time for anything else. I just let them go. I hardly ever saw them for a couple of years. And when I started to make an effort, something had changed. It was like they weren't the same."

I nodded. I wondered where he was going with all this.

"But I worked at it and, in the end, I was able to re-establish a relationship with Jane. That never really happened with Jerry. He and I never understood each other. Of course, their mother would sabotage me every step of the way. Sometimes it seemed like it was one step forward and two steps back. But I was persistent. Toward the end, I think I was building the basis . . . ." He stopped and seemed to drift back into his own thoughts.

"Toward the end?" I prompted.

He started as if he had come back from a long distance away.

"I'm sorry. I'm here to talk about Norman. There was never a custody battle over him. But he grew up without a mother. And most of the time without a father as well. Lord knows my wife's no kind of a mother, and I was on the road most of the time. He went through his adolescent years pretty much alone. But, in the end, I think I would have reached him too except for that honey trap."

"Honey trap?"

He sighed. "He got married. A little gold-digger from South Philadelphia."

"What? Not our kind?" I asked. I guess he heard the sarcasm in my voice because he looked up sharply.

"You think I don't like her because I made it to the Main Line, and she grew up in a South Philadelphia neighborhood?" he asked. His eyes narrowed, and they seemed to bore into my own.

I shrugged. "Why don't you like her?" I asked neutrally.

He sat back on the couch. "I don't like her because she's a clone of my third and present wife. Absolutely gorgeous, and not a thought in her head except money, money, money and all the things money will buy. And she had me completely paralyzed. I would do whatever she wanted, when ever she wanted."

I thought back. "Lorraine?" I asked. "Isn't that her name?"

"That's the one. You've met her haven't you?"

I remembered a very blonde, very beautiful woman at some party about six or seven years before.

"Yes, I think I have. I don't remember if I spoke with her much or not."

"That's Lorraine. Memorable visually and physically, but not intellectually. Anyway, when Norman brought Mary home, it seemed like an exact reenactment of my own past with Lorraine."

"But you and Lorraine are still married, aren't you?"

"Not for long, I hope. It took me five years before I could get out from under her spell, and it's been five more years trying to be rid of her. But," he shrugged. "I think the property settlement is wired, and the final decree should be along any time now."

"And you thought you could keep your son from making the same mistake?"

"Of course I did. Why should he make the same mistakes that I did? But you can't tell your kids anything. I knew that, but I couldn't help myself. The upshot was, we had a big blow-up, they ran off and got married anyway, and Norman wouldn't have anything to do with me after that."

"I'm not sure I see how I can help you, Norman. If they're both adults and married . . . ."

He waved his hand. "I'm not done yet. It turns out that little Mary didn't just have money on her mind. When Norman met her she was organizing for Robert Reynaud."

"Reynaud?"

"Yeah. You know him?"

"Well, I know of him. His little crusade started in New Jersey didn't it?"

"That's right. Tell me what you know about him."

"Not much. He's the founder of "Return to the Roots," which, I gather, is sort of a nativist, right-wing return to our Aryan purity sort of thing. Almost a cross between a cult and a political organization."

"That's about it. The RTTR's a cult with political aspirations. Norman started going to meetings about a year ago. That's where he met little Mary. Then he went away on one of their retreats. The last straw was when I found he was giving substantial sums of money to the organization."

"Was it his money?"

"Yeah, I know. He's an adult, and it was his money to do with as he wished. The more fool I for giving it to him in the first place."

"So how can I help you, Norman?"

"I want you to represent me."

I shook my head. "I'd be glad to do that Norman, but I don't see any claim. You want me to sue Robert Reynaud to get your son back?"

"Ah, not exactly. But before we get into that, I want to make clear that I have retained you."

"Well, to do that I have to know what it is you want me to do, and we have to work out a fee arrangement."

"Of course," he said, and he got out a pen and a checkbook and started to write out a check. I was about to interrupt him with an objection, but I held my tongue. Never interrupt a client, or a potential client, when he is writing out a check. He finished and passed the check across to me. It was for twenty-five thousand dollars. For a moment I was speechless, staring at the check. I looked up at Norman's blue eyes. For the first time the blue was a little less icy and there even appeared to be a little twinkle.

"Have I got your attention, counselor?"

"Ahh," I stammered. "Yes, I think you do. This is too much."

He put up his hand. "Never say that. And you don't know what I want you to do."

Now it was my turn to narrow my eyes and lean forward. "That's true," I said. "What do you want me to do? Kidnap Norman?"

"No." He smiled. "I want you to defend me from the charge of kidnapping him."

"You're going to kidnap Norman? You have to realize . . . ."

He stopped me by raising his hand again. "I know counselor. Your ethical obligations don't permit you to participate in any illegal activities."

"That's right, and furthermore . . . ."

"Would you let me finish?" He interrupted. "I didn't say I was going to kidnap Norman. I'm not. But I might be put into a situation where Robert Reynaud's organization accuses me of having kidnapped him. Reynaud might even convince one of his pocket politicians to pursue the matter."

"Pocket politicians? Who do . . . ?"

"That's not important now." He shook his head impatiently.

I looked at the check again. "Why me? I'm not a criminal lawyer. I'm not even a litigator. You must have a bunch of lawyers at that big Philadelphia firm that does your legal work."

"Sure I do. And good lawyers they are. But I have a feeling that the action is going to be here in New Jersey. And I have my reasons why I don't want to use them for this. Are you saying that you don't want my business?"

"Of course we're interested in your business."

"Well, there you are." He got up as if to leave. I got up as well.

"That's it?" I asked.

"That's all for now."

I turned to look out the window at his big blue sloop. "Where are you going to do the de-programming? On 'Far Cry'?"

"Who said anything about de-programming?" He said with a little smile. "Norman and I are just going to take a little sail together. Taking the boat south like I do every year."

"Yeah, right," I said.

He stood up. "You're right about the money, Pete. It is too much. But I'm not sure what is going to happen in the next few days. Reynaud's group is a rough bunch, and I'm not sure whom I can trust any more. You're my ace in the hole. If it all goes sour, I'm counting on you to have something more than a moral obligation to ferret out the facts." He looked straight at me. "Be my representative if something happens to me."

I felt a cold knot growing in my stomach.

"That sounds pretty serious."

He smiled and the twinkle was back in his eyes.

"Not to worry. It's all going to turn out just fine." He turned and walked towards the door. "I'll keep in touch, counselor."

And with that he was gone. I went to the window and watched him cross the street to the boat hunched against the rain and wind. His trench coat looked incongruous as he climbed over the rail and stepped into the cockpit. He stood there a moment, next to the wheel, looking out the inlet to the open sea.

"Anything I can do for you this afternoon, Pete?"

I started. It was Donna. Clearly she wanted an update on why Norman Hawkins had been calling. She would have to remain curious for the moment.

"I guess not, Donna. Is Linda around?" Linda Stevens was my other new partner at Stockard & Stevens. Dave Stockard is the first part of the masthead. Up to a month ago, he handled the corporate nuts and bolts of the operation. If there's a client who needs someone familiar with the inside of a courtroom, that's Linda.

"No. She's up in Newark on the Johnson deposition."

"OK. Thanks, Donna. I don't think I'll have anything else today."

She gave me an annoyed look and retreated from the room closing the door a little too loudly. I turned back to the window. Hawkins was still standing there in the cockpit. He must have been soaked by that time. Then it seemed like someone spoke to him from the companionway. He turned his head to reply and disappeared down below. The wind rattled my window again, and I shivered involuntarily.

* * *

I left the office shortly after that. There was no use trying to get to any of the work in my in-basket. My thoughts were too full of the meeting with Hawkins, and the questions I should have asked but had not. Normally, I walk to work. North Beach is a small enough place. There's about two miles of it on one of the barrier islands that forms Barnegat Bay in New Jersey right at the Cranberry Inlet. The town and my office sit on the south side of the inlet right by the inlet bridge. There's not much in the town itself. Dalton's Pier is just west of the bridge right where the inlet starts to open up into the bay. Across the street from the marina are the combined firehouse, police station and town hall and a couple of buildings housing a grocery/deli and the law offices of Stockard & Stevens. The beach cottages stretch south from the inlet. Norman Hawkins' wedding cake is about a mile down the beach. Around the bay side is the North Beach Yacht Club. My new house is about a half-mile south of the Club. It's a little bit of a walk, so when the Weather Channel predicts rain, I drive. Today, I hadn't needed the Weather Channel. I ran for my car, and put Norman Hawkins out of my mind.

At least, I did for a while. But after dinner I started to think about Norman again. I couldn't concentrate to read, and I was too restless to settle down to the lassitude of watching television. I pulled on my raingear, ran out in the rain to my car and headed for the Dunes. The

Dunes is the only bar in town. It's located in the basement of the North Beach Inn, a monstrosity right on the inlet at the beach. I pulled into the parking lot and made a dash for the door. Inside it was dark and warm. I found a place at the end of the bar. The place was almost empty. Two fishermen were nursing beers at the bar and a foursome was in one of the back booths. I ordered a beer and studied the collection of beer bottles that decorated the back of the bar. I was on my second beer and making no progress on the Norman Hawkins puzzle when someone sat down on the bar stool next to me.

"Peter. Drinking alone on a Friday night?"

I turned to see Dave Stockard's daughter, Sarah. In her mid-twenties and working for some bank in Philadelphia. I knew her from my earlier life in North Beach when I had been a sailing instructor at the Yacht Club, and she had been a brat in the program.

"Sarah. Buy you a drink?"

She indicated the booth in the back. "I'm with Freddie."

I turned to look. Her boyfriend, Fred Wooding, was a local sailmaker. He saw me and waved. I waved back. "And the Briggses I see," I said.

She made a face. "Yeah. Fred's trying to sell them on a new mainsail. It's pretty deadly."

"So stay and talk to me for a moment." I waved to the bartender to get her a drink. I got her talking about her job persuading her to stay for a moment, until I got to what I really wanted to say.

"Sarah, did you know Norman Hawkins, Jr.?"

"Harry? Sure. What's up with Harry?"

"Harry? That's his name?"

"Well, he hated the name Norman. He had pretensions that we ought to call him Hawk. It didn't take long for us to corrupt that to Hack. Finally we all settled in on Harry."

"How'd you know him?"

"The sailing program at the Club."

"You're kidding. I don't think I remember him at all."

"That's possible. He may not have been there when you were an instructor. If you were I think you only overlapped with him for one year. And he was pretty unmemorable, especially that first year."

"I'm just drawing a blank."

"He was actually in the program for a couple of years. He was never very good. I guess his balance was a little off, I don't know. He never did get the hang of going downwind in a Laser." She laughed. "He had some spectacular wipe-outs when it was windy."

"What kind of guy was he?"

"Loner. Never talked too much. Especially he didn't talk to girls. I think he went to one of those all-boys private schools. You know. Where they teach you girls are a different species of being."

"So you didn't know him very well."

"Not then. Then he quit the program, and no one saw him for a couple of years. He reappeared at about age sixteen or seventeen."

"I don't remember him being around the Club then."

"No, he never hung out at the Club. It was at his house. It was party time every weekend."

"Really? His parents didn't mind?"

She laughed. "Who ever saw the parents? Mr. Hawkins was never there. Mrs. Hawkins always seemed to be on a different planet. I think she was drunk half the time, if not all the time."

"So Harry gave a lot of parties?"

"Sort of. They weren't really parties. We all just went there. There was beer on tap in the basement and a pool table and about fifteen thousand records and tapes. A big home entertainment center, TV, tape player, you name it."

"So you never saw his father?"

"I wouldn't say never. I do remember one night Harry and his father got into a fight."

"What happened?"

"Not much that I saw. We were sitting around listening to music. Some of the guys were drinking beer. Harry's father came in and started yelling at him about something."

"Did Harry yell back?"

"No, he just took it for awhile and then walked out."

"What happened then?"

"Not much. We all split. The next night it was as though it had never happened. Same party. No sign of the old man."

"Did Harry have any particular friends?"

"Not really. Like I said, he was pretty much a loner."

"Did he date?"

She laughed. "None of us dated in those days. We just went around together."

"How about Harry? Have you seen him recently."

"As a matter of fact, yes. I saw him on the beach this summer with his new wife. What a knock-out."

"Do you know where he is now?"

"Yeah, I think he's living at the beach house. His mother's living there too, although I guess it isn't his real mother."

"He's living at the Wedding Cake?"

"Yeah, the step-mother's got the south end of the house, and Harry and his wife the north end. I doubt they ever meet in the middle."

Sarah and I chatted for another couple of minutes and then she headed back to her table. I sat and thought for a time as the wind continued to gust against the windows of the bar. I could begin to guess why Norman thought he would need a local lawyer. If he was going to take his son from North Beach, the investigation would begin here and any charges would be brought in the County.

So, it came to the point that I had to order another drink or go home. Neither option sounded really enticing, but I certainly didn't need another drink. I went outside and, for some reason I walked around to the front of the Inn to look at the inlet. The rain had let up, but the wind was still blowing a gale. I couldn't see much except the lights on the bridge and the blinking green light of the sea buoy. The sound of the waves breaking on the rock jetty was overwhelming. Usually, when I stand on that spot looking out at sea, it is with some longing to be in a boat and heading out. To be going somewhere, anywhere. But not on that night. On that night I was glad to be going home to my warm bed. The rain started to spit again, and I ran for my car. I was home and shedding my coat when the phone started ringing. I picked it up.

"Hello."

"Hello. Is this Peter Gordon?"

"Yes."

"My name is Jane Turner. Jane Hawkins Turner actually. My father is Norman Hawkins."

"Yes. How may I help you, Mrs. Turner?"

"I'm not sure. Did you speak with my father today?"

"Ahh . . . . Yes, as a matter of fact, I did. Why do you ask?"

"My father called me today. He was in this strange, euphoric mood. But at the same time he said some odd things."

"What kind of things?"

"Like he was saying good-bye, but didn't really know how. He gave me your name in case something happened to him. At least, that's what he said."

"Did he tell you that he thought something might happen to him?"

"No. Quite the contrary. For most of the phone call he was talking about getting control of the company back and putting the family together again. Do you know what he was talking about?"

"Not really, no."

"It must be connected to the reason he came to see you. What was it about?"

"I'm afraid I'm not at liberty to talk about that." I sounded stuffy even to myself.

"What do you mean, 'not at liberty'? I'm his daughter."

"I'm sure you are. But I can't even be sure of that, can I? And even if I was, I couldn't tell you what we talked about without his OK."

"That's ridiculous." She sounded angry.

"I'm sorry, Mrs. Turner. If you want to find out what your father has on his mind, you'll have to ask him."

"That's just it. I can't track him down anywhere."

"I'm sure he'll turn up," I said as reassuringly as I could. I was thinking that I should end the conversation, but for some reason I didn't want to do that.

"I can tell you we didn't talk about the company."

"You didn't?" she asked skeptically.

"No, but we did have a conversation about your brother."

"Jerry?"

"No. Norman, Jr."

"Oh, you mean Harry."

"You don't sound very close to Harry." I said.

"Nobody's close to Harry. Look, Mr. Gordon. You can't really believe I'm not who I say I am. Would you please tell me what my father is up to? I'm worried about him."

"I'm sorry, Mrs. Turner. I really don't know what he's up to."

"Well tell me why, in God's name, he came to see you?"

I wasn't sure of that myself, but I wasn't about to tell that to a voice on the telephone.

"I'm sorry. You'll have to get that from him."

"Well, thank you very much," she said, angry again. And she hung up the phone.

I looked at the receiver in my hand for a moment and then I hung it up. I opened the refrigerator door to pull out a beer. I sat in the living room facing the bay and imagined the wind and waves on the water as I sipped from the glass. The storm should have blown itself out by now, but the wind seemed as strong as ever. I only got half way through my beer. Somehow it didn't taste very good. I went up to bed.

Chapter II

The next morning the phone rang at about six o'clock. It was still an hour before sunrise. I fumbled for the receiver.

"Hello?"

"Pete, it's Fred."

I groaned. Freddie Wooding. Sarah's boyfriend from the night before.

"Isn't it a bit early?" I asked. "Didn't you close down the Dunes last night?"

"Sure, but I sold a mainsail so life is good. Let's go fishing."

"Not today. The weather's lousy."

"The weather's great. The front finally came through and cleared out all that crap. It's going to be clear and sunny."

"Yes, and cold and rough."

"Come on. What else are you going to be doing?"

I groaned again. "All right. Be over here by seven."

At seven, he knocked at the front door, and I let him in. What I call the front door faces the street, but the house really faces Barnegat Bay. On the southwest corner is my kitchen. The kitchen has a counter separating it from a living room, which has sliding glass door opening onto a deck that looks out over the bay. There's a little beach and a boat dock. At the dock is a center console Grady-White, "Rebound." Fred sat down on one of the living room chairs, and I handed him a cup of coffee.

"Where's Sarah," I asked. "Doesn't she want to go fishing too?"

He grinned. "Not likely."

He started to tell me about the sail-making business in general, and the Briggs' new mainsail in particular, as I got my foul weather gear together. He was still talking as we walked out the door and down to the dock. I couldn't figure out how someone could be so cheerful so early in the morning. He had been right about the weather. The wind had shifted around to the northwest and was blowing briskly. The sun was up, the sky was blue, and there was more than a hint of winter in the air. The trees on the west side of the bay were well into their autumn colors. I jumped in the boat and, after a few cranks, she started up with a roar. Fred got the lines; I backed away from the dock and turned north towards the inlet. There were no boats on the bay. It was a little late in the season and early in the day. We passed the North Beach Yacht Club, and it already looked like it was closed for the winter. I advanced the throttle, and we cruised up to the town itself. Dalton's Pier slipped by on my right as I slowed down for the inlet bridge. I looked back at the marina. Something was different about it. Then I realized. There was no mast dominating the scene. "Far Cry" was gone. I turned the boat suddenly and headed back to take a closer look. At what, I'm not sure. If the boat was gone, it was gone.

"What's wrong, Pete?" Fred was asking me. "Where are we going?"

"Just going to check on something."

Just then Rick Dalton came out of one of the sheds.

"Hey, Rick," I called as I pulled into one of the empty slips. He waved and walked over, taking a line from Fred.

"Morning, Pete," he said. "Going fishing?"

"Yeah. Say, what happened to that big sloop that was on the end of the dock until yesterday?"

"You mean 'Far Cry'? I guess she left some time during the night."

"In the middle of that Nor'easter? Isn't that kind of odd?"

He shrugged. "Mr. Hawkins told me yesterday afternoon he wanted to get an early start."

"Do you know where he was going?"

He grinned. "South. Just where I'd be going if I had a boat like that."

"But you don't know exactly where?"

He shrugged. "No. Mr. Hawkins doesn't tell me what his plans are."

"Who did he have with him?"

"Well, I guess he had his captain, Louie."

"Anyone else?"

"I don't know, I didn't see him go. Lots of times he and Louie just take it themselves."

"Do they usually start out in the middle of a storm?"

"No, not usually."

"OK. Thanks Rick." Rick threw the line to Fred, and I nosed the boat out into the current again.

"What was that all about?" asked Peter.

"Oh nothing much. Hawkins came to see me yesterday. He told me he was taking the boat south, but I'm a little surprised that he left so soon."

"Norman Hawkins came to see you? What about?"

"Nothing very interesting," I lied.

By this time we were through the bridge and breasting the long rollers that were marching in the inlet. Fred took shelter behind the console as the spray started to blow over the bow. The leftover waves on the ocean were still quite impressive, and it took some time to get to our fishing ground. All the time I kept looking to the south as if there was the possibility that I could still catch a glimpse of "Far Cry" on her way.

* * *

The next morning I awakened to another crisp fall day. I overslept a little, but I told myself that it was a Sunday. I had had trouble getting to sleep the night before. I kept thinking about Norman and the de-programming effort that I suspected was underway. "Far Cry" had to be a couple of hundred miles to the south this time. But there was nothing for me to do but to wait and see if Norman got in touch with me when he got in. Normally on a Sunday morning I walk to the deli to get my paper, but it was a little cold so I took the car. And so it was that, as I reached the stop light on Ocean Avenue, I saw a police car with its flashing lights pulling into Skelly Avenue. Skelly is one of the cross streets in North Beach that dead-ends on the ocean. On an impulse I turned south on Ocean Avenue instead of north and followed the police car.

There was another police car already there with its red and blue lights flashing. I pulled up behind the second car just as Rich Skowronski was getting out. Rich is the police chief of North Beach. I had known him since I had been a kid here. He had grown up in one of the towns further down the beach and spent his teen-age years working at Dalton's before going off to the Navy. He's about fifty, shorter than I am and heavy-set with dark hair and eyes. I saw he was dressed in blue jeans and a flannel shirt. Obviously, he had been called out directly from home.

"Well, Pete," he said. "Isn't it a little early for ambulance chasing?"

"I don't see any ambulances," I replied.

"It'll be along."

"Someone hurt?"

"They're not hurt anymore. Old Mrs. Reznick over there," he pointed to the first house on the beach just north of Skelly, "reported something in the surf. Stark came to investigate, and he tells me it's a stiff."

A cold foreboding settled in my stomach at this news. I looked up at the Reznick house, and there was Mrs. Reznick out on the front screen porch peering over the dune at us. I looked back at her and then at the beach. The dune blocked any view of the beach from the street.

"Do you know who it is?"

"I just got here, didn't I?"

"Stark didn't make an identification?"

"Stark's only been on the job three months."

"You mind if I come take a look?"

He shrugged. "Be my guest. It's probably some drunken fisherman who fell in the surf."

He turned and walked to the steps that led over the dune and down to the beach. I followed slowly. From the top of the steps I could see down to the water. Officer Stark had pulled the body clear of the waves and was standing there uncertainly. Rich joined him and stood looking down at the body. I reached the beach, and my shoes sank into the sand. As I plodded towards the surf, the sand seemed to cling to my shoes as if to hold me back. My legs grew heavier as I approached the two policemen. I couldn't bring myself to look down at the form that lay with its feet still in the water. Rich turned to look at me as I came up.

"It's Norman Hawkins," he said.

"Which one?" I managed to croak. As I did I forced myself to look down. It was Norman, Sr. He had changed his trench coat for a bright yellow foul weather gear outfit of jacket and pants. His hair was plastered against his head. His fingers were bleached and bloated and seemed to be outstretched as if he were grasping at something.

"The old man, of course," said Rich.

I looked at him in puzzlement, not realizing for a moment that he was answering my question.

"Drowned?" I asked. Somehow my voice was still not working properly.

"Looks that way to me," said Rich. "The medical examiner will tell us for sure." He turned and peered down the beach.

"You suppose he went for a swim in that outfit?"

I turned to see what he was looking at. Anything was better than staring at the body. There, about five houses south of us, was the Wedding Cake standing out in lonely white splendor against its gray, shingled neighbors.

"You think he was at the house?" I asked.

"You got a better idea?"

"As a matter of fact, yes. His boat was at Dalton's Friday afternoon and left some time that night."

"In the middle of the storm?"

"So I understand."

"And he was on the boat?"

"I imagine so. That would explain the foul weather gear. He's got no safety belt," I pointed out. "He could easily have gone overboard in the storm."

"Who else was on the boat with him?"

"I have no idea," I lied. "He had a captain. I suppose he would have been on board."

Rich turned to Stark. "Tony. Go get on to the Coast Guard. Find out if there have been any distress calls from . . . ." He looked at me. "From . . . ?"

"From the yacht 'Far Cry'," I said.

"Right, from 'Far Cry', and then find out where the hell that ambulance is. I'd like to get our friend here off the beach before we draw a crowd."

Stark hustled off apparently glad to have an assignment that took him away from the scene. I turned and looked out at the ocean, squinting against the sun. The wind was whipping the waves into whitecaps that seemed to string out in rows as they marched towards the beach.

"Hello," said Rich. "What have we here?" I forced myself to look down. He had rolled the body over and was inspecting a large bruise on Hawkins' forehead.

"I wonder how he got that?"

"Could have been any number of things," I said. "Most likely the boom. It's probably what knocked him overboard."

"So why didn't whoever was with him pick him up?"

"Who knows? Maybe no one else was on deck. Maybe they were busy with some other emergency and, by the time they got the boat around, they couldn't find him in the dark. It's not so easy to find someone who's gone over the side even in daylight. That's why people wear safety belts at sea."

"Yeah. And where's his belt?"

I shrugged. "So he was stupid. But it's dollars to donuts we'll find that 'Far Cry' called in a Mayday and the Coast Guard has been out looking for him since early Saturday morning."

"Hey Chief." It was Stark walking back down the beach towards us. "The medical examiner and the ambulance are here."

"So are they coming down?"

"Yeah, they just got here. They'll be right down."

"Well?" asked Rich, looking at him narrowly.

"Well what?"

"Well, what about the Coast Guard? Did you call them?"

"Oh, yeah. Manasquan didn't have any distress calls from 'Far Cry' or from anyone about someone going overboard. They're checking with Cape May."

For a moment neither of them said anything.

"They won't get anything from Cape May," I finally said.

"Why not?" Rich turned his attention to me.

"If he washed up here, 'Far Cry' must have been right offshore.

He must have gone over right after she'd cleared the inlet. Manasquan would have picked up any Mayday."

"They could have called Cape May." he said.

"It's the same calling frequency they all monitor. If Manasquan didn't hear the call, no one did."

"Or there wasn't any call," said Rich.

I nodded. "Or there wasn't any call."

The next arrivals on the beach were a couple of paramedics carrying a stretcher and a surprisingly young man with sandy hair and blue twinkling eyes.

"What have we got here, Rich?" He asked cheerfully.

"A body, Joe. What does it look like? And what are you so happy about being called out early on a Sunday morning. Somebody's dead."

He nodded, more serious now. "I know. It's my job. But this is a hell of a lot better than being called out at three in the morning for a car wreck with a couple of teen-agers dead."

He looked at me. "Who are you?"

"Ahhh, Pete Gordon." I extended my hand.

He shook it briefly. "Joe Bracey. You just a civilian?"

"Ah, yes, just."

He smiled wanly. "Sorry. No offense. Why don't you stand over there?" He pointed towards the steps leading over the dune to the street. Without waiting to see if I would comply, he turned to Rich.

"Has anyone moved the body?"

"Sure. Stark pulled him out of the surf, and I rolled him over."

They continued to talk, but that was all I heard as I was retreating, gratefully enough, to the steps. For about fifteen minutes, Bracey poked and prodded at the body and then motioned to the paramedics to load him on the stretcher. Rich started up the beach first, and I intercepted him at the stairs.

"You going to tell the widow?"

"Yeah," he looked south towards the house. "The least favorite part of my job."

"You mind if I go with you?"

He turned back and looked at me. He didn't speak for what seemed like a long time. I use the same technique when I want someone to reveal himself, so I just waited him out.

"Now why would you want to do that?" he finally asked.

"I'm Hawkins' lawyer."

"Why didn't you tell me that before?"

"No need to."

He looked at me for a while longer. "Is there something you're not telling me that I should know?" he asked.

"Of course not," I said quickly. It wasn't really a lie, I told myself. I had no idea whether Norman's visit to me on Friday afternoon had any relevance to his death. I was hoping it didn't, but I was curious enough to wonder whether it did.

"All right," he said finally. "But if you're holding something out on me, I'll crucify you."

He turned and led the way up the steps.

Hawkins' house has a gate blocking the driveway. Rich got out to open it up, while I looked at the house closely for the first time in years. It had stood on this spot for ten years, but I had never paid too much attention to it. The driveway curved up to a cobblestone circle at the central part of the house. Two wings flanked the circle. Identical, large decks poked out of the second story of each wing. I wondered why anyone would want to sit out and watch the traffic on Ocean Avenue. I guessed there was a view of the bay from that level. Above the second floor rose a majestic, cedar shake roof with dormer windows protruding. By now Rich had gotten back in the car, and we were bumping over the cobblestones up to the double front doors. One of the doors opened as we parked, and a large black woman was standing in it. She waited until we were out of the police car and standing on the bottom of the front step a little below her.

"May I help you?" she asked in an unfriendly tone.

"We'd like to see Mrs. Hawkins," said Rich politely.

"Mrs. Hawkins is not up yet," she said, planted solidly in the door. "Perhaps you could come back later."

"You'd better get her up then," said Rich. "We have to see her now." There was just the slightest emphasis on the now.

The woman started to say something, but Rich interrupted her. "It's police business, and it's important, so, if you wouldn't mind?"

The woman hesitated a moment more and then backed down gracefully. "In that case, why don't you gentlemen come in?"

She turned and led us into a two-storied foyer. Turning to the right, she went through double doors into a living room that stretched the entire length of the south wing of the house. We hesitated and then followed. At the ocean end of the room, French doors opened onto an enormous deck. There was no furniture on the deck but the living room was full of over-stuffed armchairs and couches, and the walls were covered with oil paintings. Overall, it had the effect of an over-decorated country estate rather than a shore house. Looking over all that furniture and then out at the ocean gave me a sense of unreality, as if I was on a Hollywood sound stage.

"Can I get you some coffee while you're waiting?" asked the woman.

"That would be nice," I said. Before she could leave I asked her. "Is Norman, Jr. in the house?"

She hesitated a moment before she said. "No. Mister Norman is not here." Before I could say any more, she swept out of the room. She brought the coffee in about ten minutes, but she would not say any more except to announce that Mrs. Hawkins would be down presently.

Rich sat silently on one of the couches facing the ocean while I paced, nervously. It was another twenty minutes before Mrs. Hawkins put in an appearance. Neither of us noticed when she came into the room. I gave a little start when she announced her presence.

"Well, gentlemen. How may I help you?"

I turned around to see her standing in the doorway. She had on blue jeans and a shirt. Her hair was done carefully, and she had taken the time to put on make-up. She was tall and slim. She stood there motionless for a moment and then came into the room with a quiet grace that put me in mind of an athlete or dancer. I knew she had to be about fifty, but she appeared ten years younger. Rich rose from his seat and met her in the middle of the floor.

"I'm sorry for this intrusion, Mrs. Hawkins. I'm Chief of Police Skowronski, and this is Peter Gordon."

"Yes," she said looking at me for the first time. "Mr. Gordon and I have met, although it's been some time now. Please, gentlemen, sit down. What can I do for you?" She gestured at the couch that Rich had just risen out of.

"I'm afraid I have some bad news, Mrs. Hawkins." He remained standing where he was. He plunged on before she could say anything. "There has apparently been an accident. Your husband has drowned. His body was found on the beach this morning."

I watched her face. Her eyes closed for an instant and then opened again. For a moment she just stood there showing no sign of emotion. Then she backed up and sank down on one of the armchairs. She put both hands in front of her mouth.

"He's dead?" she asked. Her voice was so quiet I had to strain to hear.

"Yes ma'am," said Skowronski. "We're not sure of the time of death yet. We won't know until the results of the autopsy."

She stirred on the chair. "Is an autopsy really necessary? I hate to see him cut up like that."

"I'm afraid so," said Rich. "It's routine in any kind of accidental death like this."

"And you say you found him this morning?"

"That's right. He must have washed ashore some time last night."

At this she closed her eyes and kept them shut for a long moment.

"I'm sorry Mrs. Hawkins. I need to ask you a few routine questions. Are you up to it now, or should I come back later?"

She sat up straight and raised her head.

"Before we do that could you give me a minute, Chief Skowronski?"

"Of course."

She rose and swept from the room, leaving us standing there awkwardly. Rich sat down again on the same couch, and I picked out the other armchair. Fifteen minutes later Mrs. Hawkins returned and resumed her seat on the chair opposite Rich. Her mascara was a little smeared, and she was carrying a handkerchief.

"You might as well ask now, Chief. I might as well tell you that, while Norman and I were still married, we were no longer living together. While his death is a shock, I'm not going to be going into any prolonged spell of mourning." She recited this like a speech she had just memorized. I wondered why she had thought it necessary to give us this information.

"Ah, thank-you for your candor, Mrs. Hawkins," said Rich. "When did you last see your husband?"

"Not for some time. It must have been about two weeks ago."

"He wasn't here on Friday night?" I broke in.

She looked over at me coolly. "No. By the way, Pete, what is your interest in this? Do you have some connection with the police now?"

"No, Norman had retained me as his lawyer."

Her eyes widened momentarily in surprise. "Why would he do that? He's been represented by Spofford & Channing for years."

Spofford & Channing is a large, Philadelphia law firm with offices all over the country. I shrugged.

"Might I ask what was the purpose of his retaining your services?"

I looked at her steadily. I needed to regain the offensive and get her off this subject. "I'm afraid I can't tell you that. But I do know he was in North Beach on Friday afternoon. Are you saying he wasn't staying here?"

"That's exactly what I'm saying. He was probably staying on that horrible boat of his with his latest little friend."

"Little friend?" asked Rich. "You mean a woman?"

"Of course, I mean a woman," she said.

"Could you tell me her name?"

"I have no idea what her name is or who she is, for that matter. She was just the most recent."

"How do you know she was on the boat?" I asked.

"I don't know. I didn't even know he was in town. Listen Chief," she turned to appeal to Rich. "Maybe this has affected me more than I thought it would. Do you think we could finish this another day?"

"Of course," he said. "Just a couple more questions. Who else is living in the house?"

"Florence lives here, of course. And Norman and his wife, Mary, live in the other wing."

"You mean Norman, Jr? That would be your husband's youngest son?"

"That's right."

"Are they in the house now?"

"I have no idea. We have separate entrances and we go our separate ways. Norman's an adult, and I don't keep tabs on him."

"Might we talk to them?"

"It's all right with me. I'll have Florence take you over." She rang a little bell, and Florence appeared immediately in the door.

"Florence, take these gentlemen over to see Mr. and Mrs. Hawkins, please."

Florence nodded wordlessly, and we took our leave.

"Ah, Florence," said Rich as we caught up to her in the foyer. "Just a moment. How long did you work for Mr. Hawkins?"

She turned and looked at him. "Did?" she asked.

"I'm sorry. Mr. Hawkins died, probably last night, in a drowning accident. Mrs. Hawkins didn't tell you that a moment ago?"

"No sir, she did not."

"How long had you been working for Mr. Hawkins?"

"Ten years, sir. Ever since he built this house."

"Then you knew the first Mrs. Hawkins?"

"There were two others sir. But he was already married to the present Mrs. Hawkins when he built the house."

"When did you last see Mr. Hawkins?"

"I can't say for sure, sir. He doesn't come around too much these days."

"He wasn't here on Friday?"

"I couldn't say for sure, sir. I wasn't feeling too well on Friday, and I went up to my room right after dinner."

"Any commotion or disturbance in the house that night?" I asked.

"Not that I heard," she said.

"Was Norman, Jr., here on Friday night?" I persisted.

"I couldn't say, sir."

"You don't know?"

"I pretty much keep to this side of the house, sir."

"When did you last see him?"

"Some time last week I understand he went away on a business trip."

"When is he expected back?"

"You'd have to ask Mrs. Hawkins that, sir."

She looked back calmly at us, a block of granite that I could not penetrate. Rich must have decided the same thing because he gestured that we should proceed. She turned and led us through the foyer and into another living room identical in dimensions to the one we had just left. In contrast to the over-crowded furnishing of the south living room, this one was almost bare of furniture. A couple of worn, wicker chairs sat forlornly down at the beach end of the room.

"Wait here," commanded Florence. "I'll see if Mrs. Hawkins can see you."

And so we sat, waiting for the second Mrs. Hawkins. This time we didn't have to wait so long. In no more than two minutes a door in the far wall banged open and a young lady entered the room. There were a number of similarities to the first Mrs. Hawkins that we had met. Like Lorraine, she was tall and slim and dressed in blue jeans and a shirt. She crossed the room with an athletic grace that was a mirror image of the woman on the other side of the house. But there were differences as well. While Lorraine had seemed reserved and passive, this Mrs. Hawkins was overflowing with energy. She started speaking while she was still halfway across the floor.

"What's this I hear? The old man's drowned himself?"

Rich rose from the little wicker chair that he had chosen to meet her. He ignored her question, introduced himself and me and asked her to sit down. She perched herself on one of the wicker chairs and repeated her question. This time Rich gave her an answer.

"That's right, Mrs. Hawkins. Mr. Hawkins, that is, your father-in-law was found this morning on the beach. He had apparently been drowned during the night."

"The dumb son-of-a-bitch."

"Why do you say that, Mrs. Hawkins?"

"To go drowning yourself like that. I expect he was out on his boat, isn't that it?"

"Ah, we're not sure of the circumstances. Are you up to a few questions?"

"Sure. There was no love lost between the old man and me."

I was struck by the similarity of the reaction of this Mrs. Hawkins and the first we had interviewed.

"He never liked me from the beginning," she continued. "I'm not sure why. I guess it was because he thought I was after his son's money. Or, to be more precise, his money. He had all the money, and he never let you forget it." She smiled. "I think I would have reached him in time, but there's no time left for that, is there?"

"Were you after Norman for his money?" asked Rich.

She looked at him sharply. "What a question to ask! This was just an accident wasn't it?"

"We have no indication that it's anything else. This is just a routine, preliminary investigation. Could you tell me the last time you saw Mr. Hawkins?"

She sat back in the chair to respond. "I think it was last weekend. He was here at the house. He and Lorraine had another big blow-up."

When she said the name, Lorraine, the venom in her tone was almost palpable.

"Mr. and Mrs. Hawkins weren't getting along?" asked Rich.

She laughed. "That's putting it mildly. They were in the middle of splitting up, and it was bitter beyond words. It's been going on for more than a year."

"Why so long?" I asked.

"Lawyers," she said. "They can spin things out forever. I guess it was about the company stock. Lorraine wanted a big chunk of it, and Norman wasn't willing to give it up. Every once in a while he'd come over and yell at her about it."

"And you could hear?" asked Rich.

"Sure. This is a big house, but not that big. Especially when they're yelling at each other right out front on the deck."

"So, Mr. Hawkins didn't live here."

"No way. He left her this house about a year ago. The only stipulation was that Harry and I could live here too. Lorraine didn't like that, but what was she going to do until the divorce became final? He lived in the house in Philadelphia and on that stupid boat of his."

"So Mr. Hawkins wasn't here on Friday night?" I asked.

"I just told you, didn't I? I haven't seen him since last weekend."

I blinked. "So the answer to my question is no?"

"That's what I said."

It hadn't been quite what she said, but I let it go. "How about your husband? Where is he?"

"Harry? He's off on a business trip."

"What's his business?"

"He's the personal assistant to Robert Reynaud."

"You mean the 'Return to the Roots' Robert Reynaud?"

"That's right."

"And when did he leave on this trip?"

For the first time in our interview she seemed unsure of herself. "Ah . . . I'm not sure. Maybe Wednesday or Thursday. No Wednesday."

"And when will he be back?"

"He's in the middle of this big political campaign in California. It's very important. He might not get back until after the election."

"How did Harry and his father get along?"

"They got on great. Why wouldn't they?"

"Mr. Hawkins didn't have any concerns about Harry's involvement in RTTR?"

"Well the old man didn't agree with a lot of RTTR's positions, but he was glad that Harry was making something of himself."

"Mr. Hawkins didn't want Harry to leave the organization?"

"Of course not."

I glanced over at Rich. He was looking at me curiously. I shrugged and turned to look out the window.

"Well, thank you for your time, Mrs. Hawkins," he said. Will you ask your husband to give me a call tomorrow?" He gave her a card.

"Of course, Chief. Anything I can do to help."

We went outside and neither of us spoke until we were sitting in Rich's car. He started the engine and then turned to me.

"Well?" he asked.

"Well what?"

"Something's bothering you. Let's have it."

I shrugged. "Norman was in town on Friday night. He came to see me that afternoon. He told me that his son was involved in this RTTR cult and that he had to do something to get him back."

"You think he was going to do some de-programming stunt?"

I nodded.

"But the kid was out of town."

I nodded again. "That's what the story is. But I had the impression that Norman was going to do something real soon. When the boat left in a storm, I figured it was because he had snatched the kid."

"But he didn't tell you that."

"No. It's just my feeling. And I think his new girlfriend was in on the plan."

"How do you know that?"

I told him about that yellow slickered form I had seen getting on board the boat on Friday as Norman was talking to me in my office.

"But you only saw her from across the street," he objected. "You can't even be sure it was a woman, let alone his girlfriend."

I thought back and pictured her as she had climbed over the rail and gone down below.

"I didn't think about it at the time, but it was a woman. The size was right and something about the way she got on the boat. Who else could it have been except the new girlfriend?"

"That's supposition upon supposition."

"So what do you think?"

He started to pull out of the drive. "I don't think anything yet."

Neither of us spoke until he had left me off at my car. The ambulance and the other police car had gone. There was only Mrs. Reznick still out on her screen porch, still watching. I turned to Rich.

"What about finding 'Far Cry'?"

"That's the Coast Guard's job."

"Are they looking? There is certainly one, probably two and maybe more people on that boat who can shed some light on this."

He smiled tiredly. "I understand that Pete. I'm not completely stupid."

"Sorry," I said. "I didn't mean that. But you'll get the Coast Guard looking?"

"I'll give them a call. The Coast Guard doesn't usually follow my instructions, but there does seem to be a missing boat, doesn't there?" He waved and spun his wheels in the sand as he turned back towards Ocean Avenue.

I walked to my car like I was in a trance and found my way back home. I think I made myself some breakfast, but I have no recollection of it. Something was bothering me but I couldn't figure out what it was for a long time. It finally came to me. I had to call Jane Hawkins Turner and tell her about her father. It would have been easier if I could have picked up the phone and made the call immediately. The only problem was that I had no idea where to find her. I started by calling Sarah Stockard. I tried her at Freddie's apartment. Freddie answered.

"Fred. Is Sarah there?"

"I don't think she's stirring yet."

"Get her up, would you? It's important."

"Your funeral."

The phone line went silent for a few minutes until Sarah came on.

"Hello."

"Sarah. It's Pete Gordon." I rushed on before she could say anything. "Sorry to bother you, but you're my expert on the Hawkins family. Norman Hawkins was found this morning on the beach, drowned."

"Norman? You mean the old man?"

"Exactly."

"How did it happen?"

"No one really knows. We think he went overboard from 'Far Cry.'"

"Jesus. This wouldn't be somehow connected to your interest in Harry the other night, would it?"

"I don't know. Right now I'm trying to get in touch with Norman's daughter, Jane. Do you know where I might find her?"

"Wow, I don't know. I heard she got married and moved to California."

"North or South?"

"Somewhere around LA, but not in LA. One of those towns with an 'Oaks' in the name. I'm not too good about the geography out there, you know?"

"Thanks."

"Peter. Tell me what this is all about."

"I'll let you know when I know something."

I told myself that it was too early in California. I would wait until eleven. Meanwhile I had to get a number. I did know a little bit about LA. I started with Sherman Oaks and struck out, moved to Thousand Oaks and struck gold. Then I sat and tried not to look at the phone. At eleven I told myself that eight on a Sunday morning was really too early a time to be calling. I stalled until about eleven-thirty. Finally I couldn't stand it any more. I had to get it over with. I picked up the phone and misdialed the number. I think I did it twice before I got it right. The phone rang and rang again at the other end. Someone picked it up.

"Hello?" It was the same voice that I remembered from Friday night.

"Mrs. Turner?"

"Yes."

"This is Peter Gordon. We spoke the other evening?"

"I remember, Mr. Gordon."

"I'm afraid I have some bad news. There's been an accident."

"Oh God. My father?"

"I'm afraid so. He was drowned. The body was recovered just this morning."

I could hear a sound like an indrawn breath and then silence.

"Mrs. Turner. I'm so sorry to be the one . . . . If there is anything I can do?"

"Please, Peter is it?"

"Yes."

"Give me a moment, Peter." There was silence.

"If you would like me to call back?" I started.

"No. I'm all right really. It's almost as if I was expecting . . . . Just hold on the line a moment, please." There was silence again. I think she had put the phone down. A few minutes later she came back on.

"Peter?"

"Yes."

"Thank you for holding. I'm sorry I'm acting so stupidly."

"For heaven's sake, don't apologize."

"Tell me what happened."

"We're not really sure. Your father was found on the beach this morning. We think he left with his boat on Friday night. In the middle of a storm."

"Where's the boat?"

"The boat hasn't been found yet. The Coast Guard's out looking for it." I hoped this part was true.

"Oh, God. Was he just washed overboard? Why didn't they pick him up? Who was on the boat with him?"

"We don't know the answer to any of those questions, Jane. We think the captain, Louie, isn't it? Was probably on the boat. Harry may have been as well."

"Harry? Why Harry?"

"When your father came to visit me, he said something about getting his son back."

There was silence at the other end of the line.

"But, why would Harry be on the boat? They weren't even speaking."

"Do you know where Harry is?

"I haven't talked to him for over a year. Last time I heard he was out here in California at that cultist camp that's in the mountains somewhere around here."

"I thought he was living here in North Beach with his wife."

"I guess he does sometimes, but mostly he's off with his guru."

"Robert Reynaud?"

"Exactly. You know about Reynaud?"

"Your father told me about him."

"Oh, you can tell me about that now?"

"I'm sorry. The situation's a little different now."

She sighed. "No, I'm sorry. I shouldn't have snapped at you like that."

"What do you know about Reynaud?" I asked.

"Not much. He's just opened a 'Return to the Roots' center out here in Thousand Oaks. Supposed to be like one of those think tanks. There seems to be a lot of marching and singing involved in the program."

"Marching and singing?"

"Yes. Kind of like a summer camp atmosphere for teen-agers. Hiking in the mountains. Singing around the campfire. Indoctrination into the RTTR creed. He's got a ranch up in the hills where all that goes on. I think that's where Harry is most of the time."

"You mean 'strength through joy' and all that stuff?"

"You said it, not me. Anyway, the great man himself is running for Congress. He won't win, but his presence has sure mixed up the race for the incumbent."

"Who's the incumbent?"

"Ted Renfrow."

I whistled. "You mean to tell me that Ted Renfrow is in trouble?"

Ted Renfrow was a Democratic congressman with probably 20 years seniority. He was chairman of a couple of committees, including Ways and Means. Captains of industry and cabinet secretaries quailed before his presence at his committee hearings. To think that an RTTR cultist could put the great Ted Renfrow in fear of retirement was news.

"Why should that surprise you?" she said. "Ted's been around too long and worn out his welcome. People are sick of politicians, and any new face that promises change is going to make some waves. Renfrow's got a strong Republican challenger this time, and Reynaud is taking votes from both sides. Ted will probably win, but he has to pay attention this year."

I sat and thought about this for a moment.

"Peter."

"Yes."

"Do you think you could tell me what my father was doing at your office on Friday before he went off and got himself drowned?"

"Yes, I guess I could. I think he was going to take Harry and do a de-programming on 'Far Cry.'"

"So Harry was on 'Far Cry' that night?"

"I don't know. His wife says he's been in California since last Wednesday." With that, I told her the whole story from the time her father had walked into my office. I hadn't intended to do that, but somehow, once I had started, everything seemed to come out. I finished with placing the phone call to her. There was silence on the end of the line for a long time.

"You don't think my father's death could have been anything more than an accident, do you?"

"Why do you say that?"

"This RTTR group has been involved in some street brawling out here."

"That may be, but going from that to murder is a pretty good stretch."

"What are you going to do?"

"I don't know."

"Peter," she said.

"Yes."

"Thank you for calling to tell me."

"It was the least I could do."

"No, you could have done a lot less. I think I have to go now."

"Bye," I said, but I think I was saying it to a dead line.

Chapter III

I spent the rest of the day doing odd jobs around the house. On Monday, I got to the office early and tried to lose myself in work. I found I couldn't concentrate and, by ten, I gave up all pretense. I called Rich to find out if "Far Cry" had been found. It hadn't been, and Harry hadn't called him. I got out the check that Norman had given to me and stared at it. Twenty-five thousand dollars. He didn't have to give me a check for nearly that amount. I would have been delighted with ten thousand. Hell, I would have agreed to be his lawyer on account. And what had he really wanted me to do for the money? I felt like I needed some advice from the senior partner in the firm. Dave Stockard was on vacation, but I decided this was worth bothering him. That took some doing because he was at some obscure fishing camp in Montana where there was only one phone. Because of the time difference, I reached him while he was still in camp.

"This better be good Pete," was his initial greeting. "I'm about to get on a horse and pack up into the mountains for the next week."

"Just some advice, Dave." I abbreviated the story as much as I could, but it still took about fifteen minutes. He let me get to the end before he made any comments.

"So what do you want to do?" he asked.

I looked at the check sitting on the desk in front of me. "I don't know what to do. My client is dead. I guess the thing to do is send the check back and forget about it."

"Is that what you want to do?"

I thought for a moment and, suddenly, I made a decision. "Hell no. I want to find out what happened."

"Good. Why do you think Norman wrote you a check for twenty-five thousand dollars?"

"I have no idea."

"Well, I've known Norman for a good many years, and he doesn't write checks for twenty-five thousand just on a whim. I think he wrote you that check to cover himself."

"What do you mean?"

"What was that you told me he said at the end? Something about you having a moral obligation to ferret out the facts if something happened?"

"Yes."

"Well, something obviously happened, didn't it? And he sure as hell can't write you a check now, can he?"

"No."

"Well, it's a damn good thing he wrote you one before, isn't it? He's as much as told you he wants you to find out what happened, and he's already paid you for it."

"He could have been a little more direct about it."

"Not Norman. He was never one to do directly what could just as well be done indirectly."

"So what do I do?"

"First take a picture of that check and deposit it in our attorney account. The money can sit there for the time being. Then I'd find out a little more about this RTTR, wouldn't you?"

"I guess so."

"Good. I hear my horse calling to me. Let me know how it all comes out."

I rang off and sat there looking at the check. Now the decision was made, I could feel the excitement building inside of me. All my doubts of the previous Friday had vanished. By noon I had deposited the check and decided on a course of action. A few calls had found me a "cult" expert at the University of Pennsylvania and one more call had gotten me an appointment for the next morning.

I set off at about seven in the morning. An hour-and-a half later I was looking for a parking spot on Chestnut Street in West Philadelphia. Professor Ralph Bartholomew had his office on Locust Walk. I found the building and then an entrance off to the side. Inside was a secretary who directed me upstairs. I climbed the stairs to find several frosted glass, closed doors opening off a landing. The door on the left had a sign that read R. D. Bartholomew. I knocked.

"Come in," said a voice.

I opened the door and walked into a small office with a window full of plants facing out on the alley. Bookshelves lining the walls were crammed with books and papers. In the center of the office was a large desk covered with more books and papers. Behind the desk sat a small, balding man with a pipe in his mouth. He spoke without removing the pipe from between his teeth.

"Yes?"

"Ah, Professor Bartholomew. I'm Pete Gordon. We spoke yesterday?"

He waved to a chair. "Oh yes. You wanted to talk about cults and such. Please have a chair." He motioned to a small wooden chair in front of the desk. It was clearly designed to intimidate undergraduates who proved bold enough to visit the Professor during his visiting hours. It was the only choice so I took it. Bartholomew took the opportunity, which I thought superfluous, to light a match and touch it to the tobacco in his pipe. I imagined that this was another defense mechanism to keep student interviews short.

"What can I do for you?" he asked.

"I'd like to get a little information about cults and their practices if it wouldn't be too much trouble."

"That's a broad subject. Do you have anything specific in mind?"

"A friend of mine has a son who has become a member of a cult-like political organization. I'm trying to get some help for him."

"What's the cult?"

"The RTTR."

He looked at me levelly. "Why isn't your friend here himself?"

"He's dead."

There was a long silence as he took the pipe out of his mouth and tapped the remaining ashes into an ashtray. I waited him out.

"Is there any connection?"

"I have no idea," I said. "I'm just curious."

Suddenly he seemed to come to a decision and got to his feet. "Maybe you better tell me the whole story," he said. "But not here. Let's get more comfortable."

Without another word he led the way out of the office and down onto Locust Walk. The walk was packed with students walking to classes or just lounging around taking advantage of the late October sun. Bartholomew worked his way expertly through the crowd while I tried to keep up. In five minutes we were ensconced in the back of a little coffee bar. Bartholomew ordered two coffees from a waitress who had greeted him by name.

"Terrible office," he said. "The Comparative Religion Department doesn't rate too much around here."

"Comparative Religion. Is what you teach?"

"That's the slot they have me in. My doctorate is in Philosophy, but I got interested in cults and most of my work has centered around the religious aspects of cults."

"The RTTR really isn't a religious cult, is it?"

"No, that's one reason that I've gotten interested in it. It's a little different than the standard mold." The waitress brought our coffees, and he busied himself with cream and sugar.

"But before we get into that, though," he said. "Why don't you tell me about your friend?"

I told him about Norman's visit, my suspicions about Norman's de-programming plan and his subsequent drowning. When I was finished, he sat there thinking for a moment.

"And where is the son now?" he asked.

"His wife says he's in California helping the Reynaud campaign to unseat Ted Renfrow."

"But you can't seem to get in touch with him?"

I nodded. "The police have been trying to get in touch with him, but, so far, no success."

"So what's your interest in this? This man wasn't really a friend of yours was he?"

"No, he wasn't. But he came to me for help. It was too late for me to give him any. He also paid me a big retainer. Now I can't ask him what he'd want me to do with it. And I can't pay it back to him."

"You could pay it back to his estate."

"That's true. I could also do something to earn it by finding out what happened to him. And maybe his son does need help."

"You mean because he's ensnared in the grip of this evil cult?"

I shrugged. "Maybe. I really don't know, do I? Which leads me to why I called you in the first place. Why don't you tell me a little about cults?"

"OK. Here's Cults 101." He paused a moment and launched off into a lecture. "There may be five million Americans right now who are more or less attached to more or less of a kind of a cult. Figures are hard to come by because cults aren't conscientious about filling out forms, and one man's cult is another man's religion. Some people think there are three thousand separate cults. No one really knows, but they have certain common characteristics. Usually they have a common religious ideology that revolves around one authoritarian leader. The leader may be God or God's messenger on Earth or simply the embodiment of salvation or all power and knowledge. The ideology of the cult, whatever it happens to be, is seen as revealed truth, which prescribes the only legitimate world-view for the members. New members are recruited with a vision of this world-view, which is said to answer all worldly questions and solve all worldly problems. Once recruited they are usually isolated from friends and family and put into a new peer group of committed members. Then they are subjected to various psychological pressures to conform to the norms of the group. The goal is to make them totally dependent on the group for all things. The member surrenders total control of his life, his finances, and his persona to the group and particularly to the leader. In return, the group, or more specifically, the leader, provides safe and easy answers for every problem that might have plagued his past life or that could possibly plague his future life."

He paused for a moment to refill and light his pipe. I was surprised that he had gone without it so long.

"What about this proselytizing on the streets?" I asked.

"Lot's of them do that. Others have small businesses that cult-members work at for virtually no pay. Imagine having a committed work force willing to work seventy or eighty hours a week, week in and week out, for no pay except the gruel they get fed in the mess and a bunk in a communal barracks."

"I guess you could make some money that way."

"A lot of money."

"Is that what all this is about? Money?"

He shook his head. "Maybe in some cases, but mostly I think no. This is really about power. Power over people. The leader probably started because he enjoyed, and was good at, manipulating people to do what he wanted them to do. Soon he got more people to do what he wanted them to do, and it became like a narcotic. The more he succeeded the more he had to continue to succeed. There grows up a psychological bond between the leader and the follower. The follower gives unstinting devotion and loyalty to the leader, thereby resolving the internal personal conflicts of the follower. They are unworthy while he is all-knowing."

"As for the leader, he's on a tread-mill. The more he dominates his followers, the more completely he must dominate them. It's never enough. The more devotion they offer, the more he must have. And every problem he encounters and every setback he receives must be laid at the door of the failings or insufficient loyalty of his followers. And so it is that the most loyal of his followers must bear the brunt of his frustration and anger."

"It sounds a little like Stalinism to me."

He nodded. "Stalinism writ small, as it were. Most cults that we have studied in the United States have been religious based. Often they have an apocalyptic side to them. Sometimes almost literally like with the Waco thing. But there is another kind of God. A political kind of God. The Communist Party had a lot in common with the features of the cults that I've just been talking about. An all-encompassing ideology. An all-powerful leader. A membership that is expected to be totally committed to the goals of the group to the exclusion of every other aspect of their lives." He laughed. "Why do you think that the communists called the phenomenon of Stalinism the 'cult of personality'? Fascism has many of the same features. Hitler and Mussolini led the same kinds of ideological, leader-driven movements."

"And that brings us to RTTR."

"Yes," he said. "That brings us to RTTR."

"What do you know about it?"

"Just a little bit. It follows from what I've already said. There are some interesting parallels between RTTR and both existing cult groups and certain totalitarian political movements of the mid-20th century. Which is only another way of saying that there are certain parallels between today's cults and totalitarian political groups."

"You mean both communists and fascists?"

"Of course. Most people see the political spectrum as a straight line from right to left. It's really more like a circle, with the middle of the spectrum at the top and the far left and the far right approaching each other and finally meeting at the bottom."

"But they are so different and so at war with each other."

He stopped to light his pipe again and took the opportunity to signal the waitress for another cup of coffee. I began to realize that the pipe lighting exercise was just a convenient interruption that afforded him a moment to marshal his thoughts.

"I'll grant you the latter. Each lives by demonizing the other. But the greatest amount of vituperation and hatred is often reserved for those on the political spectrum closest in ideological belief. Look at the battles between the Bolsheviks and the Mensheviks in the years before the October revolution. The examples of those who have made the journey from far right to far left and vice versa are not inconsiderable. Look at Mussolini himself. It's hard to imagine someone traversing the entire political spectrum from left to right as Mussolini did, unless you visualize it as not a very long trip at all. Many of the beliefs are similar if not identical. The cult of the leader. The all-encompassing ideology that provides the total explanation for life, the world and man's existence. The thugs and the terror. In the end it's all about power. It's about the total control by the leader of every aspect of the follower's life to the exclusion of every other human need or emotion. At that part of the spectrum where far right meets far left, it's all the same."

"So how does all this relate to RTTR?"

He smiled. "Sorry. Sometimes I get carried away with my rhetoric. RTTR is a far right political movement that is organizing along the lines of the fascist movements of the twenties and thirties. Which, by the way, were attributes also shared by the Bolshevik and communist parties of the same era. The leader is the all-powerful font of wisdom. The followers owe him total obedience and loyalty. There is a force of black shirts or brown shirts, or the like, who keep discipline and order through terror. New members are recruited, indoctrinated and kept in the organization by a variety of means, including persuasion, propaganda, psychological and peer pressure, intimidation and, in the end, force.

"RTTR has the same attributes?"

"Absolutely."

I stirred my coffee absently. This wasn't getting me any closer to a decision of what to do about Harry.

"So what are the prospects for Harry?" I asked.

"You mean the son, I take it."

"Yeah, the son."

"You think he is a captive of this cult?"

"Don't you think that's obvious?"

"I don't know. He may be being held against his will. He may just be a believer."

"So what should I do?"

"You want to help him?"

"Yes."

He shrugged. "Go and find him and talk to him. Try and persuade him to come out."

"That sounds like pretty weak tea compared to the psychological pressures you were just describing."

"I know. But we can get him some exit counseling, if he comes out. I'd be glad to help at that. It would be interesting to learn more about the organization."

"What about de-programming?"

"You mean kidnap the kid and hide him away for days or weeks, depriving him of privacy and sleep while you hammer at him night and day about the evils of the RTTR?"

"Well, I wouldn't put it that way."

"That's the way de-programming works."

I shrugged. "If that's what it takes."

"And how would you be any different than the cult itself?"

"Well, I guess you have to use strong measures against something as insidious as these cult influences."

"Un-huh. Like 'We had to destroy the village to save it', is that it?"

"Well not exactly."

"If you're going to go that route, you'll get no more help from me."

"I don't know what route I'm going to take, but I'd like to talk to some de-programmers."

He said nothing and just looked at me.

"Look," I said. "Helping the kid is only part of what I'm about. I'm also trying to find out what happened to the father. I'm certain he was going to do a de-programming on the kid. He must have enlisted the help of one of these de-programmers. He had the money, and he wouldn't have launched into such a venture without professional help."

Bartholomew snorted.

"OK, I know what you think of their tactics, but I'm sure that he hired one to help him. If I can find and talk to the guy, it may lead me to what happened that night. It's a long shot, but I don't have many other leads."

"How do I know you won't just hire the same de-programmer yourself?"

"You don't know that. Let me put it to you this way. I'm pretty resourceful. If I set out to find a de-programmer, I'll find one. If you help me out, I promise that I won't hire him to work his voodoo on the kid without coming back to you to discuss it. You're a persuasive guy, I'm sure you'll be able to talk me out of it."

He grunted. "I think you're the persuasive guy sitting at this table. OK, I'll help. But there are dozens of de-programmers around. How are you going to find the right one?"

"How many are there in Philadelphia? My bet is that he would pick someone local."

He sighed and signaled for the check. "Come back to my office. I'll get you a couple of addresses."

He gave me three. Two in Philadelphia and one in Newark. The first number I tried in Philadelphia produced a recorded announcement that the phone had been disconnected. The second produced an answering service and an appointment for an hour later at an office downtown on South Broad Street. I found the building easily. It looked to be one of those that had formerly been occupied by the law and accounting firms that were steadily moving to the new buildings on Market and Arch Street to the West of City Hall. The lobby had the seedy look of the not fully rented building. I took the elevator to the fourteenth floor. I found his door at the appointed hour. It had his name, Ernest Fagin, stenciled neatly on the door and one other word, Investigations, beneath his name. The door was locked, and no one came to my knock. There was a bench sitting a little way down the hall. I sat down to wait. Fifteen minutes later a man got out of the elevator and walked down the hall towards me. He was about fifty, tall and blonde with black-rimmed glasses.

"Mr. Gordon?" he asked.

"That's right. You must be Mr. Fagin."

"Call me Ernie," he said as he gripped my hand with a grip that cut off the circulation to my fingers. He turned and fumbled with a set of keys to open the office.

"Sorry I'm late. My service paged me, but I was all the way over in Jersey on a job. Took me longer to get back than I thought."

"I'm sorry," I said. "I didn't mean to interrupt your work. We could have met another time."

He waved his hand as if it were nothing and led the way into the office. There was a reception room full of old file cabinets and a secretary's desk with an old IBM computer sitting on it. The room looked like it hadn't been swept out in quite a while.

"The secretary's got the day off today as it happens," he said and fumbled to get another key to open the door to a back office. He opened the door and waved me in. It looked like a clone of the front office except it had a window looking out onto an adjoining roof. He took off his coat, hung it on a peg and sat down behind the desk.

"So what can I do for you?" he asked. "You asked about de-programming, but you don't really need a de-programmer, do you?"

I sat down in the wooden chair in front of his desk. "How do you know that?"

"Well, I used to be in the de-programming business, and I know the look. The parents who used to come to me were at the end of their ropes. There was a kind of desperation in their eyes. They'd already tried everything they knew of to get their kids back, police, psychiatrists, you name it, but nothing worked." He leaned his chair back and put his feet up on the desk. "Yup, by the time they got to me they thought they were at the end of the world." He laughed shortly.

"You're no longer in the de-programming business?"

"Nope. The authorities were making it too hot for us. Threats of prosecution on kidnapping, false imprisonment, or whatever other bullshit charge they could think up. The DA was out to get me because of some trumped up complaints. So I went back to straight investigations."

I sat and looked out the stain-streaked window at the air conditioner sitting on the roof next door. I didn't believe him for a minute. One call from me to his answering service, and he had dropped whatever he was doing to come in and meet me. I turned back to look at him.

"You're right," I said. "I don't need any de-programming for myself. But I have a friend who has a problem." I pulled out my wallet, pulled out a hundred dollar bill and put it on the table. "I don't want to hire you to do a de-programming, but I'd like some advice."

He grinned and swept the bill off the table. "You mean off the record?"

I shrugged. "I don't really know what you mean by 'off the record'. Let's just say it's a hypothetical situation."

"Yeah, I like that. A hypothetical situation."

"First," I said. "Maybe you could tell me what a de-programmer does. Not necessarily anything you yourself have done, of course, but what in your experience others in the business might do in the course of their work."

"Sure," he said. "First you got to understand that, when a parent comes to a de-programmer, the only thing in his mind is to save his child. It may be a son or daughter who has been, in effect, kidnapped by this group. They always start out easy with the promise of the perfect life. Everyone's so friendly and caring. All you have to do to have inner peace is to give yourself over to belief in the master. Then they get you away to an isolated spot where there's only cult members for you to talk to. No phones, no contact with your family or friends. And they're at you twenty-four hours a day. No sleep, very little food, endless rituals, constant pressure to join up from the other cult members. Finally, out of exhaustion, you consent and they have this big initiation ceremony, full of rituals and meaning, and everyone is hugging you and kissing you and welcoming you to the fold. And the big guy himself comes and blesses you, and you're saved. But now you're hooked. You're part of the group and subject to discipline. You can't shit without someone else's permission. You can't leave. You certainly can't communicate with someone familiar, your family, for example, who might talk some common sense into you. Your family can't reach you. You're like a prisoner."

"But surely," I said. "Anybody who really wanted to escape could find a way. I mean, don't they let them out on the street to do panhandling or to sell flowers or to otherwise make money for the group?"

"Sure they do. But they're not trusted alone. They go in pairs and there's always someone who's like a supervisor close by. But the major restraint is that they're brainwashed by the time they're let out. By that time their minds have been so manipulated by the crap they've been fed that they really have no desire to leave. They really think that they're living the perfect life."

"You think there really is such a thing as brainwashing?"

He laughed. "I know there is. It goes back to the Korean War when the North Koreans and Chicoms were doing it to our GIs. These cult leaders have adopted the same techniques. Believe me, I've seen how powerful it is."

"So what's the cure? Kidnapping them?"

"You laugh," he said. "But what do you suggest? Talk about false imprisonment. That's what these cults are all about. If you don't think mental bars are stronger than steel bars, you don't know what you're talking about. What do you think those Branch Davidians were thinking when that house was burning down around their ears in Waco. They were thinking that the time of resurrection had come, just like Peter Koresh had promised it would."

"So what's the process?"

"Basically you have to get them out of that environment so that they can see the crap they've been fed for what it really is. You take them to an isolated place, bring in their family and talk sense to them until they see it."

"Have you had success at this process?"

"Let's just say that, when properly done, the success rate is nigh on 100%."

"How long does it take?"

"Depends on the subject. Sometimes it takes a while, but in the end, they all break, believe me."

"It all sounds to me like a mirror image of the brainwashing that's practiced by the cults that you complain about."

His eyes narrowed. He didn't like the comparison. "Sure," he said. "You have to use many of the same techniques, that's true. The mind control practiced by the cults is so pervasive that, to reverse the process, it takes some radical procedures. That's why the normal psychiatric bullshit is so ineffective."

"You mean exit counseling?"

"That crap. That does nothing." His voice was raised and he had taken his feet down off the desk. "What I do . . . ." He stopped. "What I mean is, what these de-programmers do . . . the good ones, that is, works. And the thing you have to remember is, even though some of the techniques are similar, the crucial difference is, it's these poor victims' families that are doing this. It's being done for the love of the person, not for the aggrandizement of some wacko who's out to rule the world."

I sat and thought for a moment. I had enough, for the present, on his views about the cults.

"What's your background?" I asked.

"Twenty years as a Philadelphia cop," he said. "I started on the beat and then was a detective for eleven years. Finally had enough and started my own investigations business."

"How'd you get interested in cults?"

He shrugged. "I was doing a lot of trace work on runaways. I traced one to the Hare Krishnas. I managed to get her home. Then clients started to come to me because their kids had been brainwashed by one cult or another. I started to get interested and learned a lot about their practices."

"What made you stop?"

"I told you. The police and the DA can't solve the cult problem, but they sure can make it difficult for parents to get their kids back."

"And for the people who help them?" I asked.

He grinned. "You got that right." He had relaxed again and put his feet back up on the desk.

"You ever get an inquiry from Norman Hawkins about deprogramming his son?"

The instant I said the name, I could see he recognized it. The feet came down off the desk, and he leaned forward in his chair.

"What do you know about Norman Hawkins?" he demanded.

It was my turn to shrug. "He's an acquaintance of mine. It was the RTTR that had his son, wasn't it?"

He hesitated a moment and then made a decision. "Yeah, he called me."

"Did you agree to help him?"

"Haven't you been listening? I told you I'm not in that business any more. He called me, and I told him that."

"Did you refer him to anyone else?"

"No, I just told him I couldn't help him. I don't know what he did."

"Did you know he was dead?"

"Yeah, I read something about that in the paper this morning." He looked at his watch. "Look, I've spent as much time on this as I can. If you don't mind, I've got some other appointments."

Inside of thirty seconds I was back out in the corridor looking at Ernie Fagin's closed door. I didn't have anywhere to go for the moment, so I sat back down on the corridor bench to collect my thoughts. No one came for Ernie's next appointment, and Ernie didn't come out. I wondered if he had a back entrance. I hadn't seen one.

After fifteen minutes, I had had enough of the game, and I had decided on what I wanted to do next. I went down to collect my car and drove it over to Logan Circle. The new neighborhood of the fancy law firms that had fled the buildings now housing Ernie Fagin and his fellow tenants. I parked in an underground parking garage and stood on the street looking up at the office tower that housed the firm of Spofford & Channing. 'Hawkins Industries' was chiseled in granite above the door. I guessed it had been deemed a good idea by the Management Committee of the firm to stay close to a major client by moving into that client's new corporate headquarters building. I knew quite a number of the partners at Spofford & Channing from my years as an associate and partner at Davis & Piersall, which had its own new offices just across the street. I found from the building directory that Spofford occupied twelve floors of the building with reception on 41. I found the right elevator bank and, a moment later, I was in the Spofford & Channing reception area looking past the receptionist at the view down Benjamin Franklin Parkway to the Art Museum.

"May I help you?" she interrupted me.

"Ah, yes. Could I see Steve Banks, please? Tell him Peter Gordon is here."

"Do you have an appointment with Mr. Banks?"

"Ah, no, but he knows me, and I'll only take a moment of his time."

She looked at me as if I were beneath contempt, but picked up the phone and talked into it.

"If you'll please have a seat, Mr. Banks will see you," she said.

It was twenty minutes later when Steve Banks came out to greet me. He emerged from the elevator and advanced upon me with an outstretched hand. I noticed that his thinning hair from law school had advanced so that he was now completely bald, but the quick smile was the same.

"Pete," he exclaimed. "Sorry to keep you waiting, I had a client on the phone. It's been too long."

He shook my hand enthusiastically.

"I understand you bailed out of the big city. And how's the practice at the shore? Going all right? Come on in here." He gestured to a door that opened off the reception area as he kept on talking. "I'd take you to my office but it's five floors down, and it's such a mess, anyway." He kept up a constant chatter as he shepherded me into the conference room. We finally got settled and through the pleasantries of our immediate personal lives, and he asked me what he could do for me.

"I know your firm represents Hawkins Industries, and I guess represented Norman Hawkins personally. I'd like to talk to the lawyer in charge of the representation."

"Really? Might I ask why?"

That wasn't the easiest question. I wasn't exactly sure why myself.

"Ah, I have some information that may be of interest and a few questions."

He considered. "Wilfred Brunell's the guy you want to talk to. I'll go ask, but he's not the easiest guy to deal with."

My spirits sank at the news. I had never met Brunell, but I knew his reputation. Steve's characterization was an understatement at best. "I'd only take a few minutes of his time."

"I'll see if he'll talk to you."

Steve left the room and was gone for about twenty minutes. I amused myself trying to decipher the abstract painting that covered one wall of the conference room. Finally he returned followed by the great man himself. Brunell was tall and thin with shaggy white hair and shaggier white eyebrows. His suit hung about him as if he had recently lost a lot of weight. He went immediately to one of the seats at the end of the conference table without offering to shake my hand. Steve stood uncertainly as if he didn't quite know what to do.

"Well, Mr. Gordon. I'm not sure why I should see you, but Mr. Banks here thinks it would be a good idea. Of course, I knew your father quite well."

I gritted my teeth. My father had been a senior partner at yet another old Philadelphia law firm. I had never worked for him, but everything I had done from my birth to his death had seemed to be under his ever-critical eye. He had died just a year before, still active in the practice of law and still critical of everything I had ever done. Of course, one of the benefits afforded me by that relationship was the ability to resist intimidation.

"Thank you for seeing me," I said.

He nodded. "So you're no longer at Davis & Piersall?"

I knew he was trying to needle me.

"No, I left the firm about two months ago." I gave no further explanation so he moved on.

"Well be that as it may. How might I help you? You said you had some information?"

"Yes, Norman Hawkins came to see me the night he went out on his boat. He later drowned, as I guess you know, under circumstances that have not been fully resolved. I've been looking into whether there might have been some connection."

Brunell's eyes narrowed as he fixed me with a stare that must have stricken fear into the hearts of first-year associates. "I'm afraid I don't understand, Mr. Gordon. Are you saying there was something in Mr. Hawkins' death that was other than an unfortunate and untimely accident?"

"I don't know. I'm just wondering. Why do you say untimely?"

"What?"

"I said, 'Why did you say untimely?' What was untimely about his death?"

He waved his hand as if to shoo away a gnat. "The death of a man like Norman Hawkins is always untimely. But that's not the point. The point is, what right have you to wonder about this let alone go around and ask questions about it?"

"That Friday night when he came to see me he retained me to represent him in connection with a matter."

"You?" He drew himself up in his chair theatrically. "Norman Hawkins hired you to represent him?" There was a definite emphasis on the word 'you' and his tone was dripping with sarcasm. "And with respect to what matter, pray tell, did Mr. Hawkins need you for representation."

I smiled to myself. Now I was getting the full Brunell treatment.

"I guess I'd be willing to share that with you if we could work out an agreement to share information."

"Nonsense. I'm not going to share information with anyone coming in here claiming to be Mr. Hawkins' lawyer. How did he hire you, did he give you a retainer?"

"Yes."

"How much was it?"

"Enough to demonstrate his seriousness."

"Do you have an engagement letter signed by him?"

"No," I admitted. "He died before one could be prepared for execution."

"And the matter for which you were hired. Were you able to complete it before he died."

"No, of course not."

"Fine. As executor of Mr. Hawkins' estate, I hereby formally terminate your services, if you were ever hired. I'd like the return of the retainer forthwith. You can keep a thousand dollars for your trouble." He rose from the table. "Now, if there is nothing else?"

I remained seated. "I take it this means you won't be accepting my offer to share information."

"No." He leaned forward. "I understand this is not the first time you have misrepresented yourself about your relationship to Mr. Hawkins. If you persist in this, or if you ever attempt to speak to Mrs. Hawkins again, I will file charges with the disciplinary board in New Jersey."

With that he turned on his heel and strode out of the room leaving Steve looking extremely embarrassed.

"Ah, I'm sorry, Pete," he said. "I don't know what to say. That was extremely rude."

I smiled. "You mean rude even for Wilfred Brunell?"

"Yes."

He escorted me out, apologizing every step of the way. There was nothing left for me to do but get my car and point it back to North Beach.

Chapter IV

The next morning found me in my office catching up on some correspondence. My mind kept drifting to Norman Hawkins. After my enthusiasm of the day before, I was beginning to have second thoughts about my decision to pursue the matter. I wasn't an investigator. Maybe the smart thing was to do what Brunell had so rudely suggested. I hadn't done anything for Hawkins, and he certainly wouldn't be needing any representation now. I had just passed the New Jersey Bar exam. I certainly didn't need to spend time defending myself in front of the State Disciplinary Board. One thing I knew about Wilfred Brunell was that he wasn't shy about carrying out his threats. Maybe I'd just leave it alone and send the money back. I cleared my mind and began to attack the papers in front of me with a renewed enthusiasm. I had lost myself in figuring out the details of a complicated option agreement, when Donna interrupted me.

"Pete, there are three men here to see you."

"Who are they?"

"They wouldn't say. They just said it was about Norman Hawkins."

For an instant I thought of telling Donna to send them away. I had decided to be quit of Norman Hawkins. But curiosity overcame my earlier resolution, and I asked her to send them in. I needn't have bothered. They were right at the door. Donna gave a little squeal of surprise as they pushed their way past her.

"Mr. Gordon?" asked the first, as he sat himself in the chair in front of my desk.

"Pete?" Donna inquired from the doorway.

"It's all right Donna," I said while inspecting the trio who filled up my office. All three were dressed in black suits, white shirts and dark, plain ties. They all had identical short haircuts. The first one to come through the door was the oldest. He looked to be about forty. He was slightly overweight and had a bored expression on his face. The other two were in their twenties. They arranged themselves behind the first man's chair and stood, in a military stance, staring into space with their hands clasped behind their backs.

"Are you Gordon?" asked the first man with a little more emphasis.

I focused my attention on him. "Yes," I said neutrally. "Who are you?"

"My name is Richard Beck," he said.

He waited for me to respond. I didn't. He tightened his lips in annoyance and continued.

"We understand you have been seeking information about Norman Hawkins." His speech seemed somehow formal.

"Who's we?" I asked.

"I beg your pardon?"

"I said, 'Who's we?' Who's the 'we' who has this understanding?"

"Ah," he said. "You do not know who we are." He carefully removed a wallet from his jacket pocket, selected a card and handed it to me across the desk. It had his name and a title of Executive Director of Return to the Roots. At the upper left hand corner of the card there was a logo, the initials of the organization, RTTR, with the two R's diagonally slanted away from the T's."

I smiled. "Nice logo."

He didn't answer but just stared at me.

"What can I do for you?" I asked.

He remained silent for a moment longer and then spoke.

"We understand that you are interested in Norman Hawkins."

"You mean senior or junior?"

"The senior is no more."

"So you mean junior."

"I mean Norman Hawkins."

"Do you know where he is?"

"He is in California doing important work for the RTTR."

"I think our Chief of Police wants to talk to him."

"He knows nothing about this unfortunate accident that has befallen his father."

"Yes, well, nevertheless, our Chief is an obsessive kind of guy. He'll probably want to talk to Harry directly. You know. Just to kind of shut the book on the matter."

"You have not answered my question."

I thought back. "What question was that?" I asked.

"The question about your interest in Norman Hawkins."

"That was a question? I thought it was just a statement of your understanding."

His eyes narrowed, and he leaned forward in his chair. I guess he was tired of the sparring. "Mr. Gordon, you will learn to take us seriously. Now, you will tell me what is your interest in Norman Hawkins."

I thought about playing with him further, but I happened to look up at his two companions. They were no longer staring out into space. They were looking straight at me and leaning forward on the balls of their feet for all the world like a pair of attack dogs waiting for the command to kill. I sat back and held out my hands palms up.

"No real interest. I'm just curious about the events that led up to his father's death, that's all."

He leaned forward as well so that the three of them looked like they were all about to start a race.

"It is not healthy to be too curious."

"Why is that?" I ventured. "Is there something about Norman's death that you want to keep secret?"

"We do not care about the father. The son is one of the elect, and we will not permit him to be diverted from his tasks."

"I see." I looked at the card again. "Executive Director. Is that an important title in the organization?"

He drew himself up. "I am second to the Archon."

I kept a straight face with some effort. "Archon? You mean Reynaud? The leader?"

"Yes. I mean Archon Reynaud."

"So Harry is not to be diverted from his precious duties, but you, the second in command in the organization, can be diverted from your important duties to come tell a lawyer in New Jersey not to be curious?"

"My duties are to protect the organization's members from outside influences that might distract them. But perhaps you need an object demonstration of our seriousness." He paused as if for dramatic effect. "Minuteman Spiegel," he barked.

Before I could move, the attack dog on the right strode to my chair and past it and, without a moment's hesitation, thrust his fist through my window. He then returned to his place and stood looking out into space again. Blood from the wound covered his hand and dripped on the floor. It had all happened so quickly I had not had an opportunity to react, but now a little ball of horror settled in my stomach. I tried to speak but could not. Beck didn't speak either but just sat there staring at me.

"If we meet again, it will not be such a joke anymore – our little group – will it?" he asked.

I didn't think the question really needed an answer, and I didn't try to give one. He got up from his seat in a leisurely fashion.

"But there won't be any necessity for us to meet again, will there, Mr. Gordon?"

Without waiting for my answer he turned and swept out of my office. His two attack dogs remained for a moment, little smirks on their faces, then they turned in unison and followed Beck out. I sank back in my chair and a wave of exhaustion came over me. The effect of the demonstration was far more unnerving than if they had threatened me directly.

I must have sat there as if in a trance for half an hour. Finally, I roused myself and crossed the street to the police station. I asked for Rich at the desk and, after a few minutes, I was escorted back to his office. He was sitting at a chair behind a battered desk talking on the phone. He waved me in and gestured for me to sit in a chair in front of the desk. He talked for a few moments longer and then hung up the phone.

"What can I do for you?" he asked.

"Have you had any luck in contacting Harry?"

"You mean little Norman? Yeah. The kid called me this morning.

His story matches the others. He left for California last Wednesday. He's been out there doing political work for the election. He hadn't seen his father for over a week before he left. Nice as could be and nothing there."

"Have you gotten the ME's report?"

He looked at me curiously. "You've taken a special interest in this case."

"Norman was my client. I am interested."

"Well, there was nothing there either. He drowned. There was a big bruise on the forehead. Not enough to kill him. Caused by a big blunt instrument."

"Like the boom of a sailboat?" I asked.

"Yes, just like the boom of a sailboat."

"So you're calling it an accident?"

"I don't have anything else to go on."

"What about the boat?"

"No sign. The Coast Guard has done some searching. I'm not sure how much. But they haven't found anything." He paused a moment. "Well, I've done enough talking. What about you? What is it made you rush over looking like you'd just seen a ghost?"

"The RTTR just came to visit me."

"The RTTR?"

"In the person of Executive Director Richard Beck. Plus two goons."

"Tell me about it."

So I related the story to him. When I finished he sat for a moment contemplating the over-painted wall next to his chair.

"He just drove his fist through your window? Just like that?"

"Just like that. And then just stood there like it was nothing, bleeding all over my floor."

He smiled at me.

"Guess it gave you quite a turn, didn't it?"

"Damn straight it did. I thought for a moment the guy was going to attack me. Then he went right by me to the window. I think it was the matter-of-fact way that he did it that was so chilling."

"Pretty smart," said Rich.

"What do you mean?"

"I can't arrest him for assault on a window. If I did it would be laughed out of court. They'd all claim it was an unfortunate accident."

I laughed.

"What's so funny?"

"That's just what they called what happened to Norman. An unfortunate accident. I'm wondering if the two events were equally accidental."

"Why? Because some nutsos from a cult are super-protective about one of their prize catches? Norman, Jr. is a great meal ticket for them, don't forget."

"Yeah. Especially now his father is no longer around. It was his father who was so upset about the money Harry was contributing to the organization, remember? With him out of the way, no more complaints. And how about the inheritance? What happens to the stock of Hawkins Industries? Wouldn't that be a nice catch for our Archon Reynaud?"

"Archon?"

I laughed. Now it all seemed so silly. It hadn't seemed that way in my office. But now I had a little distance from the intensity. I laughed again.

"Yes. That's Reynaud's title. God knows what it means. I guess Fuhrer had already been taken, so he had to go with something."

"Well, I'll grant you that this RTTR is a little nest of vipers. But I don't have anything that tells me yet that this wasn't an accident. We'll have to wait until the boat shows up."

"What if it never shows up? If it sank it will never be found."

"That's true. And it could have been sunk in a hundred different ways from deliberate scuttling to hitting a floating telephone pole to being rammed by a super-tanker. One of those guys could have driven over that little tinker toy of a boat, driven it under, and the crew wouldn't even have felt a bump. So what do you want me to do about it?"

I sighed. "You're right. I guess I'm just frustrated because I need to know the answer and there doesn't seem to be one."

Rich got up from his desk and walked around and sat on the front of it directly facing me.

"Pete. That's what life is. You never get to know the real answers.

You know that. Why don't you take a little time off? Get a girl friend. Stop obsessing."

I smiled ruefully. "I'm not sure I'm ready for that yet."

"So you're just hanging around feeling sorry for yourself, right?"

"I've got plenty to keep me busy," I said, maybe a little defensively.

"OK," he raised his hands in surrender. "Whatever you say. But if you're so busy, get the hell out of my office and stop obsessing about this Norman Hawkins thing."

"But you'll keep pursuing it?"

"I'll pursue it if I've got something to pursue. Right now I've got jack-shit, OK?"

"OK." I got up and he ushered me out the door.

"Come back when you've got something specific."

I walked out on the front steps of the police station and stood on the steps. Across the street was Dalton's Pier and beyond that the blue of Barnegat Bay in the fall sunshine. The blustery post-storm northwest wind had shifted to the Southwest and calmed to a gentle ten to twelve knots. The late morning sun warmed the back of my neck. The west shore of the bay had turned all brown and gold. It was the last lingering remnant of the summer, a brief little interlude before the howling northeast gales and lowering gray skies of winter claimed the landscape. I looked over at the marina. Right across from me was the slip where "Far Cry" had lain the night before she had gone out the inlet. Was she now at the bottom of some canyon? Had she taken the rest of her crew with her? I shivered at the thought.

I shook off the feeling and stepped out into the street to walk the short block back to my office. As I stepped in the door, Donna handed me an envelope. It was an expensive rich cream with the name "Spofford & Channing" in fancy script in the upper left corner. It felt palpable as if the weight of its content had transformed itself into the very mass of the letter. I held it out in front of me as I walked back to my office. I sat at my desk and slit open the envelope. Inside was the trademark letterhead of the firm. It used to be that to the left and sometimes also to the right of the firm's name would be listed the names of the lawyers in the firm, or sometimes just the partners listed in the order of their seniority. As the firms grew larger, the names became listed in progressively smaller print, as the very number of the partners listed would threaten to overwhelm the entire first page of the letter. So, one by one, the larger firms abandoned the practice. The letter in my hand had one name, Wilfred Brunell, II, and a direct dial telephone number at the upper left hand portion of the letter. The letter started out graciously enough with "Dear Mr. Gordon" but then the threats began. The threats were the same as he had made to me orally the previous day. He must have gone right back to his office to dictate the letter. The gist was that if I did not return the retainer given me by Norman Hawkins and immediately stop harassing his client, Mrs. Hawkins, he would take the appropriate legal action including "without limitation" initiating such proceedings before the State Disciplinary Board as were warranted in the circumstances.

I had been standing while I read. I realized that my fingers were crumpling the bottom of the letter itself as I gripped it. I dropped it on my desk and went around to sit in my chair. I swung around to put my feet up on the radiator that is under the window behind my desk and looked out at the water. As it happened, my view just includes that empty slip that had been filled with sixty feet of sailboat just last Friday. Just five days before. So Lorraine was his client. That was interesting. I had thought Hawkins Industries and Norman Hawkins were his clients. And Mary had told us that Norman and his third wife, that very same Lorraine, were in the middle of a rather unpleasant property settlement in connection with a pending divorce. It was time I got some legal advice of my own. And since one of the partners of Stockard & Stevens was being threatened with disciplinary proceedings, it was time that at least one of the other partners became apprised of the facts.

I picked up the letter and went to find Linda Stevens. She was in her office talking on the telephone, which is what she is doing for about the entire time she is in the office. Linda and Dave had been partners for about ten years. He handles the corporate stuff and she's the litigator. Her long black hair is now streaked with gray, but her energy never stops. I'm not sure how she took to Dave's idea to take on a new partner, me. There had been a certain reserve there at first. But I had shown some interest in litigation and even a bit of a flair for it, and she had needed the help. She waved me to a chair and continued her conversation. I picked some files off the chair, put them on the floor and sat down.

"Chuck, please," she was saying. "You don't have to polish up your jury speech on me. I've heard it all before." She listened for a time and took the phone away from her ear, and rolled her eyes up in her head. I could hear Chuck continuing to argue in the background.

"Chuck, stop. You may not like what the judge did. And your client may not like what the judge did, but he granted my summary judgment motion. You may think that you'll get the Third Circuit to turn the whole thing around for you, but that will be another year from now and then you have to go back to trial in front of the same judge who just threw your case out. I think we're being pretty generous that our previous offer is still on the table. It won't be if we have to incur any more legal expenses."

Chuck talked some more.

"OK, you go talk to him again . . . . I'll wait, but not too much longer . . . . Yes, Chuck. Bye."

She hung up the phone. "Whew," she said. "That Chucky Jackson is such a pain in the butt."

I put the letter on her desk and pushed it over to her. "Speaking of pains in the butt, take a look at this."

She picked it up and read it quickly. A little smile tugged at the corners of her mouth.

"It's nothing to laugh about," I said.

"What? A threat from Wilfred Brunell? He's an old fraud."

"You know him?"

"Sure we used to pray he would be representing the other side when I was with Erv."

Erv was Ervin Fine, one of the nation's leading anti-trust plaintiff's attorneys. Linda had spent ten years carrying Erv's bag before she had decided that Erv was really a one-man show. When her husband had found a job in New Jersey she had followed along and set up a practice at the shore. She and Dave had met and formed a partnership.

"He's got a formidable reputation."

"He's a bluffer. And he's got such an intimidating manner that most people let him get away with the bluff. The problem with being a bluffer is that, once you're called on the bluff, you've got nowhere to go. All your credibility goes up in smoke. Erv used to love to negotiate with him."

"Are you saying I shouldn't take this seriously?"

"I don't know. Are you guilty of improprieties?"

"Maybe I had better tell you the story."

"Maybe you'd better."

I started out and in twenty minutes I had completed the tale.

"So the twenty-five thousand dollars is a nice little windfall for Stockard & Stevens. Showing you can earn your keep, right?"

I shrugged.

"And, naturally, you don't want to give it back. Have you talked to Dave about this?"

"Yes."

"What did he say?"

"He said 'Do what you want to do.'"

"He would." She tapped her pencil on the desk in a familiar gesture. "So you're obsessing with guilt because Norman gave you too much in the first place, and you haven't done anything to earn it."

"That's about the size of it."

"OK. Where's the money now?"

"Dave suggested I put it in our attorney escrow account."

"Good. I'm glad to see he's not gone completely senile."

I sat and waited while she tapped that pencil. "So what do you want to do?"

I was struck that Dave had asked me the same question. New partner or not, Norman had been my client.

"I think we play out the string a little."

"OK, so we leave the money there for the moment. And we decide whether to give it back after the smoke clears, right?"

I shrugged. "If it turns out that Norman's death was really an accident, and there's nothing going on with the son other than a revolt against the mores of an authoritarian father, I guess I won't have provided much value to the estate."

"Are you willing to risk some time to find that out?"

"I am now. I had almost decided to give it all up, but the RTTR visit and this letter have begun to intrigue me. People are reacting too strongly for this all to be innocent."

"Well, maybe so, and maybe not. But the first thing is to find out who Wilfred really represents."

"How do we find that out?"

"Let's call him and ask."

Without any further discussion, she picked up the telephone and dialed the number that was on the letterhead.

"Hello, Mr. Brunell please. Tell him it's Linda Stevens calling . . . . I see. Does unavailable mean he's not in the office? . . . Well it's rather important. Could you give him a note to tell him I'm on the line? . . . Yes, he knows me. If he has any trouble with his memory, tell him I used to work for Erv Fine. And it's in reference to a charge of unethical conduct . . . . That's right."

She put her hand over the mouthpiece to speak to me.

"You'd think he was actually an important person the barriers that he puts in the way of people wanting to talk to him."

"Is someone going to get him?"

"They made me no promises. He's a very busy man, you know."

We waited about five minutes before Brunell came on the line. Linda was all sweetness and light.

"Wilfred, I'm so sorry to have intruded . . . . Yes it has been quite a long time . . . . I'm doing quite well, thank-you . . . . Yes, it's about this curious letter you've just sent to Peter Gordon . . . . No, I don't represent him, but I am his partner . . . ."

A long pause followed while I supposed Brunell was laying out the bill of indictment against me. Finally Linda cut him off.

"That's all very interesting, Wilfred. If you think you have grounds to file a complaint, I suggest you do so. What I'm not clear about is, on whose behalf will you be acting? . . . . I see. It's Norman Hawkins' estate is it? But that's just what confuses me, Wilfred. This letter says that your client is Mrs. Hawkins . . . . I see. And your firm also represents the company, Hawkins Industries? . . . But my understanding was that Mr. and Mrs. Hawkins were involved in a rather messy divorce and property settlement."

There followed another long pause while Brunell must have started into another long monologue. Linda was nodding and smiling all the time, but she pulled over a pad and began to write some notes. Finally, Brunell must have run out of gas.

"All that sounds pretty convoluted to me, Wilfred. You're sure there's no element of conflict of interest in all that? . . . . Well, far be it from me to second-guess your firm's ethics committee. Let me say this. If you want a battle, please go ahead and file. We'll have every one of those ethics committee members testifying before the Disciplinary Board to personally explain your firm's position . . . . Yes, it's nice to talk to you too, Wilfred."

She hung up the phone and threw down her pencil in disgust.

"I'd forgotten what an insufferable, pompous ass he is."

"So what's the story? He represents the company, the estate and the wife all at the same time?"

"That's right. And I have been misinformed about a contentious property settlement. Sure, there were some discussions going on, but they were very professional and open, and Mrs. Hawkins had separate counsel to represent her specially in those matters."

"And Norman was fully informed of all this and consented?"

"Of course." She picked up the letter again. "You know he's so stupid."

"Why?"

"He doesn't need to mention Mrs. Hawkins in here at all. I wonder why he does? It's totally gratuitous, and, if he hadn't, we never would have realized that he might have a conflict of interest problem."

She shook her head. "Why don't you let me worry about this? I'll find out who her other counsel is and find out how contentious it really was."

"It would also be interesting to know if he was aware that Wilfred had a continuing lawyer-client relationship with Mrs. Hawkins."

"Yes, wouldn't it?"

I thanked her and found my way back to my office. I felt better that I could leave Wilfred Brunell in Linda's capable hands. With that assurance, I was able to put the whole matter out of my mind to devote myself to some work. Before I knew it, it was 1:30 and past time to take a break for lunch. Looking at the pile of papers that still filled up my in-box, I decided to walk up to the deli, bring back a tuna-fish sandwich and continue working. I went out into the sunshine and started up the street. Halfway there I heard my name being called in a curious half-whisper. I looked around and heard it again. Parked on the street was a Cadillac, and someone was calling my name through the open front window. It was Mary Hawkins.

"Mr. Gordon. Could we talk a moment?"

I walked over to the car and looked in the window. She was in the driver's seat leaning across towards me.

"Certainly, Mrs. Hawkins. Can I buy you a sandwich at our local deli?"

"No. I can't be seen with you. Please get in the car."

She reached across and opened the passenger side door. I hesitated a moment and then slid into the seat. She had the car running and pulled out into the street before I could get the door closed. Without a word she pulled up to the stop light on Ocean Avenue, and, getting a green light, took a left to take her over the Cranberry Inlet Bridge. I started to say something but she motioned me into silence. She continually looked into her rear view mirror as if she was expecting to be followed. We proceeded in this fashion north and then over the Mantoloking Bridge to the mainland. By this time I was beginning to get a bit nervous. For all I knew she was delivering me to a rendezvous with Richard Beck and his happy crew.

"Do you mind telling me where we're going?" I finally asked.

"Just to a place where we won't be seen."

"Well, all of this cloak and dagger is making me a little nervous. Do you mind if I pick the place of seclusion, if that's all we're after."

She looked at me in surprise. "You think I'm with them?"

"Well, the thought had crossed my mind. It really would make me feel better."

She agreed, and I had her turn around and head back towards the bridge. I directed her to turn right into a deserted dirt road that led into the marsh. About a mile down the road was a pull off where duck hunters parked to walk to their duck blinds on the bay. She parked the car and turned off the ignition. The turn-off was beside a little grove of trees, which bordered the marsh. Beyond the marsh was the bay. She just sat and looked at it for a moment. I waited. Finally she turned and looked at me.

"I'm not sure why I'm doing this."

"Doing what?"

"If they find out, they'll probably kill me."

"You mean the RTTR?"

"Yeah, the great Bob Reynaud, or more likely his master of dirty tricks, Dickie Beck."

"Why don't you tell me about it?"

She sighed. "I guess since I've come this far. Harry was home that Friday night."

"You mean he hadn't gone to California on Wednesday?"

"Oh, he went on Wednesday, all right. But Friday night he came back. He was all confused and upset, but he wouldn't tell me why."

"Why didn't you tell us that Harry had been home before this?"

"It was too much of a shock, hearing about Norman. I didn't think it mattered where Harry was."

"Where was Harry?"

"Oh, he was back in California by that time."

"OK," I said. "Let's take it a step at a time. Let's start with his father. Did he come over to the house that night?"

"No. Or not that I know of. Harry got a call about ten o'clock. When he got off the phone, he wouldn't tell me anything about it. He said he was going out to the Dunes. That he had to see somebody."

"Who was he going to see?"

"He wouldn't tell me. We, ah . . . . We weren't really talking."

"Why not?"

She didn't answer for a moment. She was looking away from me again. I thought I saw that her eyes were wet.

"We . . . . We had a big fight that night."

"What about?"

"The RTTR."

I waited, and finally she explained.

"I wanted for him to get out of the organization, but he is so blinded by Bob Reynaud that he can't see what it's become."

"I thought you had gotten him into the organization in the first place."

She looked at me sharply. "Who told you that? His father?"

"Uhh, yes. I guess it was."

"Well, I guess it's probably true enough. We met at an RTTR rally. I was one of the girls in the funny hats and armbands. I was handing out literature when Harry came up to the table. He smiled at me, and I thought the earth would open and swallow me up. But I was already wanting to get out. The only reason that I persuaded him in was so I could get to know him better."

"So you got him to stay for the rally."

"Sure. I became his personal guide. It was what we were supposed to do if we found likely recruit, especially a recruit for the Minutemen."

"The Minutemen? Who are they?"

"Bob's personal guard. They act as security at rallies and as Bob's personal bodyguards. If there's any strong arm stuff to be performed, it's the Minutemen who take care of it."

"Yes," I said. "I think I've made the acquaintance of a couple of them."

She looked at me, her eyes frightened. "Where? You mean here in North Beach?"

"It's all right. They've gone." I had to keep her talking now, or she might not go on.

"So your job was to find likely recruits and use your personal charm to sell them on the organization?"

She nodded. "That's right. It was a beautiful day, I remember. I didn't really take him around, we just walked and talked. Then I took him into the program. Bob was there himself." She sighed. "Harry was just blown away by the speech. Sometimes I think he fell in love with Bob Reynaud more than he did with me. Anyway, he was hooked. We both got on an RTTR bus that night for one of Bob's camps in the Pocono's."

"They took him away?"

"Sure, that's part of the program. We scoop them up at the rallies. Then it's off to one of the camps for the indoctrination period. Bob likes to get them there for three weeks. At the end of that time, they've been cut off from their family and friends and surrounded with nothing but RTTR propaganda twenty-four hours a day. They're so isolated from reality they're ready to believe anything."

"So Harry became a member?"

"Right." She laughed. "Just when I was having second thoughts about the whole thing and ready to make a break, Harry comes along and becomes a true believer. And now I'm stuck again because Harry won't leave, and I can't leave Harry."

"So your argument with Harry that night was about the RTTR?"

"Yes. I wanted him to leave. He could see some of the terrible things that Beck and the Minutemen were doing, but he would always say that it was all going on behind Bob's back. All he had to do, he said, was to let Bob know, and Bob would put a stop to it. I think he was beginning to recognize that argument was beginning to be a little hollow, but his stupid male pride couldn't come to terms with the fact that he'd made a mistake."

I wanted to learn more about the RTTR, but I wanted to find out about that Friday night even more.

"Do you think it could have been Harry's father who called that night?"

"I don't know. It could have been. They kept having the same argument. Harry was saying the same things over the phone. It got pretty heated, but then it always did with his father."

"And he went out right after the phone call?"

She thought a moment. "Well, not right after. About a half-hour later."

"And he said he was going to meet someone?"

"Yes."

"Did he come back that night?"

"No."

"Didn't that worry you?"

"Of course, but I thought he was still mad from our fight."

"So when did you see him again?"

"I haven't."

"You haven't?" I sat up and turned to look at her. "You haven't seen him since last Friday night?"

"No. The next morning I was really worried. I didn't hear from him all that day. Then, the morning after that, I guess that would have been Sunday, that little Nazi, Dickie Beck, and a couple of his storm troopers came to visit me. They said that I shouldn't worry. That Harry had been called back to California for important party work." She shivered. "That guy gives me the creeps. The way he looks at you."

"Beck came to visit you? When? Before Rich and I came over?"

"Yes, I think so. It was pretty early."

"And he told you Harry was fine and in California?"

"Yes. He told me he had met Harry the night before and sent him back."

"You believed him?"

She shrugged. "I had no reason not to. How else could Harry have gotten back to California so quickly?"

"So it was Beck on the phone who wanted to meet Harry at the Dunes?"

"It could have been."

"Did Beck say anything to you about Harry's father?"

"No, not a word."

"You don't think Harry could have gone out on 'Far Cry' with his father?"

She looked at me sharply. "No, of course not."

"And you didn't think it was important enough to tell us about this when we came to see you?"

She was crying now. "I didn't think that one thing had anything to do with the other. And Beck warned me not to tell anyone about Harry's whereabouts."

I sat back against the car seat. So, Beck was in town on Sunday morning. I wondered if he had also been in town on Friday night. Or, at least on Saturday morning. A sudden chill settled on my stomach. Rich had said he had heard from Harry that morning. But how would Rich have known it was really Harry on the phone? I looked over at Mary.

"Ah . . . . I don't know how to ask this except just to ask it. Are you sure Harry is all right?"

She looked at me quickly. "What do you mean?"

"I mean you haven't seen him since last Friday . . . ."

"Oh," she looked relieved. "Yes, he's all right in that sense. I've talked to him on the telephone. He's been in California right enough. I don't think he's doing any political work like they're saying, though."

"What do you mean?"

"They've got a ranch out in Ventura County. I think he's there."

"Being held against his will?"

She shrugged. "Your own will doesn't count for much when you join the RTTR. It's Reynaud's will that's important."

I sat back to think. If it had been Beck on the phone that night, he hadn't met Harry at the Dunes. I had been at the Dunes myself that night and I hadn't seen Harry or Beck. I hadn't seen Norman either. I had been sure that Norman had been planning to take Harry with him on "Far Cry." Why would he have left without Harry? Maybe Beck had called Harry and whisked him back to California before Norman could get hold of the kid. Maybe Beck knew that Norman was planning something. A great blue heron came swooping in to land in a little open piece of water in front to us. He looked around nervously for a moment and then bent his head to his business. We both watched him silently. Suddenly, he spread his great wings and took back to the air.

"Did anyone else know that Harry was home on Friday night?" I asked.

"What do you mean?"

"Well. You weren't expecting him, were, you?"

"No."

"Was anyone else?"

"I don't think so."

"Could he have come and gone without anyone else knowing? Like his stepmother? Or that housekeeper? What was her name? Florence?"

She thought a minute. "I suppose he could have. The garage is on our side of the house. And he came in and went out through the garage door, not the front door. There's no reason for any one else to have seen him."

"Did he tell you why he had come home unexpectedly?"

"Party business was what he said. I was so glad to see him, I didn't inquire too closely. And then we got into that fight, and he left."

"How was he dressed?"

"What do you mean?"

"Just what I said. What kind of clothes did he have on?"

"Just that stupid black suit that all the Minutemen wear."

"Did he change before he went out?"

She thought a minute. "No. He had the same suit on. I remember him pulling on the jacket as he went out towards the door."

"So Mary, the only thing I don't understand is, why are you telling me all this?"

"I thought about it for a long time. I have nowhere to turn. My parents are both dead. I can't burden my sisters with this stuff. No one in the party is going to help me."

"What do you want me to do?"

"I want to hire you to help me get Harry back."

I laughed suddenly at the incongruity of it all.

"Don't laugh at me," she said.

"I'm sorry. I'm not laughing at you. Harry's father came to see me the night before he went off on his boat for the last time. He wanted to hire me in connection with a scheme to get his son back."

"That's not funny either. Maybe you don't realize that these people aren't a happy little band of Hare Krishnas. They're serious, and they're willing to use violence to solve a problem."

"I know. I've had a taste of their tactics."

"All right." She seemed to accept my explanation. "I don't have much money to offer you."

"That's all right. And you don't need to hire me. Let's just say I'll help you." It probably wouldn't be wise to be taking more money from the Hawkins family at the moment, anyway. And it wasn't clear that Mary wanted to hire me specifically for my legal talents.

"We should go and tell your story to Chief Skowronski."

"No," she said quickly. "We can't. They'll find out."

"Look. I've known Rich for a long time. He's a reliable guy."

"What about all his deputies? Are you sure none of them have a connection to the party? They make a special effort to recruit police. Did you know that? There's no police force in the country I'd trust with any of this. If they just saw me going into the station, Beck would hear about it in an hour."

I thought this was all a little paranoid, but I wasn't prepared to argue the point now.

"So what should we do?" she asked. I realized I had been drifting. I shifted my attention back to her. She was looking at me expectantly. Now that she had passed her problem on to me, she expected me to have a plan to solve it.

"I don't know."

I spent the rest of the day working on that very problem. I had not been able to convince Mary to let me confide in Rich Skowronski. After some more arguing on the subject, I decided to leave it to a future time. She dropped me off on a side street back in North Beach. I walked back to my office and spent the rest of the day alternatively trying to get some work done and being sidetracked with how I might get Harry back from the RTTR.

Chapter V

Norman's funeral was set for Friday of that week. Rich called me the night before.

"You going?" he asked.

"I thought I would. What about you?"

"Yeah. It seems like a good opportunity to see who shows up."

"And who doesn't?"

"Oh, I think everyone will be there. What about we drive up together. That's more your territory than mine."

"Not anymore."

"That's what you say."

So the next morning I picked him up in front of the police station, and we headed towards Philadelphia. More precisely, we headed towards Bryn Mawr, to the big Episcopal Church to which Norman had contributed his money over the years. Whether he attended regularly as well is something I was ignorant about. Rich was all rigged out in a dark suit, white shirt and striped tie. I couldn't help but comment on his outfit but other than that, we didn't say much until we crossed into Pennsylvania. I spent the time wrestling with myself, trying to decide if I should tell him about my conversation with Mary despite her admonition of silence. In the end I decided I had to. After all, I rationalized; I hadn't taken her on as a client. And I needed Rich to know that Harry had been in North Beach that night. Rich took the news quietly. If he was drawing any conclusions, he kept them to himself.

We arrived early. I usually drive around and kill time in those circumstances but Rich insisted on going right in. He picked a seat near the back where he could see everyone as they came in the church. People started to file in about twenty minutes before the service was due to start. Rich questioned me about every new arrival. I knew some of them, and I could recognize a number of others. It appeared that the Philadelphia business, banking and legal communities were out in force. Just a few minutes before the service was to start a tall, dark-haired woman came down the aisle alone. She was wearing a dark dress and appeared to be in her mid-thirties. I found I couldn't keep my eyes off her. Rich elbowed me as he had already done a dozen times.

"I don't know," I whispered to him before he could ask.

The woman looked neither to the right nor the left, but walked straight to the front of the church and took the vacant first pew on the left.

"Do you think that's the sister?" hissed Rich.

"I don't know," I said again.

Just then Lorraine, Mary and Wilfred Brunell appeared in the back of the church. Lorraine hesitated a moment and then swept down the aisle with Mary a half step behind. Brunell followed a respectful full step behind them, the image of the faithful family retainer. I don't think Lorraine saw the woman who had just preceded them at first. She was still kneeling at the rail with her head bowed. It looked to me like Lorraine was headed towards the front left pew when she suddenly saw that someone was already there. She came to a full stop, and her followers bunched up behind her. There was a moment of confusion and then Lorraine changed course for the right pew. Mary and Wilfred followed dutifully behind. Maybe I imagined the whole thing, it was over so quickly. The woman in the left pew finished her prayers and resumed her seat without so much as a glance to the other side of the aisle.

"Where's little Normie?" asked Rich.

I shrugged. It appeared that whatever was keeping him in California was more important than his father's funeral. Just then there was a stir behind us, and I turned to look. A group of five men had come in the door. All of them were wearing dark suits. Three of the men peeled off and went around the other side to sit in the back. The other two started the long walk down the center aisle. One I recognized as

Harry. He was taller than the skinny adolescent I now remembered from days when he had hung around the North Beach Yacht Club. He had short dark hair and appeared apprehensive as if he didn't know exactly why he was here. The other man appeared to be in his fifties. He was tall and almost painfully thin, dressed in a pinstriped suit that any banker in the church would have been proud to own. I had never seen him before.

"Minutemen?" asked Rich, indicating the three dark suits who were just seating themselves opposite us.

"None other," I said.

"Who's the tall guy?" he asked, indicating the older man walking down the aisle. "Beck?"

"No. My guess is it's the Archon Reynaud in person come to pay his respects."

"So the other guy is Normie?"

"That would be correct."

We watched them walk down the aisle. Reynaud had his right hand about an inch behind Harry's left elbow as if he were afraid Harry would slip or forget where to go. When they were three-quarters of the way down the aisle, Mary turned to see them. Her face lit up, and she got to her feet to greet Harry. She gave him a kiss in the middle of the aisle and pulled him into the pew to sit beside her. Whether by design or not she sat down leaving just enough room for Harry. Reynaud hesitated for an instant and then made a move as if to sit in the front pew on the left. Then, for some reason, he thought better of it and retreated to the third row, causing some dark looks from the occupants of that pew as he squeezed into the space. Just as he sat down, the organist cranked up from his prelude into the processional hymn. We rose to sing and our view of the pews in the front of the church was blocked.

I didn't pay much attention to the service. The minister droned on somewhere far above my consciousness. I rose for the hymns and knelt for the prayers, but my mind kept going back to the pre-ceremony scene. It had all gone so quickly, I wondered if I had seen it right. At the end of the service the minister announced that there would be a reception at the parish house for family and friends.

"Do you think we qualify?" I asked Rich as we lined up to exit from the church.

"We're not missing this," he said. As we came out the door, a rain shower opened up so that no one stopped to talk at the door. They either ran for their cars or bent their heads against the rain to make their way to the parish house. Rich hesitated under the last bit of shelter.

"Damn. Where did this come from?"

I pushed past him. "This way," I said and double-timed across the parking lot towards the parish house. Upstairs was a little auditorium with a stage at one end. A long table had been set up against one wall with coffee urns at each end and cakes and cookies in the middle. Two Main Line matrons oversaw the dispensing of the coffee, cup by cup. By the time I had gotten a cup and turned around to face the room, it had filled to overcrowding. I looked for the woman I thought must be Jane, but she was nowhere to be seen. I wondered if I would be able to find her at all. I started to work my way around the door. In the corner by the door, I spotted the Minutemen. Mary and Harry were in the middle. The dark suits formed protectively around them. Rich was there talking animatedly with the man I had assumed to be Robert Reynaud. Reynaud was shaking his head to whatever Rich was saying to him. I started to go over when I saw Jane by the stage, a cup in her hand talking to two men in suits. I worked my way over and stood just outside the little group until the men said good-bye and moved on. I stepped forward.

"Ah, Mrs. Turner? Jane?"

She turned her head and fixed me with her hazel eyes, and I almost faltered.

"Yes?"

"I'm Peter Gordon. I want to express my sympathy for your loss."

"Ah, Mr. Gordon, of course. We've spoken on the phone. Thank-you."

"Call me Peter, please."

She nodded without saying anything or acknowledging that we had reached a first name basis on the telephone, leaving me to deal with the silence. The silence grew as I struggled for something to say and only seemed accentuated by the roar of the many conversations around us. I could see her attention start to wander.

"Ah, was that Robert Reynaud who came in with your brother?"

Her eyes snapped back to my face and seemed to flash angrily.

"Yes," she snapped.

"Did you say something to him that caused him to retreat to the third row so ignominiously?"

"I just reminded him that the front row was reserved for family. Maybe I said it a little too sharply."

"Well, he got the message."

"I'm not so sure." She was looking beyond me. I turned to see what she was looking at. It was that little group of Minuteman gathered around her brother. Rich had managed to wedge his way in to talk to Harry. Reynaud appeared to be hovering nervously at his shoulder.

"Who's that talking to my brother?" she asked.

"Why do you think I would know?"

"You were with him."

"I didn't realize you'd noticed."

"So, who is it?"

"It's Rich Skowronski. He's Chief of our North Beach police force."

"What's he doing here? More to the point, what are you doing here?"

"Paying my respects to your father."

"You didn't know him. You only spoke to him that one time, didn't you?"

"Well, not exactly. I met him when he first built the house in North Beach"

"And Chief Skowronski? Is he paying his respects as well?"

I shrugged. "Your father's death is still under investigation."

"Do you have anything that would lead you to believe that it was anything more than an accident?"

"No."

"Have they found the boat yet?"

"No."

"Well, they never will. He'd never leave the boat unless it was past saving."

"He might if the boom hit him on the head, and he got knocked overboard."

"So, I still don't get it. What do you care?"

I shrugged. "I told you. When he came to visit me the Friday afternoon before he left, he hired me."

"Yes, you told me that. And you still don't know why?"

I smiled. "He wasn't real specific about that."

"That sounds like Dad. So you got an assignment, but you're not sure what it was to be."

"Right. And ever since, I've been trying to figure it out."

A silence settled over us again. She continued to watch the RTTR group.

"You don't seem real close to Harry," I ventured.

She sighed. "Oh, we're close enough. I told him I wasn't having anything to do with him while he belonged to that . . . whatever it is."

"RTTR?"

"Yes."

"Mary told me she was after him to quit."

She looked at me in surprise. "Mary told you that?"

"Yes."

"That's the biggest load of baloney I ever heard. Mary's the reason he joined, and I think the main thing that keeps him tied to the organization."

"Mary also says he was in North Beach that Friday night. She doesn't think so, but I'd been wondering if he went out on the boat with your father."

She looked at me with her eyes wide. "That's crazy. If he did, what's he doing standing over there big as life? Why isn't he dead too?"

"I don't know."

"You've got to be wrong."

I was going to admit that I probably was wrong, but she had left me, heading right for Harry. I followed a few paces behind her. She walked right up to Harry and started talking. I was going to follow but I got intercepted by two of the RTTR attack dogs.

"Excuse me," I said, but they wouldn't budge from in front of me. I felt someone take my arm. It was Reynaud.

"Mr. Gordon, I presume," he said. He had a smooth deep voice.

I turned to face him. I'm an even six feet, but he was about three inches taller than I am.

"Mr. Reynaud," I said.

"I'm pleased you know me."

"I'm not sure I'm pleased that you know me," I answered.

"Why shouldn't you be? An attorney in a new practice. You ought to be doing whatever you can to get your name networked around."

"I was going over to pay my respects to Harry."

"You know Harry?"

"Not well, but yes, I know Harry."

"And you've met his lovely wife, Mary, I understand."

"Yes, I have had the pleasure."

"Well, I think you can understand that all of this has been an enormous shock to Harry. He's told me that he wishes to avoid the strain of dealing with anyone other than his close family."

"And you're here to see that his wishes are respected?"

"Exactly."

By now the conversation between Harry and Jane had gotten somewhat heated. I looked beyond Reynaud to see that Mary had joined in, and she and Jane seemed that they were shouting at each other, although in tones so low I could not hear their voices. Reynaud noticed the same thing, and he made a little signal to one of his Minutemen. Then he stepped smoothly to Harry's side and whispered something in his ear. Harry nodded, and the whole entourage started towards the door, with two of the Minutemen clearing a path for the rest. Jane and I were suddenly alone.

"Damn him," she said. I didn't know whether she was talking about her brother or Reynaud.

"What did he say?" I asked.

She looked at me as if surprised that I was still there.

"Oh, Peter. Did you see that? I'm having a conversation with my brother, and then that harridan steps in and starts yelling at me, and before you know it, Reynaud's got them all out of here."

"What did he say? Was he in North Beach last Friday?"

"No. He says he was out on the RTTR ranch in California."

"Why would Mary tell me he was in North Beach?"

"Mary will tell you anything she thinks you want to hear."

"Ah . . . . Do you think we could go somewhere and talk."

She didn't answer for a moment. She was staring at the door where her brother had disappeared in the midst of his RTTR guardians a moment before. The crowd noise rose around us as if no one had noticed a thing. It had all happened so quickly, I expect very few people had noticed anything.

"Jane?" I asked.

She looked up at me as if she were coming out of a trance.

"Oh, no," she said. "I don't think I'm up to any conversations at the moment. As a matter of fact I think I'd best be going myself."

"Where are you going?"

"Back to California."

"Can I give you a lift to the airport?"

"No, really. I have a car. And I'd much prefer to be alone."

She held out her hand to shake mine. "Good-bye, Mr. Gordon. I really recommend that you not get yourself involved in the affairs of the Hawkins family. We won't be grateful, and you'll only cause yourself grief."

"Thank you for the advice, Mrs. Turner."

She turned on her heel and headed for the door. I watched her retreating back until the door had closed on it.

"Looks like you get all the luck," I heard at my shoulder. I started and turned. It was Rich.

"Not bad," he went on. "You get to talk to the pretty sister, and I get to butt heads with Reynaud and his pretty boys."

"I saw you got to talk to Harry."

He grunted. "Much good it did me. Come on. Let's get out of here." He started for the door, and I followed. Most of the others were leaving at the same time. Neither of us spoke again until I had threaded my car through the traffic jam trying to leave the parking lot. Rich appeared to be lost in thought, staring out the window. I left him to his thoughts. Finally he turned to look at me.

"So she told you he was in North Beach last Friday?"

"Who? Mary?"

"Yes, cute little Mary."

"That's what she said."

"That's not what she says today."

"Where was he?"

"He says he was in California the whole time. They just flew in this morning for the service."

"That shouldn't be hard to check. Call the airlines."

"And ask what? Did you have a passenger named Norman Hawkins on your flight 99 from LAX? Dollars to donuts they say they did. But how do I know it was really Normie?"

"And Mary backs him up."

"All the way."

I shrugged. "What else is she going to do with all of them around?"

"She didn't seem the reluctant witness to me. Pretty vociferous about it."

"So why would she lie to me?"

He sat back in his seat and closed his eyes. "I don't have the first clue." He sat there apparently thinking for what seemed like a long time.

"What did you say that set off the sister?" he asked.

"You mean when she charged into the lion's den?"

"Exactly."

"I told her what Mary had told me. That Mary had said he was in North Beach, and I thought he might have been out on the boat."

"You have no way of knowing that."

"That's true, but it stirred the pot, didn't it? Could you hear anything they were saying?"

"No. Did she fill you in after they all split?"

"No. She just gave me some advice to stay out of Hawkins family affairs."

"It looks like everyone wants you out."

I sighed. "Yeah. Everyone except old Norman himself. He wanted me in for some reason. Some reason that I can't yet figure out."

"Well, when you figure it out, let me know." He put his head back again and closed his eyes. Five minutes later I looked over, and he was fast asleep.

* * *

I put the whole thing out of my mind as well. I went fishing with Freddie Wooding on Saturday. On Sunday I went into the office to clean up some neglected work and spent the afternoon watching football. I started to think about the Hawkins family again as I was getting some scrambled eggs together for dinner. I had not come to any conclusions by the time I settled down with my plate and switched on the news. I wasn't paying much attention until I realized that there was an RTTR banner on the screen. The banner appeared to be in the middle of a scuffle between contending groups. I could see a group of Minutemen in their trademark black suits fending off a shouting crowd. Then the camera swung wildly as the Minutemen formed up into a wedge and charged through the throng. I turned up the sound to hear a slightly hysterical announcer.

" . . . Hospital reports on the Congressman's condition are still sketchy. Police report that a suspect has been taken into custody and taken to the police station in Thousand Oaks."

I sat paralyzed as the announcer went on to report on a noon rally featuring Congressman Ted Renfrow and gunshots, apparently from a rifle, from across the street. The Congressman had been shot just as he was starting his speech. I switched from channel to channel to get something more specific, but it was not until 8:30 that I got the news that the Congressman was recovering comfortably, but that one of his aides had died on the operating table. The suspect in custody for the murder was Norman Hawkins, Jr.

My first call was to Mary. It took a lot of talking to get Florence to bring her to the phone, but she finally did. When she did get on she sounded faint but in control of herself.

"Hello," she said tentatively.

"Mary. It's Peter Gordon. You've heard?"

"Yes. What should I do?"

"Do you still want to help him?"

"Of course."

"Good. One thing though. I understand, at the funeral, you were telling Chief Skowronski that Harry had been in California all week."

"What did you expect me to say with all those goons around me?"

"Jane told me you were pretty emphatic about it."

"I bet she did. She never gave a damn about Harry. She never got over that her old man was leaving the company stock to Harry and not to her and her fag brother."

I thought a moment. "You mean, Jerry?"

"Yes, Jerry. Check it out, counselor."

I didn't answer.

"Peter?" she asked in a softer tone.

"Yes."

"I didn't mean that the way it sounds. I guess I'm still in shock about this whole thing."

"I understand."

"I'm sorry. They never treated me very well, and I guess it shows. I only want to get Harry out of this mess and us back together."

"OK. By the way, what happened to Harry after the funeral?"

"He had to go right back to California."

"Without you?"

"I was supposed to join him next week, right before the election. In the meantime he was going to be too busy."

"OK, I think we need to go to California."

"To help Harry?"

"Yes. Do you still want to hire me?"

"I thought you couldn't do that."

"Under the circumstances, I think it might be a good idea if you hired me to assist you in getting representation for Harry. If there ever was a conflict . . . ." I hesitated.

"Why would there be a conflict?"

"Never mind. Can you be ready in the morning?"

"Of course. There's nothing to keep me here."

"Good. I'll pick you up in the morning."

She kept thanking me. I rang off and made reservations on a United flight from Newark the next morning. Then I placed a call to Jane. I got a busy signal for about an hour, but I kept trying. When I finally got through it was an unfamiliar voice with a decidedly unfriendly tone.

"Hello."

"Hello, could I speak to Jane Turner, please."

"She's not coming to the phone, so why don't you reporters just quit calling."

"Wait," I said quickly. "I'm not a reporter. Tell her it's Peter Gordon on the line."

"Jane knows you?"

"Yes."

"Hold on a moment."

There was silence on the line and then her voice.

"Peter?"

"Yes, Jane, it's me."

"So you're still sticking with us despite my advice?"

"It looks that way. Who was that who answered the phone?"

"A friend. I asked her to come over after the reporters started calling."

"Can you talk about it?"

"I suppose I can with a friend. You're a friend, aren't you, Peter?"

"I'd like to be. Do they really have Harry in custody?"

"Yes. They've got him down at the jail, and they won't let me see him. They claim he doesn't want to see me."

"I'm coming out tomorrow, and I'm bringing Mary."

She was silent for a moment. "How is that bitch going to help?"

"They'll at least let her in to see Harry, and maybe me as well. We'll get him a lawyer. They've got to let his lawyer in to see him." I hesitated, but then asked. "Are you up to talking about it? Do you know what happened?"

"I don't really know very much that wasn't on the news. The rally was about two blocks from the office where I work. It was about twelve-thirty. None of us heard the shots, but all of a sudden there was all this yelling and then sirens all over the place. Renfrow was apparently shot in the shoulder. He's all right but the next shot got someone else on the platform. He died at the hospital. Everyone's been going crazy."

"Any word on how they apprehended Harry?"

"There was a report on the local station. They got him leaving the parking garage across the square. There was a rifle in the trunk. Presumably it was the weapon used by the shooter. The local police are all making soothing noises like they got the guy. Why would he do something like that?"

I thought back to what I knew about Harry. It wasn't much. Now that I had seen him I could remember him from my sailing instructor days. He had seemed a nice enough kid. Quiet and seemingly shy. Who could tell what was going on beneath that exterior? And who knew how he could have been changed by his association with the RTTR?

"I don't know," I answered. "What do you think?"

"I can't imagine Harry having anything to do with any of it. But I haven't been very close to him in the last couple of years. And who knows what being in the cult has done to him? If he did it, they conned him into it somehow."

"The RTTR tries to kill Renfrow to give Reynaud a better shot at winning?"

"Why not?"

"Do you think it could have worked?"

"Who knows? It would certainly scramble the race. The Democrats wouldn't have time to field anybody with any real chance. Who knows where the Renfrow faithful would have jumped?"

"Well, let's take one thing at a time. We'll get him a lawyer first and then see what to do next." I rushed on before she had a chance to answer. "I'll be coming out on the morning plane, could you meet me for lunch?" There was silence for a moment so I rushed in to fill it. "Just to get some more information that might help with Harry, of course."

"Will she be there?"

"No, I'll put her in the hotel."

"Just the two of us?"

"Ah . . . . Yes, I guess so."

"That would be nice."

"Good." We set the place at a restaurant in Westlake Village and rang off. But the night was not going to leave me alone to think. I had two more calls. The first came in just as I was hanging up with Jane. It was Sarah Stockard.

"Peter. Did you hear about Harry?"

"Yes."

"What do you think? Do you think he could have done it?"

"I don't know. You knew him better than I did. What do you think?"

"No way. He's too much of a nebbish."

"Well suppose he wasn't in his right mind. Suppose he had been brainwashed by this cult he belongs to. What then?"

"I don't know. He always was sort of open to suggestion. Anything some authority figure put in his mind he was ready to follow through on. Why do you think we had so many parties at his house? But an assassination? In broad daylight? That seems to be stretching the limits of suggestibility."

We talked some more and then rang off. Rich called just as I was deciding to go to bed.

"Pete," he said. "Did I catch you too late?"

"Not quite, Rich."

"I guess you've heard."

"Who hasn't?"

"You think there's any connection?"

"I have no idea, Rich."

"Any more contact from those RTTR creeps?"

"Not a word."

"OK. I was just calling because I had a complaint on you."

"A complaint."

"Yeah. Mrs. Hawkins called."

"Mary?" I interrupted.

"No, not her. The other one, Lorraine. She called me to say you had misrepresented yourself as her husband's attorney. That you had never represented her husband, and she didn't want you involved in any further investigation. You misrepresent yourself, Pete?"

"You know better than that, Rich. What would have been the point? Even if I was predisposed to misrepresent myself, which I'm not," I finished.

"Slow down Pete. No need to be defensive."

"Norman hired me, and I've got a copy of the check to prove it."

"No need to prove it to me, Pete. I just thought you'd be interested."

"Any news on the boat?" I asked.

"Not a thing."

I said good-bye and hung up the phone. I had not told him I was going to California the next day. I sighed and went up to bed.

* * *

The next morning was dark and rainy. The bay was black and filled with whitecaps. I stood looking out with my first cup of coffee wondering what I was getting myself into. I had offered to pick Mary up, but she still did not want to be seen with me in North Beach. She had insisted on taking a taxi to the airport. I drove myself and had some time to think as the rain beat against the windshield of my car going up the Garden State Parkway. I met Mary at the gate, and we silently watched the early morning crowds. She sat hunched over, lost in her thoughts. She didn't speak until we were somewhere over Ohio and the stewardesses were serving coffee and cereal. When she first spoke it was so softly that I didn't catch what she had said.

"What was that?" I asked.

"Do you think he did it?"

"I have no idea, Mary. I don't know him at all. If it's any comfort, no one who knows him thinks he could have." I didn't tell her why Sarah had come to this conclusion. "What do you think?"

"I don't think he could have, but I don't know what they could have done to him."

"What do you mean?"

"I mean they have these techniques. They come at you and come at you until you don't know black from white or right from wrong. They keep you awake and feed you only once in a while and parade you through endless meetings and rallies until you'd believe anything Bob Reynaud would tell you. Or do anything he ordered you to do."

"How did you get hooked up with them?"

"The same way Harry did actually. And maybe partly for the same reason. I had an authoritarian Irish father. OK, I was the princess, but it turns out that the princess wasn't allowed to actually do anything except be cute and funny and admired. If I wanted to do anything on my own, forget it. My younger brothers, they could go to college, or, if they didn't want to do that, they could be groomed for the family business, but not me. I was supposed to find some nice Irish guy and settle down and have a bunch of kids. Of course, nobody I brought home could ever measure up to the standard."

She laughed. "Maybe one reason was that I brought home a string of more and more outrageous jerks. I think I wanted my father to disapprove of them. Well, I got pulled in at a rally by this cute hunk of a guy and the next thing you know I'm up at the Pocono's at that camp singing the camp songs and clapping my hands like an idiot."

She sat back in her seat and closed her eyes. When she spoke again she kept them closed.

"No, he didn't do it," she said. "I know they have ways of making you do and believe the weirdest things, but no one could get my Harry to shoot anyone. So we have to get him off. What's the first thing we do?" She looked at me expectantly as if I could wave a magic wand and clear up the whole misunderstanding.

"Well the first thing to do is get him a good lawyer."

"What about you? Didn't I just hire you?"

"Thank you. I do think I'm a good lawyer, but I'm not a criminal lawyer, and I don't reside in California. I'm not going to do Harry any good trying to break into the local scene in Ventura County. The first criterion is someone good. The second is someone local, who's plugged into the local network."

"You have someone in mind?"

"Yes, I do." One of the things I had done the night before was to tap my own network in the legal profession to get a name. I had gotten two. My most likely candidate was Bonnie Hirsch. I relayed the details of Bonnie's career to Mary as I ate my breakfast. She had spent ten years in the Los Angeles District Attorney's office before moving into private practice where she had done a few plaintiff's class-action lawsuits and a number of semi-to-high profile criminal defense matters. The most recent had been a nationally publicized shooting of a black kid by a Hispanic motorcycle cop. She had done a superb job with a hostile press and had gotten the cop acquitted. I finished that she wouldn't come cheap.

"But I don't have any money," protested Mary. She was just picking at her food.

"What about Harry?"

"I don't know. I know he's given a lot to Bob Reynaud."

"We'll have to find out. If necessary there's a lot of money in his father's estate. We may have to spring some of it loose."

I called Bonnie from the plane somewhere over Colorado. I couldn't penetrate the receptionist, and Ms. Hirsch was too busy to meet us until the end of the week. At the mention of the magic words, Norman Hawkins, Jr., I was told to wait. I waited for some time, but when the receptionist came back on the line she said that Ms. Hirsch had been able to clear an afternoon meeting and could meet with us at her office at 2:30 that afternoon. Did I need directions? I did. I punched in another call to Jane's office and a quick negotiation with Jane's receptionist confirmed a time for my lunch date with her in Westlake Village and our hotel information. I hung up the phone and slept the rest of the way.

At LAX, Mary started to get nervous again. She looked around constantly and held on tightly to my elbow. We got the bags and the car and got out onto the 405 with no apparent problems. I don't know LA that well. I imagine there are distinct communities that the residents can recognize. To me, it all blends in to one enormous mass of traffic and congestion. But, I did know which way to go and, an hour later, we were turning off the 101 into Westlake Village. Our hotel was just off the freeway.

Chapter VI

From the hotel I could walk to the restaurant where I was meeting Jane. It was tucked away in a shopping center across the street from the hotel and featured all sorts of New York deli-style sandwiches. I got there about ten minutes early and picked out a table against the wall. The lunch crowd was just starting and the bar was already packed. I ordered an iced tea and started to look through the ten-page menu.

I was nervous. I looked up and there she was standing by the maitre-d's station scanning the restaurant to see if I was there. I don't remember getting up and crossing the restaurant, but all of a sudden we reached each other in the crowd around the bar. We shook hands a little awkwardly.

"You look great," I said.

She looked down. It occurred to me that maybe she was nervous as well. I took her arm to lead her to the table.

I seated her on the bench against the wall and took the chair facing her. I looked into her eyes and thought I could lose myself in there.

She forestalled my tendency to stare by picking up the big menu and hiding behind it. I picked up mine and leafed through the pages of selections.

"Where do you begin?" I asked.

She laughed. "It's a bit of a puzzle, isn't it?"

"Actually you're a bit of a puzzle."

She put the menu down to look at me. "Why do you say that?"

"Your manner seems so different. Sometimes it seems that you're warming up to me. Other times you seem so cold and distant."

"When for example?"

"At the funeral, for example."

"I'm sorry. That was a hard time for me. And to see Harry still stuck in the middle of those gangsters. I'm afraid I had to get away."

"You told me you were never close to Harry."

"I don't think I said never. Harry's only my stepbrother. Did you know that?"

"I think I did."

"My mother and father got divorced when I was about three. I don't really have any memories of them being together. My mother took Jerry and me away, and we never really saw my father until he got married again. By that time I was 13. Her name was Julie. She was really a lovely lady. I was prepared to hate her at first. But she was able to get my father away from the business to spend some time with his family for the first time. He had a boat then, too. Not as big as 'Far Cry' of course, but big enough to go cruising comfortably. By that time my mother was married again, and she didn't care any more if we spent time with Norman. Julie and Norman had Harry right away. I think it was Harry who won me over. He was so cute as a baby. My job was to watch him when we went sailing."

The waitress came. I ordered tuna fish and negotiated the bread type. Jane duplicated my order.

She smiled. "It seems like a travesty of something to order tuna fish with this enormous menu."

"Lunch is lunch. Maybe we can get a little fancier for dinner."

She didn't answer, so I didn't press it

"What happened?" I asked to get her back on the story.

"What? Oh, yes. Julie was killed in a car accident. I think Harry was about ten. He was in the car with her. He was all right. He had a seat belt on. It took three hours to cut them out of the wreckage. She was dead before they could get her free."

"God. Poor Harry."

"Yeah, Harry was so quiet after that. His eyes had lost the sparkle they had always had, you know?"

I nodded.

"And the family drifted apart after that. Julie was the anchor that held us together. Norman lost himself in his work again. He sold the boat. He started going out with Lorraine soon after that. She didn't have any use for his kids, of course. I was a senior at college and going with this guy. I thought I was in love with him. I'm not sure now whether I was or I just had nowhere else to go. Anyway, we got married. He was from Simi Valley, so we came out here to live. Harry and I used to write and maybe see each other once or twice a year, but not much more than that. When he joined the RTTR I really lost contact with him."

"So you don't know much about the cult?"

"Actually I've learned quite a bit. When they set up their little research center out here in Thousand Oaks I got interested because Harry was a member."

"I get the idea that it's more of a political cult than the normal religious variety."

"That's one way to look at it. The ideology is a strange mix of racism and mythology. All the ills of America can be laid at the door of a vast under-class of sub-people who live off welfare, do and sell drugs, collect food stamps, vandalize our cities, absorb our tax dollars through consumption of social services, rob our men and rape our women. The mythology revolves around a golden age when America was pure, before cities, before immigrants, before drugs and before crime."

I laughed. "And when was this mythical time?"

"Never, of course, but that isn't really important. What is important is that it paints a picture of an idyllic period in our history to which we must bend all our efforts to return."

"I get it. Don't tell me. In order to return America to her former greatness we need to end welfare, protect our borders from illegal immigrants, and put all violent criminals into prison for life, if not execute most of them. Is that it?"

She nodded. "That's a good part of the program."

"But all that is pretty much the standard litany of a lot of right and conservative groups. And many of those propositions are the subject of quite respectable political debate." I noticed I was speaking faster, and my tone had sharpened considerably. I took a breath and slowed down. "I don't think we should just end welfare. But I do think that perverse incentives perpetuate dependency. What's the difference between RTTR and a hundred other groups?"

"That's the crucial question. I've thought a lot about it. I think there is a subtle difference that is all the difference in the world. You know there's been a lot of scholarly debate recently about intelligence, bell curves and the like?"

"Of course. Who could miss all that hullabaloo?"

"Well, the significant part of that debate, in my mind, is that intelligence counts. That is, the ability to organize and prioritize information and to communicate the results of the process, are crucially important to success in society. By success I mean the ability to find and retain gainful employment. And, as typical assembly-line manufacturing jobs become more and more a thing of the past, the information age does a kind of sorting of society into two classes, the economically productive and the economically dependent. The conclusion is that if we don't do something radical to break the bonds of those trapped in the economically dependent sub-class, we will be faced with a bleak future of fortress living communities in a rising tide of hatred and violence."

"I understand the point. What's that got to do with RTTR?"

"Well, Reynaud has added a little bit of a twist. Part of it is a normal extrapolation. He says that, since the statistics show that there are differences in racial groups, particularly that blacks test about 15% below whites, we can conveniently peg who is properly in the under-class by the color of their skin."

"Sure. That's what civil rights groups are so exercised about."

"Of course, and that leads to the twist. Reynaud's vision of the new society permanently perpetuates the division. Look at it this way. Hitler had a vision of a vast empire sweeping over Eastern Europe and Russia controlled by a string of Aryan cities ruling over a rural society of Slavs, whose sole purpose was to serve the master race. Reynaud's version is the same, except it's reversed. The master race will populate the suburbs and the countryside, penning the under-class, who can be identified by their racial make-up, in cities that will look more like concentration camps than cities. The under-class will be allowed out to clean our houses and cook our meals, but then back they will go, out of sight and out of mind. And kept out of sight and out of mind by terror."

"But, that's crazy."

"Of course, but that doesn't mean that he doesn't mean it. How different is it than the apartheid solutions of the Boers in South Africa?"

"That didn't work."

"Why not? Because the whites were too few, and South Africa was so isolated in the world. South Africa transplanted to America would be a different story."

I shook my head. "It's absolutely insane."

"Of course it is. But that doesn't mean that it can't be the driving force of a cult. Weren't Hitler's ideas insane? Weren't Jim Jones'? Cults flourish with wacky ideas. The wackier the better."

Our lunch arrived, and we devoted ourselves to the food for a few moments.

"What do you do at that office where I called you?"

"What do you think? Receptionist maybe? Secretary?"

I put up my hand, placatingly. "Hey, I don't even know you. For all I know, you own the business."

"Actually I do. I started out here as the housewife. When that turkey of a husband left me, I had a down period, but it soon became clear that I had to do something. I was always interested in computers. I took a few courses and began to help people out informally. Someone suggested that I charge for what I was doing, and the rest, they say, is history."

"How many people do you have working for you now?"

"Five. One in the office and four out on the road working with the customers."

"How about you?"

"I spend most of my time on new business these days. Mostly that puts me out on the road as well."

The waiter came and refilled our iced tea glasses. There was a pause when he left. I thought it might be time to change the subject.

"Mary says that you're angry at your father for cutting you out of the will."

She looked up at me and her eyes flashed momentarily, the same way they had done when she had gone off to confront Harry at the funeral. "Is that what you think?"

"I have no information. I'm just telling you what she said. I'm just trying to figure out the family dynamics."

"Is that why you were pumping me about the family history?"

"No, that's not it at all. I'm trying to get a handle on Mary."

"If you're trying to get a handle on Mary, look where the money is."

"Yeah, I know. The problem is that's just what she told me about you."

"OK, here it is. Yes, I was angry at Norman when he told me he was going to leave all the company stock to Harry. He said it wasn't the money, but he wanted Harry to be in a position to take over the company. But, I'm all right. There are enough other assets around to spare. I've got my own business now, and it's doing fine." She paused for a moment and looked off into space. "It wasn't the money that rankled as much as it was that he picked Harry to be the one, and he never even considered that it might be me. I've got more brains and drive than Harry could ever dream about. And Norman knew it. But I'm a woman, so I'm automatically disqualified."

"I understand."

"Do you? I wonder."

"How was all this going to work with Harry a member of the RTTR?"

"That's just it. It wasn't. Norman had to get Harry free of the organization. Otherwise, it wouldn't be Harry running the company, it would have been Bob Reynaud."

I sat back to think about this. She left me alone for a moment and then she did a little probing of her own.

"So what is it with you and Mary? How has she gotten you enmeshed in her little schemes?"

"It's not as simple as that."

"It never is that simple."

"Yeah, you're right. But, apart from some rather unusual political ideas she seems pretty straightforward. She wants out of the RTTR, and she wants Harry out as well."

"Is that what you think?"

"That's what she says. And I have no reason to doubt her."

"And you're going to help her."

I shrugged. "She does need help. And your father did pay me a retainer of twenty-five thousand dollars for almost the same thing. She's my ticket to get in to see Harry. Right now, let's say we have a mutuality of interest."

"That's the way it looks to you. Believe me. Mary has just one interest, and that's Mary."

I paid the check. We walked out of the restaurant and stood on the brick sidewalk soaking up the sun.

"One other thing she said that you ought to know about," I said.

"What's that?"

"She made some comment about your brother, Jerry."

"What? Like calling him a queer?"

I shifted uncomfortably. "Ahh, yes, something like that."

She took my arm and pulled me over to a bench. "I have to start at the beginning. Jerry was always a loner. I attributed it to the problems the family was having when he was growing up. Not even Julie could really bring him out of his shell. He didn't do very well in college. He spent his time with the drama club and avoided going to classes. Anyway, he got married to a nice girl and things seemed to be going well for him. They weren't. The marriage lasted barely eighteen months, and then he left her. He came out here to try to get into acting full time. By that time I was out here too, but I didn't see very much of him. I was too busy being the perfect wife to my new husband. I didn't think I had enough time in my own life to pay any attention to my wayward brother. Then I got divorced. I told you I had a little down period. Well, that was a bit of an understatement. I was drinking myself to death alone in that house. I thought I was the worst person in the world, and I had succeeded in driving away everyone who loved me because I didn't deserve their love. Jerry came to see me, and he told me his story. He was gay. He'd always been gay. His marriage had been predicated on a monumental act of denial of his very nature. It was no wonder it hadn't worked. He came to Los Angeles to make a new start and become a star. Of course he had only succeeded in becoming a waiter.

And he started to drink. In a few years he had given up the acting classes and any pretense that he would become an actor, and he could barely keep a job as a waiter."

"How did you feel about this?" I prodded.

"I had decidedly mixed feelings. At first, it was a real shock. I had a real problem with the picture of my brother doing those things with another man. But, at the same time, the fact that he was gay somehow clicked. I mean he was so at ease with it, and we could talk for the first time in our lives. He would talk about his gayness and his alcoholism. It was just at the time when I was at the bottom. I was even thinking about suicide. He took me out of that big house to come and live with him. And, he literally loved me back to life. I don't know if I would be here today without him. For the first time since Julie had died, I began to feel that I wasn't alone in the world. Maybe I wasn't the scum of the earth after all. I began to live again." She stopped and looked at me. "So you have to understand."

"What's that?"

"Jerry saved my life."

I nodded. She wiped her eyes with a handkerchief.

"And now he has AIDS."

I just sat there for a moment. I didn't trust myself to speak. I took her hand.

"Why are you telling me this?"

"I don't know." She smiled. "Maybe it's to help you with our family dynamic."

"Touché."

She looked at me. "How do you feel about it?"

I thought for a moment. "He's your brother, and he saved your life. My experience of gay men is pretty limited. If there are any in North Beach, they're still pretty much in the closet. I only had one . . . ." I stopped.

"One what?" she asked.

"Nothing. I don't really want to talk about it."

"Come on. You have to tell me now."

"I haven't thought about it for years."

"And this brought it to the fore?"

"Yes."

"Tell me."

I hesitated for a moment and then plunged right in. "I was in college. Or, I was flying home from college. It was about Thanksgiving, but it wasn't that weekend. I don't know why I was coming home. I was sitting on the plane next to this man. I had the window seat. We struck up a conversation. Or he did, and I responded. He was very friendly. There was a snowstorm, and I was going to get a taxi home. He offered me a ride. In the car he got even friendlier. He put his hand on my leg and said how nice the material of my pants was. They were just pants for Christ's sake. Then he wanted to stop for a drink. It was late. I just wanted to get home. The snow was coming down in buckets. He grabbed my leg again. I asked him to stop. Then he asked me if I wanted to put my hand on his penis. I said 'No'. How about if he put his hand on mine? 'What harm could it do?' he asked. He put his hand on my leg again. I thought I was going to be sick. The car seemed like an oven. He kept pressing me."

I stopped. The telling of the tale had taken me back into that stifling car, and I felt like I was sweating just as I had been then.

"What did you do?"

"I got out of the car at a traffic light. He's asking me to get back in and saying that it's all a mistake. He'll just take me home. The snow was up around my ankles, and the wind blew right through me, but I wasn't going to get in that car again. Fortunately, we were about a mile from a train station. I walked to the station and called my parents. I still remember standing on the train platform waiting for the train and shivering. I don't know if it was from the wind or from fear."

"Did you tell your parents?"

"I never told anyone until now."

She squeezed my hand. "Poor baby. Now you know how we girls felt at the drive-in when you were making your moves."

"At least you were supposed to have an attraction for the opposite sex."

"Most of the time I did."

We sat for a moment, not speaking. Finally, she broke the silence. "Jerry's not like that, you know."

"Of course I know that. It's my problem to resolve, and I can do it. How's Jerry's health?"

"That's the problem. Until about a month ago it was very good. Of course, he'd have his ups and downs, but he never had to go into the hospital. He got this infection that he couldn't shake. He's been in the hospital for about a week."

"What's the prognosis?"

"Good, I hope. I know Jerry thinks this is just another interlude. The doctor is more cautious, naturally, but he seems to be getting slowly better. Of course, they have him plugged into all sorts of IV lines, and the drugs he's taking are all incomprehensible to me."

We got up at the same time, and I walked her to her car.

"Were you serious about dinner tonight?" she asked.

"I thought you had forgotten about that."

"No. I just didn't respond."

"Yes, I was serious."

"Will you come with me to see him tonight?" she asked me as she opened the door to her car.

I suppose I knew this was coming because I didn't hesitate.

"Of course."

"Good." She kissed me on the cheek, got in the car and drove away. I walked back to the hotel thinking of old nightmares, and how much I hated hospitals.

By the time I got back to the hotel, it was time for our meeting with Bonnie Hirsch. I picked up Mary from her room, and we drove into Thousand Oaks. Bonnie's office was on a little side street. The office itself was a sprawling, one-story building with pitched roofs like a ski lodge and lots of windows. An orthodontist and an accountant occupied the front of the building. At the back of the lobby we found a door with a sign that read "Law Offices of Roberta M. Hirsch". I opened the door, and we went in. The reception area was light and cheery with abstract paintings on the walls. A receptionist sat behind a wall with a sliding glass window. I asked for Ms. Hirsch, and she asked us to take a seat. We each took a seat at the opposite ends of a large couch that offered a view, through the magnificent windows of the building, of the cars in the parking lot.

After several minutes a woman about my age opened the door from the back of the office and walked over to greet us. She was small with brown hair cut very short.

"Mr. Gordon?" she asked.

I got up. "That's right. Pete Gordon. And this is Mary Hawkins."

We shook hands, and she led us through the back of the reception area to her office. She also had windows looking out over the parking lot, but there was also a view of the mountains beyond. On her desk and scattered all around the office were stacks of files, boxes of documents and binders full of papers. To the right was a small conference table. She motioned us to sit down at the table and pushed some files away to give us room.

"I apologize for the mess," she said. "I just finished a trial yesterday, and I haven't had the energy to get all this stuff put away."

Mary looked around. "All this is for one trial?"

Bonnie laughed. "That's right. And a pretty simple one at that. Just a breach of contract case. Of course, my opponent's theory was that it was a whole lot more complicated than that." She laughed again. "That's the kind of case I like, when my story is simple, and the other guy has to explain all the complexities of life."

"Did you win?" I asked.

"Don't know yet. We finished last night, and the jury is deliberating today."

"But what do you think?"

She looked at me as if I had said something extraordinarily stupid. "I don't make a practice of predicting what juries will do."

I studied the mountains. I really didn't care what this jury would do. I was already into my interview. I looked back at her and leaned back in my chair crossing my legs.

"Really?" I asked. "I would have thought that it was your job to predict what juries will do. Otherwise, how do you know when to settle a case rather than try it?"

She narrowed her eyes briefly then looked at Mary. She looked back at me and seemed to make a decision.

"I think the worst case is a walk-away," she said. "The other guy has a fraud counter-claim for big numbers but it's a make-weight. He spent most of his case trying to convince the jury that it was my client's fault that he couldn't deliver the product, not that he couldn't make it. Like I said, my case went in short and sweet. The jury is going to like my guys. His case went on forever and got more complicated with every witness he put on. Plus, I got something out of every one of his witnesses that contradicted something another one of his witnesses had already said."

"So you feel pretty good about it?"

"I feel good about it. But there are no sure things. My case went in as well as I could have hoped for, and I still could lose."

"Why didn't the case settle?"

"Arrogance. Arrogance on the part of a defendant who didn't have the imagination to think he might have made a mistake. Arrogance on the part of the big name, big firm lawyer who thought he was going to bury little sole practitioner me. We spent a lot of time trying to settle it before we filed suit. But they sent the guys who had screwed up in the first place to negotiate. They weren't about to actually pay my client's money back. That would have been an admission that they had screwed up. Who knows what the ramifications of that admission would have been in the coin of promotions, career path and annual bonus. So the best they would offer was a walk-away. That wasn't good enough so we sued."

"And they never put any money on the table after that?"

"No, never. By the time they got to trial they had painted themselves into a corner. They had spent a fortune on discovery and hadn't come up with anything worth spit. But, it was the same guys who screwed up in the first place still running the litigation now with the lawyer who had advised them not to settle. During the whole trial they never sent any senior executive out to take a smell test of how things were going. So, no. The answer is they never put any money on the table."

Mary was getting restless. "This lawyer talk is all very interesting," she said. "But didn't we come here to talk about Harry?"

I turned to her. I had gotten enough to draw some early conclusions about Bonnie Hirsch. "Sorry, Mary. I guess the shop talk can get a little boring."

I looked back at Bonnie and gave her a brief recitation of the facts that had gotten us here. I left out my conversations with the elder Norman Hawkins. I think I just mentioned that he had recently drowned at sea. Bonnie asked some quick questions and then sat for a moment thinking.

"You know the RTTR?" I asked.

"Sure, they've gotten a lot of local publicity. About a year ago they bought a ranch up in one of the canyons. They kept pretty much to themselves at first. They put up a big fence around the property and kept people away. They would set up tables around town and solicit money and sell or give away literature."

"What kind of literature?"

"I never read any, but I understand it was of the 'Feed Jane Fonda to the whales' kind of stuff. Lot's of stuff promoting guns and nuclear energy. Recently it's been more and more anti-immigrant. Whatever political controversy is currently running on Night Line and Crossfire, they're in it, but they take it one step beyond, if you know what I mean."

"And Bob Reynaud has political aspirations?"

"In spades. He ran in the Republican primary for Congress and lost, but did OK. He had a virtual army of political solicitors getting the vote out. Then he filed as an independent for the general election. He won't win, but he might well have prevented Renfrow from getting in again. Renfrow has been having political problems with this anti-Washington, anti-incumbent mood."

"Who's running on the Republican side?"

"A guy named Eric Perkins. He's a lawyer in town. Does defense work for insurance companies. Been a city councilman for years. He always had the bug to go to Washington. Beautiful wife, two tow-headed kids, a boy and a girl, a photogenic smile, and he doesn't have the brains that God gave chickens."

"I would have thought that with Perkins and the RTTR splitting the conservative vote, Renfrow would have had a walk."

"That would be the conventional wisdom. It didn't seem to be working out like that though. Reynaud was targeting some of Renfrow's main constituent bases. Reynaud's big on defense spending, and the defense cutbacks have cut a swath through the employment out here.

He's anti-immigrant, and that's striking a popular chord. He's just plausible enough that people are listening to him a little. And if they're concerned that he isn't respectable enough, well Perkins sure is, and he's been well enough advised that he's saying many of the same things Reynaud is but in a more civilized way. The pros thought that Renfrow was in trouble."

"So what's your take on it now."

"It looks like Renfrow will survive one more time."

"Reynaud doesn't have a shot?"

"No. He's just a spoiler. He can't win. Especially now that one of his flock is tagged with murder."

"But Harry couldn't have done it," cut in Mary.

"That may be so," said Bonnie. "Or if he did, it may have been under some extreme influence, but we're talking about people's perceptions with an election only two weeks away. By election time, chances are people will still be believing it was your husband. And that's not going to help Bob Reynaud's chances of getting elected."

She looked at me. "So you want me to represent Harry?"

"Yes, will you do it?" I asked.

"I'll need to talk to him."

We talked about her fees. She would do the job on her hourly rates or for a fixed fee, a large one, payable up front. We settled on the hourly rate through the arraignment. I didn't want to commit to the fixed fee until both of us had some more facts. She asked for a retainer to start, and I convinced her that the heir to Hawkins Industries was good for the money. With that, we shook hands and were out on the street again.

* * *

Jerry's hospital was back in West L.A. Jane and I drove there together and in silence for most of the whole way. I drove, and she provided directions off the 405. She got me there by a back street, and we spent some fruitless minutes looking for street parking before giving up and putting the car in the hospital parking lot. From there she led me through a maze of corridors and elevators until we came out on a brightly lit patient floor that seemed full of people. Jane guided me past the nurses' station to a room at the end of the corridor. She walked right in. I hesitated at the doorway to the room until I began to feel conspicuous just standing there. I took a breath, and I went in too. Inside the lights were dimmer and there was Jane talking to a man sitting up in a hospital bed. She waved me over.

"Pete. Come meet Jerry."

The man was thin to the point of emaciation. He had thinning black hair and the beginnings of a beard. He reached out one of his stick arms to shake my hand. His grip was stronger than I would have expected.

"Pete," he said in a deep voice. "Jane has been telling me a little about you."

"Really?" I asked. "I've heard a little about you too."

"Meet Steve, my partner," he said, indicating a chair on the other side of the bed. I looked over to see another man I had not noticed before in the dimness. As he got up, I could see he was short and slim. We shook hands awkwardly over the bed.

"Let's get Pete a chair," said Jerry. Steve indicated I should take his and went off to fetch another one from the corridor. Jane perched familiarly on the foot of the bed.

"So, I understand you've come to LA to save the Hawkins family," he said.

I shrugged. "Not really."

"It's what I hear. Tell me about it."

I don't know whether it was my nervousness or whether it was Jerry's easy manner that inspired confidence, but I sat down and told him the whole story right from the time his father had come into my office seeking my help. When I had finished there was silence for a long moment in the room. Jerry was the one to break it.

"Well our old friends, the RTTR, seem to have a finger in everything, don't they?"

"You know them?"

"Oh, yes."

"Did you know Harry was a member?"

He waved his hand. "Yeah. Jane keeps me up to date on family matters. I don't think I've actually seen Harry in more than ten years, though."

"Tell me how you've run into them."

"A big part of their shtick is anti-gay propaganda. On one hand, we're unnatural beings cursed by God. And I don't mean 'cursed' in any figurative sense. The curse is the AIDS virus that God has sent down to wipe us from the face of the earth. On the other hand, even if the virus is incurable, our sexual orientation isn't. We have chosen to be gay, and, given the right influences, we can make another choice to be straight again."

"Well that has its own inner logic," I said.

"What do you mean by that?" he asked me sharply.

"Well, it would only make sense for God to send down a plague to punish gays if the act of being gay was voluntary. So we have sin, punishment for the sin and the possibility of redemption. Let me guess. Does Reynaud offer up his organization as an agent of redemption?"

"I guess you know quite a bit about them."

"Not really, but I'm beginning to learn. Tell me about it."

He shrugged. "There's not much to tell. We've developed a sort of political action organization here in LA that is active in gay political issues. Anti-discrimination and so forth. From time to time we organize a little demonstration to dramatize our views. Nothing so dramatic or forceful as some groups, you understand, but maybe a quiet little picket line. All of a sudden we were getting counter-demonstrations from RTTR members. They started off peacefully, but then from time to time some of our members got beat up on the way home. Then the RTTR began to find out where a number of us lived, and they came to harass us at our homes." He looked at me. "Are you really interested in all this?"

"Actually, yes I am. Did you complain to the police?"

"Of course. They sent someone out to investigate. Naturally, the RTTR denied that any of the violence was connected to them. I think they said something sanctimonious about how it was inevitable that our parading of our ungodliness was bound to bring a reaction among the God-fearing folk of Southern California. They themselves wouldn't stoop to such measures, of course. They were only interested in our best interests. In bringing us peacefully back to God before it was too late."

"And the harassment at your homes?"

"Simple proselytizing. Exercise of their inalienable rights of free speech. They were careful to stay off private property. The police said there was nothing they could do."

"Do you know Richard Beck?"

Jerry's eyes widened briefly. "You are well informed."

"What do you know about him?"

He shrugged. "He's a scary guy. Reynaud's security chief from what I understand. He always seems to be in the background. You never see Reynaud himself except at a carefully choreographed event. Beck always seems to be there hovering in the background."

He leaned back against his pillow and closed his eyes as if suddenly tired. Almost immediately a nurse came in and started bustling about with his tubes.

"Another blood test, Dearie," she said cheerfully. "One from the shunt and one from your arm this time."

Jerry roused himself. "OK, wait a minute." He looked at me. "If you're really interested, Steve can take you to a guy who's been through the Reynaud cure for gays."

I hesitated. "I'm interested."

"Good. Stevie, take him to see Frank. He's probably working tonight."

"Sure Jerry," said Steve.

He turned to Jane. "Thanks for coming by, Sis. You might as well go. I think I'll try to get some rest after this vampire gets through with me."

He gave her a kiss, and we all crowded towards the door. I looked back to see him leaning back against the pillow with his eyes closed again as the nurse was beginning to probe for a vein in his arm.

We met Steve in the front of the parking garage. He had retrieved his car from the street. He led us to Wilshire and then right towards Santa Monica. Somewhere west of the 405, he turned left to get to Santa Monica Boulevard, and then he turned into one of those little strip malls that seem to be everywhere in Los Angeles. He parked his car and got out. I found a space near the back of the lot, and we joined him in front of a storefront with a lighted sign that announced 'Lisa's' in red script. Jane took my arm.

"What's this?" I asked Steve.

"Lisa's. Best French restaurant in a strip mall in Los Angeles. Frank is a waiter here. Let's go see if he'll talk to us."

He opened the glass door and led us into the restaurant. Inside was a maitre d's stand right next to the door behind which were about twenty little tables jammed into the converted store. A bar was against the back wall. The room was about three-quarters full and buzzing with noise. Steve was talking to a waiter in a white apron standing by the bar. The waiter looked over at us and shook his head. Steve seemed to talk faster. Finally the waiter shrugged, picked up the drinks he had been waiting for and went to deliver them to a table. Steve wended his way back to us.

"Well?" I asked.

"He'll talk to us, but he's pretty busy right now. How about we have some dinner."

I looked at Jane.

"I guess we have to eat."

"I'm not very hungry," she said. "How about you? It's getting pretty late for being on East Coast time."

"I'm all right. Let's talk to this guy before he changes his mind."

The maitre d' had been standing, patiently waiting throughout this colloquy, and now led us to a table for four towards the back. Jane and I took the bench seats against the wall, and Steve took one of the chairs facing us. Frank came over to take our order. He was tall and blonde, and looked about thirty. Steve introduced us.

"Steve said you want to know about the RTTR," he said.

"That's right," I answered, wondering how to approach this. "Ah, we have a friend who's a member of the group. Actually it's this lady's brother. We're not sure if he's a willing member any more or not. We're trying to find out as much as we can to see if we can get him out."

"I can't really help you with that."

"I know, but any information you could give us about your own experiences would be helpful."

He looked doubtful as he took our orders and left us alone.

"How long have you been with Jerry?" I asked Steve.

"We've been together about three years. We met in a gay AA group."

"There are gay AA groups?"

"Well, not specifically. Every AA group is generally open to any drunk who wants to come, but anyone can start a group. So many of the groups take on a personality. You shop around for a group that's comfortable for you. There are women's groups, smokers' groups, yuppie groups, gay groups. You name it, there's a group for it."

He reflected a moment. "Actually, Jerry got me into the program. I was in this counseling program for DUI's."

"DUI's?"

"Sure. One of the things they do with drunk drivers out here is to force them to go to counseling. It's usually pretty ineffective. You've got a group who are basically in the worst stages of denial. Maybe the other schmucks in this group might have a problem, but I don't. I was just unlucky to get caught this one time. Of course, every one of them has the same opinion. It's really pretty hilarious." He shrugged. "At least it appears that way now. It didn't seem hilarious at the time."

"And Jerry was in the same group?" asked Jane.

"No, he wasn't, but the group leader happened to be gay. I guess he recognized a kindred spirit. He called Jerry. Jerry called me and suggested a better way to serve my sentence."

"What was that?" asked Jane.

"You could go to AA meetings instead of these counseling groups. You just needed some responsible person to confirm that you'd actually gone to the meetings. I thought it would be great. Jerry seemed like a guy who would understand. I'd go to one or two AA meetings, and then he'd let me slide. After all, anyone could see that I didn't have a problem."

"But Jerry wouldn't let you slide?"

"No not Jerry. He knew right from the first day what I was thinking. And he told me the first time we talked that I would go to every meeting. I, of course, didn't believe him, but in the end, I did."

By now Frank had brought our dinners, and we fell to eating silently. Jane and Steve picked up a conversation, but I was lost in my own thoughts and paid no attention. With the coffee, Frank came to sit at our table. The rest of the restaurant had mostly cleared out. There were a few couples sitting with coffee, but the noisy buzz that had filled the room when we had entered was gone.

"I can only stay a few minutes," he said. "And there really isn't much I can offer that will help you."

"We appreciate you talking to us at all," I said.

"I wouldn't except that Jerry asked me to." He looked at Jane. "You're Jerry's sister, right?"

She nodded. "Yes."

"And it's Jerry's brother that's in the group?"

"That's right," said Jane.

He laughed. "That's pretty ironic. Is he gay as well?"

"No," she said. "But we're just looking for information about them."

He took a deep breath and nodded as if he had made up his mind.

"Are you afraid you're not quit of them?" asked Jane.

He laughed bitterly. "You're never quit of them. They make a big thing about making a lifelong commitment to the cause. It's like a blood oath. And you swear that the tie to the Archon will never be broken."

"The Archon? That's Reynaud?" I asked.

He nodded. "Right. Every member has a personal bond of loyalty to him."

"How did you get involved with them in the first place? You're gay, right. I understood part of their ideology was demonizing of gays."

"Sure it is. But that was part of the attraction. You think that my gayness wasn't part of the basis for my hatred and contempt for myself?"

"I don't know."

"Look. When they pulled me off the street, I was taking every kind of drug known to man. I was doing blowjobs in back alleys and back seats just to keep me in drugs from day to day. It was a race whether I would overdose or starve myself to death. They picked me up and took me to this ranch they have in the mountains. They cleaned me up, fed me and got me off the drugs."

"How did they get you off drugs?" asked Jane.

"Love. They loved me to death. They loved me in shifts, day after day, night after night. They convinced me I wasn't a piece of shit, and I had a value. They gave me something to believe in. When they put me back out on the street I was still hustling, but I was hustling for God. For the God Robert Reynaud."

"You brought in money?"

"Sure. We all could get more or less a hundred dollars in a day. At three hundred and sixty-five days a year that's close on $40,000. And it doesn't cost very much to house us all in those barracks they had up at the ranch and to feed us the slop that they fed us. And we did it, day after day, for love. If you went along with the program, you got lots of positive reinforcement. If you complained, there was immediate negative reinforcement."

"What was that?"

"Reynaud's precious Minutemen. First they'd take you aside and talk to you. Four or five of them. They could be pretty intimidating. Next they roughed you up a little or put you in the hole."

"The hole?"

"It was basically a box buried in the ground. Not much bigger than a coffin. They'd put you in there to think for a day. When you came out, everyone would love you to death again. You'd be repentant for your misdeeds, and you'd be forgiven."

"Suppose you persisted?"

"I don't know. Sometimes people just disappeared. Word would be put about that they had been kidnapped by the FBI or forces of the anti-Christ. There was constant propaganda that the FBI or the CIA was constantly trying to infiltrate the group and forcibly kidnap our members."

"What about you being gay?" asked Jane.

"That was the most diabolical part. They convinced me that I was gay for the same reason that I had been a drug addict. My self-hatred had led to my drug addiction and my sexual preference as well. It was all a manifestation of my lack of self-worth. And just as I could be cured of my drug addiction, I could be cured of my gayness. I really believed it. Of course, I couldn't cure my feelings, and my very failure made me feel as though I just had to try harder. Confess my sins more openly. Purge myself more thoroughly. Enter into the activities more energetically. I even set my sights on becoming a Minuteman. What a laugh. One of them disabused me of that idea in one of their discipline sessions. A little fag like me could never aspire to the requisite purity of becoming a Minuteman. I think that was what first set me back on the road to sanity."

"What do you mean?" asked Jane.

"It was like a revelation of how they really viewed me. I was once and always a little fag to them. Even if I could cure myself, it would always be the same. I could never enter the elect. From that time on, I began to plot my escape."

"How did you escape?" asked Jane.

"Actually it was easier than I thought. We were doing a lot of anti-gay demonstrations then. I think the Minutemen took delight in having me participate in all the anti-gay activities. It was good for my cure, I was told. I got to listen to a lot of Jerry's speeches because we were demonstrating against his group. One day we were picketing outside his gay rights office. Someone went through our picket line and up the steps to the door. I just followed like I was going to harass him all the way to the doorway. We weren't supposed to do that. There was some injunction proceeding going on, and we were supposed to be on our best behavior. I just walked in the door after the guy. Two big guys collared me immediately and were going to throw me back out into the street. I did some fast-talking and asked for Jerry. Fortunately he was there and I told him my story. Meanwhile there was a riot going on outside. Beck himself showed up and claimed I'd been kidnapped. They were demanding I be returned. The police came, and I had to convince them that I really wanted to stay. In the end they let me stay, and Jerry snuck me out the back. I hid out for about six months, but I still have nightmares about them coming to get me."

"How long were you with the RTTR?"

"Almost eighteen months. And I've been free for almost a year now. I've been straight as far as drugs goes ever since, but I've given up trying to straighten out my sexual preferences."

I started to ask another question, but he interrupted me. "Look,

I've already taken too much time. I've got to get back to help put the place to bed."

I looked at Jane. She shrugged and said, "That's great Frank. You've been a tremendous help, and we appreciate it."

He got up, shook hands and headed off to the back of the restaurant. We thanked Steve in the parking lot and fifteen minutes later were back on the 405 headed towards Ventura County.

"What do you think?" I asked trying to keep my attention of the river of taillights that stretched, seemingly endlessly, in front of me.

"I think this RTTR is a pretty spooky group. I guess there are a lot of people who believe that homosexuality is a voluntary choice. Reynaud doesn't just believe it, he acts on it."

"Yes, and he can exert such psychological pressure on someone that they believe it as well. How about Frank's comments about the FBI?"

"It didn't really surprise me," she said. "The RTTR appears to have all the aspects of a proto-fascist organization. Simple answers to complex problems. Constant repetition of the ideology. A bunch of brown-shirts to maintain discipline. I'm sure there's a whole mythology of conspiracy theories to explain the pickle Western civilization finds itself in. The FBI or the CIA or the Trilateral Commission or the terrorists or the gays or a combination of all of the above."

"So you see them as sort of comic book Nazis?"

"I'm not sure 'comic book' is the way I would put it. Don't forget, both Hitler and Mussolini were regarded as buffoons in their early years."

"I know. And buffoons with a private army can be just as dangerous as any other thug."

"Exactly."

We spent the rest of the drive in a kind of awkward silence. It was like we knew too much about each other, yet not enough at the same time. I turned off the Ventura Freeway in Westlake Village and around to the hotel. I dropped Jane at her car in the parking lot. We said good-bye, shaking hands a little hesitantly, and I walked up to the large, brightly lit overhang of the hotel. In front of me was a black van with smoked windows. At the passenger door of the van was a young man with a crew cut, white shirt and tie and dark slacks. I looked at him curiously as I went through the electric glass doors and into the hotel. I had left my bag with the bell captain after registering that morning. I stopped there to retrieve it, and he went into a back room to collect it. I thought about calling to check on Mary, but it was after midnight. With the time change I concluded that she would already be asleep. I would call her in the morning and maybe, by that time, Bonnie would have some news for us about Harry. One of the elevators opened in the back of the lobby and five men and a woman got out. All the men were dressed with the same white shirts and dark slacks. Just like the guy out front, I thought. The woman was right in the middle of the group. I thought she looked familiar, and then a shock ran through me. It was Mary.

The men were walking quickly towards the door. One of them led while two others held Mary's arms as they hustled her along. The other two brought up the rear. Without even thinking, I stepped into the path of the leader.

"Wait a minute," I said.

The leader tried to go around me, but I stepped in front of him again. He stopped.

"Get out of our way," he said, quietly.

"Wait a minute. Where do you think you are taking her?"

"Who are you, sir?"

"I'm Peter Gordon." I looked at Mary. Her eyes had an unfocused look. "Mary. Are you all right?"

She looked vaguely in my direction. "Peter?" she asked.

"What's the matter with her?" I demanded.

"Nothing." he said. "She's just a little tired, that's all."

"Fine," I said. "Let's just take her back . . . ." I never got to finish my sentence. All of a sudden my legs got weak, and I felt very dizzy. I felt someone's hand on my arm guiding me into a large armchair. I shook my head and looked around and saw the backs of the white shirts as they were leaving through the front door. I struggled to my feet and wobbled as another wave of dizziness swept over me. Someone was at my arm.

"Are you all right sir?"

For a moment I couldn't speak. "Those men. Where did they go?"

"What men, sir?"

"The men who were just here, damn it." I suppose I was shouting. I shook off his hand and walked as quickly as I could manage out the front door. The van was gone.

"Peter. Are you all right?"

It was Jane. Suddenly I felt a pain in my head and reaching up felt a growing bump on the back of my skull.

"I think someone hit me," I said.

She got me back inside and sat me down on the same armchair.

"Tell me what happened."

I related the tale, and she said she was going off to call the police. I lay back and must have dozed off because the next thing I remembered was someone shaking my arm. It was Jane with a police officer. I told him the story, and then he went away. Jane bundled me into a car and to the emergency room of the local hospital. I don't remember very much after that. There were bright lights and low voices. Someone came and prodded my head. I kept drowsing off. Then Jane took me out of there.

Chapter VII

The next thing I knew, it was morning and I was lying in a four-poster bed with the sun streaming in the window. I could smell coffee. There was a bathroom just off my bedroom. My bag was by the bed. I took a shower, changed into some clean clothes and went down the stairs to find the kitchen. Jane was cooking eggs at the stove.

"I thought I heard some life up there," she said.

"What happened last night?"

"I guess the phrase is, 'you crashed.'"

I fingered my head. There was still a bump that was sore to the touch, but, otherwise, I felt all right.

"I guess I got hit on the head."

"Apparently you did. No concussion. The doctor said you'd be fine. I could have told him what a hard head you had."

"How did I get here? What happened after I left you in the parking lot?"

"Well, I was driving out, and I realized I had left my glasses in your car. So I turned around to come back. I found the glasses and was leaving again when all these men came out of the front door of the hotel. They were all in a bunch, but there looked like there was a woman in the middle of the pack."

"Mary?"

"Yes, Mary. I recognized her as they hustled her into the back of the van. I figured they were Minutemen. I ran into the hotel to see if I could find you, and there you were, arguing with the bellman. You weren't making much sense."

"You called the police?"

"Yes, and then took you to the emergency room. I thought, under the circumstances, that I couldn't just leave you back at the hotel, so I brought you here."

"And you got my stuff?"

"All of it. Fortunately, you hadn't done any unpacking."

"What about the police?"

"I talked to Sheriff Martin this morning. He wants to see you."

"Sheriff Martin?"

"That's right."

"Are they going to get Mary back?"

"I think there's some disagreement about the need for that."

"What do you mean?"

"Apparently she went voluntarily. She called the RTTR last night and asked them to come pick her up."

"That's a load of crap."

"Maybe. Here, have some coffee."

She poured me a cup. "Go sit out by the pool and soak up some sun."

I noticed some French doors for the first time. Out back was a little pool with a high stucco wall all around. There was a table and some chairs right outside the door. I sat down and drank the coffee. I had to think. I thought for about thirty seconds and then was back inside asking for a phone. Jane gave me a portable and shooed me back out the door. I returned to my coffee and called Bonnie Hirsch. It took some persistence with the same receptionist but I finally got Bonnie on the line.

"Bonnie, it's Pete Gordon."

"Pete. Thanks for calling. I was trying to get you all afternoon yesterday. I thought you were staying at the Hyatt."

"Ah, well I was, but the plans changed. Right now, I'm at a private home."

"Well, no harm done, but I have some bad news."

"What's that?"

I tried to get in to see your Norman Hawkins. He wouldn't see me. He already has a lawyer."

"He what?"

"You heard me. He already has himself a lawyer."

"Who is it?"

"A guy named Roy Corbin."

"Has he got any criminal experience?"

"I guess you could say that. He defends RTTR members on all the trespassing and assault beefs they keep getting involved in locally."

I couldn't believe what I was hearing.

"He's an RTTR lawyer?"

"That's right. You'd better get that wife of his down to the jail fast to change his mind. Otherwise, there's nothing I can do for the poor schmuck."

"Ahhh . . . . There may be a problem with that."

"What could be the problem?"

"Well, a bunch of RTTR goons came and took her out of the hotel last night. God knows where she is right now. Probably up at that ranch they have."

"How do you know?"

"I was at the hotel when they were bringing her out. I got a bump on the head for my pains."

"Did you call the police?"

"Ahh . . . yes. Apparently, the police are saying that Mary called the RTTR and asked them to come pick her up."

"That sounds odd."

"Of course it's odd," I exploded. "It's more than odd, it's a damn lie."

"OK, OK, calm down. You don't have to yell at me. What are you going to do?"

"Apparently this Sheriff Martin wants to talk to me at ten."

"Martin. Good. This is beginning to sound interesting. Are you retained as Mary's counsel?"

"Yes," I said. This was true only in a limited sense, but the facts were a little complicated to explain over the phone.

"OK, you have just retained me as your local counsel. I'll meet you at Martin's office at ten. Got to go now." And she rang off and left me with a dead phone in my hand. Jane came out with a plate of eggs, and

I found I was ravenous. I gobbled them down while she sat down opposite me.

"Who was that?"

I explained between bites.

"So now you have a local lawyer?"

"Right. I don't think that I have any clout to move the local establishment. Let's see what clout the renowned Bonnie Hirsch has."

Jane drove me over to the Sheriff's office at about five minutes to ten. We waited by the door for about fifteen minutes before Bonnie arrived. Then, we waited another twenty minutes before we were escorted into the presence of the Sheriff himself. The Sheriff was sitting behind an enormous desk in an equally enormous wood paneled office. Lining the walls were dozens of pictures of Sheriff Martin posing with a variety of political and show business figures and dozens more plaques, awards and certificates all honoring Sheriff Martin. Bonnie walked over and engaged the Sheriff in small talk while we loitered at the entrance to the room looking at the pictures and mementos. Bonnie waved us over to introduce us.

"Chet. This is Peter Gordon and Jane Hawkins."

I stepped forward to shake his hand. The Sheriff didn't get up, so I had to walk around the side of his big desk to shake his hand. He appeared even in his seat to be well over six feet in height, and I would have guessed that he was closer to three hundred than two hundred pounds. He had a large head and a red face, and he was perspiring although the air conditioner on the wall was struggling mightily.

"I'm glad to meet you, Sheriff."

"Thanks for coming in Mr. Gordon. Ms. Hawkins. Please sit down."

He looked at Jane narrowly. "Hawkins? Are you another relation to the Norman Hawkins we've got cooling his heels down in the holding cells?"

"I'm his sister, Sheriff."

He grunted. "I understand you're interested in one Mary Hawkins. That would be his wife, right?"

"Ahh, yes sir," I said. "I have reason to believe that she was taken against her will last night by members of a cult that operates around here."

"Would you mean the Return to the Roots organization?"

"Yes, I would."

"And what makes you think that Mrs. Hawkins was taken against her will?"

"I was there. I saw them taking her."

"Did she cry out? Ask for aid in any way?"

"No. I think she had been given some kind of sedative or drug."

"Oh, really. And how do you know this?"

"She wasn't really walking. She was between two of the goons. One on each arm. They were kind of dragging her along. And her eyes were kind of unfocused. She was mumbling."

"I see. They were 'kind of' dragging her along. And her eyes were 'kind of' unfocused. And from that you allege she was drugged?"

"Sheriff, all I'm doing is trying to tell you how it looked to me. I flew out here with Mrs. Hawkins, at her request, to try to help out with her husband. It just seems a little funny to me that she would, all of a sudden, run off with these RTTR guys without a word to me. We would just like you to look into the matter."

He picked up a typewritten page from his desk and scanned it briefly.

"Well, as a matter of fact, we've already looked into it, Mr. Gordon. I've personally spoken to Mr. Richard Beck. Mr. Beck tells me that Mrs. Hawkins called Mr. Robert Reynaud last night at approximately 10:00 PM and asked if she could return to the fold so to speak. At her request, Reynaud sent someone around to pick her up."

"He didn't just send someone around," I interrupted. "He sent at least six goons in a van. If this is all so innocent, why didn't he just send one person in a car to meet her at the hotel's front entrance? Why does he need to send five of the goons up to her room to collect her?"

"Mr. Beck says that they were concerned about adverse public reaction growing out of the attempted assassination of Congressman Renfrow."

I started to say something else, but he continued on.

"We also interviewed the Bell Captain who was on duty at the hotel. He remembers nothing of this, but he does remember you creating a disturbance, Mr. Gordon. He believes you were intoxicated."

"That's ridiculous," broke in Jane. "I was with him all night. He wasn't drunk; he got hit on the head by those gangsters. I took him to the emergency room myself."

Martin looked at her briefly and then consulted his sheet of paper again.

"Yes, we checked that out also. Mr. Beck claims that Mr. Gordon attacked his people and punched one of them."

Jane started to react, but I motioned her to be silent. I leaned back in my chair.

"Really?" I said. "And what else has Mr. Beck told you that's on that little sheet, Sheriff?"

"Not much," he said cheerfully. "Only that Mr. Beck says that you're being investigated back east for misrepresentation by some New Jersey ethics board and that you have, for some reason, instituted a one-man hate crusade against the RTTR."

"A one-man hate crusade?"

He put the paper down as if it had served its function.

"That's what Mr. Beck charges."

Now I was about to retort angrily, but Bonnie interceded.

"And what's your take on all this, Chet?"

He moved himself in his chair as if he were suddenly uncomfortable.

"My take is that, unless Mr. Gordon here makes a formal complaint, there's not much I can do."

"And if he makes one, this Richard Beck is bound to make one as well."

"That would be my guess."

"So it's no harm, no foul, right?"

He shrugged.

"Except for one thing," she continued.

"What one thing is that?"

"The one thing is that one Mrs. Mary Hawkins, who happens to be my client, was brazenly and openly taken against her will out of her hotel room last night, and once again they've buffaloed you into taking no action against them."

Martin's face got redder and redder as she spoke.

"Now wait a minute."

"No, you wait a minute. Anyone with half a brain could see where the truth lies here. This isn't some little fracas over who's got rights to the sidewalk. This is a kidnapping. If you think we're going to let this slide, you've gravely miscalculated."

Martin's eyes had turned into slits. For a moment, I thought he was going to explode out of his chair. Then he thought again and subsided.

"So Mrs. Hawkins is your client as well?"

"That's right. She was in my office yesterday. Beck may be able to throw around accusations about Mr. Gordon here. They're easily made and hard to check. So let's forget about Mr. Gordon. Let's deal with me. I'm telling you that Mary Hawkins is my client and I want some action out of this office."

He leaned back. "What do you want me to do Ms. Hirsch?" "Send in a SWAT team? Call out the National Guard and storm the place?"

She leaned forward in her chair. "Those are all good ideas Sheriff. But before going to those extremes, why don't you just call this Richard Beck on the telephone and tell him to get his butt into your office pronto and to bring Mrs. Hawkins with him. Her lawyer wants to consult with her. If there's nothing to this abduction charge, what better way to prove it?"

"All right, Bonnie. I'll call him. Why don't you give me a call in about an hour, and I'll see what can be arranged."

"Good." She got up and leaned over the desk. "Be persuasive, Chet."

She turned and walked out of the room. There was nothing left but for us to follow. We caught up to her out in the parking lot.

"What an asshole," she steamed. "Sometimes I think he's intimidated by them. Sometimes I think he's on the payroll."

"You really think so?" asked Jane.

"Who knows? Come on. Let's go back to my office."

We drove back to Bonnie's office. An hour later, on the dot, she called Sheriff Martin. He told her Beck and Mary would be in his office at two. Jane went back to work. I sat by myself in Bonnie's conference room until a quarter of two. I think someone sent in sandwiches, but I don't really remember. Finally the waiting was over, and Bonnie and I were back in the reception area of the Sheriff's office. There was a black van with smoked windows in the parking lot. Martin kept us waiting for fifteen minutes. Finally, we were escorted back into his office. The Sheriff was behind his desk with his feet up. Mary sat in a chair in front of the desk, looking down at the floor. Beck was leaning against the wall by a window to the right of the desk. He was smoking a cigarette, and he gave me a slow wink as I came into the room. Martin started before we had gotten fully into the room.

"I've spoken to Mrs. Hawkins, and she assures me that she initiated the call to the RTTR, and she returned to them of her own free will."

Bonnie spoke up before I could say anything.

"Sheriff. I want to speak to my client alone, please."

"Mrs. Hawkins has told me that she no longer wishes you to represent her. In fact she's doesn't believe she ever engaged you to represent her. Mr. Gordon here seems to have a history of exaggerating who his clients are."

I started to react, but Bonnie put a restraining hand on my arm.

"Sheriff, we need to talk to Mrs. Hawkins out of the intimidating presence of Mr. Beck here."

Martin affected an amazed expression. He was clearly enjoying himself.

"Intimidating? Mr. Beck hasn't been intimidating in the slightest. He's cooperated with this office in every possible way. Including taking up his valuable time to bring Mrs. Hawkins here to straighten out this misunderstanding."

"Sheriff, have you interviewed Mrs. Hawkins out of the presence of Mr. Beck?"

Martin shot a glance at Beck.

"Ah, no. I do not see the point in that."

"The point is, if we're right, and the RTTR is putting undue pressure on Mrs. Hawkins, she might be able to speak more freely with Beck out of the room."

Martin's face was getting red again just as it had that morning.

"You asked to speak to Mrs. Hawkins, and here she is," he said. "I'm not going to listen to any special conditions you want to impose."

"Let me talk to her a moment," I said to Bonnie.

I went over and sat next to Mary. During the entire colloquy she had remained with her eyes fixed on a spot on the floor.

"Mary," I said. "Mary. Can you hear me?"

She nodded.

"Look at me," I asked.

She shook her head and kept looking at the floor.

"Mary. All you have to do is say so, and you can leave here with us. We'll see that the RTTR doesn't bother you again."

She finally raised her head and looked at me.

"It's all right," she whispered. I leaned closer to hear her better "I called them to come and get me. I realized that my rightful place was with them."

"What about Harry?"

"They are the only ones who can get him freed."

"Mary. In New Jersey you thought they had set him up for the murder."

"I was wrong. What reason would they have to do that to one of their own?"

I couldn't answer. That very same question had been bothering me.

"I'm sorry to have gotten you all the way out here. I see that was wrong now."

"How did you see? Did Beck explain it to you?"

"Oh no. The Archon Reynaud lifted the blinders from my eyes. I see now where I was wrong. This was all a plot by the FBI to get rid of Congressman Renfrow and throw the blame onto the RTTR. Only Archon Reynaud understands the inner workings. With his help we will get Harry back."

She turned and stared at the floor again.

"Satisfied?" asked the Sheriff.

"Actually no," I said. I pulled Bonnie over to the door.

"Did you hear all of that?" I asked.

"Not all of it, but enough."

"There's not much we can do, is there?"

"Not if she sticks with that story."

"We could insist that we interview her alone."

"I don't think we're going to win that one today."

"How about if we get a court order?"

"We might be able to get a hearing. But the judge is going to want to hear her in person. And probably Beck will be allowed in the courtroom. And she's probably going to tell the same story, don't you think?"

I felt defeated.

"Yeah, I think she'll tell the same story."

"And if she does, Beck is going to pursue this nonsense about assault on his poor, helpless Minutemen. I know it's crazy, but without corroboration of the abduction, you could come off looking guilty."

"Well?" asked the Sheriff from across the room.

"Under the circumstances we're withdrawing the complaint," said Bonnie. "We still think that Mrs. Hawkins is under undue pressure, and we reserve the right to pursue this matter again if we find the facts warrant."

"Pursue away," said Martin.

Bonnie led me out the door. Beck turned and gave me a big smile as I went out the door. As it closed, I could hear his loud laugh.

Neither of us said anything on the way back to Bonnie's office. We sat down in her office and, for a moment, we still were silent. It was Bonnie who spoke first.

"I hate that."

"What?"

"Having an asshole like Chet Martin get the upper hand on me. That Beck is a cute customer, isn't he?"

"Yeah. He just smirks in the background while the Sheriff does his dirty work for him."

"Look, I know it's a long shot, but I can get a hearing before Judge Weinstein tomorrow. He was never an admirer of Martin's, and you can be sure this Nazi, RTTR stuff isn't going to play with him."

I put up my hand to stop her. I had come to a decision.

"No. I'm going to do what my ex-wife is always telling me I can't do. And that's 'Let it go.'"

"You're just going to drop this? Mary is your client."

"It was her father-in-law who really hired me. And anyway, it sounds like we've just been fired. It doesn't matter that we have suspicions about the influences that may have caused her to fire us. The fact remains that she did. In front of witnesses, yet. No, I feel like spending a few vacation days out here in the sun and forgetting I ever heard about Norman Hawkins."

"I've got a little invested in this as well. To whom do I send my bill?"

"Send it to me. I'll take it out of the original Hawkins retainer, pay myself and send the balance back to the executor of the estate."

"So the going gets a little tough, and you bail out, is that it, Gordon?"

"It's not my fight. I had a client, but he's dead. The death may not have been an accident, but we'll never know for sure."

"What about the RTTR? Don't they scare you a little?"

"Sure, but just a little. We've always had violent fringe groups in this country. RTTR is just another one. Maybe a little odder and more violent, but maybe not."

We sat there glaring at each other over the desk. The phone rang. She picked it up said a few words and then handed me the receiver.

"It's Jane."

"Hello," I said into the receiver.

"I take it that it didn't go well."

"Sorry. Was I barking at you?"

"A little. A guy named Rich Skowronski just called me. He needs to talk to you urgently."

"OK. I'll call him from here, then come over and fill you in."

"Don't tell me the darling Mary is delighted to be back in the arms of her old comrades."

"That's the story."

"OK, I'll expect to see you soon."

I hung up and dialed Rich hoping I could still catch him in the office. He was still there. He got right to the point.

"Pete. They've found the boat."

For a moment I drew a blank.

"The boat?"

"The boat. You know, the Hawkins boat. 'Far Cry.'"

"Where?"

"Drifting at sea. The Coast Guard's towing her in to Cape May. She's dismasted and almost sunk."

"There was no one aboard?"

"No. She'd been abandoned."

There was silence on the line.

"So," said Rich. "You interested?"

"In what?"

"In Hawkins? What's the matter with you? Do you want to see the boat, or not?"

No. I wasn't interested. I had just given up on any interest in Norman Hawkins or his problems. I just wanted to do nothing for a few days.

"Of course I'm interested," I said.

"Well, then you better get your butt back here tonight. I'm going down to see the boat tomorrow morning at the Coast Guard Station in Cape May. If you come with me, I can probably get you on board. Otherwise, who knows?"

"All right. I'll catch the red-eye."

We arranged to meet in North Beach the next morning, and I hung up. Bonnie was looking at me with an amused expression on her face.

"Don't say anything," I said.

She held up her hands, palms out.

"They've found Norman's boat," I said.

"So I gather. And you're going back on the red-eye to take a look at her."

"Right."

"So you're still acting as Norman Hawkins' lawyer?"

"Looks like it," I said.

"What about Mary?"

I smiled ruefully. "We'll have to see if she really meant to fire us."

"You want me to do anything while you're gone?"

"No. Just pick up whatever information you can."

"And what will you be doing?"

"They have us stymied here for the moment. We need to get something to pry them open. I have a feeling our best shot for that right now is on the East Coast."

"By them, you mean the RTTR?"

"Who else? They're the bad guys, aren't they?"

With that parting shot, I left to find Jane.

What I found was an argument.

"I'm coming with you," she said.

"There's no need for that. I'm just going to look at a boat. I'll let you know what happens."

"Yes, but it's my father's boat. He's dead and it sounds as if Louie is as well."

"Don't you think you should try to get in to see Harry?"

"Harry will keep. He's got his precious Mary to visit him. And I don't think he'll be any more anxious to see me than he was when I tried to visit him before."

"How about Jerry?"

"Jerry will be all right. Steve's there, and there's a whole network of people eager to help out. No, there's something going on here that I don't understand. It's like we're behind the curve on it, where everybody knows more than we do. You know what I mean?"

"Yes." I knew exactly what she meant.

"I think that's what my father hired you to find out. He hired you, and I'm holding you to the deal. And furthermore, I'm along for the ride until the end."

I held up my hands in surrender. I think I was really glad she wanted to come.

"OK, OK, you've made your point. Let's call the airlines and get some tickets."

She picked up the phone on her desk.

"Alice," she said into the phone. "Make two reservations on that United red-eye to Newark . . . . Yes, tonight . . . . That's right. Me and Mr. Gordon."

Back in the days when I had worked for Davis & Piersall in Philadelphia, I had gotten to Los Angeles fairly frequently. Over the time I had developed a routine for catching the red-eye. The routine was more fun with Jane than it had been all those years by myself. The first step was to have dinner in a restaurant in Marina del Rey or Santa Monica. We opted for one of the quieter restaurants in Santa Monica on this trip. Jane suggested an Italian restaurant on the promenade downtown. I ordered some wine, and when it came, she took a sip and looked at me over the rim of the wineglass.

"Well, Mr. Gordon. You know about everything there is to know about the Hawkins family. I know practically nothing about you. So it's time to give."

"I don't talk about myself very easily."

"That was not a request, counselor. I want the information and I want it now. We have our ways of making you talk, you know."

"OK," I said. "Where do you want me to start?"

"At the beginning. Give me the life story."

"The life story. All right, you asked for it. I was born 40 years ago outside Philadelphia. My father was a Philadelphia lawyer, who intimidated practically everyone he met, with the possible exception of my mother."

"So you were bound to the law from the beginning?"

"Yes, it seems that way, although nothing I ever did quite measured up to the accomplishments of my father. I got good grades, but never the top. Whatever I did there was always an expectation level that was always just slightly higher. I went to law school as a path of least resistance. It was always expected of me, and I didn't have any pressing reason why I shouldn't go. As it turned out, I was pretty good at it. Law Review and all that. Of course, he had been Notes Editor, so just making Law Review was expected but not something to lavish praise over. Finally I wised up a little. When it came time to take a job, I did go to one of the big Philadelphia firms, but not his. I went to one of the competition. I kept my head down, worked my tail off and made partner in the requisite number of years. Mostly pretty boring stuff."

"What made you leave and go to North Beach?"

I sighed. I had been avoiding this part of the story. "Dad had a house on the beach there when I was growing up. It's where I learned to sail. My first job was sweeping up around the club and later as sailing instructor. We spent summers there right up through last year."

"At your father's house?"

"Yes."

"Maybe you better tell me about the we."

"That would be Joanne."

"If you say so."

"I met Joanne in Law School. We got married right after I graduated.

We never had kids, but we did the whole other suburban bit. In the summers she moved to North Beach and I commuted. But somehow after ten years we stopped communicating. I'm not sure how it happened. It's like one day I turned around and looked at her and felt nothing. I realized that I had been feeling nothing for a long time, but I never realized it, or maybe I just wouldn't admit it to myself. But I didn't know how to change it. It's like inertia. You know you're not going anywhere but you have no power to do anything about it. Then last year it all changed. First my father died."

"What about your mother?"

"Oh, she died twenty years ago."

"And your father never remarried?"

"No. He had a sort of companion to take care of him."

"A companion?"

"I just don't know how to explain it. A friend. Family really. She was my mother's cousin."

"And he never married her?"

"Oh, it was nothing like that. She was already married."

"Where was the husband?"

"Oh, he was around too. They both stayed in the house in North Beach in the summers. The husband was a great old guy. He was a teacher so he got the summers off."

"And you think there was nothing going on?"

I stopped eating and looked at her, my fork frozen halfway to my mouth.

"I never even thought about it."

"My, you were a dull boy, weren't you?"

I put the fork down. "I guess I was. They were always just kind of around."

She reached across and patted my hand. "Of course they were. How did Joanne get along with the old guy?"

"Oh, they got along great, of course. She could do no wrong and neither could he."

"So what happened when your father died?"

"It was like a month later that Joanne told me she wanted a divorce."

"Was there another guy?"

"Of course. Joanne's not one to take a leap of faith. She has to know where she's coming down. But she knew enough to get a hotshot lawyer. She got the house, and I wound up in an apartment."

"Soon you're going to get to the part about how you moved to North Beach, right?"

"I'm almost there. The divorce was final sometime last winter. By spring I knew I felt the same way about my job as I had about my marriage. I took a sabbatical in July to write a book."

"You? Write a book?"

"Don't laugh, it was kind of fun. Anyway, I got to know this local lawyer in town. His name's Dave Stockard. He offered me a job. I never would have taken it if my father had been still alive. But with him gone, it was like I didn't have to prove myself any more. I didn't have to be the Philadelphia lawyer. You know what I mean?"

"I think I know exactly what you mean."

I looked at her. "Yes, I guess you do. So it seemed like a great lark. I started in September. Maybe I was beginning to have second thoughts. But then your father walked into my office. And here I am."

We had finished our dinner. I asked the waiter for some coffee. My routine called for finishing up at about that time, so we drank our coffee and got back on the road. The schedule called for arriving at the airport at about nine o'clock, checking in, purchasing and consuming the obligatory ice cream cone, hoping the plane wouldn't be delayed and waiting for departure. We did all the obligatory stuff, the plane was not delayed, and we lined up for boarding at about ten. I took the window and Jane the aisle. Fortunately there was no one in the middle seat. We held hands as the plane trundled down to the end of the taxiway, and the big turbine engines roared to accelerate the plane down the runway. The plane bumped once and then what had been a huge, lumbering beast became suddenly graceful as it launched itself into its proper element. I looked out the window at the lights of Santa Monica and the mountains behind, and followed with my eyes the necklace of lights that were Malibu as they led out towards Ventura County. I wondered what Harry Hawkins was doing tonight. I wondered if I would be able to help him. I wondered if he had tried to kill Ted Renfrow. I wondered if he had killed his father.

The view faded to my right as the plane took a big swing to the south to turn back to the east over Palos Verdes Estates. Then I was looking south into Orange County, and the stewardess was making an announcement about drinks and a movie.

Chapter VIII

The next thing I remembered was a bell sounding and the cabin lights switching on. A stewardess was passing around a tray of orange juice. I took one gratefully. My mouth was dry and foul tasting.

"Well, you certainly slept," said Jane.

I stretched and began the laborious process of putting on my shoes.

"I guess I did. How about you?"

"On and off. I never really sleep on airplanes."

"That's good. Someone has to be responsible for keeping the plane in the air."

"Very funny. What does the routine call for now?"

"Well, normally it would call for me to go home to take a nap for about an hour. Then a shower and off to the office. But I've got to meet Rich and go to Cape May to look at the boat." I looked at her. "Are you sure you want to do that part?"

"I've been having second thoughts about that. I think it was over Nebraska that I decided that maybe I don't want to rush down to look at the boat."

"I don't blame you. In that case, I'll drop you off at my house, and you can do the nap and shower bit."

The stewardesses were making sure everyone had their seat belts fastened and seat backs upright, and the pilot banked the plane and brought her around to land to the south. I had a quick view of downtown Newark, and then we were over the runway, bouncing once and then on solid ground as the thrust-reversers roared. Jane had taken my hand again and now she squeezed it.

"Be careful."

"Why?"

"These RTTR guys may seem like buffoons, but I have a feeling that they don't view themselves the same way."

"No." I thought about Beck ordering one of his Minutemen to put his hand through my window. "I think they take themselves very seriously."

"Right. And you're putting yourself in their way. They're not averse to solving their problems through violence. And you're a potential problem."

"Don't worry. They don't even know which coast I'm on. And how could I be safer than to be with the police?"

She squeezed again. "Just be careful."

I promised and then we were standing in the aisle waiting for the plane to empty. We got the bags and found the Garden State Parkway. Jane proved that she was capable of sleeping in cars even though she had difficulty in airplanes. In an hour and a half, we were going over the inlet bridge into North Beach. I showed Jane to the guest room, had a quick shower, and by 8:30 I was parking my car in front of the police station. Rich came down the front steps of the station, zipping up a fleece-lined jacket that came down over his thighs.

"Is that all you've got?" he asked. I had quickly pulled a windbreaker off the rack on the way out.

"I'll be all right."

He looked at me doubtfully and motioned me to an unmarked police car that was standing in front of the station. I hesitated and looked out over the bay. A blustery northeast wind had blown a sheet of cloud in from the ocean to cover the sun and was kicking up whitecaps on the water. The temperature was in the mid-forties, but the wetness in the wind off the ocean made it seem colder. I shivered in my jacket. I'd be fine in the car. I opened the door and got in.

"Glad to see you, Pete. What have you got from your end?"

"What am I? Your unpaid investigator?"

"Actually, that's just what you are. And if you want me to help you, you'll help me too. Or, do you want to get out right here?"

"No, that's all right," I said placatingly.

He started the car, and I told him about Southern California. By the time he had picked up the Garden State Parkway in Tom's River, I had finished the tale.

"This Beck character seems to keep turning up, doesn't he?" he commented.

"Yeah, I noticed that."

"It doesn't make sense."

"Why not?"

"If little Norman did try to kill Renfrow, why would the RTTR want to get him representation with their pet mouthpiece? Why wouldn't they want to stay as far away from him as they could?"

"Because they need to keep control of him." I replied. "They're going to paint this as a set up orchestrated by malign forces. The CIA. The FBI. The Gays. Who knows? It will be someone."

"But your theory is that he was set up. By whom? The RTTR?"

"Who else?"

"I don't know who else. I don't think it was the CIA. But why would they set up Harry? If they wanted some schlump to take a fall, I'm sure they could have arranged someone not so close to Reynaud. And they set him up and then provide a defense pointing the finger somewhere else?" He shook his head. "It's all too complicated. We're missing something. There's a whole lot going on here that we don't understand."

He kept on talking, but I was too tired to concentrate. I drifted off, and didn't wake up again until we were going over the canal bridge into Cape May. The summer tourists had long since departed, and the town seemed deserted. Rich negotiated our entrance to the Coast Guard base and got directions to the dock.

"When did she get in?" I asked.

"Sometime last night."

He parked the car at the foot of the pier, and we walked down to the end. A buoy tender was tied up to the dock with an enormous green bell buoy perched precariously on its stern. The wind blew across the harbor and right through my jacket. I shivered.

"I don't see her," I said.

He pointed to a knot of men standing on the tender.

"She's tied up to the tender."

"There's no mast."

"Yeah, I told you. She was dismasted. Could be in the same accident that knocked old Norman overboard."

I looked closer, and now I could see a part of "Far Cry's" hull, riding low in the water. A large pump had been set up on the tender. It gave off a constant growl as it pumped water from the boat into the harbor. Rich climbed down a ladder attached to the pier to the deck of the tender. I followed somewhat clumsily. Rich walked over to join the group of men, and I followed to look over the rail of the tender. He introduced himself while I looked down at the sailboat. The mast was snapped off about six feet above the deck. The boom, with a piece of the mainsail still attached, lay along the rail. A hose from the pump on the tender led down the main hatch into the bilge. The noise of the pump was overwhelming. Several men were on the boat inspecting the damage. Without thinking, I climbed down to join them. I walked over to one of them who was inspecting what remained of the starboard stays. He was dressed in a suit, tie and winter overcoat and looked quite out of place standing on the deck of a boat. He was holding one of the turnbuckles and examining the ends of the wire.

"Cut," I said.

He looked up. "Yes," he replied. "Looks like it was a bolt cutter."

"It's what you would expect."

"What do you mean by that?" He asked.

"When you lose a mast like this. The first thing you have to do is get rid of it. The whole rig would have been dragging in the water. It was bound to be rough. Banging around like that, that mast's a danger to the crew and to the boat. It could punch a hole in the hull or take somebody's head off."

He nodded. "I get it. So you have to cut it free?"

"Right. Every boat like this will carry a set of bolt cutters for just that purpose. In a situation like that you'd cut all the stays at the turnbuckles, then cut away the mainsail. If you had enough people and it wasn't too rough you might be able to save the rig. With a mast this big and the number of people who must have been on this boat, they would have just let it go. It would fill up and sink pretty quickly."

"Thanks," he said. "By the way, who are you?"

"My name is Peter Gordon," I said. "I'm Norman Hawkins' lawyer. Or, I guess you could say I was when he was alive." If I were guilty of misrepresentation before about the relationship, I had just compounded the situation.

"Hawkins' lawyer?" He looked at me doubtfully. "You shouldn't be on the boat."

"Why not? Who are you, by the way?"

"My name is Dick Corville. I'm a special agent for the FBI."

"The FBI? What's the FBI's jurisdiction in a case like this?"

"I'm afraid I'm not at liberty to talk about that at the moment." His manner had become markedly more frigid. "You'll have to get off the boat. We're still in the middle of our investigation."

"Sure," I said and walked back to climb aboard the tender. Rich reached down and gave me a hand up.

"You can't get on the boat yet," he said.

"So I was told. What did you find out?"

"She was spotted by a fisherman at dawn yesterday morning. He called it in. A cutter went out to get her. They had her hooked up before dark and got her in here about midnight last night."

"So she was pretty far at sea?"

"Yeah, maybe thirty or forty miles."

"What are they doing now?"

"Finishing pumping her out."

"Has anyone been down below yet?"

"No. Not since the first inspection when they were hooking up the tow. I guess no one wants to get their feet wet." He stood with his hands in his pockets watching as the pump coughed to a halt, and two sailors pulled the hose out of the main companionway. Corville and another man disappeared down the hatch.

"What's the FBI's interest in this?" I asked Rich.

He looked at me sharply. "What do you know about the FBI?"

"That guy who went down the hatch. Or one of them. He's an FBI agent."

"How do you know that?"

"He told me he was."

There was silence as Rich concentrated on the empty hatch.

"Did you know the FBI was involved?" I demanded.

"I was just officially informed."

"And what's the basis of their interest?"

He shrugged. "I'm told it's federal jurisdiction because the boat was found in international waters."

"It's not in international waters now," I pointed out. "And doesn't the Coast Guard usually do the investigation at least up to the point where there's evidence that there's been a crime committed?"

"Yeah, that's usually the case."

"So why all these big guns?"

"They were a little vague on that."

"Don't you have a right to know?"

He looked at me angrily. "Pete, give me a break. I've got jack shit on this case. If it's a case at all. If the FBI wants to do an investigation with all their resources, I say terrific. I'll be delighted with a few crumbs from the table because that's a whole lot more than I've got now."

Before I could respond there was a shout from down below. Corville stuck his head out of the hatch.

"Jack," he called to one of the men standing on the tender. "Get the ME. And get the lab boys down here."

"What was that?" asked the man.

"You heard me. Get them here pronto. And we need some lights down here. Let's get something rigged up." His head disappeared down the hatch again. Jack turned and started to climb the ladder back to the pier.

"What's going on?" I asked Rich.

"Looks like your evidence of a crime committed may have just come to pass."

"Is there a body down there?"

"Yeah. It looks that way. Or maybe more than one."

A chill went through me that was not from the wind. We fell into silent watching. After a half an hour, I could not stand the wind any longer. I climbed back up on the pier and found my way back to Rich's car. I hunched down in the front seat and, in ten minutes, I was asleep.

I was awakened some time later as the car door opened and someone put a hand on my arm.

"Mr. Gordon?"

I snapped awake and looked up to see one of the Coast Guard ratings from the tender.

"Yes?" I asked.

"Come on. Special Agent Corville would like to see you."

He stepped back and let me out of the car. An ambulance now sat on the edge of the pier with its lights flashing. Two other cars had arrived and, as I got to the edge of the pier, I could see that the number of men on the tender had doubled.

"Right down there," said the man. He pointed to Corville who was standing talking to Rich at the far rail of the tender. I climbed down and walked over to them.

"Mr. Gordon," said Corville. "Did you know Hawkins' captain?"

"You mean Louie?"

"Was that his name?"

"Yes, Louie. I didn't really know him. I've seen him around the marina when 'Far Cry' was tied up there."

"But you could identify him?"

"Sure. So could Rich here."

"Rich says he only saw a guy on the boat from a distance."

"OK. You think it's him on the boat?"

He compressed his lips as if he was dealing with a slow child. "It's a logical guess, don't you think?"

"Ah, yes. I would guess so. There's only one body?"

"Should there be more?" he asked sharply.

"I don't know. I'm just asking."

"No. Just the one. Come on. Let's get this over with."

He turned and climbed down onto "Far Cry". Rich and I followed him onto the boat and down the companionway ladder. At the foot of the ladder was a huge stateroom. Wires ran everywhere to lights that had been fixed to the overhead with duct tape. The lights threw off a harsh, unnatural glare. The room was a mess. The water had obviously covered the settees, and the cushions were a soggy wreck. A man was kneeling at the forward end of the stateroom at an open door. The door to the head, I guessed. Corville was leaning over his shoulder and waved me forward impatiently. I remembered Norman Hawkins' waterlogged body, so I thought I was prepared for what I would see as I went forward. The kneeling man got up to give me room. Beneath him was a body lying on the cabin floor and wedged halfway into the head. His head was butted up against the toilet bowl. I felt the urge to vomit, but forced it down. The smell in the confined cabin was almost overpowering. The back of the man's head was covered with blood.

"It could be him," I managed to say, my voice cracking. "I can't see his face."

"Doc. Can we move him?" asked Corville.

The man who had been kneeling must have given his assent because Corville reached in and roughly pulled at the man's shoulder exposing the face. It was enough. It was Louie. I backed out of the doorway into the stateroom.

"It's him," I said to Corville.

"It's Louie, the hired Captain of this vessel?" asked Corville formally.

"Yes," I said. "That's what I said. Now can I get out of here?"

He made a dismissive gesture. I don't remember climbing back topside. The next thing I knew I was back on the pier looking down at the men on the tender. I stood there a minute watching them and then the wind got to me. I retreated once more to the uncertain shelter of Rich's car. This time I couldn't sleep. I kept thinking about Louie with his head up against the toilet bowl. Something about the picture bothered me. Finally I had it. The hose from the bowl leading overboard had been cut. Someone had tried to scuttle the boat.

Rich didn't come back for another half hour.

"Fire up the heater," I said as he got into the car.

He was whistling.

"Why so cheerful?" I asked.

"You're the one who ought to be cheerful," he responded. "You've got your wish."

"Why's that? Because now there's some evidence that Norman was murdered after all?"

"What evidence is there of that?"

"Now we've got another body, and he was clearly murdered."

"How do we know that? Maybe that conk on the head just happened when the mast came down."

"That's possible," I said. "But why would Louie try to scuttle the boat?"

"Very good," he said, starting the car. "I thought you were too out of it down there to notice the cut hose."

"I almost was. I haven't been seasick in twenty years, but the stench in that cabin almost did me in."

"So how do you see it?" he asked.

"That hose was cut with a knife. Did you find it down there?"

"No."

"Any other hoses cut?"

"Very good again. Yes. The hose under the sink in the galley had been cut."

"Was the seacock on that hose shut off?"

"Not all the way. It was leaking, but someone had tried to shut it."

By now Rich had gotten us out of the base and was approaching the town. I pictured it on a summer day with the crowds and the traffic. We cruised through the yellow flashing traffic light and turned right towards the Parkway.

"So what do you think?" he prodded.

"How long does the Doctor think Louie could have survived with that head wound?"

"We won't know anything very definitive until the autopsy, but he thinks quite a while. It probably knocked him out, but he could have come out of it and been conscious for some time. Maybe drifting in and out."

"Conscious enough to realize the boat was sinking? Conscious enough to crawl around shutting off seacocks?"

"Maybe."

"So suppose someone got on board the boat and over-powered the crew. They chucked Norman overboard, and hit Louie on the head. They cut the hoses to sink the boat and then they abandoned it. Louie woke up and realized the boat was sinking. He got to the seacocks but passed out in the head like we found him. He saved the boat, but he never woke up again. How about that?"

"That's about how I figure it. So who did it?"

"Reynaud. Norman took his son off in the boat like he planned. Reynaud found out about it and found him at sea somehow. They took the kid back and then decided to leave no witnesses."

"Harry claims he was in California all the time."

"What else is he going to say? He's back in their control spouting the party line."

"What about the mast? How did the boat lose the mast?"

"I don't know."

"Well the Coast Guard is saying that they lost the mast in the storm, and someone came to help them out. But these weren't your normal Good Samaritans. These were some bad guys who decided to rob the boat and dispose of the witnesses. They bungled the sinking of the boat just like you say, but it's basically an opportunistic crime."

I sat and thought as Rich sped north. We had gotten to Atlantic City before I spoke again.

"The pirate thing just doesn't get me," I said.

"Of course not. You're too hung up on Reynaud being the bad guy here."

"Yeah, but I just can't get over how Norman washed right up on our beach. And the boat was a thirty miles offshore and closer to Cape May than North Beach."

"It could have drifted a long way before someone found it."

"It had to be pretty far off or it would have been found sooner."

"At this time of year?"

"Sure. There's plenty of commercial traffic and, even at this time of year, there's still a lot of fishermen. No, I think the boat was way offshore when it was taken. And, it's too big a coincidence about where Norman came ashore. Someone wanted him found and that kills the random pirate theory."

"Why would Reynaud want him found?"

"To get at the inheritance. If he controls the kid, and he's going to control Hawkins Industries, isn't that motive enough to take out the old man? And Reynaud needs Norman demonstrably dead. He doesn't need a lot of speculation about him being somewhere off in the South Seas."

Rich thought a moment and then went off on different tangent.

"You still think whoever you saw in that yellow slicker wasn't Louie?"

I pictured again Louie's thick shoulders as Corville shifted him off the floor. They just didn't fit with that slim form that had stepped aboard "Far Cry" on that rainy afternoon. I shook my head.

"No, it wasn't Louie. I still think it was a woman."

"So how does she fit in?"

"I have no idea. Maybe they took her off with Harry. Maybe she drowned and never washed ashore. How do I know?"

Rich drove for a while longer, apparently thinking.

"If this is all an RTTR abduction scheme to get the kid, and then the inheritance, how does the assassination bit fit in?"

"That's a puzzler. It's what Jane was saying yesterday. There's too much going on that we don't know about. We're way behind."

There was a silence, and I realized he was looking curiously at me.

"Jane? You mean the sister?"

I felt the blood rush to my face.

"Yeah," I said. "The sister."

"OK, we'll leave that for the minute. Do you think the kid shot Renfrow?"

"I don't know why in the world he would, and I can't figure out why Reynaud would set him up for it."

We were both silent for about twenty miles before Rich spoke again.

"How'd you like to be the unofficial representative of the police department of the Borough of North Beach?"

"And do what?"

"Go talk to Junior and see what you can find out. Interview Reynaud and find out what's happening in the RTTR organization."

I stared at him in amazement. "You want me to do your job?"

"Well, the next logical step in the investigation is on the West Coast. I don't think the Mayor is going to spring for a plane ticket for me to go out there unless I've got something a little more concrete. You could get me something."

"I can't do that Rich. In the first place I already have a client. Well, two clients actually. So far there hasn't been any conflict between them that I can see, but I'm in an impossible situation if I take on a third."

"What's the problem? The first client is dead. He won't care. And didn't you tell me this morning that the second had fired you? So, you don't have a client. And I'm not engaging you to be my lawyer. I'm just asking you to help out a friend."

"No. It can't work that way. Even if I don't have a client any more, which I'll accept for the sake of argument, I still owe loyalty to the client. I can't use information I gained for them to help you." I sounded pompous even to myself.

"Why not?" he asked. "You've been doing it up to now."

"That's different."

"Why?"

"I've been sharing information with you for the purpose of helping my clients. Not for the purpose of helping you. Besides, they're not going to let me in to see Harry. And what do you think I could find out talking to Reynaud? You think he's going to reveal the innermost secrets of RTTR politics to an outsider like me? You're crazy if you think that. If I do get to see him, it'll be all sweetness and light and Potemkin villages."

I slumped back in my seat.

"So which is it?" asked Rich. "You won't do it because of your moral scruples? Or, you can't do it because of all the difficulties."

"Both."

"OK. Have you given up on this?"

"What do you mean?"

"I don't know why you started out on this crusade. Maybe something in Norman Hawkins touched you. Maybe you were feeling guilty because you were going to keep his money, and you thought you ought to do a little something so that you could tell yourself that you were earning it. Maybe you were just curious that a guy could talk to you one day and be dead the next. And you had to find out why. But for whatever reason you went ahead. My question is, 'Have you given up?' Do you still feel an obligation to Norman? Are you still curious? Or are you quitting?" The last was said in almost a shout. As he was speaking Rich had, consciously or not, speeded the car up to more than 90.

"Hey, slow down," I said. "How would it look, the Chief of the North Beach Police getting a ticket."

"I don't think I'm going to get a ticket," he said, but he slowed down to a more sedate speed.

The silence grew until he broke it again.

"So are you going to give me an answer to my question?"

"Which question? It seemed like you asked a whole bunch."

"No. There was only one. I just asked it in a couple of different ways."

"I've quit on this project a couple of times already. Something always seems to come up that draws me back in. The latest thing was your phone call that the Coast Guard had found 'Far Cry.'"

"So I called at just the right time."

"Yeah, you did. And I un-quit when I heard about the boat. And I haven't quit again yet."

"Good, so you're still in."

"I'm in to the same extent that I was before. And that is not as your representative."

"All right. I understand that. But if you think it's in your client's interest, whoever the hell your client is now, you'll continue to keep me informed?"

"That's a fair statement."

"Great. So when are you going back?"

"Back? I just got in this morning."

"Best not to get acclimated to Eastern Time at all. Just get back on that big bird this afternoon. I have a feeling the tide is running fast now."

"Well, this tide will wait for this man. I've got a few things to do before I head back west."

"Really? Care to tell me what they are?"

"Not at the moment."

He must have gotten all he wanted, or all he thought he could get, out of me because he left me alone for the rest of the trip. I wasn't ready to go back to LA just yet. I had just arrived, and I had a feeling that the keys to the identity of the mystery woman in the yellow foul weather gear were on the East Coast.

Rich dropped me off at my house, and I found Jane making eggs in the kitchen.

"Just in time," I said. "Did you manage a nap?"

"Managed isn't the right word. I just crashed. What shape was the boat in? Pretty bad?"

I told her as she served the eggs, and we ate them sitting in the living room and looking out over the bay. Or, she had started to eat them when I began the story. As I got into it, she stopped and just listened. When I had finished, she just sat there for a long time.

"I'm glad I didn't go," she said. "Poor Louie. A nicer guy, you'll never want to meet. And he never thought about hurting anybody. All he wanted to do was go sailing." She stopped, and I could see tears in her eyes. "And 'Far Cry,'" she went on. "Do you think there's any salvaging of her?"

"Yes, I would think so. Structurally, she's all right. She's a mess, and there's a lot of water damage down below. But, she's not a total write-off by any means."

"Good. I'm glad I didn't have to see her in that condition."

She sat up straight and made another stab at her now cold eggs. "It just gets curiouser, doesn't it?"

"Yes it does."

"Well, it gets curiouser yet. Have you seen the morning paper?"

"No."

She got up and went into the kitchen returning with the Business section of the Asbury Park Gazette. The lead story was about Hawkins Industries and featured a picture of Wilfred Brunell. I looked up in surprise.

"That's right," she said. "Your close friend Wilfred Brunell is now Chairman of the Board of Hawkins Industries. Also CEO by the way. He's leading the search committee to find a President to run operations. Every one is saddened by the tragic death of the founder, Norman Hawkins, but this is a great company and it will continue to achieve the growth goals propounded by the great man while providing total customer satisfaction with due regard to respect for the individual." She breathed heavily pretending to be out of breath from the recital. "Did I leave any clichés out?"

I was reading as she was talking. The piece had been written from a press release issued by the company the day before. It ended with the normal tag line that Hawkins Industries was a diversified manufacturing company with products in the aerospace, transportation and general industrial markets. I looked up.

"No, you seem to have gotten the gist of it. This must be Brunell's dream. He finally has a client who will assuredly take all his advice. Himself."

She laughed. "Yes. Can we sell the stock short?"

"No reason why not."

I got up to put the dishes in the dishwasher.

"So what's next?" She called in from the living room.

"Rich wants me to go back to LA. He thinks the action is back there."

"Isn't he right? That's where Harry is, and that's where Reynaud is."

"I don't think I want to go back right away. Maybe in a day or two. Right now I want to ask some questions around here."

"Of whom?"

"Maybe I'll start with the widow Hawkins."

She gave a short little laugh. "That bitch."

* * *

I didn't get to see the widow Hawkins that day. My travel schedule caught up to me, and I slept for the rest of the afternoon and a good part of the evening. The next morning I made a quick visit to the office to return some telephone calls before finding myself driving up the cobblestone drive to the Hawkins house on the beach. I remember thinking that it was only Lorraine and Florence living there now. It would seem pretty empty to me, but maybe they were used to it. I parked the car by the door and rang the bell. I could hear the chime faintly as if it was ringing a long distance away. It probably was. Nothing happened, so I rang again. Finally, the door opened, and Florence stood in the doorway, as before, as if she would block my entrance with her body.

"Could I speak with Mrs. Hawkins please?" I asked.

"She's not receiving," replied Florence, and she started to close the door. I managed to get my foot in the crack.

"Wait a minute. I think she'll want to see me."

"Why would she want to see you?" she asked, but she released some of the pressure on my foot.

I was prepared for this initial unwillingness so I had an answer ready.

"Why don't you tell her that the police now know that her husband was murdered?"

Her eyes widened fractionally as I said the word murdered.

"I have some ideas about who might have done it that she might be interested in hearing."

Florence didn't move for a moment and then looked down at my foot.

"If you'll remove your foot from the door, sir, I'll go ask Mrs. Hawkins if she will consent to see you."

I nodded and retrieved my foot. Florence shut the door in my face. I stood there as the minutes rolled by feeling more and more foolish. Fortunately, I had thought to put on a warmer jacket than I had worn to Cape May. But the wind whipping around the sides of the house still penetrated directly to my bones. It must have been twenty minutes later that the door opened again. This time it swung wide, and Florence stood aside.

"Mrs. Hawkins can give you five minutes."

She shut the door behind me, turned and led me to the south wing. The living room was just the same, except that Lorraine Hawkins was already there, sitting at a sofa by the French doors. I imagined the doors opened to the summer breezes and the soft sounds of the summer ocean. Now they were tightly shut against the wind, and the surf pounded in the background. Lorraine was staring out the doors at the surf, and she started to speak without looking over at me.

"I hate this place in the wintertime. The wind howls unceasingly. Day after day. Week after week."

I walked right over to stand in front of her. "Why don't you go somewhere else?"

She turned her head to see me hovering over her.

"I do, of course. By now, I'm usually safely ensconced in our beach house in Palm Beach. Under the circumstances, my departure has been a little delayed."

I didn't move, and she began to be bothered by my proximity.

"Why don't you sit down, Mr. Gordon." She indicated the sofa across from her.

"Call me Pete," I said in my most friendly tone, as I retreated and sank into the over-stuffed pillows.

"Pete, of course. There's no formality here in North Beach, is there? But why should I be talking to you at all, Pete? I'm told you misrepresented the facts when you were here last. Telling me that you were my husband's lawyer."

"Where did you hear that?" I asked. "From Wilfred Brunell?"

"Wilfred had been a great comfort to me in this difficult period."

I decided the time had come to press a little.

"Yes. And now he's Chairman of Hawkins Industries. And you no longer have an unpleasant divorce proceeding on your hands. What's been so difficult about it?"

Her head jerked around as if she had been struck.

"That's an outrageous suggestion."

"What is?" I responded. "I don't think I suggested anything."

"You certainly did. I think that you should know that Norman and I were going to get back together. There wasn't going to be any divorce. He was coming back to me."

"When did he tell you this?"

"The night before he went out on that awful boat."

Bingo, I thought. "So he *was* here that night."

She hesitated. She had said more than she had intended.

"Yes, he was here."

"You told the Chief and me that you hadn't seen him."

"So what. It was an accidental drowning. What difference would it make if he had stopped by? But what's this about murder?"

"The police now have evidence that Norman's death wasn't just an accident. So his whereabouts on that Friday night have more than an academic interest."

"What evidence?" she asked sharply.

"I'm sure the police will explain it all."

She turned her head back and resumed her inspection of the ocean. "I think you'd better leave now. I have nothing further to say to you."

"The police might have a few additional questions."

"So let them come and ask. You're not the police. You have no legitimate interest in any of this."

"That's what Brunell says. I just have one question, and them I'll go."

She didn't answer, but she turned her head back to look at me.

"Who was Norman's new girlfriend?"

There appeared a flicker in her eyes.

"He didn't have a girlfriend. He and I were getting back together."

"Actually, I think you said he was coming back to you. To me, that implies he was coming back from some other woman. The other woman you told us about when Chief Skowronski and I were last here. Who was she?"

She had turned away again.

"Lorraine. I'm going to keep asking the question until I find the answer. You can tell me, or someone else can. In the end, it will all be the same." I got out of the chair and started to walk towards the door.

"All right," she said. "You're right. There was one. Tell me how the police know Norman was murdered, and I'll tell you her name, the little bitch."

I came back and stood over her again.

"They've found 'Far Cry.'"

There was that flicker in the eyes again. "Where?" she asked.

"At sea. She'd been dismasted. Louie was aboard. Someone had bludgeoned him to death."

"Who could have done it?"

I shrugged. "The Coast Guard thinks someone came upon them when they were disabled and took advantage of their plight."

"You mean like pirates?"

"Something like that."

"That seems so . . . so Elizabethan."

"The rules are breaking down on land. It shouldn't surprise us that the same thing is happening on the water." I paused. "So what's her name?"

She turned to me as if she had come back from a great distance.

"What?"

"Norman's girlfriend. What's her name?"

"Oh yes. Her. Her name is Annie Shelburne. She was a secretary at the company."

"At Hawkins Industries? Norman's secretary?"

"Not his. That would have been too tacky even for Norman. No. She was some little slut who worked in accounting or something. I never paid that much attention."

"Where's she live?"

Lorraine waved her hand dismissively.

"In Philadelphia, I think. You can find her. She still works for the company. Maybe not too much longer, though." She smiled. "No. Probably not for too much longer." Then she looked up as if out of a reverie. "And now, Mr. Gordon. I think our business is finished. I think you can find the door."

"Yes, I suppose I can. Thank you for seeing me." I turned to leave again. I had gotten half way across the floor when she spoke once more.

"And Mr. Gordon."

I stopped and turned. "Yes?"

"Don't come again."

I didn't respond, but just continued on my way to the foyer and straight out the front door. Florence was nowhere to be seen. But someone else was. A silver-gray Jaguar was pulling up the drive as I came out the front door. The driver pulled in behind my car, opened the door and got out. It was Wilfred Brunell. He saw me, and I could see his jaw clench. He walked quickly over and stood in front of me.

"Gordon, this is outrageous. You have no right to be here."

"Hello, Wilfred. It's so nice to see you too."

"I would have thought you were smarter than to continue to misrepresent yourself as Norman Hawkins' attorney."

"I'm probably not as smart as you give me credit for. But I don't think I said anything about being Mr. Hawkins attorney. The subject never came up."

"Why would Mrs. Hawkins see you then?"

"You'll have to ask her that. I understand you've been a great comfort to her in this difficult period."

He glowered at me.

"By the way," I continued. "Congratulations on your new position. The Hawkins Industries board must have great faith in your judgment."

"I fail to see how any of that is your business," he said.

"Oh, but it is. I'm a shareholder, you know. Fifty shares, I think it is. And furthermore," I leaned forward as if I was going to impart a confidence and lowered my voice. "I still consider myself to be Norman Hawkins' attorney, and I take a proprietary interest in the affairs of the company."

He had leaned forward as well to hear me better. He straightened up as if he had received an electric shock. His face was red.

"Get off this property," he hissed. "If I ever catch you here again, I'll call the police."

"Better you should stick to your disciplinary proceedings, Wilf. This is my town. I don't think the police are going to be arresting me." I turned and walked to my car. He continued to stand there staring at me as I turned the car around and drove off down the drive. I went back to my office and had made some phone calls when Linda Stevens found me sitting at my desk with my feet up.

"So where have you been?" she started. She deposited herself on my couch. I started to bring her up to date. She raised her eyebrows when I told her Jane had come back with me from California, but she kept silent through my recitation of Lorraine's revelations about the identity of the girlfriend and my confrontation with Brunell.

"I don't think you should play with him," she observed. "You know he's pushing ahead with this disciplinary board thing. There's a hearing next month."

"That's certainly quick action. He must be pressing it hard."

"He is, and you ought to take it seriously."

"I take it seriously. But the question it raises for me is why is he doing it?"

"I don't know. Because he's a public spirited citizen trying to protect the public from malfeasing scoundrels like yourself?"

"I doubt it. He knows as well as you and I do that the disciplinary board is a blind old dog. If you steal from your clients, and you steal a whole lot, maybe they'll sniff around your ankles a little."

"So, what's he after?"

"I think it's a blocking action. He's trying to divert me from something. And the more he tries to divert, the more interested I get."

"So you're going to find this Annie Shelburne?"

"I've already made some calls. I've called the company. It turns out she isn't a secretary after all. She's an accountant. Something to do with the internal audit function. And she hasn't been to work for over a week."

"I'm surprised you could get all that from the company."

"The company didn't give me crap. I got all that from her roommate."

"How'd you get her number?"

"There were only two 'A. Shelburnes' in Philadelphia. Pine Street it turned out to be."

"What else did the roommate tell you?"

"Not much, except she may know where Annie is."

"Well, don't just sit there. Give. Where is she?"

"Roomie wouldn't tell me. Not sure that Annie would want me to know. But she's agreed to meet me tomorrow morning to check out my bona fides."

"You think one look at your honest face, and she'll tell you everything?"

"No question about it."

She got up to leave the office. "Take my advice," she said at the door.

"What's that?"

"Take Jane with you."

Chapter IX

And so it was that early on Friday morning, just two weeks after Norman first came to visit me, Jane and I were on the road to Philadelphia. The roommate worked for Hawkins Industries as well, so nine o'clock found us entering the parking garage of the Hawkins Building. We took the elevator to the lobby and searched the building directory for Joy Marasco. She wasn't on the board, but the company's Human Resources Department, where she worked, was on fourteen. The elevator was crowded and had one of those annoying computer voices that announced the floors. We stepped off the elevator directly into a reception room that was apparently supposed to be a copy of an old English drawing room. The walls were paneled with prints of hunting scenes. An oriental rug covered the hardwood floor. I let Jane interrogate the receptionist while I went to seat myself on a slip covered sofa. Although I doubted whether Wilfred Brunell kept track of whatever visitors came into the Hawkins Building, I felt better not using my name. Jane came to join me in a moment.

"She'll call Joy. We're supposed to wait."

We waited for about ten minutes when a young woman came in from a side door, asked the receptionist a question and then came over to us.

"Ms. Hawkins?" she asked, the question apparent in her voice. She was tall and very blonde, although I wasn't certain that her hair color was the one with which she had been born. She appeared to be about thirty.

"This is Jane Hawkins," I said. "I'm Peter Gordon. We spoke yesterday on the telephone."

She looked at Jane. "Hawkins?" she asked. "Any connection . . . ?"

"Yes," said Jane. "Norman Hawkins was my father."

"Oh, well I'm really not sure . . . ."

"Is there somewhere we could talk, Ms. Marasco?" I asked.

"Well, I guess it would be all right. Why don't we get a cup of coffee at the cafeteria?"

She led us back to the elevator and down a couple of floors. It took us about ten minutes to negotiate our way through the line of employees getting coffee to take back to their desks. We finally paid and found a booth near the back.

"Why so crowded?" asked Jane.

Joy wrinkled her nose. "A cost cutting move by our new Chairman. Everyone has to pay for coffee now. And come down here to get it on an approved break."

"That must be doing wonders for morale." Jane continued.

"Morale hasn't been too robust around here since Mr. Hawkins . . . er, your father died." She looked at Jane uncertainly. "Then since Mr. Brunell was named in his place, we've had a blizzard of memos about everything from company policy to paper clips."

"Including coffee breaks?"

"Yes," she looked at Jane. "Including coffee breaks. But what's your interest in all this?" She turned to look at me. "What do you want with Annie?"

"Do you know where she is?" I asked.

"Maybe I know where to find her. Maybe I don't. I don't want to do anything to hurt her."

"Joy." It was Jane who cut in. "Is she afraid of something?"

"She's afraid. She wouldn't tell me why."

"Something to do with my father? Or what happened to him?"

"I really can't say any more. She told me not to."

"Look, Joy," I said. "Norman Hawkins came to see me the day before he died. He hired me to help him with his problems. But he went out on that boat and was killed, probably murdered, before he could tell me the whole story."

Joy flinched visibly when I spoke the word 'murdered'.

Jane leaned forward. "Do you think he was murdered too, Joy?"

"Yes. I . . . No . . . I don't know. All I know is that Annie thinks he was murdered. That's why she disappeared."

"Maybe you'd better tell us, Joy," said Jane. "Annie and I want the same thing, don't we? To find out what really happened to my father? And it looks like Annie needs a friend."

"But how do I know I can trust you? She told me not to tell anyone."

I was planning to let Jane take the lead in convincing Joy of our good intentions. Linda had been right in suggesting I take Jane along. As Jane started to speak again, I was distracted by a little commotion in the coffee line. I glanced over and froze. Two young men in the black suits and crew cuts of the Minutemen had pushed to the front of the line.

"Jesus," I said and slid over to the wall where I could not be seen. Both Joy and Jane were looking at me curiously.

"What's the matter?" asked Jane. "Suddenly you went white as a ghost."

"Those men in the black suits, Joy." I asked. "Who are they?"

Joy turned to look. The two men had either smoothed, or intimidated, their way out of the mini-disturbance that had caught my attention. They were paying for their coffee. Joy turned back quickly.

"Oh them," she said, the contempt apparent in her voice. "It's the new security."

"New security?" I asked. "How new? Just this past week?"

"Oh, not that new, but I would say its been about six months that they've been nosing around." She looked at me appraisingly. "They really gave you a start, huh?"

"Yes, I've seen their type before."

"Yeah, well they're all arrogant creeps and the new security chief is the worst."

A little thrill of anticipation ran through me.

"Ah, Joy," I asked as calmly as I could manage. "What's the name of this new security chief?"

"His name is Beck."

"Richard Beck?"

"That's it." Her face lightened up and then suddenly darkened. "You know him?" she asked.

"Yes. Mr. Beck and I have met. He came to see me a few days after Norman Hawkins was drowned to warn me not to pursue the matter any further."

"Oh."

"Yes. Beck and I are not exactly friends. He brought some of his goons with him to the meeting. Intimidating goons. They looked just like those two in the coffee line. In fact it's possible that one of them was with him that day."

"I guess you must be telling the truth about that. It would be hard to fake what a start they gave you."

"So tell us the story, Joy," jumped in Jane. "Annie really could be in some danger, and she needs to put some trust in someone."

"That makes sense," she said doubtfully. "What would you want to know?"

"What was Annie's relationship with my father?"

"Well, it started out about six or seven months ago. She was in the accounting department, and he tapped her for a special research project. One day she got called up to his office and, from then on, she was off her regular duties working on this project."

"What was the project?" I asked.

"She wouldn't tell me. It was this big secret."

"Was there anything . . . ahh . . . personal between Annie and my father?" asked Jane.

"No. At least not then. But they started to spend a lot of time together. She would do the work on the project during the day and then they would meet in his office after hours. At first it was all professional. But I could tell she was getting this thing for him. He never noticed her in that way at all. But then something happened. She didn't come home until the next morning and there were like stars in her eyes, you know?"

"How long ago was that?" I asked.

"About three months."

"And she continued to work on this secret project?"

"Yes."

"When was the last time you saw her?"

"She came home late one night. It was just before Mr. Hawkins disappeared. She was excited. She said it would all be over soon. When we heard he was dead it's like she went to pieces. She told me that they'd gotten him, and they'd get her next. She paced around the apartment for about an hour then she went to her computer and downloaded a lot of stuff. She packed up a whole carton of documents, put it all in her car and took off."

"Where did she go, Joy?" asked Jane.

Joy looked away. "Ahh, I don't know. She wouldn't tell me."

"She must have left some way to get in touch with her."

"She calls me every once in a while. She told me it would be safer for me not to know. They would be looking for her."

"Has anyone come looking for her?" I asked.

"Only security when she didn't show up for work."

"Wasn't that unusual?"

"A little, I guess. I hear Beck went to her office the next day and had it searched. I hear they took everything off her computer. A couple of days after, a couple of his goons came around to ask me if I knew where she was. I told them I didn't. I'm glad I didn't know. They were kind of spooky."

"Joy." It was Jane again. "Even if Annie didn't tell you where she was going. You have an idea, don't you?"

Joy was avoiding her eyes. "Well, I don't know."

"Joy. Annie thought she might be in some kind of trouble because of her relationship with my father and whatever she had found out in this research project. We think she might be as well. But wherever it is, she can't hide out there forever. And sooner or later, Beck's boys are going to find her. They are nothing if they're not persistent. She needs some help and, right now, we're the only ones available to help her. If you have any ideas, please tell us."

"Well," she looked at Jane. "You should know. They used to go to this hunting camp he had somewhere down south."

"He took her to the hunting camp?"

She nodded. "Yes, four or five times."

"And you think she's there?" I asked.

Joy nodded.

"Great," I said, looking at Jane. Something in her face stopped me. "What?"

"Maybe great," she said. "All I know it's down on the Eastern Shore of Virginia. I have no idea how to get there."

"You've never been there?"

"No, it's a male bonding kind of place. Norman and his cronies would go to drink and slaughter ducks and the occasional deer. I never had any interest."

"Damn." I turned to Joy. "Can you call her there?"

"There's no phone in the place. Annie used to say that was why she and Norman liked to get away there so much. No one to bother them."

"Can you tell us anything about it?" I persisted. "Was it on the bay side or the ocean? Did Annie ever mention any towns?"

"I don't know. The bay, I think. There was a town. I don't know the name. Something funny, Painter, I think."

I sat and thought. I had been down that way several times. I was sure we could find Painter. But finding the town would be a long way from finding one cabin.

"How often does she call you?" I asked.

"She's called twice since she left."

"When was the last time?"

"Last night."

"Damn. And she didn't leave any way for you to get in touch with her?"

"No. She said it was too dangerous. Look, if we're done here Mr. Gordon, I've got to get back to work. I've already been away from my desk for too long."

"All right, Joy. Thank you for all your help. Would you do one more thing for me?"

"What is it?"

"If Annie calls you again, tell her we came to see you and we would very much like to talk to her." I wrote my work and phone numbers in North Beach on a napkin and gave it to her. "Ask her to leave a message for me at one of those phones."

Joy looked doubtfully at the numbers. "Please, Joy," said Jane. "There may not be a lot of time for her."

"All right." She got up. Jane motioned for me to stay where I was and walked Joy to the elevator. In two minutes she was back.

"What was that? A little girl talk?" I asked.

"I got her home number and the direct dial number for her desk. We may want to call her back to see if Annie does call her." She sat down. "What next, Sherlock?"

"I don't know. I'm really confused now. Why would your father agree to having Beck as his security chief?"

She nodded. "To say nothing about letting those thugs have a free run inside his company. Do you think Reynaud was using Harry to put pressure on him?"

"There's got to be a connection. And it looks like Annie is the key. We've got to find her."

"What do we do? Comb the marshes of the Eastern Shore?"

"Are you sure you don't have any clues about where that hunting cabin is?"

"I told you. I never paid any attention to it at all."

"What about your father's records?"

"The bitch or Wilf will have those. I don't think they're going to tell us anything, do you?"

"No. But, we've got to narrow it down a little bit. I need a map and a telephone. And it would also be nice to have a little consult about cults, don't you think?"

"You have a counselor in mind?"

"Yes, I do. Shall we go?"

We got up and walked out of the cafeteria towards the elevator. As we were going out, two of Beck's Minutemen rounded the corner and headed towards the cafeteria. I ducked my head as they passed and continued walking towards the elevators. Had one of them stopped to look at me? I repressed the almost overwhelming desire to turn and look back. I felt an almost physical pressure in the small of my back as I imagined them watching me. Jane punched the button for the elevator. We waited. I was in agony. Had they gone in the cafeteria? Finally, I could bear it no longer and made a half turn to look down the hall out of the corner of my eye. I breathed an audible sigh of relief. The hall was empty.

"What's the matter?" asked Jane as the elevator doors slid open.

"Nothing," I lied.

Our next stop was to visit Ralph Bartholomew. I parked the car on Chestnut Street, and we walked over to Locust Walk past the Law School and the Library. Fortunately, Ralph was in and, more fortunately, he remembered me. He made a big fuss over Jane, getting her settled in the only comfortable chair in his office and then settled himself behind his desk fiddling with his pipe.

"So, Mr. Gordon," he said when he had gotten the pipe going. "Are you back for more about the RTTR? Some excitement there recently with one of their Minutemen shooting Congressman Renfrow."

"Please. Call me Pete," I said. "And we're not sure it was as simple as all that."

"Really? The press thinks it's pretty simple."

"The man that they have in custody for the job is the same man that I was concerned about when I came to visit you last week. His name is Norman Hawkins. This is his sister."

"You don't say." I had his interest now. He had even set down his pipe.

"Yes. I don't think it was really young Norman who pulled the trigger."

"You know," he was playing with the pipe stem now. "When you were here you never said, but is this Norman Hawkins any relation to the Norman Hawkins of Hawkins Industries?"

"The very same. The father was the Norman Hawkins. And the kid is his son. And the son is the heir to, or already the owner of, a substantial chunk of the company."

"I see."

"The question I have is whether cults or these political groups have ever had any interest in business. Or more precisely, in taking over legitimate businesses."

"Well, you have the Moonies and the Washington Star. I think that was as much a ploy about getting a piece of the media as anything else. Other than that most cults are into real estate and small businesses.

They can use their members as virtual slave labor. That gives them a great competitive advantage against legitimate businesses that have to pay market scale for their labor. And give them benefits and decent working conditions to boot. As for a major company like Hawkins Industries, I don't know of any case. The competitive advantage is lost if you can't use cult members as your employees. I would imagine it would cause too much disruption to displace the employees of a major corporation with cult members. And with union shops it would be even more difficult." He had been staring off into space as he had been musing. Now he looked back directly at me.

"I assume this isn't a hypothetical question. Do you know something specific about Hawkins Industries and the RTTR?"

"We know a fair amount," said Jane. "We know that my father was killed and probably murdered. We know that my brother is under the influence of the group. We know that some months ago, the security chief of the RTTR began moonlighting as the security chief of the company. We know that clones of the Minutemen are now security officers at Hawkins Industries. We know enough to make us curious to know more."

"I would think so," said Ralph. "I think I'd like to know more myself. How are you going to proceed?"

I told him about my lead to Annie and how I proposed to find her. He sat and thought a moment.

"Painter, eh? Well, why don't you use the phone to see if you can get a lead, and I'll scrounge you up a map of the lower Eastern Shore." He got up and offered me his chair and the telephone. I got to work. It took about an hour. I started with a lawyer I had worked a case with in Baltimore. He had a partner whose classmate at Washington & Lee practiced in Accomac, Virginia. The Accomac lawyer knew Painter and told me it was little more than a crossroad stoplight. But he had a brother-in-law who was a real estate broker in a neighboring town. I got the broker on the line. Brokers love to talk, especially about real estate and who owns it. I had all I needed in about two minutes of what turned into a twenty-minute conversation. I put down the phone to see that Ralph had returned and he and Jane were poring over a large-scale map.

"I think we found it," said Jane.

I got up to see what they were looking at.

"Here it is," she said pointing to a little crosshatch on the map about twenty-five miles north of Cape Charles.

"I see," I said. "And here's where the cabin is." I pointed to a spot at the end of a narrow strip of land where a creek met the Chesapeake Bay. Right at the end this neck where the this little creek empties into Chesapeake Bay."

"So the broker knew Hawkins?" asked Ralph.

"Sure. He sold him the property about ten years ago. It had nothing on it. Norman built a little cabin. Just two bedrooms overlooking the creek. He's got the point here," I pointed to the entrance to the creek. "And about a mile of beachfront all the way up to the next creek north."

"How do we know she's still there?" asked Jane.

"The guy is going to call me back. He knows the people who live across the creek."

Just then the phone rang, and I picked it up. I said a couple of words and put the phone down again.

"That's it," I said.

"What?" asked Jane.

"The neighbors say there have been lights on in the cabin for about a week. It's got to be her."

"So, what next?" asked Jane. "As if I didn't know."

I smiled at her. "Have I ever told you how beautiful the Eastern Shore is this time of year?"

"No, you haven't. But I have a feeling that I'm about to hear all about it."

"You think she's the key?" asked Ralph.

"I don't know," I said. "But she certainly knows some things we don't."

"So let's go," said Jane.

"Not so fast," I said. "Don't you think tomorrow is soon enough?"

"Actually," she said. "I do not."

Twenty minutes later we were on the road to the Eastern Shore. Most of the twenty minutes had been occupied with an argument between Jane and me as to whether we should retreat to North Beach, pack a proper bag and set out afresh for Virginia. Jane pointed out that a one-and-a-half hour car trip in the wrong direction, adding a three hour detour to an already four hour trip at night would not be a good idea.

"It's already after noon," she had pointed out. "If we put seven hours in the car, it will be dark before we get there. We'll never find it in the dark."

"So we'll leave tomorrow morning. Or we'll bunk out in a motel," I said. "What's the difference?"

"The difference is that I have a feeling that we don't have much time. We may already be too late."

"A feeling?"

"Don't take that tone with me," she said. "Yes, I have a feeling. And if I'm wrong, so what? If I'm right and Beck beats us there because we wasted three hours on some detour . . . ." She didn't finish and just stared at me.

"How could he find her?"

"Don't be stupid. He isn't. If we can find Annie so can he."

"But we don't have any clothes or anything," I said, plaintively. I knew she had won. Hell, she was right.

"Come on," she said, heading for the door. "That's what credit cards are for."

There was nothing for me to do but bid good-bye to Ralph and follow her out. The threatening sky had opened up, and we left Philadelphia in a driving rainstorm. The weather mirrored my mood as Jane had transmitted to me her anxiety that we were indeed too late. We stopped at a mall outside of Wilmington for lunch and a change of clothes. Then we picked up Route 13 and headed south. The rolling hills of Pennsylvania and Northern Delaware soon turned into flat farmland with a string of little towns. We went through a strip of Maryland and then into that little piece of Virginia that sits on the bottom of the Eastern Shore. It was a little after six that we found the turn-off in Painter. It consisted of a hardware store, a railroad siding and a flashing yellow light on Route 13. I took a right and began following the directions that Jane read to me. In twenty minutes we came through a stand of pine trees and stopped at the end of the paved road. In front of us were three gravel tracks and a wide open expanse of farmland leading down to a creek on the left about a mile away and another stand of trees directly in front of us, which stretched around to the north as far as we could see. The track to the left led down to a little group of houses on the creek. The track to the right went on for several hundred yards and then seemed to take a turn farther right. The center track seemed to end at the tree line right in front of us.

"We must be close," I said. "I guess those trees ahead of us extend out to the bay. Which way are we supposed to go?"

"The directions say keep going straight."

"OK. On we go." I wheeled the car out off the paved road and on to the gravel track. A ditch full of water ran along one side of the track. The track skirted another stand of trees, turned left at the head of another field and, there on the creek, stood a small house. It was a two story wooden house with a porch looking out over the creek. Just beyond the house was another stand of trees leading down to a point of sand that extended for about half a mile to the southwest. Beyond the point was the Chesapeake Bay and one of the most spectacular sunsets I have ever seen. The rain had stopped about a half-hour before. The clouds still covered us, but in the west they were breaking up and providing a backdrop for the sun to paint its colors. I drove up to the back of the house, and we got out of the car and stood transfixed for a moment. It was Jane who returned us to reality. She walked up to the back door of the house and knocked. She knocked again. There was no answer. There was a separate garage over to one side of the house. I went over to look. Inside there was an ancient Ford tractor and a much newer Honda. I returned to Jane who was still knocking on the door.

"No answer?" I asked.

"No sign of life at all," she replied.

"Well there's a car in the garage. Someone must be here."

"Maybe she took a walk to look at the sunset."

"Or maybe she's just hiding inside." I said.

"Why don't we walk down to the beach to see if we can find her?"

"What and have her run out of the house, jump in her car and be gone?"

Jane stepped away from the door to look at the garage. "Pull your car in front of the garage and block hers in." She continued around the house and walked towards the woods. "Look," she called. "Here's a path. I bet it leads to the bay. Come on."

She started off. I shrugged, moved the car over to the garage and followed her. She was waiting for me at edge of the trees. A clearly defined path cut through the undergrowth.

"Isn't it getting a little dark?" I asked.

"Nonsense. The water can't be far, and we have plenty of time to see the sunset." Without waiting she plunged into the trees, and I followed. Fortunately the path was wide and well marked because the gloom under the pines quickly closed off most of the light. And a magnificent stand of trees they were. Someone must have taken the time to thin them out at some point in their growth, saving the best ones. It had the feeling of being wild and yet cared for. It turned out that Jane was right. A hundred yards along the path the trees abruptly ended with beach grass, a little drop off and a narrow beach. Beyond the beach the Chesapeake Bay stretched west to the horizon. And on the horizon was the final act of the sunset. Jane sat down on the dune to watch the end of the day. I plopped down beside her.

"It's not that often that us Easterners get to see the sun set over the water," I said.

"Poor baby. If you come to visit me in California, I can arrange this every day."

We sat and watched the top half of sun's great red orb sinking visibly in to the water. The bay was restless from the passage of the storm, but there was almost no wind and no sound except for the calling of the gulls. And suddenly, the barking of a dog. Jane gripped my hand and a springer spaniel ran into sight around a curve in the beach. The dog immediately saw us and stopped to bark again.

"Here boy," I called to it softly. It stopped barking and looked at me with its head cocked to one side. I called again and went out on the beach and got down to its level on my haunches.

"Be careful Pete," called Jane.

I waved her to be quiet and continued to talk to the dog. It came up suspiciously, smelled my offered hand and allowed its ears to be scratched. I reached through its legs to scratch its belly all the time talking and now she, because I could see it was a she, rolled over on her back to let me scratch some more. Then she rolled over again and launched herself at my face to lick me. I had found a new friend.

"Pepper?" called a woman's voice from up the beach. "Pepper, come here. Here Pepper."

Pepper pulled to go, but I held her, saying her name. A woman came around the point and stopped.

"Pepper," she called again with some urgency in her voice. Pepper pulled away from my grasp and ran towards her.

"Who are you?" she asked uncertainly. It looked as if she were about to turn and run back up the beach or bolt into the woods.

"Friends," I said. "We just want to talk to you."

"How do I know that?" she asked, taking a step back.

"Annie, don't run away." It was Jane, who had gotten off the little dune and was standing beside me. "This is Peter Gordon. He is going to go over there and sit down." She waved me back to the place where she had been sitting. "I am Jane Hawkins. Norman was my father. We don't wish to harm you. In fact we came here to help you if we can." She put up her hands, palms out and took a step towards Annie. Meanwhile, I had retreated to a seat on the dune and was trying to look non-threatening.

"Don't come any closer," said Annie.

Jane ignored her and kept walking slowly forward talking soothingly, much as I had done with the dog. Annie didn't run. Jane stopped about five paces away from her and continued to talk. She talked steadily for about five minutes. They must have come to some resolution because Jane went over, took her by the hand and led her back to where I was sitting. Pepper was running circles around them, barking madly. When they got up to me I could see that Annie was crying. They sat down next to me with Jane's arm around Annie, and we just sat there silently. Pepper found a place with her head in my lap and seemed perfectly content.

Slowly Annie gathered her composure. Jane offered her a handkerchief. She looked over at Pepper's head in my lap and laughed.

"That dog," she said. "She's got to have a man. She's never acted like that since Norman . . . ."

She stopped, and I thought she was going to start crying again but she didn't."

"I'm sorry for my behavior," she said. "I've had to hold myself together by myself for so long. The idea that I might have someone to help me just overwhelmed me for a moment."

She looked directly at me. "You're that lawyer who Norman went to see the afternoon before he left on the boat."

"Yes, and you're the woman in the yellow slicker who I saw getting aboard the boat that afternoon."

"You saw me?" I could just make out a smile in the gathering darkness.

"Yes. I could only see your back, but it was enough to know you existed. And if I knew you existed, I knew you could be found. And voilá." I gestured expansively.

"That's the good news," said Jane. "The bad news is that if we could find you, so can the bad guys. I think we need to get out of here."

"I agree," I said. "What do you think Annie?"

"I just came here to get away. When I heard Norman was dead, I didn't know what to do. I just ran. I had just decided today that I was finished running. I just hadn't figured out what to do."

"Do you have any food in the house?" I asked.

"Yes. Not much, but enough for some dinner."

"Let's go back and plot what to do."

By this time it was almost full dark. We found our way along the path mostly by following Pepper. She repeatedly raced on ahead and dashed back to see what was taking us so long. In the end she kept us on the path, and we broke through to the house. Annie unlocked the door and led us inside. The lower floor was mostly one room with a kitchen towards the back, an eating area in the center and a sitting area in the front where there were two large windows, which must have afforded a view of the creek in the daylight. I went over to see if I could see anything, but there was nothing but black outside.

"It's a great view," said Annie. "I guess you know that Jane."

"Actually, I don't," said Jane. "I've never been here." She was in the corner looking at the collection of photographs on the wall. "Look at this," she said. "Here we all are on Norman's first boat."

I walked over to look. Norman was at the tiller of what looked like a forty-foot yawl, with a woman standing by his shoulder and three kids in the cockpit. The woman had her arm on Norman's neck, but she was looking down at the children. Jerry looked to be an awkward seventeen. Jane was holding Harry who was wearing a life jacket.

"Is that Julie?" I asked.

"Yes."

"How old is Harry?" I asked. "About three?"

"About that," she said.

Annie interrupted us. "There's some liquor in that cabinet. Why don't you get us all a drink, Pete?"

"Good idea." I busied myself with accomplishing that task while Jane and Annie started to make preparations for dinner. By some unspoken agreement none of us mentioned the events that had brought us together until we had finished with dinner and cleaned up the dishes. Annie made coffee, and we all took our cups to the sitting area overlooking that magnificent but invisible view. Annie pulled down the shades to block out the night.

"I always imagine them out there looking in," she said.

I took a sip of the coffee. "Why don't you tell us about it?" I asked.

She sighed. "I suppose I've been procrastinating long enough. It all started last spring. I was an accountant in the internal audit department. Norman came in one day and asked my boss for someone to do a special job for him."

"Norman didn't pick you out himself?" I asked.

"You mean like, did he have his eye on me from the beginning? I don't think he even noticed me at the beginning. He was too tied up with the company and what was happening to it."

"What was happening to it?"

"Well, he was in the middle of a major restructuring of the business."

"What was he trying to do?" Jane asked. "Get into e-business and internet like everyone else?"

"That's part of it. But he said that everyone was doing that so you had to move in that direction just to survive. He was trying to move the company into electro-mechanical systems at the same time. He said that in five years the company would be a completely new company with new products, systems and customers. But in the meantime, the stock was taking a beating. He was constantly frustrated that Wall Street wouldn't give him enough time to complete his strategy."

"Is that what he had you working on?" I asked.

"No, that's just the background. He came to me because he thought someone was buying up company stock. He wanted someone he could trust to find out what was going on."

"Why not just go to the stock watch section of the New York Stock Exchange?"

"He was concerned about publicity. And he had no facts to take to them; he just had this feeling that the stock was acting funny. You know as if there was someone accumulating a position that he didn't know about."

"How much stock in the company did he own?" I asked.

"He had about twenty-five percent. His son, Norman, Jr., has about ten percent."

"Really," I said. I looked at Jane. "Norman gave his son ten percent of the company?"

"No, not really. That block came from Norman's father. The kid's grandfather. The old man had financed the company in its early stages. He had had that stock from the beginning. When he died he put it in a trust for his grandson. When Junior got to be twenty-one he got the shares."

"What about you and Jerry?" I asked Jane.

She laughed. "Jerry was beyond the pale, of course. Granddad wasn't about to waste an inheritance on him. I got some cash. Harry was the one who got the stock. Of course, it wasn't such a big deal then. The stock wasn't worth very much."

I looked back at Annie. "Were there any other big holders?"

"No, not really. A group of individuals from the early days and some institutional holders. No one with any significant percentage of the shares."

"So what did you do?"

"I was detached from my regular duties and went to work for Norman exclusively. I hit the stock records and transaction sheets trying to find correlations and new shareholders. It takes a while if you have no official authority to get behind all the street name transactions, but I finally came up with something. First, I found various accounts that had been net buyers. I traced the majority of them back to a broker in Southern California."

"Don't tell me," I said. "Was he in Ventura County?"

"Yes, as a matter of fact he was. In Camarillo."

"And did you make a connection to the RTTR?"

"Norman did. I got him all the trading records and got them on a database. We could sort them in all different ways. Harry was hooked up with the RTTR by that time. Norman figured it was them."

"How much of the company did they own?"

"Norman figured it was about twenty-two percent."

"Really? And they had made no public announcement of their position?"

"Well, the position was held in about fifteen different accounts with each one a different partnership with different names as the partners. That's what took so long, tracing back the beneficial owners to some connection to this one broker."

"But if they are acquiring these shares for a common purpose, and they don't make a public filing of their holdings and intentions, they're in violation of about ten different SEC rules. Norman could have blown the whistle in them."

"He knew that. He went to his lawyer and got primed with about twenty-five thousand dollars in legal advice."

"Who was that? Wilfred Brunell?"

"Yes. Mr. Brunell was all ready to go with lawsuits and injunctions, and I don't know what all."

"So what happened?"

"Norman went to talk to Reynaud. When he came back it was like he was a different man."

"Why?"

"Because they had his kid indoctrinated into the cult. Reynaud told him that with the stock he controlled in various partnerships, plus the kid's ten percent, he controlled the company. Or, he could anytime he chose. He showed Norman an undated stock power he had that the kid had signed transferring the kid's shares over to the RTTR. He said if

Norman sued or took it public, he would have the transfer effectuated, and Norman would never see his kid again."

"So Norman did nothing?"

"For awhile he just quit. By that time our relationship had gotten to a more personal level. He stopped taking any interest in the company's operations. Reynaud suggested that Richard Beck should move in as security chief. Norman didn't seem to have the energy to object. He told me that Reynaud was pushing him to retire and turn over the reins of the company to him."

"Did Reynaud continue to buy more stock?"

"I don't think so. I don't know if Norman convinced him not to or whether he was afraid the Stock Exchange or the SEC would discover the purchases."

"What happened then?"

"Norman couldn't stand it any longer. That company was his baby, you know. He started it in his garage. He had to get out. He brought me down here, and we just stayed for about a month. One day, Norman just turned back on again. It was right after one of those morning news programs. They had Reynaud on for an interview. Norman didn't say a word, but he took Pepper out for a walk on the beach. They were gone for about four hours. I was beginning to get worried. But when he came back he was just like the old Norman. Full of energy. We packed up the car and drove back to Philadelphia the next day."

"What was he going to do?" Jane asked.

"He wouldn't tell me the details. He just said he was going to get his son and his company back. Both of them."

"How was he going to do that?" I asked. But I already had an idea.

She shrugged. "Some kind of intervention with Junior. Pull him away from the cult. And with the kid on his side he would have a good chance to sue to get the kid's stock back or to block any transfer. And Wilfred could be unleashed with his writs and injunctions to sterilize the stock held by the partnerships. He was also going to begin using his own money, plus borrowing to the hilt, to buy stock for himself. He said on the way back, that if Reynaud wanted a fight, he had come to the right place."

"Do you remember anything about the TV interview with Reynaud."

"Not really, I wasn't paying much attention. Maybe I should have been."

"Think carefully. Did they talk about the election in California?"

She thought for a moment. "Yes, I guess they did. In fact I think that was the main part of the interview."

"Was he consulting with Brunell on all this?"

"Yes, he spent a whole day at Brunell's office when we got back."

"Then what?"

"He started lining up financing to buy company stock and phoning old shareholders to see if they would remain loyal to him in a proxy fight and, if not, would they sell him their stock. It was like a rejuvenation to him."

"And he was arranging to get Harry on 'Far Cry', right?"

"Yes. He had set the boat up to go south. He was going to get Harry aboard. He said, by the time they got to Florida, Harry would be cured or else."

She dabbed a napkin to her eyes. I could see that she had started to cry.

"You don't have to go on if you don't want to," said Jane.

"I'm sorry. I keep forgetting this is just as difficult for you. I just never thought that the 'or else' would be that my Norman would never come back."

"So, how was it set up?" I asked.

"It was simple really," she said. "Norman called Harry and persuaded him to meet him."

"How did he do that?"

"He had a story that he wanted to settle everything with Reynaud, and Harry could be the go-between. Harry was reluctant at first, but eventually Norman convinced him."

"How did Norman know Harry was even on the East Coast?"

"Oh, Florence told us that."

"Florence? I thought she worked for Mrs. Hawkins."

"Technically she does," said Jane. "But she's worked for Dad for years. Back to when he was married to Julie."

"So Norman had a source inside the house," I said.

"That's right," said Annie. "We had the whole thing set up for about a month waiting for Harry to show up in North Beach."

I got up to pace and think about this. It hadn't been Beck who had called Harry that night. It had been Norman. I stopped pacing.

"How did you spirit Harry off?"

"The old damsel in distress trick. Harry didn't know me. I pretended to have a flat tire right outside the driveway. It was easy to get Junior to volunteer to help me. Once he got out on the road, Norman and Louie and the de-programming guy hustled him into the van that we had."

I sat down again. "OK. What happened next?"

"Well, they got him in the van. Then the other guy had some sort of a syringe to put him out. They pretended he was just drunk to get him aboard the boat. There was no need really; no one was at the marina at that hour. I took the van back to Philadelphia, and they took the boat out some time that night. I should have gone but Norman needed someone to take back the van and to take care of Pepper, he told me. I wasn't to worry. I can't get it out of my mind that if I had been along it might have been different."

She stopped, and I thought she was going to start to cry again.

"You shouldn't think that," I said. "If you had gone along, you'd be dead too. So tell me. Who was this other guy who had the syringe?"

"He was the supposed expert, the de-programming expert. I forget what his name was."

I felt a cold weight in the bottom of my stomach.

"It wouldn't have been Ernie Fagin, would it?" I asked.

She looked up in surprise. "Maybe. They might have called him Ernie. How did you know?"

"I've spoken to Ernie. He seems to be surprisingly healthy for someone who has gone through a marine disaster."

"You mean he's not drowned too?"

"Not drowned at all. And disclaiming any knowledge of Norman and his problems."

"Are you sure he went off with them on the boat?" asked Jane.

"Well, I didn't see them actually leave, but they were all on the boat and getting ready when I drove off."

"Was Ernie in it from the beginning?" I asked.

"Sure. He was kind of in charge of the whole thing. Norman was sure of himself when it came to the company and what to do. But when it came to his son, he had kind of turned the whole project over to this expert, Ernie." She shivered. "He was really spooky. And too sure of himself by half. But he had Norman convinced that he could bring the kid around. 'One hundred percent,' he kept saying."

"Did he suggest the boat as the place to take Norman?" I asked.

"Not specifically. I think he just suggested someplace isolated and quiet. Norman thought about doing it here, but later decided on the boat."

"Here?" I asked, alarmed. "Did Norman tell Ernie about this place?"

I don't think so. He may have mentioned that he had a place on the Eastern Shore, but no details. He focused in on the boat pretty quickly. And Ernie agreed it would be an ideal spot. Why?"

I said nothing.

"You think Fagin might tell Beck where Annie might be?" asked Jane.

I shrugged. "The only way I can think that Ernie got off that boat alive is if he and Beck were working together. If they were, Beck had a pipeline into the whole plan and plenty of time to set up his countermeasures."

"So what do you think we ought to do?" Jane asked. "Get out of here tonight?"

"I don't think that's necessary," I said. "But certainly first thing in the morning. Right now, I just think I'll take a look around."

I put on my jacket, took Pepper and slipped out the back door. Any idea I had of being silent was immediately shattered as Pepper ran around the yard barking at shadows. She calmed down as we set off down the road. It took a little over ten minutes to reach the three-way fork where we had first seen the cabin. By now the sky had cleared and a half moon hung in the sky. There was no sound except for a soft rustling of the wind in the trees. I stood at the fork and stared through a tunnel of pine trees down the road that led to Route 13 and eventually home. I felt like a rat in a trap. Annie had already confirmed that there was only one road leading down the neck. I wondered if Beck was already out there waiting for us. If he was, all he had to do was wait for us to come out. I stared as if my concentration could disclose his whereabouts. Of course, I could see nothing, so Pepper and I turned to walk back to the house. Jane and Annie were having another cup of coffee and chatting in the dark. I got the last of the pot and joined them.

"We felt better with the lights out," said Jane. "Find anything out there?"

"No."

"Don't you think that we ought to leave now?" asked Jane.

"I don't know. If I weren't so tired, maybe I'd say yes. But I'd really like to get some sleep." I turned back to Annie. "Is there a window that gives a good view of the driveway all the way to the end?"

"Yes. There's a bedroom on the second floor that does."

"I think we ought to keep a watch on the drive tonight. Say two hours for each of us. One watch each will give us until about four in the morning. I think that would be a good time to get out of here."

We all agreed, and Annie showed us the bedroom with the view. A little ribbon of driveway showed in the pale moonlight. Jane took the first watch, and I opted for the last. Annie showed me a bed, and I was soon fast asleep.

Chapter X

It seemed an instant later that someone was shaking me awake.

"Pete. Wake up." It was Jane.

"Is it my time?" I mumbled.

"No. But I've seen something."

I sat straight up. All thought of further sleep was gone.

"What? What was it?"

"Down at the end of the lane. I saw some headlights. Then they went out."

"How long ago?"

"Just a minute. Do you think it's some couple, parking?"

"Did the car turn around."

"No. It came down the road to the fork and stopped. And then the headlights just went off."

I got quickly out of the bed. Fortunately, I hadn't bothered to undress.

"We've got to get out of the house. Where's Annie?"

"Already at the back door."

"Good."

I ran down the steps with Jane just behind me. Annie was there at the back door with Pepper jumping on her in excitement.

"Do you have a leash for the dog?" I asked.

"No. We never put her on a lead down here."

"How about a rope?"

She gestured towards a utility closet next to the back door. Inside was a clothesline. I quickly fashioned a lead for Pepper.

"All right. You two go directly to the beach. Then walk a hundred yards north and go back into the brush from there. Keep the dog with you and, for God's sake, keep her quiet."

"Where will you be?" asked Jane.

"I'm going to watch for awhile. Now please go, and go quietly."

We crept out the back door, and the women made directly for the path. I went to the shelter of the garage and watched until they had disappeared into the shadows of the woods. The half-moon had swung all the way around to the west. With Jane and Annie gone there was no sound. I couldn't see the driveway from where I stood, but I didn't want to walk around the house and chance stumbling into someone. I waited for a few minutes and then made my way to the path to the beach. I managed to find it after some false starts but without making any noise. I found a tree just off the path to shelter behind and settled down to wait. Waiting is something I've never had the patience to do very well. After five minutes I got cold. After ten I began to feel fidgety. I tried sitting down, and I tried standing up. After twenty minutes there was still nothing. I could see nothing, and I could hear nothing. If anything it grew darker as whatever light had been provided by the moon began to fade as it continued its passage to the horizon. After thirty minutes I had had enough. Whatever Jane had seen, it couldn't have been anything that had to do with us. I stepped out from behind the tree and watched for a moment. There was still nothing to be seen. I moved further into the path and then to the edge of the field. I thought I saw shapes moving and I froze, but then they vanished as suddenly as they had appeared. My imagination was playing tricks with me. I would wait here another five minutes and then go down the driveway to see if I could find anything.

The five minutes drifted slowly by and, at the end of it, I was dancing from one foot to another in impatience to start walking. Enough. I did start walking. And then I heard it. Just a little tinkle of glass. I stopped in my tracks. There it was again. And then a little pinpoint of light at the back door of the house. My stomach tied itself in a knot in an instant. Slowly, I began to walk backwards towards the shelter of the path I had just abandoned. Four steps, five. I was back in the woods. I knelt down to watch. Whoever held the light was now inside the house. I could see the little point of light going from room to room. I stepped further back into the woods. What should I do? Run? Would they come looking for us? For some reason, I just stood rooted to my spot. I had to know what they would do next.

The light disappeared for a time, and then lights began to come on in the house. They had discovered we were no longer there. And then I had another shock. A group of five men assembled at the back door from all around the house. They had had the house surrounded in the darkness, and I had almost blundered right into the middle of them. Someone was talking to them at the back stoop. I couldn't see who it was. I strained to see as they split up. Two went around the house in the direction of the driveway, and the rest disappeared inside the house. By this time it seemed as if every light in the house was illuminated. I took the opportunity to resume my position behind my friendly tree and sat back to watch. Five minutes later a van that was a clone of the one I had seen in California drove up to the back door. Two men got out and went inside the house. For another thirty minutes nothing happened. Then two men came out and started to search our cars and the garage. They were looking for something. Annie's records of the stock transactions, I thought. Ten minutes later two men came out of the house holding boxes that they loaded into the van. Five minutes later all the men were assembled at the back door once more. The house lights had all been turned off, except for the outside light at the back door itself. That light cast an eerie projection of light and shadow against the night. Someone was speaking to them again. Now I could recognize him. Richard Beck. There was no mistaking the way the light glinted off his almost shaved head. He looked up as if he had heard something, and I could see his face clearly. Yes, it was Beck. But what had he heard? Then I heard it too. The quick barking of a dog. Damn. It was Pepper. The barking was quickly snuffed out. It was enough. Beck gestured to two of the men. They ran off towards the sound. Fortunately, they ran to my left as the women's hiding place was somewhere to the north of the path. They would find no path there. With any luck they would find nothing but brambles and underbrush. And so it proved for after some shouts and the sounds of crashing of underbrush they returned and rejoined the group. Beck had apparently made a decision because he was giving orders again. His men split up and again and set about various tasks. One of them pulled the van away from the house and set it on the drive as if for a quick getaway.

In a few moments they all reassembled by the van and stood watching expectantly. I stood to get a better view. I had no idea what was happening. Then there was a flash of light at the back of the house and a little 'whump'. They had somehow set off the propane tank that sat behind the house. Immediately flames ran up the back of the house to the roof. Now I saw that another fire had been set in Annie's car in the garage. In a few minutes both the house and the garage were burning fiercely. The men gathered in a little semi-circle at the van admiring their handiwork and cracking jokes. I felt a slow rage building inside of me. Up until that point, I had been following the leads out of curiosity and maybe for the fun of it. And because Wilfred Brunell had as much as challenged me by filing an ethics complaint. It had seemed a little dangerous, but the danger had been abstract, a little removed from me personally. I could hear the laughter of the Minutemen, if that is what they were, floating across the yard over the roaring of the fire. I clenched my fists in frustration because there was nothing that I could do that night.

At that moment Beck called out an order, the men climbed into the van, and it quickly disappeared down the driveway. By this time the fire had spread throughout the house. With a loud crash, the roof caved in. The van turned on its headlights at the far end of the drive. It had stopped. The headlights of another car suddenly snapped on. The new car turned around and led the way out on the road back towards the highway. I stood watching for another five minutes in the flickering light to see if they would come back. I could see no sign of them, so I turned into the path to find Annie and Jane. That proved to be quite easy. The path took me to the beach, and I walked north along it calling softly. About a hundred yards up the beach there was an answering call and, a moment later, a dog was at my feet jumping up on my legs. I bent down, and she licked my face. Jane and Annie came out of the brush. Jane ran over to me and grabbed my arm.

"Peter," she said. "We were so scared. What happened?"

"They burned the place," I said. "Look." I gestured back in the direction of the house where the glow from the fire flickered above the trees.

"Oh my God," said Annie, and she started to run down the beach. Jane started to run after her but I caught her after a few steps.

"Let her go. There's nothing anyone can do. We'll get there soon enough."

And so it proved. When we got back to the house, we found Annie standing there as if mesmerized, and Pepper running around barking wildly. Jane went over and gave her a hug, and she responded fiercely.

"It's the only thing of him that I had left," she said. "It was our place. Lorraine never came here. For a few months it was just us. And that's all I ever had. Just a few months."

Jane looked at me. "What do we do now?"

I shrugged. "Not much for us to do except wait for the fire company. Someone from across the creek will see the fire and call it in."

"No," said Annie fiercely. "We've got to get out of here. I've got to get my records to a safe place. They're the only hope we have to catch these bastards."

I took her by the arms. "Annie, you don't understand. They took your records with them. And if they missed any," I gestured towards the house, "they've burned to a cinder."

She pulled away from me and reached into her coat pocket to pull out a floppy disk. "Not all the records are gone," she said. "I've got the best ones on this disk. Records tying all the partnerships together. On here is a road map that will lead right to Bob Reynaud's door."

She put the disk back in her pocket. "Do you understand why we've got to get out of here? They won't be satisfied with this. They'll want to get us to make sure that there's nothing that can be traced back to their precious Archon."

She looked around at my car, which the Minutemen had searched but not burned.

"Come on. Do you have your keys?"

"Yes," I said. I looked at Jane and shrugged.

"I'm ready to get out of here," she said.

We all got in the car and it started right up. Man, I thought. That

Beck had been pretty dumb not to sabotage my car somehow. Then I shut off the ignition. Whatever Beck was, I didn't think he was dumb. I was the dumb one for even starting the car.

"What are you doing?" demanded Annie. "Let's get out of here before they come back."

"They're not coming back," I said.

"What do you mean?"

"There's only one way back to the highway?"

"Yes."

"Well dollars to donuts, that van is waiting somewhere on that road for us. Why wouldn't they burn this car too? Or disable it somehow? It would have been easy. No, they left this car as bait. We make our escape and they pick us right up on the road."

I opened the door and got out of the car.

"What about the fields?" said Jane. "Aren't there any farm roads?"

"No good," said Annie. "All these fields are bordered by drainage ditches. With how wet it's been, we'd be stuck in no time. Maybe there's a connection of farm roads that would get us around, but we could be a week finding it."

"So I guess we wait for the firemen after all." I said.

"We do not," she replied. "There's another way."

She started walking around the house towards the creek. She quickly disappeared out of the glow cast by the fire, and Jane and I hastened to catch up.

"Where are we going?" I said. But by the time I said it I could see for myself. At the water's edge was a little dock. And tied up to the dock was one of the prettiest little motorboats I ever saw. I could just make out the lines from the glow of the fire.

"It's 'Firefly.'" said Jane.

"What is it?" I asked. "It looks like a Maine lobster boat."

"That's just what it is," she answered standing beside me. Annie had already jumped down into the cockpit. "Norman found it up in Rockport and had it completely restored. I'd forgotten he kept her down here in the fall."

"God damn," I said. "We could take this thing all the way to North Beach. Ahh, have you got the keys?" I called to Annie.

"Right on the inside of that piling," she pointed. "The spare key should be hanging there on a hook."

It just took me a minute to find the key and jump into the boat. Jane and Pepper followed, the engine started right up and, a moment later, we were nosing our way slowly out into the creek. I stopped the boat, and we watched the remains of the house burning. One of the walls caved in with a roar and a shower of sparks.

"Let's go," said Annie. "I can't bear to watch it." I pushed the throttle ahead and turned the boat away from the house. I left the running lights off and felt my way southwest through the entrance. At the lighted buoy off the point, I turned north and opened up the throttle. The diesel roared and the dog barked in response. The bow rose and the boat went up on a plane. My spirits went up as our speed increased, and I settled comfortably on the stool behind the wheel.

"Any way to get any coffee on this vessel?" I asked.

It turned out that the cabin had a little galley and coffee was available. Jane fixed a pot and brought a steaming mug to me at the wheel. By that time I was well out in the bay heading north at about fifteen knots, which I judged to be the boat's best cruising speed.

"Where's Annie?" I asked.

"She's had it. She crashed on one of the bunks."

She came and stood next to me at the wheel. I experimented with putting my arm around her shoulder, and she slid neatly in against my chest.

"What about you?" I asked.

"I'm tired too, but I'm not as emotionally worn as she is."

"Why don't you go down and get some sleep as well?"

"What about you?" she asked. "Why don't you pull up some creek, drop the anchor, and we can all get some sleep."

"It's tempting, but I want to get clear of the area. Besides I have some thinking to do."

"You'll be all right?"

"I'll be fine."

So she gave a quick kiss on the cheek and left me to the starry night, the purring of the diesel and my thoughts. Norman had thoughtfully provided an autopilot as well as every navigational aid and gadget currently available on the market. My main pre-occupation was making sure we didn't get run down by a careless container ship.

And it left me plenty of time for my thoughts. For a while, I just thought about how easily Jane had fit into the fold of my arm and wondered what that kiss had meant. Then my mind came back to the problem at hand. It all seemed pretty clear, at least up to a point. Norman had come up with a plan that could have worked. If he had been able to turn his son away from the RTTR, or at least taken him out of the game, he would be able to go to court over Reynaud's SEC violations. At the least, he could get an injunction preventing Reynaud from buying more stock. That should have gained him enough time to shore up his own position if he had financing. Annie seemed to think he had financing in hand. Maybe he wouldn't have even had to go to court. The threat of exposure with the upcoming election might have been enough to get Reynaud to back off. And it all would have worked except it appeared that Norman's chosen de-programmer, Ernie Fagin, had really been working for the other side. It would have been easy for Beck to follow "Far Cry" by motorboat if he knew her departure time. He could have just waited outside the inlet. It would have been uncomfortable in the storm, but no more. Then he could have followed keeping track of his quarry by radar. Maybe the Coast Guard had had it almost right. Maybe Fagin had dismasted the boat and Beck's Minuteman came by to render assistance. Once a few of them were on board, it would have been easy to overpower Norman and Louie. Then they could open the seacocks and leave Louie for dead. It would be a simple matter to dump Norman right off of North Beach where he would be likely to be found. They miscalculated when they left Louie alive to turn off the seacocks and save the boat.

But why did they care if Norman showed up dead or not? They had Harry back as their hole card. And as long as Norman was out of the way, and they knew he was out of the way, they could make their move to take over the company, and no one would be able to stop them. Since he did show up dead, the board had moved to put Wilfred in his place and start the process towards a succession. Why would Reynaud want that? And why hadn't he made his move on the company?

Was he waiting for the election? Was he so concerned that a curious lawyer and a former employee who still had the trading records could stop him? Maybe that was it. They had to slow me down and find out where Annie was and what she knew.

The biggest unknown was Harry. If they had taken him off the boat and gotten him back to California, why hadn't they kept him incommunicado on this ranch that they had? Why let him out to be arrested in that parking garage with a rifle in his car? Why set him up for an assassination that tarred the RTTR with violence? Clearly there was a major piece of the puzzle that I still didn't have. But where was it, and how would I find it?

The moon had long since set in the west, but the stars revolved over my head as I worked the boat north and wracked my brain for an explanation that fit all the facts I knew. Jane woke off the Pautuxent River and spelled me for an hour. By nine in the morning I had the boat anchored off the Naval Academy in Annapolis harbor and gone down below for a proper nap. Jane shook me awake at about noon. I was in the forepeak in a little bunk that was too small for me. I could smell more coffee brewing in the galley.

"Wake up, Captain," said Jane. "Where are we anyway? Is this Annapolis?"

"Yes. What's the weather doing?"

"It's going to be a nice day. Maybe a little cold. Come and get some coffee. I'm afraid that's all we've got."

She left me, and I struggled to get out of the bunk. I felt like a ninety year old man. Nothing the matter with me, I thought that a good ten hours sleep wouldn't cure. Jane and Annie were sitting at the table in the main cabin of the lobster boat drinking coffee. I sat down and looked around. This was the first time I had really been able to see the boat properly. It had obviously been completely stripped, and a whole new cabin built into the hull. A complete galley had been installed with a little settee and table all in brightly varnished mahogany. Annie didn't let me admire the joinery work for very long. She plopped a cup of coffee down in front of me.

"Why did we stop?" She demanded. "I thought you said that this boat could take us all the way back to North Beach."

"It can," I said sipping my coffee. I made a face. "Whew that's strong. I guess we don't have any milk."

"No milk. Please answer my question. Aren't we wasting time?"

"Hey, slow down Annie. I had some time to do some thinking last night. If we want to get back to North Beach, and pushed on straight through, it would take more than a day in this boat. Maybe we'd be coming into Cranberry Inlet this time tomorrow. Maybe not until late afternoon tomorrow, I don't know. But I do know that renting a car and driving will get me there a hell of a lot quicker."

Jane looked quickly over at me. "Get you there?"

"Ummm, yes. Do you think you could drive this boat to North Beach?"

"In my sleep, but why bother? Let's stick the boat in some marina, and we can all drive to North Beach."

"Beck is looking for you and one of the places he is going to be looking is North Beach. Right now the safest place for you and Annie to be is on this boat."

"Do you think that Beck knows we were down at Norman's house last night?"

"We have to assume he does. My car was there."

"Then maybe we don't want to go to North Beach at all." "We can't just stay on the run."

"So, maybe we should all take the boat to North Beach. Why split up?"

"I'd like to get some police protection arranged and turn Beck into the hunted instead of the hunter. It will take a little time to do that, and meanwhile you two will be out of the line of fire so to speak."

"Norman told me not to trust the police," cut in Annie. "A lot of them are RTTR sympathizers."

"I think I can find one who isn't," I said.

I finished my coffee and went topside. A brisk wind was blowing out of the north. The harbor was almost empty of boats. Most of the larger ones had departed for Florida and points south. The smaller ones were covered and put away for the winter. I started the engine and let it run, sheltering in the cockpit from the gusts blowing over the bow. I called Jane to take the wheel, and she kicked the throttle ahead while I went up in the bow to recover the anchor. The anchor broke free from the bottom, and I waved her to go into neutral as I pulled in the line, sluiced off the Chesapeake mud and put the anchor in its chocks. I waved Jane to turn the boat south away from the wind and joined her in the cockpit. I went to take the wheel but she wouldn't let me in.

"Let me drive," she said. "Where are we going?"

I pointed at a drawbridge ahead of us. "There are a couple of marinas up the creek a little ways. You think you can park this thing?"

"Maybe I'll let you do that part. In the meantime, wouldn't this be fun to do some time?"

"What?"

"Take a boat like this. Just two people and just go. I could do without the excitement of RTTR goons chasing us, of course."

I looked at her inquiringly. "Is that a hypothetical, or do you mean you and me?"

She looked at me quickly and then away. I could see a little blush starting on her neck. "Just hypothetical," she said. "I was just thinking I might buy this little beauty out of the estate. Harry has no interest in boats."

"Maybe when this is done a little vacation might be an idea." I shivered in the wind. "Maybe a little farther south might be better."

By this time Jane had us through the bridge, and I pointed to a marina on the right. She gave me the wheel, and I put the boat into a slip on the inside. A young man in blue jeans and a ski jacket came out to take our lines. I asked him where I could get a rental car. He offered to call and have one sent down. Two hours later the car had arrived, we had gone uptown for some lunch and done a little grocery shopping for the boat. We had renewed the argument over my plan during lunch, but I must have been persuasive, because in the end they both agreed. I was standing on the dock with Jane while Annie stowed the stores in the galley. I think neither of us knew what to say.

"You've got the disk?" she asked.

I patted my pocket for the thousandth time. "Yes, it's right here in my pocket." We stood silently. "You're sure you don't want me to hire you someone to go with you?"

"We've been all over that. I'm familiar with the boat, and I'm a Jersey boat rat. I think I can find North Beach all right."

"When you get to Cape May just be sure to go up inside. Don't try to go out in the ocean."

"Pete, don't worry. We'll spend the night in Chesapeake City, leave early tomorrow morning, and I'll have this boat tied up at your dock by three tomorrow afternoon."

"OK, radio me on 68 when you're at Tom's River. I'll be able to give you the all clear."

"We've been over this, Pete. If I don't get you, I go into Tom's River and call Rich Skowronski. If I don't get him, we rent a car, drive to the airport and get the hell back to California."

With that she leaned over and gave me a kiss. Before I could respond she had jumped down into the boat. She started the diesel with a roar and waved at me to let go the lines. I threw the lines on the boat, and she backed the boat out of the slip, let her turn in the current and headed downstream towards the bridge. I stood on the end of the dock watching the transom get smaller and felt about as alone as I ever had in my life. She turned to give one wave and then drove the boat through the center of the bridge span and was gone. I turned and walked slowly up the dock to the car.

I called Rich Skowronski from a rest stop on the New Jersey Turnpike.

"Pete," he said. "Where the hell are you?"

I told him roughly where I was.

"Do you know the Virginia State Police are looking for you? For questioning about an arson somewhere down in Virginia?"

"No, but it doesn't surprise me."

"You want to tell me about it?"

"Not over the phone. I'll be there in about two hours. Why don't you meet me at my house?"

"Sure. It's been a slow news day."

"I think it will be worth your while. Oh, and Rich."

"What?"

Maybe you should send a police cruiser by the house a few times just to see if it's being watched."

"Watched? By whom?"

"Maybe by some of our RTTR Minutemen friends."

"You've still got a bug about them, have you?"

"More than ever. See you in about two hours."

And two hours later I drove over the inlet bridge into North Beach. A quick right and a left, and I pulled into my driveway where there was a police cruiser parked.

Rich got out of the driver's side of the car and someone else got out of the passenger side. It was the FBI agent, Dick Corville. I got out and walked up the drive.

"Right on time, Pete," said Rich. "You know Special Agent Corville?"

"Yes. We've met," I said. "What's he doing here?"

Rich shrugged in apology. "A little inter-service cooperation."

"I see. Did you have to shoo anyone away from the place?"

"Not a one."

"Mr. Gordon," said Corville. "Why don't we go over to Chief Skowronski's office to talk?"

"I don't think so," I said. "I think we'll be more comfortable here."

"I'm afraid I must insist," he said. "There are serious crimes we are investigating here."

I turned and looked at him as if for the first time. "You can insist until you're blue in the face. We're not going down to any police station. We are going into my house, and I'm going to tell Rich what I know about this. You're welcome to join us if you like, but don't be an asshole, all right?"

I turned and started up the walk. Rich took Corville's arm and said something to him to forestall any further argument. I unlocked the front door and walked inside to a nightmare. I froze for a moment unable to immediately comprehend what I was looking at. Someone had been in the house and had turned it upside down. There was a big pile of stuff in the middle of the living room floor where it seemed that all the contents of every drawer and closet in the house had been unceremoniously dumped.

"What is it Pete?" asked Rich from behind me. I realized I was standing in the doorway blocking the scene. I stepped out in the walk and sat down. Rich brushed by me and went into the house.

"Oh shit," he said.

After that I don't remember very much. I think Rich looked around and then came out to his car for the radio. A number of other police cars appeared at the scene, sirens blaring. There seemed to be a lot of traffic in and out of the door. Then I found myself sitting on the couch with a lot of men milling around the room.

"Pete." Someone was talking to me. "Pete. Can you tell me what's missing?"

"What?" I asked, looking up.

It was Rich. "You've got to help us, Pete. What's missing?"

I looked around the room as if for the first time. "The TV used to be over there." I waved towards a corner of the room. I got up to walk around. "The computer, that's gone. And an old short-wave radio that I had." I walked over to my little office in the corner of the room where the computer had been. The computer had been set on a table with a view of the bay. Underneath had been a small, two-drawer filing cabinet. It was gone. "And all my records seem to have walked out the door."

The slow rage that had built in my belly as I had watched Norman's house burn returned and, for a moment, I didn't trust myself to speak. If Richard Beck had been in front of me and I had a loaded gun in my hand, I think I would have emptied it into his chest without a second thought. I clenched my fists.

"What's upstairs?" I asked hoarsely.

"More of the same," said Rich. "Anything of value up there?"

"Not really. Another TV." I turned and walked up the stairs. Rich was right. The drawers had been emptied onto the middle of the bedroom floor. The TV was gone, but nothing else seemed to have been taken.

"I could kill the guy who did this," I said.

"I know," said Rich. I turned around, startled. I hadn't realized he had followed me up the stairs. "Don't think about that. This doesn't change anything."

"What do you mean?"

"Violence is their way. It's not yours. They're better at it than you'll ever be. The way to pay them back is to just keep on doing what you're doing."

I laughed bitterly. "And what is that? I wasn't doing anything."

"Of course you were. You're not very free with your plans, but I assume what you were doing was finding out what Reynaud and Beck most wanted trying to prevent them from getting it. Wasn't that it?"

"Something like that."

"Of course. And all this," he waved his hand around the wrecked room. "All this is the best evidence that you're succeeding. Or evidence of their fear that you will succeed."

I laughed again. "So all this is actually good?"

"Well, I wouldn't go so far as to say that. But if you weren't in a position to hurt them, why would they fool with you at all?"

I shrugged and went downstairs. Corville met me at the foot of the stairs.

"Now do you think it would be convenient to talk at the police station, Mr. Gordon?"

I looked at him. "Actually, I don't."

Rich noticed that sparks were about to fly. "It would be a lot easier than talking here," he said.

"My office will do nicely. I've got something to show you on my computer. I think you'll be interested."

Corville was about to say something but decided against it. I was afraid my office might have been ransacked as well, but no one was there on a Saturday and everything looked to be in its place. I led them back to my office and offered them the couch and a chair to sit down. I flicked on the computer and slid the disk into the slot.

"What's that?" asked Corville. He had taken the chair opposite my desk while Rich sat on the couch.

"Norman Hawkins had become suspicious of the trading activity in his stock. He started an investigation on his own with an employee from the audit department of the company. Her name is Ann Shelburne. This disk contains a file of information that Ann assembled while she was working for him," I said. I proceeded to tell Corville the same story Annie had told Jane and me the day before. I pretended to have difficulties with the computer as it copied the information from the disk to my hard drive. While I talked, I finished copying, named a new file, passworded it and parked it. Then I opened the file that was still on the disk.

I had finished with Annie's story and started to shift gears to tell them about what I had gleaned about Harry's kidnapping. I turned my attention directly at Corville, and something made me break off the story at that point. There were certain details of the story I didn't want told yet. I'm not sure why I made that decision, except that with the trashing of my house the matter had become personal. All my training cried out that if I held back some information I could stay in the game until the conclusion. If I told the FBI everything, I would be lucky to read the story in the newspapers. I wanted to be in on the conclusion and to do that I had to start to control the information.

"You pretty much know the rest," I said. "Norman took the kid out on his boat to convert him and the next thing you know he's washing up on our beach, the boat is a derelict at sea with a body aboard, and Junior is somehow magically out in California at Bob Reynaud's ranch. They've been looking for Annie and these records ever since."

Corville couldn't hold himself back any longer. He got up and walked around my desk to the computer screen. On the screen was a list of names, addresses and trade information. It happened to be sorted chronologically by trade date. He reached over and scrolled down the page. The list went on and on.

"How was this compiled?" he asked.

"I told you. Norman and Ann Shelburne compiled it from the company's stock trading records. They made copies of the records and had them in a bunch of big file boxes. But Annie took the important trade information and put it all in this file. You can sort it by name, trade date, shares purchased, whatever you want."

"Where are the actual records?" he asked.

"They were taken by Beck or burned in the fire."

"You mean that arson down in Virginia?" asked Rich.

"That's right," I said. I described our efforts to find Annie and the events of the night before. All the time Corville was playing with the database. I think he was only half listening to what I was saying.

"So how do you tie these records back to the original trading data?" he asked.

Annie had explained it to me, but that was without the benefit of having the data up on a screen. I pointed at the screen. "I'm not really sure about this, but I think that this column shows the source of the information. If we still had the file you could look on the index to pull out a copy of the record. Since that's gone, you'll have to go into the New York Stock Exchange records for each individual trade. It will be a lot of work but not nearly as much as it took to originally find the trades."

"And where is this Ann Shelburne?"

"I'm not exactly sure, but she should be here in North Beach some time tomorrow."

"What do you mean you're not sure?"

"I mean exactly that. If you want to talk to her, you'll have to wait until tomorrow."

"We'll put that aside for the moment. Are you telling me that all these trades that are shown here are still in the stock exchange files?"

"Sure, they don't throw them out."

"And how does this all get traced back to RTTR?"

"Annie and Norman apparently traced enough of them back to the same broker in Thousand Oaks to figure out that there was a pattern." I tapped the screen. "The records coded 'A' they could trace back. Codes 'B' and 'C' meant they were less sure. I think with your investigative resources and this as a base you should have no trouble making the connection."

"No," he said and he reached out, ejected the disc and put it in his pocket. I gave a shout and grabbed at his arm to stop him, but I was too late.

"You can't take that," I said. "It belongs to Miss Shelburne."

"It's evidence," he said.

"I'll give you a print-out of it. You can't take the disk."

"If you don't like it, you can complain to my superiors," he said.

"At least let me make a copy," I asked.

"Miss Shelburne will get the disk back undamaged at the appropriate time."

"When?" I asked.

"Maybe when we get a chance to interview her. Look, Gordon. We've had an investigation going against the RTTR for mail fraud for over a year. He's been defrauding widows of their life savings and pensioners of their pensions. He's got a whole bucket shop operation going out there in California. Phone banks manned twenty-four hours a day, scaring people about the coming crash and taking their money. You don't even need to send in a check any more. All you need to do is give them your Visa card number."

"So what's that got to do with Hawkins Industries?"

"This is icing on the cake. Investments like this are where the money is going. And these records will show that the investments are being made illegally in an effort to take over American businesses."

"Take over American businesses?" I asked.

"That's right. You don't think it will end with Hawkins Industries, do you?" He had gotten up and put on his coat. The disk was safely stashed in his coat pocket.

"I still think you could let me make a copy of it." I persisted. "What's the harm in that?"

"Miss Shelburne will get her property back when we have finished with it," he repeated. "Just you make sure she gets in touch with us as soon as she shows up, or you're going to be the target of an obstruction investigation." He looked at Rich. "Are you coming, Chief Skowronski?"

"Ah . . . . You go ahead. I'll be along in a little bit."

Corville looked as though this plan suited him just fine and, without any further ceremony, went out the door. There was silence when he left. I went over to the window and watched Corville at the curb. He waved his arm and a brown Ford pulled out from up the street and stopped in front of him. He got into the passenger side and the car headed towards the bridge. I turned back into the room.

"I don't think he's waiting for you Rich," I said.

"No," said Rich, leaning back in his chair. "He's so damned excited about that disk, he couldn't wait to get it out of here. In fact he was so excited he didn't seem to notice all the holes in your story."

"What holes?" I asked.

"Like how did Beck find the 'Far Cry' out at sea without help? Like how did they know about Miss Shelburne, let alone find her all way down in Virginia?"

"I don't really know the answers to those questions, Rich."

"Maybe you do and maybe you don't, but I bet you've got some ideas. And that little charade about wanting to make a copy of the disk when you already did it."

"I don't know what you're talking about."

"We may be a backwater police force here, undermanned and understaffed, but we do have a computer. I could have read that disk in my office as well as you could, but we had to do it here so you could make a copy, didn't we?"

I sat down. "You didn't fall for my acting job?"

He grunted. "I was almost sorry for you the ham-handed way you pretended to grab the disk before he had got it out of the computer."

"It was good enough to fool Corville."

"He's got different priorities. He'll be a hero if he pins some penny-ante white-collar beef on Reynaud. I've got a murder on my hands, and I get damned annoyed when someone withholds evidence in my murder investigation."

As he said this, he half-rose out of his chair, and his voice went up half an octave. I put up my hand placatingly.

"Take it easy, Rich. I was going to tell you. I just didn't want that FBI puke to hear the whole story."

"So tell me," he said.

"I think I know who has been feeding Beck with information."

"So tell me," he repeated.

"If I do, will you let me go with you to talk to him?"

"I can't do that."

"Sure you can. It's out of your jurisdiction. If you go talk to him directly it will be sort of semi-official anyway, won't it?"

He shrugged. "What makes you think I won't do it all officially?"

"Because I know you a little bit, that's why. So, do you want to continue our little cooperation game or don't you?"

He glared at me. "Tell me who it is."

"When Norman came upon his idea of splitting his son away from the RTTR, he thought he needed some expert advice. He consulted some people on cults and de-programming and finally hired a de-programmer to do the job for him."

"I know. And he was going to do the de-programming on the boat."

"That's right."

"But doesn't the de-programmer have to . . ." He stopped and slapped his hand to his forehead. "I'm so stupid. The de-programmer was on the boat too."

"Right."

"Where is he now?"

"Back in Philadelphia denying all knowledge of Norman Hawkins."

Rich's eyes narrowed into slits.

"Are you sure he was on the boat?"

"Ann Shelburne told me he was here that night. According to her, he planned the whole kidnapping."

"What's his name?" asked Rich."

"It's an ex-Philadelphia cop named Ernie Fagin who's gone into another line of work. Selling dreams to parents who think they've failed. And charging quite a lot for it, I would guess."

"You've talked to him?"

"Yes. He claims he's out of the de-programming business. And he claims he refused to help Norman with Harry."

"Maybe we should have a talk with Ernie."

"That's just what I was thinking," I said.

Chapter XI

There was no point in going to see Ernie until Monday. In the meantime I had a lot of work to do at home. Before I got to that, Rich put out an all points bulletin for Richard Beck. Next, we spent an hour on the phone with a sergeant at the Virginia State Police. He was a little exercised that I had left the scene to say nothing of the state. Fortunately, Rich was able to get him calmed down a little. Rich vouched for me, and I gave him a statement over the phone. By the end of the conversation, he and Rich were discussing Beck's possible whereabouts and how best to go about tracking him down. After that, there was nothing left for me to do but go back and face the wreckage of my house. I found I couldn't do anything but go to bed.

The next morning I started on the clean up. The only way to proceed was to start in one corner of one room and work through until the room was finished. If I had thought about the enormity of the entire task I never would have had the heart to do anything. At about 11:00, I turned on my VHF radio to channel 68, and its squawks followed me around from room to room. By noon, I had finished the kitchen and living room and made a major dent in my bedroom. Rich called to report Corville had been around to pester him about Annie, and where was she? I told him she would be in town in the afternoon, and I'd call him. There was no news on Beck and no Minutemen had showed up in town. By one o'clock, I had given up all pretense of cleaning up and just sat by the radio listening to the static. Finally, I could stand it no longer and went down to crank up my Grady-White, "Rebound". Twenty minutes later I was through the Seaside Bridge idling the boat at the mouth of Tom's River. The day was a delightful sunny day with a light northwest wind. There weren't many boats on the bay, but there were a few. I inspected every one, but nothing matched the profile of what I was looking for. I continued to listen to the radio and about three-thirty, I heard, very faintly the code words that we had agreed on.

"'Endeavor' calling 'Rainbow'. 'Endeavor' . . ." and then a lot of static.

I grabbed the microphone. "'Rainbow' calling 'Endeavor'. 'Rainbow' calling 'Endeavor'. Come in please." I picked up my binoculars and scanned the horizon to the south. There were no boats in my view at all. I tried calling again and turned up the gain on the radio. I heard another faint call "'Endeavor' . . . . in . . . . berry Inlet . . . ."

Damn, I thought. She came up outside after all. Here I was down at Tom's River, and she was coming into North Beach through the Cranberry Inlet. I turned the boat around to the north and pushed the throttle as far forward as it would go. A little chop had built up and I wondered how long my kidneys could hold out from the pounding. In what seemed like an hour, but was more like fifteen minutes I could see my dock. There was a boat tied up in the slip. As I got closer, I could see it was "Firefly", and there was a figure on the end of the dock waving at me. I pulled up to the end of the dock at full speed and rammed the boat into reverse. Jane was there to take my painter with a big smile on her face and Pepper at her side barking furiously. I don't remember getting from the boat up on the dock, but suddenly I was beside her embracing her. She kissed me quickly and then again. I would have gone on but she pushed me back.

"Glad to see me sailor?"

"I thought you were going to go up inside." I accused.

"It was too nice a day."

"You were going to call on the radio."

"I did. I was a little worried when your boat wasn't here, but then I saw you tearing up the bay like a mad man."

All this time Pepper was jumping around my legs, demanding attention. I stooped down to pet her.

"Where's Annie?" I asked.

"Right here," Annie called from behind me. I turned to see her in the cockpit of the lobster boat. "You still have my disk, don't you?"

"Well, let's just say, I've got the data. The disk's been taken by an FBI agent who wants to talk to you."

I led them up the dock with Pepper alternately racing ahead and running back to see if we were coming along. The two women were talking about their trip. They went suddenly quiet when I led them into the house. Somehow, I had forgotten all about the break-in in my anxiety and relief. The evidence was still plain to see.

"What happened?" It was Jane who first regained her voice.

"A little break-in," I said. "Looks like Beck's boys are real eager to make sure there's no further evidence to be had."

Jane sank down on a couch. "This is awful."

"Believe me," I said. "It's a lot better than it was."

"Poor Peter. Here we are chattering like magpies about our big adventure, and they've destroyed your house."

"Actually it's not that bad. And I was so glad to see you'd made it all right that I'd completely forgotten about it."

"Really?" she asked and she smiled in a way that seemed to stop my heart. Before I could answer, she was off the couch. "No more moping. Come on Annie, let's finish cleaning this stuff up."

With that we set to work. An hour later Rich called again and an hour after that, he and Dick Corville were over to talk to Annie. Corville had someone else with him who had apparently loaded Annie's information on a laptop. He also had reams of information that I took to be trading records for Hawkins Industries. They sat in the living room and went to work. Jane and I continued what we were doing. In two hours we had finished up. Corville and his FBI buddy seemed to be finished as well. They were gathering up papers and stuffing them into a big briefcase. Corville had the smile of a man whose life's ambition is about to be fulfilled. He seemed to be giving Annie some last instructions.

"Get all you want?" I asked.

He looked at me and his face resumed his normal FBI guardedness. "We're finished for the moment," he said. He nodded to Jane, and he and his computer friend left by the front door.

I looked at Rich. "If he had a personality, I might learn to like him."

"He's all right. A little intense, maybe."

He got up to leave. "We still on for tomorrow?"

"Bright and early," I said.

He said good-bye to Jane and Annie and followed Corville out into the night. I made us all a drink, and we agreed on a pizza to be delivered. Annie told us about her session with Corville and tried to remember all the questions he had asked. By the time the pizza had been eaten, she was nodding off. After a few more minutes, she said goodnight and went up to bed. I made another drink for Jane and myself and went over to sit with her on the couch.

"What's so bright and early with our police chief," she asked.

"We're going to Philadelphia to see Ernie Fagin."

"The de-programmer?"

"Yes."

She sat there silently looking out at the dim moonlight on the bay. She started to tell me about 'Far Cry'. She and Annie had stopped by the boat in Cape May and sweet-talked the Coast Guard into letting them pull alongside to take a look. They weren't allowed aboard. She started into plans for putting the boat into commission again, while I put in a suggestion from time to time. She fell silent again and we both watched the water. I turned her face towards me and then we were kissing. It seemed to go on and on, and then she was pushing me away.

"No, we can't."

"Why not?"

"We haven't even had a proper date."

"This is the twenty-first century. Do people date anymore?"

"Yes. As a matter of fact, I think they do."

"I think with what we've been through, we know more about each other than any date would produce."

She gave me another kiss. "That's true, but that's all been in a different context. I need a little time to start thinking about you in this context."

"The date context?"

"Let's say the romantic context. Besides, Annie's upstairs."

"She's an adult."

"Yes, but somehow I don't feel right about it. I need a little time."

"How much?"

She kissed me again, briefly and then harder. Then she put her hand on my chest and pushed me back. "I said a little, didn't I?"

"Yes, you did."

"And now I'm going up to bed as well." She kissed me one last time, and then she went upstairs. I went to the refrigerator and got myself a beer. I took it to the couch and sipped it while I looked out on the bay by myself. It was something that I had done innumerable times in the few months that I had been a permanent resident of North Beach. Drinking a beer and watching the bay alone. But somehow the emptiness of being alone wasn't with me any more.

* * *

Early the next morning Rich and I were on the road to Philadelphia. Rich had called Ernie posing as a distraught parent and made an appointment. At a quarter of ten, Rich and I were waiting on that bench in the corridor of Ernie's South Broad Street office building. We waited until ten-thirty before Ernie showed up. He got off the elevator and slouched down the hall towards us in the same dirty trench coat that I remembered from my last visit. Rich got up to greet him while I stayed seated on the bench.

"Mr. Skowronski," he said. "Sorry I'm a little late. I hope you weren't waiting too long."

He looked at me curiously. I tried to avoid his gaze.

"Come on in," he said unlocking the door. "Sorry there was no one here to greet you. I don't know where my girl could have gotten to."

My guess was that there was no girl. Ernie was on his own. He led us into the back office, hung up his coat and sat behind his desk. Now that we were inside, I felt free to look him in the eye. He looked at me again, quizzically.

"Have we met?" he asked.

"Yes," I said. "As a matter of fact we have. Don't you remember?"

"What is this? Some kind of a game?"

"Actually it's not a game," said Rich. "It's a murder investigation."

He looked back at Rich. "I thought you . . . ."

"Yes, you thought I was a parent at the end of my rope. I guess you'd have to say I'm here under false pretenses. Actually, I'm a policeman." He showed Fagin his identification. Fagin looked at it quickly and then at me again.

"I remember now," he said. "You're that guy who was asking about Norman Hawkins. Well I told you everything I have to say on that subject."

"When did you first meet Norman Hawkins?" asked Rich.

Fagin turned his attention back to Rich. "I told you I've got nothing to say. You're out of your jurisdiction and if you've got something to ask me, you can ask my lawyer."

"Oh, is it a lawyer you want now?" asked Rich, almost purring. "We thought you might want to cooperate with our investigation as a matter of, shall we say, civic obligation? As long as you've got nothing to hide, of course."

"I got nothing to hide."

"So tell us. When did you first meet Norman Hawkins?"

"I told him." He gestured at me. "I never met the guy. I just talked to him on the phone."

"Ernie, we know that's not true. We've got a witness that tells us you planned the whole de-programming for the kid. Even puts you in North Beach and on the boat that night. Why don't you just tell us about it?"

"I told you I got nothing to say." He was on his feet now. "Get out of this office now, or I'm calling the police."

Rich stayed where he was for a long moment, then he too got to his feet. "If that's the way you want to play it, it's all right with me. Personally, I'd prefer that you didn't cooperate. I want to make sure you go away for a long time."

"Get out," ordered Fagin, his face red.

"Oh, we'll be going," said Rich. "But you can be sure we'll be back." He turned and left the office. I got up, gave Ernie a smile and followed Rich out to the hall.

"Well we didn't get very far with him," I said.

Rich shrugged. "Far enough."

"So what now?"

"Well, if you were him, what would you do now?"

"I guess I'd report to whomever I was accustomed to reporting to."

"And if you were scared of exposure, would you use the telephone?"

"Probably not."

"No. But if the guy was close by, maybe you'd hustle over and have a little chat in person."

"So we wait and follow to see where he goes?"

Rich turned away and went towards the elevator. "No, he'd probably expect that. Let's assume he's reasonably sly. If we're right, he'll go to see Beck, won't he?"

"Yes."

"So let's beat him there and see if our boy, Ernie, shows up."

"You think Beck will be over at Hawkins Industries?"

Rich shrugged. "Why not? He's head of security there. He won't know yet that the Virginia State Police are looking for him. And even if he does, Ernie might expect to find him there."

By this time the elevator had arrived, and we descended to the street. I led him up Broad Street and through the panhandlers at City Hall and over to the Hawkins Building. We sat down at a little coffee shop in the lobby where we had a good view of the elevators. We were on our second cup of coffee when a man in a dirty trench coat slipped in off the street and got on one of the elevators.

"Well, well," said Rich. "That didn't take long, did it?"

"What do we do now?"

"Let's wait until he comes down and see where he goes next."

It was half an hour before Fagin reappeared at the elevator bank. We followed him out into the street and then down into one of the many entrances to the underground warrens of Suburban Station.

"Aren't you afraid he'll spot us?" I asked.

"No. He's run his errand. He won't be careful now. And even if he does spot us, it doesn't matter. We've already seen where he ran. Seeing us will just put more pressure on him."

Rich was right. If Fagin had been careful about being followed to the Hawkins Building, he was not being careful now. He walked straight through the station and into the connecting passages for the Broad Street subway.

"He's headed back to his office," I said.

Rich nodded. "Looks that way. We'll beard him again in his den."

We followed him at a distance through the graffiti filled corridors and into the arcade that underlies Broad Street. At that point, we held back so that we were about fifty yards behind him. He was headed for the stairs that led to the street at the corner where his building was located. A homeless man was seated on the floor of the arcade just at the stairs, his back leaning against the wall and a blanket stretched around his shoulders. Fagin had just reached the foot of the stairs when the man stood straight up, threw off the blanket and stepped up beside him. Fagin looked over at the man in surprise or annoyance. There was a little pop and Fagin slumped to the ground. Rich yelled and started running. The man looked quickly back and turned, extending his arm in Rich's direction. I yelled, and Rich dropped to the ground. There was another little pop. The man took a quick look at Fagin and ducked into the stairwell. I had been rooted to the spot where I had been when I had heard the first pop. All of a sudden the life seemed to come back to my legs, and I started running.

I stopped to help Rich to his feet. He was cursing.

"Did he hit you?"

"No, I just banged my damn elbow when I went down. Let's go see the damage."

Rich walked quickly over to Fagin and felt at his neck. He straightened up, took my arm and hustled me to the stairwell.

"He's done," he said.

"Shouldn't we wait for the police?"

"Not unless you want to get stuck in a station house for about four hours answering dumb questions."

We emerged out onto Broad Street. There was the sound of sirens in the distance. There was no sign of Fagin's killer. Rich led the way to our car and didn't speak again until we were out of the garage and working our way through the Center City traffic towards the Ben Franklin Bridge to New Jersey.

"You think it was a mugging?" I asked.

"No. A mugging is a little too convenient. I think Beck got him over there to find out what was going on and had him hit on the way back to his office."

"There wasn't very much time."

"There was enough."

"So where are we going now?"

"Back to North Beach. I told Fagin there was a witness. If Beck has half a brain, he'll figure out who it is, and where she might be."

"You think he might send someone to get Annie?"

"He moves pretty quick. He's just proved that."

"Why don't we call ahead to get one of your men to cover the house?" I suggested.

He looked at me quickly and pulled out his cell phone. Neither of us spoke for the trip back. Rich took us directly to my house. There was a police cruiser in the driveway. We both jumped out of the car and met the officer in the driveway.

"Did you see anything unusual?" asked Rich.

"Just one of those vans you told me about, Chief," he said.

"When?"

"It cruised by twice about half-an-hour ago. I haven't seen it since."

"I think we need to keep someone here with you for the time being," said Rich.

By now Jane had come out to join us on the front step.

"I can't stay here, anyway," she said. "I need to get back to California."

"Why?" I asked.

"Jerry called while you were gone. He's back home, but he's not getting better. In fact he's concluded that he's never going to get better again."

"That wasn't the feeling I had when we just saw him," I said.

"I know, but he's been getting progressively worse. They don't have any drugs to treat him now that won't do more harm than good. Basically, they just have him on a maintenance regimen to prolong the agony. That's what he says, anyway."

"So what's next?"

"He demanded that they take him home. He's taken all the IVs out, and he says it's just a matter of time. He wants to see me before he goes. I've got a reservation on the five o'clock from Newark."

I looked at my watch. "That means you have to leave right away."

"That's right."

"I'm coming too."

She smiled. "No need for you to come. I'll be all right. These jerks aren't really after me. And they're not going to find me in California."

"Don't be too sure. They're pretty quick on the draw. But even without them, you'll need some support to get through this yourself. How long does he have?"

She shrugged. "No one can say. He might go tonight, or he might linger for a couple of weeks."

"No arguments. I'm coming too." I looked at Rich. "Can you take care of Annie?"

"Sure. I'll call Corville. He'll be dying to baby-sit her anyway. I'm sure he can get some federal marshals to cover her."

"Good." I went to the phone to get on Jane's flight before she could think of any reason I shouldn't go with her. I got what little stuff I would need and we threw it all in the back of the car. Rich came by just as we were about to go.

"Maybe I'll give you an escort out of town just to make sure you aren't followed. There's no telling if that black van is still around or not."

"Don't you think that will just add notoriety to our departure?" I asked. "Wouldn't it be better for us to just slip out of town?"

"Trust me," he said and climbed back into his car.

I shrugged, Jane and I got into the car, and we set off down the street with Rich following.

"This is like a parade out of town," said Jane. "Are you sure he knows what he's doing?"

"Well, usually he does, but this does seem a little crazy."

Rich followed us right through town and straight to the bridge over the inlet. At the base of the bridge he pulled across the road and started his police light going. We drove up on the bridge and the bridge bell started to gong. There was not a boat in sight, but Rich was going to have the bridge open behind us. Jane laughed.

"I guess he does know what he's doing after all."

I drove by the bridge tender, and he gave me a wave and a big smile. The gates started to close and the bridge started to go up just as we went by.

"I guess it will be a little difficult to follow us now," I said.

* * *

We got into LAX about 8:00 PM local time. Jane drove us to Jerry's apartment in Santa Monica. Jerry's partner, Steve, met us at the door and gave us both a hug.

"He's stayed up to meet you," he said. "But don't be long. He needs to get some sleep."

"Steve. Who's that?" We heard Jerry's voice from somewhere deep in the apartment.

Steve looked at us. "He hears everything," he said. "It's Jane, Jerry." He called out in a louder voice.

Jane hurried back to the bedroom. I walked more slowly into the living room. A window looked out onto the street.

"How is he?" I asked Steve.

"As well as can be expected," said Steve. "A trifle grumpy today. We just got rid of the bitch nurse, as he calls her."

"He doesn't like his nurse?"

"Most of them, no. He thinks they're fascists. This one was actually very good, but, like I said, Jerry is a little cranky today. Why don't you go in and say hello."

Going in and saying hello was just what I had been trying to avoid, but there seemed no help for it. Towards the back of the apartment there were two bedrooms. Jerry's was off to the left. Inside there was a hospital bed against the wall with a chair on either side. Jane was sitting in one chair and holding the hand of the form in the bed. I was shocked at how much Jerry had changed in the short time since I had seen him last. He was propped up in the bed on his back with the sheet pulled up over his thin chest. His arms looked like little sticks on the bedclothes. He turned his head to me and it seemed like he was all teeth and eyes with skin stretched over the skull.

"Pete," he greeted me. "Come sit down for a moment."

I walked across the room as if I was in a trance and sat at the chair across from Jane. He took my hand in his thin fingers.

"Thank you for coming to support Jane."

"What else would I do?"

"Stay away. Lots do. I'm not exactly a pretty sight."

I smiled. "No you're not that."

He turned and Jane and he began talking about some events in their childhood. Pretty soon he drifted off to sleep. Jane motioned towards the door, and we tiptoed out into the living room. Steve was sitting on one of the couches. Jane sank down next to him. I picked the armchair opposite. Jane had started to cry.

"I didn't think he'd be so thin," she said.

"In Africa, they call it the slim disease," said Steve. "That's what it does. It just wastes you away."

"Is he in any pain?"

"He has been. The nurse started him on a morphine drip tonight. We can adjust the dose to keep him comfortable."

"And we don't know how long it will be before he goes?"

Steve shrugged. "It could be any time or not for a week. Or two weeks. He's ready, but his doctor says his heart is strong. It could go on beating for a long time."

We sat and talked for some time. Steve got us coffee. We talked about funeral arrangements and family.

That night was the first night. From that night for a week, the days seemed to blend into one another. Jerry had some bad nights and some good ones. Each day he seemed to get a little weaker. A string of visitors came and went through the apartment. Some he was glad to see, and some he was not. He began to drift in and out of consciousness.

On the second day, the minister from the local church came to plan the memorial service. Jerry was still lucid, but he had begun to slow down. We sat around his little room, the five of us. I had a chair just at the foot of the bed. From where I sat, I could just see a little patch of ocean out the window and around the corner of the building across the street. It seemed peaceful being able to see a little piece of water from that room.

The others were discussing hymns and psalms. I guess I was drifting in and out and not paying too much attention. I picked up as the minister was asking Jerry what he should say about him at the service. Jerry turned to look out at the water as if that would give him inspiration.

"Tell me a little about your life," said the minister.

Jerry turned and looked back. His eyes looked enormous in his head.

"My life," he said. "There's not much to tell about that. There's more to tell than there would have been before I came to Los Angeles. That was, what Steve? Ten years ago?"

Steve nodded.

"Ten years ago. I met Steve three years later. At that time, I would have told you that my life had been worthless. That I was worthless. I had no meaning. My family would have nothing to do with me." He looked at Jane. "Except for Jane, of course. But the last ten years have changed that. I have learned that I am loved, and that I love others. In the last ten years I have meant something to others and that has meant something to me, too."

"Do you believe in God?"

"I do now. For many years I didn't. I struggled with the whole idea. But I'm beyond that now. I'm through fighting him."

"What do you think it will be like?"

"I have no idea, and it doesn't really matter. I'm ready to go, and I trust he'll be there on the other side to take me."

Jerry closed his eyes as he said the last and seemed to drift off. We all just sat there for many minutes. Finally, I got up and went into the living room. It was another twenty minutes before Jane came out. She was crying.

"Is he sleeping?" I asked.

"In and out. He comes to every once in a while and picks up the conversation where he left off." She sat down and put her head on my shoulder.

"It's not fair to you to keep you around here during all this."

"It's OK. It's pretty amazing to see the courage that he has in facing this. I hope I'll be able to do it half as well."

"It's his faith. The faith and the courage go together."

* * *

I think it was the fourth day that Bob Reynaud called. By that time the days had already started to run together in my mind, but I remember that it was two days after the minister came. Steve answered the phone and called that it was for me. I thought it must be Rich. No one else knew where I was.

"Hello," I said.

"Peter Gordon?"

"Yes."

"Good morning, Mr. Gordon. This is Robert Reynaud."

All of a sudden my stomach felt hollow. I looked around as if he might be somewhere in the room with me.

"I guess you must be surprised to be hearing from me," he continued.

"How . . . ? How did you know where to find me?"

"That doesn't really matter, does it? I have found you. Don't you think we ought to talk?"

"What about?"

"Don't be coy, Mr. Gordon. I'm right down the street. How about right now?"

"Ahh . . . I don't think now would be convenient. We have a sick man here."

"Yes, I know. Jerry Hawkins. Please extend my deepest sympathies to Mrs. Turner."

"Isn't it a little odd for you to have sympathy for a gay man about to die of AIDS?"

"Mr. Gordon, whatever I may believe about his lifestyle, doesn't change my sympathies at being taken by this terrible epidemic. Please, it's important that we talk. You have nothing to fear from me."

I hesitated. I didn't know what to do.

"Just you," I said. "I don't want any of your Minutemen in here."

"Of course not. I just have my driver with me. He'll stay out in the car."

"Well, maybe just for a moment."

"Thank you, Mr. Gordon." And he hung up the phone before I could change my mind. I just sat there for a moment looking dumbly at the phone in my hand. Jane walked into the room as I was sitting there.

"Who was that?"

I looked up, startled and put the phone in its cradle.

"It was Bob Reynaud."

"What?"

"It was Bob Reynaud. He wants to come over to have a talk."

"Here? How did he know where to find us? You told him he couldn't come, didn't you?"

"Well no," I stammered. "He's on his way."

"But he can't come in here."

"He says he wants to talk to me."

At that moment the buzzer at the street door of the apartment rang.

"It's all right," I said. "He's not bringing any of his thugs with him. I think we're perfectly safe. He wouldn't let anything happen while he was here himself."

The buzzer sounded again. We both looked at it as if it were a live thing. She turned back and stepped next to me.

"That may be. But this is Jerry's house. Jerry just got finished telling us yesterday that he loved everyone, even the ones he didn't like. He still loved them. I'm not going to have that faith stretched by having Robert Reynaud in his house, do you understand? With all the rest he's going through, I don't have to put him through that too."

The buzzer rang for a third time. Steve came into the room.

"What's the matter with you guys?" he asked. "You can't hear the buzzer?"

He went over to buzz the caller in.

"Wait," said Jane. "Don't touch it." She turned to me. "If you're going to be stupid enough to talk to him, don't do it here. Take him to that coffee shop across the street."

"All right." I went to the intercom and called down to Reynaud that I would come down for him. I opened the door to go down, but Jane grabbed my arm.

"Are you sure this is a good idea?"

"He found us. He could have sent in his goons without giving us any warning. Instead, he came himself. I think it would make sense to hear what he has to say. What can we lose?"

"Lose? He could have a dozen men out there to beat you up or take you away."

"I don't think so. Look. You can see the coffee shop from the window. If I go off with him, call Rich. Have him get that FBI guy, Corville, involved. And you go some place safe."

"Are you sure?"

"Yes."

"All right. You be careful."

I turned and went down the stairs. Reynaud was waiting in the little lobby of the building. He was dressed in a dark businessman's suit. If he had a briefcase he could have passed for a downtown or Century City lawyer. He held out his hand.

"Mr. Gordon. So nice to meet you again."

"Is it?"

"Of course. Can we go up to talk?"

"No. Mrs. Taylor is reluctant to have you up to the apartment. Why don't we get a coffee at the shop across the street?"

"That would be an excellent idea."

There was a long, black limousine parked in the no-parking zone right in front of the apartment house. Reynaud made some sort of signal to the driver who was invisible behind smoked windows. I suddenly felt all exposed out on the street. Maybe it would have been better, after all, to have him up in the apartment, whatever Jerry's feelings would have been. It was too late for that now. I followed Reynaud in front of the car and across the street, resisting the urge to turn my head around to see what the chauffeur was doing. Reynaud went in the coffee shop and was inspecting the long list of specialty coffees with a look of distaste on his face.

"Just coffee, please," he said to the girl behind the counter. He turned to me. "You?"

"Ah . . . . Coffee, that would be fine."

Reynaud paid while I picked out a table next to the window. The chauffeur had apparently stayed in the car, although I couldn't be sure if there was anyone in the car. I could see what must have been Jerry's apartment on the fourth floor of the apartment building. There was a white shape in the window. I guessed it was Jane trying to watch us.

"Well, Mr. Gordon," said Reynaud. I jerked my attention back to him. "May I call you Pete?"

"Of course, Bob." I smiled and took a sip of my coffee. A silence settled over the table. That was all right with me. This was his meeting. Until I had an idea what the agenda was, I wasn't going to say anything.

"I've thought for some time that we needed to get together and talk," he said.

"Have you?" I said unhelpfully.

"Yes. I understand that Norman Hawkins retained you as his lawyer before he died."

I shrugged. "There are those who don't choose to believe that, but yes he did."

He smiled. "You mean Wilfred Brunell, I expect."

"Among others, yes."

"Well since Norman reposed such confidence in you, I would like to discuss with you the resolution of a rather embarrassing situation that I find myself in."

I leaned forward. This was getting interesting.

"And what embarrassing situation might that be?"

"Come, Pete. There's no need to be coy. I think you know about my position in Hawkins Industries. I'd like to get out of it with as little fuss as possible."

"Why? Why not buy some more shares and take control?"

He waved his hand. "Without Norman Hawkins the company is not worth the break-up value."

I sat back again. "Then why did you set out to take it over?"

"I never wanted to take it over. I thought I could do a deal with Norman, but he proved obstinate."

"So you had him killed?"

Now he sat back in his chair as if offended.

"Of course not. Why would I want to do that?"

"I don't know. Maybe so you could put someone else in his place."

He laughed. "Like who? Wilfred Brunell? He'll run the company into the ground faster than if there was nobody in charge."

"Maybe like Norman, Jr. You certainly have him in your pocket. And I understand he has a nice chunk of shares to contribute."

He shook his head. "Norman is a nice boy, but he's not what his father was by any stretch. No, I admit I thought I could put pressure on the father through the son, but that turned out to have been a mistake. It proved effective for a time, but, in the end, I fear it was counterproductive."

"You still haven't convinced me, Bob. Norman wasn't doing what you wanted him to do, and Richard Beck's fingerprints are all over Norman's death."

He sighed. "I'm afraid Richard has been rather a loose cannon through all of this, but he had nothing to do with Norman's death."

"Look, Bob. I'm not sure what you want from me, but this conversation's not going any farther if you are going to lie to me. I know Harry was on the boat that night. I've got a witness that puts him there. And the next time he turns up is at your ranch in California. Now how do you suppose he got off a boat that otherwise produced two dead bodies and all the way across the country without you having something to do with it?"

"Oh we had something to do with the transportation aspect of it. One night I got a call. If we wanted the kid back we could have him for ten thousand dollars. The exchange spot was a rest stop on the Garden State Parkway."

"Someone called you?"

"That's right."

"Ernie Fagin?"

He looked surprised. "You are well informed."

"It was a wild guess, but I'm not sure I believe it. Isn't he your worst enemy? Why would a de-programmer be supping with the devil so to speak?"

He laughed. "You really are quite naive, you know. It's true that Ernie and I don't talk much, but we do keep track of each other. You have to understand that the de-programmers and the cults exist in a strange sort of symbiosis. We each need the other. I need the de-programmers to scare the faithful into obedience. Ernie needs the cults to scare the money out of the parents. So, we each say the most terrible things about the other, but we need each other."

I didn't know what to say to this, so I said nothing and drank the dregs of my coffee.

"You look shocked," he said. "Well you shouldn't be. And you ask why Ernie would call me? That's easy. For the money. He thought he could get ten thousand dollars out of me, and he was right. Of course, he asked for twenty."

"And you paid?"

"Of course. I didn't pay the twenty, but I did pay the ten."

"Why?"

"I didn't know Norman was dead. Ernie neglected to tell me that part of it. I still thought the kid would be valuable."

"And you sent Beck to pick him up?"

He nodded.

"Now who's being naive? How do you know Beck wasn't working with Fagin the whole way through?"

He shrugged. "I can't be sure of that. I don't think so."

"Maybe you better tell me what you meant when you said Beck was a loose cannon."

"Richard wants to take over the RTTR. To do that, he needs to discredit me or get me out of the way somehow."

"How was he going to do that?"

"Initially by cooperating with the FBI in their investigation of the group. But that was moving too slowly for Richard's plans. He thought it would go much quicker if he set up poor Harry for the crime of attempting to assassinate my opponent in the California congressional race."

"It was Beck who wanted to have Renfrow killed?"

"Actually, he didn't want the Congressman killed at all. He wanted to have him stay in the race and beat Perkins."

"I don't understand."

"The idea was to have me discredited and have Renfrow around for another two years as a convenient target for the next leader of the RTTR."

"Meaning Beck."

"That's right. He arranged for the kid to be there with the weapon in his car. An RTTR member, and one who is known to be close to me, takes the fall, and I get tarred with the brush."

"How do you know this?"

"I have the real triggerman. He's made a full confession."

"Under duress?"

Reynaud shrugged and said nothing.

"So why don't you trot the guy over to the Sheriff?"

"I think it would be more telling if Junior's lawyer did that, don't you?"

"But I'm not the kid's lawyer. You've got some RTTR mouthpiece representing him."

"Yes, I know. Richard arranged all that. I think you'll find that there will be no problem with you undertaking the representation."

"So I get the kid off. Then what?"

"Then I'd like to negotiate the sale of my shares in the company."

"I assume you'll want a release from any claims arising out of any SEC violations committed in connection with their acquisition?"

"Exactly."

"You'll have to talk to Brunell about that end of it. I don't represent the company, and I never did."

"I understand that. But you will be representing the holder of the largest block of shares. And it appears you have a special relationship with the rest of the family." He looked up at Jerry's window in a way that I didn't like. He looked back at me. "I'm sure you'll be in a position to be influential as far as Wilfred is concerned."

"Why would I want to influence Brunell in that fashion?"

His eyes narrowed dangerously. "Because it will be in the best interest of your client. Don't forget, he's sitting in a jail cell right now, and I have the means to get him out. I don't think he'll be adverse to doing a deal to get some shares back that only dilute his control of the company, do you?"

"You mean you'd keep the witness back and let the kid take the rap for Renfrow?"

He didn't answer, but held up his hands, palms up.

"I don't think so," I said. "You need to get him off to rub the stain off yourself."

"If you want to take that risk go ahead. In the meantime, why don't you go talk to your new client? I'm sure he'll be amenable to helping me out."

"What's the deal?"

"The company buys out my shares at $38 a share. RTTR gets a full release from any claims."

"Thirty-eight? Isn't the stock down to twenty-eight now?"

"Yes, but it was at thirty-eight before Norman's untimely accident."

"No deal. We want a standstill. You can't buy any more shares. And you give an irrevocable voting proxy to Harry for as long as you own the shares. You agree to sell them on the open market over a period of a year. That ought to give you enough time to get out without taking too much of a loss. I'm damned if we're going to guarantee you a profit."

"We can't do that," he said. "With that overhang on the market the price is going nowhere but south. I'd take an enormous loss."

"But the rest of it is all right?" I asked.

"You mean the stand-still and the proxy?"

"Yes."

"That would be OK if we can work out the price."

"What's your average cost for the shares?"

I knew he would have it right at his fingertips. He did.

"Thirty-two dollars."

"OK. I'll recommend this to my client." I smiled. "Or to be more precise, to my client to be. We'll work together to find a buyer over a six-month period. The buyer must be acceptable to Harry. If we can't, the company will buy the shares from you at the higher of market or your average cost."

He sat back in his chair, considering the offer.

"How are you going to get Brunell to agree to this?"

"Like you said. I'll have to be persuasive."

"You're going to take over the company for the kid, aren't you?"

I looked at him. "Maybe. You dangled the bait. I just took it. As you say, I have a special relationship with the family."

"Some bait," he said. "Control of a Fortune 500 company. So." He reached his hand across the table. "Do we have a deal?"

I hesitated. "What about Mary?"

"She'll be joining her husband, of course."

And Harry will be able to go wherever he wants?

He held up his hands. "Frankly, he's of no more use or interest to me."

"And Mary's kidnapping? I suppose that was Beck as well?"

"Of course."

I took his hand, and we shook. "Pending me clearing all this with my client, I think we can do business."

"Good."

"I suppose you want all this resolved before the election next Tuesday?" I asked.

"Yes, I do, but not for the reason you think."

"I suppose it wouldn't look to good too have all this public on the eve of the election."

"I would prefer not to have it public, of course, but the election no longer really matters."

"Why not?"

"I was nothing more than a spoiler in a three-way race. I'm not running to win this time around. Next time it might be different." He laughed. "Norman thought he could pressure me because of the election. He couldn't but, now with Renfrow a sure bet to beat Perkins, the election doesn't really matter any more. I can use Beck's strategy as well as he can. Except he'll be the one discredited, not me."

I wondered if he was protesting too much, but now wasn't the time to press it.

"What's next?" I asked.

"I think you ought to go and talk to your client."

We got up and walked out onto the street. I could see Jane's face was still in the window.

"Can I give you a lift?" he asked.

"No thanks. I'll take my own car. When will you bring in the real killer?"

"Call me from the jail as soon as you've cleared all this with your client." He wrote out his private number on a slip of paper. "I'll be there inside a half an hour."

We shook hands again, and he made another signal to his limousine. It pulled away from the curb, made an illegal U-turn and slid to a stop right in front of us. The back door opened. Reynaud slid in, and the car sped away.

I stood there for a moment, my head spinning in the attempt to absorb the implications of everything I had heard. Jane was waiting to open the apartment door for me.

"What happened? You were down there so long."

"Reynaud wanted to do a deal."

"What kind of a deal?"

"A deal to get your brother out."

Her eyes widened, and she literally pulled me into the apartment. We sat down on the couch in the living room, and I told her about it. When I finished, we both just sat there for a moment.

"Do you believe him?" she asked, finally.

"I think I believe most of it."

"I mean let's not look too many gift horses in the mouth. It's wonderful we can get Harry out. But isn't it rather convenient to put all of the blame on Beck? How do we know it wasn't Reynaud all the time?"

"We don't know that. We'll probably never know that. But the bottom line is that we have no choice but to go along with him. Should we wait for the FBI to make a case while Harry stays in jail?"

"No, of course not. But, why should Reynaud be so nice to us all of a sudden? Just to beat the rap on some penny-ante SEC violations?"

"The violations might not be so penny-ante if the FBI has some other counts. With multiple counts they can make a racketeering case under RICO and create some real problems for him. If he settles with the company, it takes a lot of the sting out of any SEC reporting violations. I bet he has a game plan to shed the responsibility for the other counts onto Beck as well. If he pulls it off, he comes out of it in full control of the organization with no loss on sale of the Hawkins stock, and the FBI investigation is back at square one."

"Corville will be furious."

"Corville isn't our concern. The Hawkins family is."

"Since when did you become our guardian angel?"

I shrugged. "I guess ever since your father walked into my office that afternoon."

I picked up the phone and called Bonnie Hirsch. I asked her to meet me at Sheriff Martin's office in an hour, and to call him to make an appointment to see Harry. She started to ask me questions, but I told her I'd fill her in when I got out there.

Jane walked me to the door and held me there clinging to my shirt. "You've been pretty good to the Hawkins family, haven't you?"

I didn't know what to say. I looked down at her, and I could see tears glistening in her eyes. She was looking at my shirtfront. "I don't know what it is with me," she said. "Maybe it's Jerry, maybe it's everything, but every so often I just burst into tears." She looked up at me again. "Well, there's one member of the Hawkins family who's grateful." And she kissed me, a little butterfly of a kiss and then again, a real kiss this time. We stood there for a long moment, and I felt like I was going down into a deep pool. Suddenly she pulled away, and I came to the surface. "Now, go get my brother out of jail and get him back here," she said. "And be careful."

Chapter XII

She pushed me out the door, and before I could think very much about my errand again, I found myself on the road to Ventura County. Sheriff Martin seemed to have undergone a personality change since the last time I had been in his office. He got coffee for Bonnie and me, and made pleasant small talk as he escorted us to a small conference room where Harry was waiting for us. There he excused himself and let us alone. Harry sat at the end of the conference table looking small in the over-large prison cover-alls he was wearing. He was in his mid-twenties with short black hair and horn-rim glasses. He looked quite pale and was slumped down in the chair in a posture that brought the word "defeated" to my mind.

"Who are you?" he asked.

"Hello, Harry. I'm Peter Gordon. Maybe you remember me from your North Beach days. This is Bonnie Hirsch. We'd like to represent you."

"I've already got a lawyer."

"We know. A fellow named Roy Corbin, isn't it?"

He nodded.

"Roy been in to see you much?"

He shrugged. "Maybe a couple of times."

"You happy with the representation?"

"Why? Shouldn't I be?"

"You know the RTTR picked him out for you?"

"Sure. The RTTR will take care of me."

"Well, as a matter of fact you're right. Bob Reynaud was the one who suggested that we take over the representation."

For the first time he looked interested. "Really? Bob did?"

"Yes. And your wife, Mary, hired me to be your lawyer as well."

"Mary? Why hasn't she been in to see me? Is she all right?"

"She's fine. She's been out at the ranch. We'll get her in to see you soon. Or if we're lucky, we'll get you out so that you can see her on the outside."

He sat up in his chair and looked interested in the proceedings for the first time. "If you have an idea to pull that off, counselor, you're my lawyer and that asshole Corbin can go to hell."

"I don't think that will be necessary."

"So what's the deal?"

"First tell me what happened the day of the shooting."

He shrugged and slumped down in his chair again. "I've been all over that with Corbin."

"Humor me. You've got nothing better to do, have you?"

"Yeah. I guess you beat the soaps. There's nothing much to tell. I was supposed to be part of Bob's honor guard at the speech."

I interrupted. "Reynaud was there?"

"Sure. He was giving a speech too. In fact he had given his speech when Renfrow got up to give his, and he and the other guy got shot."

"Where were you?"

"Well, I was supposed to be right by the podium with the other Minutemen guarding Bob. At the last minute I was put on a special assignment to work the crowd."

"Was that unusual?"

"No, we often had people in the crowd to try to pump up enthusiasm for Bob, or to be hostile to the other guy. Then we would report back on what the crowd reaction was. It was pretty typical."

"So you weren't surprised to be given that detail?"

"Well, I was pissed off. It's usually something that the junior members do. It's several steps down from guarding the Archon."

"Was there anything unusual about the assignment otherwise?"

"Well, usually the guys working the crowds would all go together in vans. I was given a car, and they told me to park in the parking lot across the street. And if anything happened just to get back to the car and head back to the ranch."

"Who gave you these instructions?"

"Richard Beck."

"And what happened?"

He shrugged. "Just what I've said. I was working the crowd, trying to get the boos started for Renfrow when the shots were fired. First one and then the other. There was a moment of almost stillness, and then this mad scramble. I stayed around for a while to make sure Bob was all right. I saw the Minuteman detail hustle him into a van so that was fine. I puttered around for a few extra minutes, and then I went to get my car. The police stopped me at the exit to the garage. They asked to look in the trunk. I had no reason not to let them, so I opened it up. There was this rifle inside. That's it. They say it's the rifle that killed the guy. So here I am."

I looked at Bonnie. I had had a brief moment to fill her in outside.

"It all fits together," she said.

"Ah . . . . At least as far as it relates to Harry here."

"What fits together?" he asked. "Tell me what's going on."

"What's going on is that Reynaud came to see me. He said that Beck set you up to embarrass him and use that as leverage to take over the organization."

Harry looked at me incredulously. "Richard take over? That's crazy. Richard wouldn't be able to hold it all together."

"Well, Richard might have a different opinion about that. Anyway Reynaud has the real shooter, and he's willing to produce him to clear you."

"Good. So what are we futzing around here for? Where is the guy?"

"One little problem. Reynaud wants to do a deal on Hawkins Industries in exchange for his help in getting you out."

Harry sat back again in his chair as if tired.

"What does he want?" He asked in a low voice. I explained the deal. When I was finished he was sitting up straight again.

"That's all? He's giving up his chance to control Hawkins Industries and just get his money back? Why would he want to do that?"

"Because he has a Department of Justice investigation on his hands. Part of his problem is that the shares he accumulated were not reported in accordance with SEC rules. He's worried about damage control and holding onto his RTTR power base. If he can get out of these problems and break even on the investment, he can live to fight another day."

"But the Justice Department must have a bunch of other stuff on mail fraud and so on with his fund raising."

"They may. And I'm sure he has a game plan to take care of those charges as well. But that doesn't concern us. All we need to care about is that this deal will get you out of jail and put you in control of a hefty chunk of Hawkins Industries stock."

"How much stock does he have?"

"We estimate about twenty-two percent of the company."

He looked up, surprised. "Twenty-two percent? That's more than I would have thought. With my ten that would give me thirty-two. That'd be effective control of the company. I could tell old Wilfred Brunell to go to hell."

"That's right. And that's how you deliver on the deal with Reynaud. Wilfred will have to go along or he won't be Chairman anymore."

"I don't get it," cut in Bonnie. "Why doesn't Reynaud just make his deal with Brunell?"

"Because Reynaud's got nothing to offer Brunell," I said. "Brunell already controls about twenty-five percent as the executor of Norman's estate. He doesn't need Reynaud's shares. All he has to do is to go into court to get an injunction to neutralize them."

"So why was Reynaud so stupid as to acquire the shares without filing with the SEC?" she asked.

"Because he couldn't afford to let it be known that he, or the RTTR, was behind the purchase," said Harry. "He much preferred to stay in the background. What he tried to do was to acquire the shares and then negotiate in secret with my father."

"So if we do this deal, why can't Brunell still get his injunction?" persisted Bonnie.

"He may try," I said. "But he'll have a much tougher time. Reynaud will already have agreed to dispose of the shares and given up the voting rights to Harry here. We would argue that an injunction would be moot."

"But it's no sure thing."

"No," I said. "It's no sure thing. But Harry will be out of jail. The risk is all Reynaud's."

"As long as his patsy doesn't change his story," said Harry.

"One step at a time," I said. "Let's first get you out of jail. Then we can concentrate on keeping you out."

"All right," he said. "Let's do it."

"OK," I said. "Let's be clear. From this point on you are retaining us to represent you and authorizing us to act on your behalf to complete this deal with Reynaud."

"I think that's what I said."

"I just want to be clear."

"We're clear."

"Good. Bonnie, why don't you get the DA down here? And call Reynaud and tell him it's a go, and he should get the shooter here as well." She started towards the door. "Oh and call Corbin and tell him he's history. Harry can notify him officially later."

Bonnie left, and I turned back to Harry. He was slumped down in his chair again, but somehow the effect was different than it had been when I came in. Now he looked relaxed rather than defeated.

"How do you feel about the RTTR now?" I asked.

He opened his eyes and looked at me. "I guess the word would be indifferent," he said. "You have a lot of time to think in here. Not that I would recommend it to anyone, but that's one of the side effects. Ever since Dad died its like I've come out of a trance. I look back at that person who was so caught up in the mystery and the ritual of the organization, and I can hardly believe it was me."

"Do you think your father's death had anything to do with that change in attitude?"

"Who knows? Maybe. All I know is that, even before I got in here, when I was back at the ranch it all seemed different. Like a new set of lenses had slipped into place, and I was looking at the world with new eyes."

"Tell me what happened on the boat."

"There's not much I remember. My father called me that night and asked to meet me at the Dunes. He said he wanted to make peace with Bob. I remember going out to meet him, and there was this woman with a flat tire. Then, suddenly, my father was there, and we were yelling. Then I got real tired and everything became fuzzy. The next thing I remember I wake up, and we're at sea. I'm in this quarter berth. It's all dark and the wind is howling in the rigging. We're heeled at a pretty good angle. Dad's driving her pretty hard. For a moment, I don't have any context. I think I'm back, years ago, on an ocean race, and I'm about to be called out on watch. The last thing I want to do is to be called out on that wet deck. I look for my watch and try to figure out what the watches are and how long I have before someone comes to get me. Then it comes back to me. I'm not on any race. I'm on 'Far Cry', and my father must have kidnapped me. I start to get out of the berth, but then I stop. What's the point? There's nowhere I can go. And it's kind of comforting that no one is going to insist that I go out on deck in the wet and cold. So I pull the blanket back over my head and go back to sleep."

He stopped and seemed to be staring at nothing.

"So what happened next?" I prodded.

"I was still asleep. I was awakened by an enormous bang. Suddenly the boat was upright and dead in the water. There was a lot of shouting on deck. I stumbled out of the berth and started up the companionway. Outside, it was a mess. The wind was blowing the rain horizontally across the deck. I was drenched immediately. Someone was shining a spotlight around crazily. It was lighting everything up in this unnatural glow. The mast was over the side. It had broken about eight feet off the deck. Dad and Louie were struggling to cut it free. There was this other guy standing at the helm kind of helplessly. He was the one with the light. I asked him how it had happened, and he gave me this dazed look. He looked scared to death. I went to help Dad and Louie cut the mast loose. The boat was rolling sideways in the seas. We worked for awhile and then I went to get the engine started so I could at least point her into the wind. The guy was still standing there with a death grip on the wheel. I pushed him aside and tried the starter. Nothing. It was completely dead. I went back to help again. We finally got it loose and rigged a sea anchor to let us ride it out better."

"Why didn't you radio for help?"

"We tried, but all the electronics were out. We had the little handheld radio, but that didn't have the range. Louie tried for an hour while we all sat down in the main cabin."

"Did you talk to your father?"

"For awhile we all just sat there like we were in shock. Louie was trying to work the radio. Finally, my Dad started to talk to me, but I wasn't listening. I was angry again that he had kidnapped me."

"Do you remember anything he said?"

"Not really. I think I really was in shock. I wasn't paying much attention to anything."

"Was he saying anything about the company?"

"You know, I don't think so. It's crazy, but I seem to remember him talking about times when I was a kid. I don't know." He stopped and I could see that he was a little teary. "You know that was the last time I had a chance to talk to my father, and I didn't say anything. I just pretended to be angry."

"Weren't you?"

"No. I don't think I really was. But I wasn't about to let him know that."

"So what happened then?"

"Well, after a while, Louie picked up something on the radio. It was another boat. They said they were coming to help us."

"Did it have a name?"

He gave me a quick look as if he was just remembering something. "You know that's a funny thing. Over the radio he said his name was Fade something. Fade . . . . away. That's it, 'Fadeaway'. But I don't think that was really the boat's name."

"Why not?"

"Well about a half-hour later they came up to us. We couldn't see much, but they maneuvered around and got a line aboard. I was on the bow taking the line and their captain backed the boat down close enough so I could see the transom in our spotlight. I couldn't see the name but it wasn't 'Fadeaway'."

"Could you see anything about it?"

He stopped and closed his eyes as if he was trying to visualize the scene. "I couldn't read it, but it looked like it started with J."

"A big script J?

"That's it. Do you know the boat?"

"Sport fisherman about forty feet? More like a charter boat than a yacht?"

"That could be right."

"Could it have been 'Justine'?"

He closed his eyes and thought. "It could have been. I can't remember more than the J. You know her?"

"Let's not get carried away. There's a charter boat named 'Justine' that works out of Brielle. It might be the one."

He jumped up from his chair and started to pace around the room, pounding one hand into the other.

"We've got them," he said.

"Take it easy. We're a long way from having anybody. Our first task is to get you out of here. Then we'll see who we've got. Tell me what happened next."

"Well, they told us they were going to tow us to Cape May. They started out. The guy who had been in a daze all of a sudden like comes to life. He says he couldn't sleep anyway, he'll steer the boat while it's being towed. Dad was uncertain, but I could see he was exhausted. Finally, he agreed, and the rest of us went down to get some sleep. The next thing I knew there was a loud roar of engines like a guy was backing them down hard, then the pounding of a lot of feet on the deck. I was trying to get out of my berth when a bright light flashed in my face and someone put a gun to my head. I heard someone say 'That's him,' and they dragged me out of the berth and out on the deck. The rain had stopped, but it was still blowing like hell. The sport fisherman was alongside banging against the rail. They didn't even have any bumpers out. They threw me into the cockpit of the boat and someone else grabbed me and hustled me below. They locked me in a little cabin. For a while I yelled and banged on the door. Someone finally came. He grabbed me around the throat and punched me in the stomach. He told me if I said another word they would pitch me overboard. I think

I was sick on the floor. Anyway, I kept quiet after that. Pretty soon the engines started up, and we got out of there. It was hours later that they slowed again, and I figured we were tying up somewhere. I'm not sure how long it was. I'd lost my watch. I guess everyone left the boat because it was quiet for a while. Maybe I dozed off. A little later they came and took me. We were tied up in a little creek. I don't know how there was enough water. They put a blindfold over me before I could really see anything. I was led up this raggedy dock and into, I guess, a house. They put me in a bedroom and locked the door. I probably went to sleep again. I don't know how long I was there. I guess the whole next day. No one spoke to me. They all wore masks. It was dark when they came to get me again. They tied my hands and put me in the back of a van. We drove for about forty-five minutes. They pulled me out at a rest stop somewhere. There were some other guys there. I didn't know them, but I knew who they were. Minutemen. The RTTR had come to reclaim me.

"They took you back to California?"

"Yes. I guess we drove straight through. Then it was all sweetness and light and welcome back to the fold. Everyone rallying around providing support. And then it was get right on a plane to come back for the funeral."

"But didn't you call Chief Skowronski from California?"

"No, that was from a pay phone somewhere in Indiana or Illinois."

"Why did you tell him you were in California?"

"When they picked me up on the Parkway, they took me to this motel. Beck was there. He told me that my father had kidnapped me to get me out of the RTTR. He said the de-programmer my father had hired had double-crossed him and ransomed me back to RTTR."

"The guy you didn't know?"

"Yeah. He said the guy had killed my father so he could keep the de-programming money and then sold me back to the RTTR for a little extra cash."

"And you believed all this?"

"It seems crazy now, but I was still a little in shock and exhausted to boot."

"What else did he say?"

"He said they would take care of the de-programmer, but I had to tell the police that I had been in California all the time."

"Why lie about it?"

"He said that the police might try to tie me into the murder if I told anyone I was on the boat. They'd protect me by saying that I'd never left California."

"What about Mary?"

"I called her to say that I'd gone to the Dunes to meet Richard and he'd convinced me to return to California with him. And I was supposed to convince her to say to anyone that asked that I had been in California all the time."

"So she didn't know you'd been out on the boat at all."

"No, she had no idea."

"And at the funeral you were sticking to the same story?"

"Yes."

At this point Bonnie came back into the room followed by a Sheriff's Deputy.

"The DA's here, and we're waiting for Reynaud. It will probably be a couple of hours until the whole thing gets straightened out. Meanwhile, you're going to have to stick it out in your cell for a little while longer."

Harry shrugged. "Now that I see maybe there's an end to it, it won't be so bad."

He got up, and the Deputy led him out.

"How will it go?" I asked Bonnie.

"The DA will want to interview this guy, but that's really a formality. He's already authorized an all points bulletin to pick up Beck for questioning. Oh, and Corbin's here. He was raising a ruckus about us interfering with his client. I suggested he might want to talk to Reynaud before he started getting too frisky. That shut him up. He's downstairs waiting in the lobby, quiet as a lamb."

She sat down. "We might as well make ourselves comfortable. This might take awhile."

Surprisingly, it didn't take that long. After an hour a serious looking man with a crew cut came in and, ignoring me, said a few words to Bonnie. Bonnie nodded and he walked out again.

"Well?" I asked.

"That's it. We can pick Harry up in the lobby in about five minutes."

"And he's free to go?"

"Free to go. They want him available for the grand jury, but the DA's convinced." We went down to the lobby to find Mary waiting on a bench. When she saw me she jumped up to run over.

"Pete? What's happening?"

I didn't have time to answer when Harry appeared out of a side door. Mary gave a little cry and abandoned me. I left them five minutes for the reunion and then hustled them out to the car to drive them back to Los Angeles. They sat in the back seat, and I couldn't get them back fast enough. I stashed them in a little hotel in Westwood on Wilshire Boulevard. They registered and disappeared up to the room without a backward glance at me. I got in the car and went back to Jerry's apartment. Jane was there at the door to meet me.

"Where's Harry?" She asked, anxiously.

I explained and her eyes narrowed. "You mean you let that bitch get her claws into him already?"

I shrugged. "She is his wife."

* * *

At Jerry's apartment everything was much the same. Everything except Jerry was a day weaker. He continued weaker day-to-day as one day once again ran into the next. I checked on Harry and Mary every day at their motel, but they were oblivious to everything but each other. Harry showed no inclination that he wanted to see Jerry, and Jane suggested that I leave it alone. Reynaud called every day to find out when we would progress on completing the deal. I kept putting him off, but each day, he became more insistent. Election day came and went, and Reynaud lost as he had predicted. He lost, but he got nearly twenty percent of the vote. I think it was the day after the election that he started making veiled threats. By Thursday of that week, I decided I needed to do something. Whether it was the need to get out of that apartment, where Jerry was slowly dying, or because of Reynaud's insistence, I don't know. In any case, that night, Harry, Mary and I got on the red-eye to Philadelphia.

Back in North Beach, I put Harry and Mary in my front bedroom for a nap. Annie was glad to see me, and Pepper almost had a nervous breakdown. I took a shower and went off to see Rich Skowronski. I found him sitting at his desk talking on the telephone. He waved me to a chair. He finished and hung up the phone.

"Where have you been, counselor?"

"On the West Coast. What's going on here?"

"Not much. No leads on our friend Fagin. The Philadelphia police are writing it off as a mugging. Anything happened on your end?"

"A few developments." I started to tell him. After a few sentences he straightened in his chair and started to pay attention. After five minutes he took out his notebook and started to take notes. When I was done, he threw down the notebook with a little shout of glee.

"Goddamn. The 'Justine'. Good old Captain Rolf Jacobsen. Where is the kid now?"

"Sleeping off the red-eye at my house."

"I need to take a statement from him. Wouldn't I love to take a shot at Rolf, that arrogant little asshole."

"We don't have very much, remember. Harry didn't see anybody. And he didn't see the whole name."

"We've got enough to split Captain Rolf like a melon. We got enough to make him beg to tell the story."

"Do you know where he is?"

"No. He takes the boat to Florida in the winter. I don't know where he goes, but I can find out. What are you going to do?"

"I'm going to pay a visit to Wilfred Brunell. Maybe I'll be able to split him like a melon too."

"Be careful. Beck is still out there somewhere."

Unfortunately, Brunell proved to be a little tougher than a melon. I got on the road to Philadelphia, and I went to call on Wilfred in his elegant law offices. They told me I had come to the wrong place. Brunell was in his Hawkins Industries office. I remembered that the firm occupied the same building. The closer to the golden goose the better, I thought. I just had to change elevator banks and go back up to the Hawkins Industries floors. Then started the tedious negotiation process with the receptionist. No, I didn't have an appointment with Mr. Brunell. I understood he was busy, but it was very important that I speak with him. Finally, I persuaded the receptionist to have a note taken back to him and, twenty minutes later, I was ushered into a magnificent conference room. A long table with plush chairs filled the room. Behind the table was a floor to ceiling window wall looking out on the Benjamin Franklin Parkway and the Art Museum. A portrait of Norman Hawkins was hung at one end of the room, and, at the other end, there was a portrait of an older man, dressed in an old-fashioned suit, but definitely a Hawkins. The nose and the eyes were unmistakable.

"The original Norman Hawkins," said a voice behind me. "The real brains behind this company."

I turned around to see that Wilfred Brunell had come in a side door at the other end of the room.

"Norman's father?" I asked. "I thought Norman started the company in his garage."

"Sure that's the myth. The old man was an investment banker. He was ruined in the depression. But he still had enough contacts to get financing for his son. How do you think Norman ever got out of that garage?"

He sat down at the end of that long table, making me walk the length of the room. As I approached, he pretended to read the note I had sent back to him. I reached him and sat down one of the chairs. He threw the note theatrically on the table.

"What in God's name is this supposed to mean?"

"I represent Norman Hawkins . . ." I began, but he cut me off.

"We've been through that. Norman is dead, and I think you'll find, if you ever get back to your office, the notice of a hearing before the New Jersey Bar Ethics Committee that is investigating your conduct in that matter."

I leaned back in my chair and half-turned it to look at the Grandfather, who was staring at me from the far wall.

"I know it's confusing with all these generations of Hawkins, Wilf, but I wasn't referring to the father, I was talking about the son."

"The kid?" He picked up the note and held it by the corner as if it carried some deadly disease. "That's the major stockholder you were talking about in this note? Don't make me laugh. The kid's going away on a murder charge. What possible interest could he be to me?"

"Actually the kid's out. Someone else has confessed to shooting Congressman Renfrow and killing his aide."

If this news was a shock to him, he gave no sign of it. He sat back in his chair and smiled.

"Am I to understand that you had something to do with this?"

"In a small way."

"Well then, let me congratulate you on your little victory. But you didn't come here to tell me this. My time is important. What do you want?"

"Harry wants to come back to have a role in his father's company."

"Sure. We'd be delighted to have a Hawkins back in the company. I'm sure we can place him nicely as a Vice President in sales."

"Actually. I think he had the job as President in mind. You would, of course, stay on as Chairman of the Board."

Wilfred started laughing before I was even finished. I waited for a moment until he was done with his little bout of merriment.

"You may think it's funny," I said. "But actually, he's quite serious."

"Look, Pete," he said. "I know you don't want to take advice from me, but you should stay out of this. You already have enough trouble with your misrepresenting yourself about the father. Now you're going to try to slide a twenty-five year-old kid, an RTTR wacko, who just got out of jail, into the presidency of a Fortune 500 corporation? I know the kid has ten percent of the stock due to the senility of the first Hawkins." He gestured towards Grandfather. "But don't think the Hawkins name will get you anything in a proxy fight. Did you forget that the estate starts fifteen points ahead of the kid? As sole executor, I'm not at liberty to say how the estate's shares would be voted, but, I don't think you're stupid. What would be your guess?"

I sat and pretended to think. "I wouldn't want to hazard a guess as to what your fiduciary duties might be," I said. "But I wonder what a court might think about your voting the shares against the wishes of the ultimate beneficial owner."

He laughed. "And who would that be, Pete?"

"Harry, of course. He gets the shares when they are distributed from the estate."

"Not quite. Norman was smart enough not to leave the shares

directly to the kid while he was involved with Reynaud. The shares go into a trust until such time as the trustee is assured, in the unfettered exercise of his own discretion, that the kid is no longer subject to the influence of the cult."

My stomach sank as he told me this news. I hoped I gave no sign of my dismay. I smiled.

"I'm sure you're right, Wilf. I take it the you are the sole trustee?"

He smiled. "The trustees are me and a local bank. But since I represent them too, I think my influence will be persuasive, don't you?"

"How convenient. But the kid, as you call him, has a few more shares than that. Harry also has a proxy for the RTTR shares. I think he starts with a higher base than you give him credit for."

"The RTTR shares? Don't make me laugh. In a proxy fight I'll have an injunction to prevent the voting of those shares quicker than you're going to be out of here."

He rose as he said these last words. I stayed planted firmly in my seat.

"What are you going to do?" I asked. "Get your own RTTR goons to throw me out? Why don't you call Richard Beck to do it personally?"

"Mr. Beck no longer works here. One of the first things I did when I took over this company was to get rid of him and his little police force."

"Smart move. When he gets indicted on a murder charge, you wouldn't want to be too closely associated with him."

"Pete," he leaned down. "I'm not associated with him at all. If you still have this delusion that Norman's accident was murder, and you manage to pin the rap on Beck, I'll applaud you as a concerned citizen. But it's got nothing to do with me or Hawkins Industries. Now you've wasted enough of my time. In five minutes, I'm sending security in here. If you're still here, they'll throw you out on your ass."

With that, he turned on his heel and walked out the side door. I looked up at Norman, who was right above my head looking endlessly across the room towards his own father. I wondered what he thought about the prospect of having to look at the old guy, day after day and year after year. I couldn't ask him so I got up and left.

I was angry for half of the way back to North Beach and depressed for the balance of the trip. Once again I had been ambushed by a piece of information that I should have had but didn't. I hadn't counted on a trust. Wilfred might be able to hold the shares due to Harry in the estate, and later in the trust, for years. At home, Pepper greeted me at the door with a lavish display of affection. I scratched her ears. At least, someone was glad to see me. I found the rest, Harry, Mary and Annie sitting in my living room, drinking coffee. They all looked up expectantly at my arrival.

"Well I screwed it up," I said.

"What do you mean?" asked Harry.

"Wilfred won't play. I think he likes being Chairman of a large corporation, and he's not about to give it up. He'll vote your father's shares to keep his hold on the company."

"But those are my shares," said Harry plaintively.

"Not while they're still in the estate. And Wilf tells me your father set up a trust to protect the shares while you were associated with the RTTR. Did you know about that?"

"Yes, he told me that. I think he did that right after one of our fights. But so what? I'm not in the RTTR any more."

"You'll have to prove that to a judge. And proving a negative is not the easiest thing in the world."

"But, I thought we still had enough shares to outvote him. Don't I have 32% with the proxy on the RTTR shares?"

"That doesn't seem to scare him. He says he'll be able to keep those shares from voting in a proxy fight. Plus, I think he's counting on his clout with the institutional holders to put him ahead."

"Is he right about that?" asked Mary.

"He probably is. He's management now, and they usually go with management on these things, unless there's a buck in it for them. They won't like a bare-knuckled proxy fight with no prospect of a big premium on the sale of their shares."

"So what do we do?" asked Harry.

"I think that, first, we give the bad news to Reynaud."

"Do you think that's a good idea?"

"Better he gets the bad news from me."

"Suppose he goes back on our deal?"

"How would he do that?"

"All of a sudden the confessed shooter will change his story. And a dozen RTTR members will swear he was somewhere else entirely."

"You think Reynaud could have that much influence on him?"

He laughed bitterly. "You don't know the first thing about it, do you?"

I got up and took him by the arm. "Harry, I want the truth about this. Do you have any reason to believe that guy's story isn't the way it happened?"

He tried to pull his arm out of my grasp. "So now even you don't believe me."

"Harry." I was almost shouting now. "It's no time for games. Did it happen the way that guy confessed?"

"Yes," he said, a little whine in his voice now. I took a breath the say something.

"OK," he said. "As far as I know, yes. But I don't know for sure. Did that guy actually pull the trigger? Or, is he just another poor jerk who's been given the opportunity of a lifetime to prove his loyalty, to give up everything, even his life, for Reynaud? I have no idea. All I know is that he'll say anything Reynaud tells him to say. And so will ten thousand other RTTR members."

I sat and considered. It was still better that Reynaud hear it from me. I dialed the phone and, in a few minutes, had Reynaud on the line.

"Well, how's it going?" he asked, jovially.

"Not so good," I said. "Brunell's not going for the deal."

"Why not?"

"I guess he likes running the company."

"I'm disappointed, Pete. This could upset our whole arrangement. You were so sure you could convince him to go along."

"Wait a minute. I was never sure I could convince him. I thought I had a good shot at it."

"So you messed up."

"Maybe. I guess I over-estimated the effect on him of us having more shares than he controlled through the estate."

"How would you have more shares?"

I stopped, confused. "Ah well . . . . Maybe this is a stupid question at this point, but how many shares does the RTTR control?"

"I don't know exactly. But it's about fifteen percent."

"Fifteen?"

"That's right. What did you think?"

"More than that." I had thought he had twenty-two percent. Where were the missing shares? "Ahh . . . Look Bob," I stammered. "I have to do some re-thinking. In the meantime, I wouldn't be surprised if Brunell started a lawsuit for violations of SEC regulations in connection with the RTTR shares."

"If he does that, our whole deal is off."

"What does that mean?"

"Your new client may find himself behind bars again."

I was about to react angrily, but it was too soon for that. "Bob, let's not over-react to this. Brunell is being a hard-ass, but he has a reputation for that. Give me a little time to work this out. In the meantime, I need the listing of all your holdings. I should have asked for that before."

"Why should I send them to you?"

"Because your best shot is to work with me and finish off our deal. Fax them to me at my office. And I would also suggest that you consolidate them all into one partnership with Harry as the general partner. He'll be empowered to vote the shares and the partnership agreement will provide for the buy-out of the shares on the terms we agreed."

"Why should I do that? If Harry doesn't get control of the company, he won't have the wherewithal to make good on the purchase."

"So he'll default, and the shares will revert to your control. You'll be no worse off than you are now."

"I don't know. I'll have to think about it."

"Well, you think about it. In the meantime, send me that list." I gave him my fax number. He didn't say he was going to fax the list, but he took the number down. He closed with a threat.

"If you don't pull this off, Gordon, not only will your client go away for murder, but you'll be sorrier than you ever could imagine."

"Threats aren't going to . . . ." But he had already hung up. My hand was shaking as I put the phone down.

"Will he go along?" asked Harry.

"I don't know."

"Why wouldn't he cut a deal directly with Brunell?"

"I think that's exactly what he'll try to do."

"Then we're finished."

"Not quite. My guess is that Brunell will be too arrogant and too greedy. He'll try to push Reynaud too far."

"But eventually Reynaud will have to go along with whatever he wants, won't he?"

"Eventually, that's right. But, in the meantime, we have some time. Brunell won't file his lawsuit while he's using it as a lever in the negotiations. I'm counting on both of them being too obstinate to come to an agreement quickly."

"So what do we do?" asked Annie.

"First. Reynaud told me the RTTR only has fifteen percent of the company. I thought you told me it was twenty-two."

"That's what we assumed from the data. We were still in the process of tracing the buys back through the various partnerships. We assumed from the timing and the similarities of the partnerships that they all would trace back to the same source. But we couldn't actually trace them all back. I suppose there could have been another buyer out there doing the same thing."

"Damn," I said. "Suppose the buyer was Brunell. Suppose he controls that missing seven percent. No wonder he's so damn cocky. Even if he can't get an injunction he's in the catbird seat."

"So what are we going to do?" asked Annie.

"I don't know," I said. What I did do was to call Jane to pour out some of my frustrations and then go to bed.

Chapter XIII

The next morning the phone woke me. It was Rich Skowronski.

"Hey Pete. I got a line on Rolf Jacobsen."

"In Florida?"

"That's right. Fort Lauderdale. He hangs out at that charter boat pier next to Bahia Mar."

"Are you going to go talk to him?"

"As a matter of fact, I am. I even got the town to spring for a plane ticket."

"Mind if I come along?"

"I thought you might want to do that. I'm leaving out of Newark tonight."

We made arrangements to drive up to the airport, and he hung up.

"Who was that?" asked Harry.

"It was Rich Skowronski. He may have a line on the boat that took you off 'Far Cry' that night."

"In Fort Lauderdale?"

I hesitated. "Yes."

"I want to go too."

"I'm not sure that's a good idea."

"Why not? I'm the only one who can identify the boat."

In the end he convinced first me and then Skowronski. That night we were in Fort Lauderdale. We got in about ten and rented a car to take us over to the Bahia Mar. Before going to bed, Harry suggested taking a walk down to the fishing pier. None of us were very sleepy so we agreed. The night was a balmy one. There were about fifteen charter boats tied up stern first at a pontoon dock. Spotlights lit up the scene, but the dock itself was almost deserted. A gangway led down to the boats. Harry went immediately down the gangway and halfway along the dock. He stopped behind what looked like a forty-footer. Rich and I followed more slowly. As we came up to him, I could read the name on the transom. "Justine".

"This is it," he said.

"Are you sure?" asked Rich. "It must have been pretty dark that night. And you never saw her in the daylight, did you?"

"No, but I recognize the script of the 'J'. It's pretty distinctive."

"You guys want to go fishin'?"

I looked over to see two men smoking in the shadows of the cockpit of the boat next to "Justine".

"Maybe," called Rich. He turned to us and whispered for us to continue on down the dock to the other end. Then he turned and walked towards the transom of the other boat. "What's running this time of year?" he asked.

Harry started to say something, but I took his arm and hustled him down the dock.

"We don't want to show too much interest in that boat or draw too much attention to ourselves."

"But those guys might know where to find this Rolf."

"Let's let Rich figure that out."

We climbed up from the pontoon dock and waited up on the pier itself. Rich came along about ten minutes later.

"Let's go," he said. "That was too close."

"Why?" asked Harry.

"One of those guys was Rolf's mate. Fortunately, it's a local guy, so there's no way he'd know me. And it's worked out all right. We've got a charter for tomorrow morning."

Next morning we breakfasted at Bahia Mar. There wasn't much conversation. By eight o'clock we were walking down towards the pier.

"You stay up on the pier, Harry," said Rich. "It's possible he might recognize you, and I don't want to spook him too early."

"Won't he know you?" asked Harry.

"Yeah, he will. It'll put him a little off balance, but he won't know for sure that we've got something on him. If he sees you too, he'll know."

We left Harry on the pier and stepped down the gangway to the boats. Two tourists off for a day of fishing. The mate saw us and gave a wave. Rolf was nowhere to be seen. Rich walked down the dock and right aboard the boat.

"Where's the skipper?" he asked.

"Right here," said a raspy voice, and a large man in a Captain's hat stepped out of the cabin. He wore khaki pants and a long-sleeved khaki shirt. He looked about sixty, but he still looked in good shape. If he was surprised to see Rich, he didn't show it.

"Well, if it isn't Rich Skowronski," he said. "What brings you down here to Florida? Don't tell me you're on a vacation?"

"Why not?" asked Rich. "Things are kind of slow at home this time of year."

"Who's this?" asked Rolf, looking at me.

"This is Peter Gordon. He's from North Beach too."

"So you're my charter party? I thought there was to be three."

"The other guy's a little delayed," said Rich. "Actually we're really not interested in fishing."

"No?" Rolf's eyes narrowed. "Then what are you interested in?"

"Norman Hawkins."

"What about him?"

"We're looking for people who might have seen him the night he died."

There was the faintest flicker in Jacobsen's eyes, but no more.

"We'll, you've come a long way for nothing. I was taking the boat south when all that happened."

"Anyone with you?"

"Some kid I picked up. He was going to mate for me down here, but he took off the minute we got in. I had to scramble to get Ronnie here."

"This kid have a name?"

"Who knows from names? Joe something. I don't know. The kid was a pick-up off the dock. He's just as well gone. He didn't know shit."

"So what was the date you left?"

"How should I remember? All I know is, when I got here . . . ."

Suddenly he stopped in mid-sentence. He was looking up on the pontoon dock, his eyes wide. Rich and I both looked to see what had caught his attention, and in that instant, he bolted. In one step he was up on the transom and vaulting to the pontoon dock. At his first step, I tried to reach for him, but he was too quick. Rolf landed on the dock and staggered for a moment as the dock went down taking his weight. He regained his balance and started to run towards the far gangway. Before he could take two steps, Harry appeared beside him and gave him the slickest hip check I ever saw. It was just enough to push Rolf off course. He stumbled again, couldn't stop himself and went headfirst into the little strip of water between the pontoon dock and the bulkhead.

"Goddamn it Harry," Rich was yelling. "I thought I told you to stay up on the pier."

"You did Chief. But I thought maybe a little stirring up was just what our Captain here needed."

By now Rolf had surfaced and thrown an arm up on the dock.

"Now, Captain," said Harry. "I'm Norman Hawkins, Jr. But I guess you knew that, didn't you?"

"I don't know nothing," spluttered Jacobsen.

By this time Rich had followed Rolf by jumping to the transom and from there to the dock. I took the more traditional route, and by the time I got there, Rich was yelling at Harry again. Harry continued to watch Rolf in the water. He answered quite calmly. "OK, OK, You told me all that, but I thought this slime ball needed his composure pricked a little."

"You thought? You thought? Where the hell do you get off thinking in all this?"

Rolf took this opportunity to try to climb back up on the dock. Harry put his foot firmly on Rolf's shoulder and pushed him back.

"I think you ought to stay right there until the police come." He turned and addressed the mate on the boat next to "Justine". "Hey you," he called. "Go call the police." The guy just stood there staring. "Do it now!" Something in Harry's tone galvanized the man into action. He jumped off his boat and fairly flew down the dock towards the phone. Rich fumed until the police came, but then he became immediately professional, flashing his badge and talking earnestly to the officers. Together, we fished Rolf out of the water. While we had been waiting he had been completely silent. As the officers started to take him off, he started to complain loudly. Rich turned to us.

"You guys better head back to the hotel. I'm going to be awhile."

He was. Harry and I walked around the docks and looked at the boats for about an hour, then parked ourselves by the pool. We sat for some time watching the bathers, before I spoke.

"That was a nice little move you threw on Rolf."

He looked at me. "You think I'm a useless jerk, too, don't you?"

"No, I don't," I protested.

"Sure you do. People have been underestimating me all my life."

"Is that why you joined the RTTR?"

"Mary was why I joined. I was so in love with her. But it was partly to spite the old man too. Or at least to get him to pay attention to me."

"But it got a little more complicated once you were in?"

He nodded. "Those guys play for keeps. Mary and I have been trying to get clear of them for over a year." He laughed. "My father didn't need to de-program me. He just needed to talk to me."

"Why didn't you just leave? Your father could have kept them away from you."

"It's not so simple. I wasn't about to ask him for help. That would have been the same old pattern. Dad has to help stupid me out of another jam. Anyway, Reynaud never let both of us out at the same time."

"Until right before your father was killed."

He nodded. "That's right. Mary and I couldn't believe they would do that. We had our chance to break free."

Some chance, I thought. Orchestrated by Fagin and Beck to get at Harry's father. It was just then that Rich called. The pool attendant found us, and I took the call.

"He may be ready to deal," said Rich.

"What have we got?"

"I think we can get Beck. It's all been hypothetical up to now. The DA back in New Jersey is negotiating a deal with his lawyer now."

"That was quick."

"Yeah. He wasn't such a tough nut as I thought he'd be. He wants to talk to Harry."

"Harry? Why?"

"I don't know. Just get down here."

Twenty minutes later we were walking into a drab interview room at the Fort Lauderdale police department. Rolf was sitting behind a plain table in the middle of the little room. A single chair was opposite him. He was wearing a prison cover-all in place of his wet khakis. His hair was still wet. He looked up at me suspiciously.

"What's he doing here?"

"He's with me," said Harry, sitting down in the empty chair. "If it wasn't for him, I wouldn't be here at all."

Rolf seemed to deflate. He shrugged his shoulders.

"You wanted to see me?" asked Harry.

"Yeah. I wanted to tell you how sorry I am about all this."

"Sorry you killed my father?"

He flinched as though he had been hit.

"I had no idea that was going to happen."

"Why don't you tell us what did happen?" I asked.

He looked over at Rich.

"Is my deal set?"

"Just a minute."

Rich stepped out of the room, and we sat silently, waiting. Or at least Rolf and Harry did. I stood trying to restrain the impulse to pace impatiently around the little room. Ten minutes later a squirrelly little guy with black, slicked back hair came into the room. He crossed and whispered into Rolf's ear. Rolf whispered back. They seemed to be having an argument. Finally, the guy made a motion like he was washing his hands of the matter, turned and left the room. He hadn't so much as given us a glance. As he stepped out the door, Rich came in, closed the door and stood with his back to it.

"That's it then," said Rolf. He looked at Harry and smiled apologetically. "My lawyer doesn't want me to talk to you at all, but what do lawyers know?"

"So tell me what you called me over here for," said Harry.

"This whole thing has been driving me crazy ever since that night."

"The night my father was killed?"

"Yeah, that night. I was getting the boat ready to go south. This was in the evening. The night before your father . . . . Anyway, this big guy came down the dock and said he wanted a charter. I told him it was a little late in the season. He said he wasn't interested in fishing, he wanted to rescue a friend of his who'd been kidnapped."

"What was the guy's name?" I asked.

"I don't know. He said Al Smith. I don't think that was his real name, do you?"

I turned to look at Rich. He made a gesture that I should wait. I turned back to Rolf.

"And this was Thursday night?" I asked. "Are you sure?"

"I don't know what night it was. It was the night before we went out. We went out at about ten the next night."

I was about to say more, but thought better of it. Harry gestured for Rolf to go on.

"Well, he said this kid who was a friend of his had been kidnapped, and they were going to do this de-programming thing on him at sea. He wanted to charter my boat to get the kid back."

"How were you going to find the boat at sea?" I asked.

"Smith said they had a guy on the boat with a radio. And we could wait outside the Cranberry Inlet until the boat came out. It was just a sailboat. There was supposed to be just a couple of them on the boat. We could follow with our radar until the guy Smith had on board was alone on watch. Then he would radio us to come in, and we'd take the kid. You've got to understand," he said, talking directly to Harry. "No one was supposed to get hurt."

"Weren't you concerned about the storm?" I asked.

"Sure. I told him it would be tough. In fact I didn't think it could be done. But he promised me cash up front. I met him later that night at the Brielle Grille. He and this woman were having dinner. He gave me the money, or half of it anyway. It was no skin off my nose if he couldn't pull it off."

"Woman? He had a woman with him?"

"Yeah."

"Did you know her?"

"No, it was just some broad."

"So what happened next?"

"I got the boat ready for them the next day and waited. I paid off my mate and told him I wouldn't be needing him any more. At about nine o'clock that night, Smith came aboard with three other guys. We left and went out the Manasquan Inlet and down to wait off Cranberry. We just waited out there rolling our guts out. All the guys except Smith were sick as dogs. Finally, Smith tells me that the boat is coming out. I pick it up on the radar all right, and we follow it for about three hours. I keep asking what are we waiting for, but Smith tells me to shut up. We're riding a little easier on the course we're on, and the goons that Smith had are feeling a little better. It was blowing like hell, and the rain felt like a fire-hose. Then we get a distress call over the radio. Smith says, 'That's it,' and tells me to move in. I find the boat without any trouble, but this is the first time I see that it's 'Far Cry.'"

"You knew Norman Hawkins?"

"No, but I knew the boat. It's been in at Brielle plenty of times. I'd done some drinking with Louie at some of the local bars."

"Did you tell Smith that you recognized the boat?"

"Hell no. I was getting a little concerned about the demeanor of those guys. You know what I mean?"

"I have an idea. What happened next?"

"I got Smith up close enough to hail. The boat had lost its mast. By the time we got there they had most of the rig cut away. I guess there was some trouble with the engine. Smith said we would take them in tow. We got them hooked up, and Smith told me to head for Cape May. We could make about four knots. There was a following sea, and the tow rode kept slackening and snapping tight. I asked Smith what the plan was, but he just told me to shut up. We went on for about an hour, when I guess Smith got another call over the radio. They cut the towline, and Smith told me to take them alongside. I said that the weather was too bad, and that's when he pulled a gun." He shrugged. "I got them alongside. There was one guy topside on 'Far Cry', who was helping them out. He took a line, and the three goons managed to get aboard. Smith stayed right there with the gun on me. I tried to keep the boats from banging too much. Pretty soon the goons came back on deck with . . . ." He looked at Harry. "With you in tow. I got the boat alongside again, and they all got on board. Along with the other guy that had been on the boat. He got on, too. They cast off and took you down below. Smith told me to get out of there."

"What about my father?" asked Harry.

"I didn't see him, or Louie."

"Are you sure?" I asked. "Someone must have pushed him overboard."

"If they did, I didn't see it."

I looked quickly at Rich. He made a motion with his hand that I took to mean not to press the point.

"Where did Smith have you go?" I asked.

"In Barnegat Inlet. We had to lay off the inlet for a couple of hours, until full light, before we could get in. Smith kept threatening me, but I wasn't going to shoot that inlet in the dark with the way the weather was. As it was, when we did go in, it scared the shit out of him. Scared me a little too, those following rollers coming over the transom."

"Where'd you go?"

"They told me to go up the Forked River. There was a little house on the water and a little dock. We tied up and they took Harry off. Smith and this other guy were having an argument. They took it up to the house. They told me to stay put, but then I guess they must have forgot me. I waited for about half an hour, and then I just untied the lines and got out of there."

"Leaving the rest of your money?" I asked, sarcastically.

"You're Goddamn right. Money or no, I didn't want to be part of that operation any more. I left and headed for Florida." He talked directly to Harry. "It wasn't until I got down here that I heard about your father. I swear I never saw him on that boat. Or Louie, for that matter. I guess those goons must have slugged him down below. I didn't see it."

"But you were scared enough to bug out without your money."

He looked directly at me. "You didn't see this guy."

"Who, Smith?"

"Yeah. He was one scary guy. When he had me by the throat and the gun pointed at my head, I knew he would shoot me as easily as he was breathing. The only reason he didn't was he needed me to drive the boat. On the way in, I made a promise to myself that I would bail out as soon as I could. And I did."

"Could you find that house again?"

"From the water? Sure, no problem."

"Why didn't you call the police when you got down here?" I asked.

"When I found out about Hawkins and then Louie, I was even more scared. I figured Smith would want to shut me up."

"So why didn't you just disappear?"

"I got to make a living. This is as good a place as any. I figured if I smelled something I could be out at sea in no time."

I looked around at Rich. He jerked his head towards the door. We got up and went out into the corridor with him.

"That's about all I got from him," he said.

"How'd you get him to talk?"

"A combination of bluff that I knew more than I did and threats to let him go with enough publicity to get the bad guys down on him. Then I got the DA on the horn and we worked out a deal."

"What's he going to get?"

"If his story checks out, and we get Beck, he'll get a walk."

"You figure Smith is Beck?"

"It was Beck all right. I had his picture faxed down, and Rolf here identified him. And the other guy was Fagin. Rolf jumped on his picture as well."

"But who killed my dad?" asked Harry.

"That's one string we need to tie up. I pressed him hard on that, but he never wavered from the story he told you. He couldn't identify anybody on the boat when he first came up to make up the tow. And later he saw Fagin and then you. That's it."

"You believe him?" I asked. "It doesn't hold water from what I can tell. From where Norman washed ashore, Rolf must have taken them back to Cranberry Inlet to dump him before going in Barnegat."

"I don't know. He could be just trying to limit his involvement by lying about that part. Or Fagin could have pushed Norman over just after they cleared the inlet."

"No way," said Harry. "My father was aboard that boat when we lost the mast. I helped him cut the rig away. Then we all went down below. Fagin volunteered to drive while we were being towed."

Rich's eyes narrowed. I could see he was angry.

"Let's go talk to Rolf one more time," he said.

We walked back into the room. Rolf looked up in surprise.

"Deal's off Rolf," said Rich.

"You can't do that," said Rolf.

"The hell I can't. It's a condition of our deal that you tell the truth. You haven't told us about Norman yet."

"I told you everything I know."

"Well, either you're lying or Harry here is. And I guess if I had to pick the liar, I'd pick you."

"What does he say?"

"He says that his father was on the boat when you took them in tow and when your pals boarded it."

"He might have been. I don't know. It was dark. They could have pitched him over, and I didn't see it."

Rich had been angry up to this point, but now he lowered his voice and adopted a friendlier tone.

"But that's not what happened, is it Rolf? They brought Norman aboard your boat too, didn't they?"

"No, I've told you."

"How many miles at sea do you figure you were at this point?"

"I don't know, thirty or thirty-five."

"Thirty or thirty-five. And a good bit south of the Cranberry Inlet, wouldn't you say?"

"I guess," Rolf agreed, looking wary at the questions.

"Well, Norman had been heading to Florida, and you were towing him to Cape May, so I guess you were heading in a southerly direction, isn't that right?"

He shrugged. "Yeah."

"And the wind. What was it? East going to northeast during the night, right?"

"I don't pay much attention to the wind."

"Well, we can find out easily enough. So, how do you explain that Norman's body washed up on shore some time on Saturday night right at North Beach when it started out thirty miles to the south and a north wind blowing. You see my problem, Rolf?" Rich's voice had risen again and the tone of anger had returned.

Rolf looked at the table. "I can't account for the currents out there," he said sullenly.

Rich lowered his voice again. "Rolf, we're not stupid. You can tell us. We have to know. You can still have the deal, unless you pushed him in the water yourself. You didn't do that, did you Rolf?"

He shook his head.

"Speak up Rolf. I have to hear you say it."

"No," he said.

"But you saw Smith do it."

He nodded.

"Say it Rolf."

Rolf looked up for the first time. "I still have my deal?"

"I said so, didn't I?"

"Yeah. But it wasn't Smith. It was one of the other goons. It's like you said. They brought him aboard and they threw him in the cockpit. Smith told me to take them back to North Beach. When we got there, they just up and threw him in."

He stopped.

"Was he still alive? I asked.

"Yeah. He had a bump on the head but he was still breathing."

"All right," said Rich. His voice sounded tired. "We'll get the stenographer in here for a supplemental statement."

He waved us to the door. In the hall I stopped him.

"One thing I still don't understand."

"What's that?"

"Reynaud told me that he had a call from Fagin to pick up Harry on the Garden State Parkway. There was no mention of Beck being involved."

"Either Reynaud's lying or he didn't know that Beck was part of the plan."

I sat and thought a moment. "So we know that Beck and Fagin were working together. When we went to Fagin, he panicked and went right to Beck to tell him. Beck figured Fagin was a weak reed and had him killed on the way back. Suppose Reynaud doesn't know Beck's part in this? What's his game?"

"Take-over of RTTR?"

"That's an interesting thought. But why take Harry back to California?"

"Because Richard has to appear like he's still working for Reynaud. And he's got his own plan to discredit the Archon. And suppose he's decided that he wants to take over Hawkins Industries just as much as Reynaud did. He takes over RTTR, and he comes into control of all the Hawkins stock it controls. And with Hawkins dead, no one is standing in his way except Wilf. I think he figured he could handle Wilf. He winds up with the whole pie."

"You think so?" I asked. "I can see Richard wanting control of the RTTR, but somehow I don't see him in the role of corporate mover and shaker. Plus, we're no nearer to a way to wrestle control of Norman's shares out of Brunell's hands."

"Well, we've all got our problems," said Rich. "I don't know what you guys are going to do, but I'm going to take Rolf back to New Jersey. We'll see if he can find this house and if anything turns up there."

"Meanwhile, what about Beck?"

"Disappeared. The last time anyone's seen him that I know about was you while he was burning down Norman's house in Virginia. We've got an all points out on him."

"I think Reynaud is looking for him as well."

"Yeah, I know. And I think Beck should hope it's us who catch him."

Harry and I headed back to the hotel while Rich stayed at the police station to clean up the final details of transferring Rolf to New Jersey. I was feeling strangely depressed. We had worked out the details of how Norman had been drowned, but it was as if the curtain had come down just before the final scene. We knew how he had gone into the water, but I doubted we would ever find out why. And, we were no closer to getting Brunell out of Hawkins Industries. I considered our limited options in silence until we had pulled into the gate at Bahia Mar and parked the car.

"What's the matter?" asked Harry. I didn't want to burden him with my thoughts, such as they were, but, if I was really his lawyer, he had a right to my views.

"I just don't see how we get you control of your father's estate, and control of the company, without a long court battle."

"What do you mean by long?"

"I mean years. And maybe a lot of them. Brunell is both executor of your father's estate and trustee under the trusts set up under that will."

"You mean the trust that keeps the shares from me as long as I'm a member of RTTR?"

"Yes."

"But I no longer have anything to do with RTTR."

"That's not what Brunell will claim. He'll claim that your separation is only a ruse to defeat the terms of the trust. Who knows? With what we know about Beck's involvement, he may claim that you were part of the plan to kill your father and try to get you disinherited for good."

"But that's outrageous."

I shrugged. "There's a lot of money involved. Then there's Lorraine."

"What about her? I thought Dad did a new will to cut her out."

"Maybe he did, but they weren't divorced yet. She might try to take against the will. She could claim up to one-third of the estate even if she gets nothing out of the will. That's why the deal with Reynaud was so attractive. It gave you the ability to control the company while all this was being sorted out. Now Brunell will have control, and that's a big advantage."

"So none of this thing with Rolf helps us?"

"Well, it helps you to be able to sort out what happened that night, but it doesn't do much else."

"And I still don't know who pushed Dad in that water."

"Well, we know it was Fagin or Beck who ordered it. But we don't know why, other than pure cussedness."

"It can't be that," he said. "What would have been the point of taking him all the way back to Cranberry Inlet to push him in?"

I got my key from the desk and there was a message from Jane. It said urgent. I called from a pay phone in the lobby. The phone rang in Jerry's house, and Steve answered. He put Jane on the line.

"Pete, is that you?"

"Yes."

"Thank God I found you."

"What is it?"

"Jerry's going. I don't think he'll make it through the night."

"I'm sorry. What can I do?"

"I think I need you."

"I'll be on the next flight."

"I don't have the right to ask that of you."

"I'm just glad you did."

"Good. I . . . ." she hesitated.

"I know," I said. "We'll talk when I get out there. I'll call you when I have the schedule."

"Is Harry there with you?"

"Yes."

"Put him on."

She talked with Harry for about twenty minutes. When he got off he was silent for a long time.

"You know," he finally said. "I haven't even seen Jerry in years."

"I know," I said.

He just sat there staring off into space.

"So are you going to go now?" I asked.

He looked up at me with a jerk. "Yes. I think I want to see him now. And, besides, I think the next chapter is going to be in California anyway. I think it's time I saw Bob Reynaud again."

Chapter XIV

We got a plane out of Miami early the next morning. It got us to LAX at about noon. We rented a car and got to Jerry's apartment before two. I parked the car and looked up at the window. Jane buzzed us up and was waiting at the door. I gave her a hug, and she clung to me and then to Harry.

"How is he?" I asked.

"He's drifting in and out. He's been out most of the day." She led us into the living room.

"Where's Steve?"

"He's sitting with Jerry."

"How are you doing?"

"I don't know. I thought I was all right until you got here. I just want his pain to be over."

"Can we see him?" I asked.

"Yes, but one at a time."

"You go ahead first, Harry," I said. "Let me catch up with Jane here."

Harry looked like he would just as soon have me go in, but he nodded and went towards the back. Jane and I sat down on the couch, but there didn't seem to be much to say. I picked up her hand and held it, and we just sat there. In about a half an hour Harry came out.

"Was he awake?" asked Jane.

"Just for a few moments. Then he drifted off again."

We all sat together for some time and then Harry announced he was going off to find a motel. Then it was my turn to go and visit Jerry, and I was as reluctant as Harry had been. I walked back towards the bedroom and went inside. One lamp was lit on the dresser that afforded a dim light in the room. Steve was sitting at the head of the bed. He looked up to see me come in and gave a little wave. The atmosphere seemed heavy and oppressive. Jerry was lying on his back with his eyes half open. He was breathing intermittently and heavily.

"How's he doing?" I whispered.

"No need to whisper," said Steve. "Sometimes he gets a lucid period, but mostly he's been like this for the last twenty-four hours."

"You've just been sitting here watching him?"

"Well, actually, I've been talking to him and playing some of the music that he likes. Do you want to take a turn?"

"He can't hear you, can he?"

"I think he can. The doctor said the body would begin to go, but the mind would still be active. We should keep talking to him right to the end. I have the feeling that he's down at the bottom of a well, and I'm at the top talking down to him. He can't respond, but he hears me as if I'm at some great distance. Every once in a while, he squeezes my hand." He shrugged. "Maybe it's all baloney, but it makes me feel better to think it, and if it's true, then he's not alone in his last hours."

"Why don't you take a break, and I'll talk to him for a while."

I sat down and started to talk. I didn't know what to talk about. I just started to talk about myself. Steve listened for a few minutes and then got up to go into the living room. Pretty soon, I began to tell the story of his father and brother. Norman Hawkins, father and son. I started with that Friday afternoon that the father had come into my office and traced the story down to my present dilemma. How to make sure that Harry stayed free of the charges on Congressman Renfrow, and how to beat Wilfred Brunell? In the telling, I picked up a new perspective on my own motivations for meddling in the affairs of the Hawkins family. Maybe it had started with the too much money that Norman had laid out on the table, and continued with my curiosity to get to the bottom of a puzzle, but those were all by the board now. I had most of the story, and the money was an incidental. But two things were continuing to drive me. One was Brunell. There was no way I was going to quit and leave him in command of the field. The other was my growing feeling for other members of the Hawkins family. I hadn't much liked Harry at first, but he had started to grow on me. And I had also begun to feel something for his sister. And the telling, and my concentration on Brunell, kindled a memory, the significance of which I had not appreciated before. We had only assumed that Fagin had run to talk to Beck when he had gone into the Hawkins Building. Wilfred Brunell was in that building as well. Wilfred had two offices in that building, one at Hawkins Industries and the other at his law firm. Maybe the elusive parts of the puzzle remained elusive because I was not casting my net broad enough.

I was close to the end of my story. I was savoring the deliciousness of these new possibilities when I heard a loud crash from the other room. I jumped up just as I heard Jane scream. I stepped to the door and there was my worst nightmare. Steve was on the floor holding his hand to his head. A man all in black had Jane in a hammerlock. And there, in the doorway, stood Richard Beck with a large pistol in his hand and a smile on his face.

"Come in and sit down, Pete," he said waving towards the couch with his gun. The man holding Jane pushed her down on the same couch. Beck stepped inside and closed the door behind him. I could see the doorjamb was splintered. Someone must have just burst the door.

"Move it," said Beck in a more peremptory tone of voice. I moved and went to sit beside Jane.

"You," he said to Steve. "You get over there as well."

Steve pushed himself across the floor so that his back was against the couch. Jane bent down to look at his wound.

"Leave him," said Beck. "He'll be all right. Chuck, take a look in the next room."

"There's . . ." I started.

"Shut up," he said. "You can speak when you're spoken to."

Chuck went to the back of the apartment and, in a moment, was back whispering in Beck's ear. I thought he looked a little sick. Beck nodded and went back to look for himself. He was back inside of a minute.

"Is that your brother back there?" he asked.

"Yes," answered Jane.

"How interesting," he said. "You mean the great Jerry Hawkins has come to this?" He laughed meanly. "You know the main problem about AIDS?" He continued. None of us answered. "It's not working fast enough." He laughed again. "But I'm not here about washed up faggots. I'm looking for your other brother. Little Norman, Jr. Where is he?"

"I don't know," I said. "How did you know I was here?"

"Easy. We've been watching the apartment. We knew as long as your little chickadee was here, you'd come back, or she'd lead us to you."

"What do you want with me?" I wondered how they had missed Harry.

"Well, you're a little pest. But I really would like to talk to little Normie."

"Why?"

"I have a proposition to make to him."

"Why don't you tell me what it is? I'm his attorney. I'll see that it gets passed along."

"With all due respect, counselor, I'd like to pass it along personally."

"I don't know where he is."

"I think you do."

"So what are you going to do?" I asked. "Beat it out of me?"

He smiled. "Actually no." He gestured at Jane, and his buddy, Chuck, came over and pulled her off the couch and into the middle of the room. There he whirled her around into a hammerlock and faced her towards me. She didn't cry out, but I could see her face was white.

"What's it going to be counselor?" He nodded at Chuck, and Jane gave a quick gasp.

"All right," I said. "All right. I'll tell you whatever you want to know."

"Good. Although Chuck here might be a little disappointed."

"Let her go, and I'll tell you whatever you want to know." I could hear the desperation in my voice. I'm sure Beck could hear it as well. He smiled.

"Chuck will hang on to her for the moment in case you have any more 'I don't know answers.'"

A cold fear took me. "I may not know everything."

"Then it will be too bad for your friend's arm, won't it? Now tell me where he is. Is he back at your place in North Beach?"

For a moment a light of hope surged through me. They had missed him. I looked quickly in Beck's face and something there made me sense the trap. "Ah . . . no, he's not." I said.

"Good. You can see it won't pay to lie to me. Was that him that drove you up here and then left?"

"Yes."

"Where did he go?"

"Look, Richard," I stalled. "I think you should know that the police are on to you. Your best bet is just to disappear."

"Oh really? Are they going to come and beat the door down again and effect a heroic rescue? I don't think so."

"I don't think so either, but they know about you being on the 'Justine.'"

I could see the name of the boat rocked him a little.

"What are you talking about?" he asked.

"Harry and I just came from Fort Lauderdale. The police have Rolf Jacobsen in custody, and he's singing like a bird. He thinks your name is Smith, but he picked your picture out. Yours and Ernie Fagin's, by the way."

"Nonsense. A pack of lies cooked up between him and Fagin."

"I see. So you do know him. And Fagin."

"Sure, I know Fagin. De-programmer extraordinaire. Or, at least if you hear him tell it."

"He's not telling it to too many people now, is he?"

His eyes narrowed. "No, he's not."

"You see your problem, Richard. Too many bodies, and your name connected with all of them in one way or another. But, I think I would be more concerned that your former boss, the Archon Reynaud, will find you. I don't think he'll be so observant of the constitutional niceties, do you?"

Beck sat down and said nothing for about five minutes. Chuck continued to stand there holding Jane in an awkward position. I could see little beads of perspiration had formed at her hairline. The room suddenly seemed hot and oppressive. Finally Beck seemed to come to a decision. He got up from the chair as if it were a great effort.

"Let's get back to business," he said. "Where's little Harry?"

"Richard," I said, desperate now. "It's no good. Leave us here. Tie us up somehow. The best thing for you is to get away without . . . ."

I never got to finish my sentence. He took one large step across the room and backhanded me across the face. At least, that's what Jane told me later. As far as I was concerned, one moment I was talking and the next moment I was lying back against the sofa with my hand at my cheek and bells ringing in my head. I opened my eyes, and there was Beck's face right against mine.

"I'm not interested in any more of this shit, asshole. Tell me where he is, or Chuck breaks her arm, right now!"

"OK," I said. "He's in a hotel on the beach. Not more than fifteen minutes from here."

"What's the name?"

I gave him the name of a big hotel in Marina del Rey, and he straightened up.

"He won't be using his right name," I volunteered.

"What name is he using?" Beck's face was in mine again.

"I don't know. I don't know."

He grabbed me by the neck. "How in hell are you going to get in touch with him if you don't know what name he's using."

"I wasn't going to get in touch with him. He was going to come by tomorrow morning. There was no reason to get in touch with him."

"How do you suggest we find him then?"

"He just checked in. It shouldn't be too difficult."

"You better be right."

Suddenly his face was no longer in mine, and he was giving instructions to Chuck. Then he was back.

"Chuck is going to stay here to make sure you don't get any heroic ideas. If you've been lying to me, you're going to be the sorriest puppy that ever shit on the living room rug. Do you understand what I'm saying to you?"

"Yes."

"Good. I don't want any of you to move until I'm back."

He said a few more words to Chuck, and then he was gone. Chuck pulled one of the dining room chairs into the middle of the room and turned it around to sit on it, resting his hands and the gun on the back of the chair. He was trying to look nonchalant, but he seemed to be strangely uneasy. I thought I knew why. I let the silence grow for some minutes, and then I started.

"Say Chuck," I said.

"Shut up."

"Ever seen an AIDS patient before tonight?"

He licked his lips and looked around the room as if Jerry would somehow appear. "I told you to shut up."

"All right, but Steve here needs to go and adjust Jerry's medicine."

"No one's going anywhere."

"Well, if we don't he's going to wake up and be in pain."

He tried to imitate Beck's laugh, but he couldn't quite pull it off.

"What do I care? He's just an old queer."

"Actually, he's not that old," I said. "I think he's about forty. How old are you Chuck? You couldn't be more than twenty-five yourself."

"That's none of your business."

"Of course not. But look. If Jerry wakes up and is in pain, he's going to start yelling for Steve and making a lot of noise. And the neighbors are going to start wondering what's the matter."

"Or maybe he'll get on the phone and start calling people," said Steve.

"There's a phone in there?" asked Chuck.

"Sure."

"Well that settles it. You think I'm stupid, don't you? No one's going in there where there's a phone."

"We can all go in," I suggested. "Steve really has to adjust the medicine."

"No one's leaving this room."

"OK," I said. And I let it ride for about a few minutes. Then I started in again.

"You're not afraid, are you Chuck?"

"What?"

"You're not afraid to go in there again, are you?"

"That's crazy. Why would I be afraid?"

"You really can't catch AIDS from being in the same room with an AIDS patient or even casual contact."

"I know all that."

"So what's the problem?"

"There's no problem. Mr. Beck told us to stay here, and here we're going to stay."

"OK," I said again. I subsided to give him another few minutes to think about it before I tried again. Jane beat me to it. For most of the time since Beck had left, she had been sitting on the couch as if in a trance. As I had started to talk to Chuck, she had started to come out of it, and by this time she was back and following the by-play with interest. Now, before I could start in again, she took over the scene by standing up. Chuck raised the gun.

"Sit down," he said.

"This is stupid," she said. "My brother needs medication, and I'm not going to let him wake up in pain. I'm certainly not going to let your ignorance and cowardice stand in the way."

Without waiting for an answer, she turned and started from the room. Chuck yelled at her and got to his feet, bringing the gun up to bear on her back. The blood was rushing in my ears with a great roaring sound. I got to my feet as well and started to take a step towards Chuck. He saw me out of the corner of his eye, and swung the gun over to cover me. I froze and, for a moment, we stared in each other's eyes. The roaring in my ears reached a crescendo, and all my attention focused on the little black orb of the mouth of that pistol. Suddenly, he swung the gun back towards Jane, but it was too late. Jane was out of the room. He hesitated for a moment, and then he grabbed me by the arm and jammed the gun in my ear. The pain of it rocked me for a moment. He was saying something.

"What?" I croaked.

His voice was a low hiss. "You tell her to get back in here, or I'll splatter your brains all over the wallpaper."

"Chuck, you heard her." It was Steve. "She's going to adjust her brother's medicine. She'll be right back."

Chuck responded by shaking me like a rag doll. "You tell her to get back in here now."

"Look," I said, my voice a little steadier now. "If you're concerned about the phone, let's all just go in there."

He hesitated a moment, not knowing what to do.

"All right," he said, waving the gun at Steve. "Let's go."

Now that he had made the decision, he hustled Steve to his feet and shoved us both ahead of him. We burst into the room and there was Jane calmly arranging Jerry's IV lines.

"Where's the phone?" demanded Chuck.

"Over there," said Jane, pointing to the corner of the room. Chuck took one step over to the phone and ripped the line out of the wall.

"That should take care of that," he said. He was trying to look tough and in control, but I could see he was nervous. He kept looking at Jerry and then quickly away.

"Are you finished in here?" he asked.

"Not really," said Jane. "We need to turn him over."

"Do that later," said Chuck. "We're all going back to the living room."

"We're doing it now," she said. "I'm not going to have him get bed sores just because you're squeamish."

Chuck opened his mouth to say something and then closed it again. Jane stood glaring at him for a moment and then bent to the task. Steve and I moved over to help. I got under Jerry's hips, while Steve took the weight off his shoulders. He weighed almost nothing. We tried to be gentle, but he cried out as I bumped his butt on the bed. He groaned as we settled him down on his right side. I looked up, and Chuck had disappeared.

"Big hero," laughed Jane.

"Quick," I said. "He'll be back soon." I looked around the room for a weapon. The only thing I could see was a heavy lamp on the bureau.

"Steve. You pick up the phone and pretend to be talking on it."

"But it's dis . . . ."

"Just do it." I looked at Jane. "Jane, you stand away from him on the other side of the bed."

"What are you going to do?" she asked.

I took up a position between the bureau and the open door with my hand around the neck of the lamp and my back against the wall. "I'm going to try to break his head with this lamp."

And so we waited. It couldn't have been very long, but it seemed like time was standing still. The only sound was Jerry's heavy breathing. He would take a ragged breath, and then there would be a long silence until he took another.

"Hey," yelled Chuck from the other room. "What's going on in there?"

I motioned that no one should answer.

"Answer me," he yelled. "What are you doing in there?"

There was a long silence. I pressed my back against the wall. I could feel the sweat beading at my hairline and running down my back. I felt enormously exposed right beside the door. Then Chuck was in the doorway.

"What the . . ."

He saw Steve with the phone in his ear, and he started to raise the gun. It seemed to me that I was watching the slow rise of the gun from some far distance, as if through the wrong end of a telescope. The proportions of the room seemed suddenly all wrong. I had intended to hit him in the head. But without even seeming to will it, my arm swung in a long arc and came down on Chuck's hand and the rising gun. At the contact, everything returned to normal speed. The gun clattered to the floor. I tried to pull back my arm to hit him again, but, before I could recover, Chuck stepped inside and grabbed me around the throat, slamming me back against the wall. I dropped the lamp and tried to pull his fingers from my throat. I might as well have been pulling at steel bands. I started to get weaker. Suddenly, there was a loud explosion and a shout in the background. The hands loosened from my neck and fell away. I slid to the floor.

I must have blacked out for a moment, because someone was pulling at my arm. I shook my head and opened my eyes. Jane was bending down over me.

"Are you all right?"

"I think so. Where's Chuck?"

"Steve's got him in the living room."

"Is he all right?"

"I should think so. Steve's got the gun this time."

I shook my head again and rubbed my neck.

"Does Steve know how to use a gun?"

"Yes. Apparently he's an ex-Marine. Or as he says, 'Once a Marine, always a Marine.'"

I struggled to get up. "A Marine? Why in hell wasn't he the one trying to bash Chuck in the head. At least, he might have known what he was doing."

I stood on my feet and immediately the room started to spin. I reached out to Jane for support.

"What happened?"

"After you hit him on the arm, Chuck went crazy. I thought he was going to choke you to death. All the time he was yelling like a wild man. I was screaming. Suddenly, Steve was there at his shoulder, and he shot off the gun right in his ear. He must have scooped it up off the floor. He dragged Chuck off you and put the gun right up under his nose." She laughed. "Chuck calmed down real fast after that. Steve hustled him into the next room, and here we are."

"Well, let's go see about what we do next."

I rubbed my neck again and followed Jane into the living room. Chuck was sitting on the same chair that he had occupied before, except this time it was not reversed. His arms were pulled behind the back of the chair and his hands were tied with what looked like extension cord. Steve was sitting on the sofa with the gun balanced on his knee.

"You OK?" he asked.

"Yeah, I think so. Thanks for pulling this guy off of me."

"Thanks for knocking the gun out of his hand. It took you long enough. So what do we do now? Call the police?"

"Maybe I have a better idea." I went across the room, picked up the phone and dialed a private number that I had committed to memory. A woman answered. I hesitated and looked over at Chuck.

"Who is this?" asked the woman.

"One moment," I said and gestured for Jane to take the phone. I told her to stay on the line and quickly went into the kitchen to pick up the portable.

"Sorry for the delay," I said. "I'd like to speak to Bob Reynaud, please."

"Who wishes to speak to the Archon?"

"Tell him it's Pete Gordon, and it's important."

"I'm afraid the Archon is engaged at the moment."

I lowered my voice and spoke as urgently as I could. "Well if he's engaged, then get him unengaged. I need to talk to him on a matter that is of the utmost importance to him, right now. Nothing he could be doing is as important as this. Do you understand?"

"I'll speak to him," she said. In a few minutes Reynaud came on the line.

"Peter," he said. "This call had better be to tell me that you have everything set on our deal."

"Actually, it's not," I said. "It's on a different subject."

"I can't imagine what other subject I would want to talk to you about."

"How about the subject of Richard Beck."

There was a silence at the other end of the line. I waited.

"What about Richard?"

"Suppose I could tell you where to find him?"

"You mean now?"

"I mean in the next half hour."

"Suppose you could?"

"Actually I can. Here's the deal. You let the kid off on the murder rap. That guy who's in jail did it, right?"

"So I am led to believe."

"So he takes the fall, and Beck ordered him to do it." I paused. "And I tell you where to find Beck."

"What about the deal with Brunell and the shares?"

"I'll still try to deliver on that. I've got my own reasons for wanting to pursue it. But if I can't, I can't. None of it reflects on the kid."

"I'd have to trust you on that?"

"Unfortunately, we both have to trust each other. It's kind of a prisoner's dilemma. But if we do trust each other, we get the result we both want. Or, we get the best shot at it."

There was a silence. I began to sweat again. "OK," he said. "Where's Richard?"

"One last thing. On your negotiations with Brunell."

"Who said I'm negotiating with Brunell?"

"Bob, what do you think I am? Stupid?"

He laughed. "All right. You want me to cut off contact with Brunell, right?"

"Actually no. I want you to keep on negotiating with him. I just don't want you to agree."

He laughed again, harder now. "That won't be hard. The son-of-a-bitch wants the sun and the moon and the stars."

"So, don't give them to him. But I don't want you to suddenly cut off contact. He'll wonder why."

"You got it. Now, where's Richard?"

I told him, hung up the phone and went back into the living room.

I pulled Jane over to the window, where I could look out, and Chuck couldn't hear. There was nothing unusual going on in the street.

"Reynaud's going to send a team here to get Beck."

"How soon?"

"They're coming from the ranch. It will take about an hour."

"But that will be too late. Beck's sure to be back here by then."

"I know."

"Where did you send him?"

"The Ritz Carlton down in Marina del Rey."

"But he could be there and back in forty minutes. He might be back at any moment."

"Probably not. It's going to take him a while to figure out that Harry's not there."

"So you're betting that Reynaud's guys get here first?"

"You got a better idea?"

"Sure. Call the cops."

"I know. But then it wouldn't be over. They don't have enough on Beck to hold him for very long."

"Sure they do. I thought you had a witness that put him on the boat that night."

"He puts him at the scene, but he doesn't know who put your father in the water."

She looked at me, and her eyes were like marbles. "And you think that Reynaud will have something more permanent in mind for him, is that it?"

I shrugged. "I don't know what Reynaud has in mind."

"The hell you don't."

I thought back to that day in North Beach when Beck had nonchalantly ordered that kid to drive his hand through my window. His eyes had never wavered from my face. It had been a chilling and purposeful display of his willingness to use violence to get what he wanted.

"The police can't protect us," I said. "Yes, Reynaud's will be a permanent solution. Whether he kills him or eliminates his power base in the party or puts him back in his place in the fold, it will be a solution that takes Beck out of the game. The police can't give us that in time to matter."

"How do you know you can trust Reynaud?"

"I don't know it. There are no guarantees. My gut tells me this is our best shot, so I'm going with it."

"OK, OK," she said. "Let go of my arm."

I looked down and realized I had grabbed hold of her arm as I was talking. I let go.

"Sorry, I didn't mean to get so intense."

The phone rang. I stood and watched it as if it were a pit viper. There was nothing to do but answer it. I picked up the receiver praying it would not be Beck at the other end. It was Harry. A great feeling of relief washed through me.

"Harry," I said. "Where are you? Wait, don't tell me." I held the phone away from my ear and looked at Chuck. I could hear Harry talking faintly in the background. I motioned to Jane.

"Get the portable phone and hold it up to Chuck's ear."

"What?"

"Get the portable phone. I want Chuck to hear something."

I waited until she had gotten the phone from the kitchen. She turned it on and held it up to his ear. I got back on my own line.

"Can you hear me, Chuck?" I asked.

"What's going on?" asked Harry.

"Harry, this is very important. Please do not say anything unless I ask you a question, OK?"

"If you say so."

"Chuck. Can you hear all right?"

Chuck grunted an affirmative.

"OK, Harry. Do not under any circumstances say where you are. Richard Beck was here, and he's looking for you."

"What? How . . . ."

"Don't talk yet. One of Richard's little buddies is on the line."

"Does he have a gun on you?"

"Actually no. Quite the contrary. We've got the gun on him. But I want him to hear the answers to a few questions. The first is, do I know where you are?"

"No, of course not. I was just calling to tell you."

"Well, don't tell me. It's better that I don't know. I want you to call me back," I looked at my watch, "in forty-five minutes."

"Shouldn't I come over there?"

"No. Beck will be back. I don't want you here when he comes. But I do want him to be able to talk to you."

"All right, forty-five minutes."

I hung up and looked at Chuck.

"You expect me to believe all that?" he asked sullenly.

"Why not? It's the truth. And all you have to do is tell Beck what he said. You don't have to say you believe it."

I sat down, and we waited. Jane went in to sit with Jerry, who was breathing in an ever more intermittent and ragged fashion. The room began to feel hot and oppressive again. Steve went to open a window. Suddenly, the door banged open, and there was Beck in the doorway. He saw me on the couch and started across the room towards me.

Steve yelled, "Stop." But Beck seemed not to hear. He reached down to jerk me to my feet. I tried to fend off his hands, but he grabbed me by my shirt and had me halfway off of the couch, when he stopped. Steve had apparently crossed the room, and now he had the gun jammed in Richard's ear and was talking to him in a conversational tone of voice.

"Let him go, Richard," he was saying. "I swear, I'll blow your fucking head off in one second if you don't let go and back off."

Beck let go of me, and I fell back to the couch. He straightened up and looked around as if he was coming out of a trance and seeing the room for the first time.

"What the hell?" he asked.

Steve backed away from him, but kept the gun leveled at his head. "Sit down over there." He pointed at an armchair.

"What's going on here?" asked Beck.

By this time, I had regained some of my composure. "The worm's turned a little Richard. Why don't you sit down a moment, and we'll talk some."

He looked at Chuck, tied up in the chair and back at the gun in Steve's hand. He shrugged and walked over to sit in the chair. I looked up to see Jane standing in the doorway to Jerry's room, watching.

"What are you going to do?" he asked. "Call the police? Go ahead. They've got nothing to hold me on. I'll be out before you can get that door fixed." He pointed at the splintered front door. "And I'll be real unhappy that you lied to me about where your buddy Harry was."

"Well, that's true enough. I did lie to you that he was at the Ritz. But the fact of the matter is, I don't know where he is. He did call, however, and I asked him to call back."

His eyes bored into mine, and I could see the hate reflected in them.

"It's been you from the beginning, hasn't it?"

"What do you mean?"

"Interfering. Getting in the way. I was right. I should have taken you out from the first."

"You were right?"

He waved his hand as if it didn't matter. "So you think you have the upper hand? What are you going to do about it?"

Actually, I didn't know what I was going to do about it. My little trick with Chuck and the phone seemed rather silly now. Richard sensed he was regaining control of the situation.

"So you haven't called the police, or they'd have been here while I was off on that wild goose chase. Chuck," he snapped out. "Did they call the police?"

Chuck raised his head up to look at his leader. He had not been able to look at Beck before this.

"No," he said. "I don't think so. But he," he made a gesture towards me with his chin. "He called someone. I don't know who it was. He made the call in the kitchen."

Beck looked at me again. "So you do know where Harry is. You called him."

"I don't think so," said Chuck. "The kid did call later. I know it was him because he put me on the line."

"What for?" asked Beck.

"So I could hear him tell me that no one knows where he is."

"Did you believe it?"

"Not really."

I was happy to let this by-play go on. If Beck thought I had cooked up a fake phone call with Harry, he wouldn't guess whom I had really called. He was now ready to return his attention to me.

"So did you think your little charade was going to fool me? Now I'm certain you know where he is."

"Maybe you are," I said. "But if I knew where he was and called him, the first thing I would have told him to do was to move. In any case, it doesn't matter. He's going to call back in about twenty minutes now."

"So what?"

"It's time to make a deal."

His eyes narrowed. "What kind of a deal?"

"Well, you can't kill Harry now. We know too much. You'd have to kill all of us."

I could see from his eyes that he had already been entertaining this possibility.

"That would be a mistake," I went on.

He smiled and leaned back in his chair.

"Would it?"

"Yes. There are beginning to be too many bodies, even for you."

He didn't answer. He just stared at me.

"It would be a little difficult to arrange a convincing accident for all of us, don't you think? Too many people know too much for it to be convincing."

"I don't know," he said. "A little robbery went wrong. Maybe a druggie looking for drugs. A lot of drugs here, I bet. What you got the fag on, morphine?"

Jane took in her breath suddenly, and I looked at her warningly. Beck laughed.

"So what's this deal you mentioned? Better make your pitch fast because I got a couple of guys in the street who are going to start to get curious pretty quick now."

"Actually, it's a proposition I need to make to your boss."

He looked disconcerted for a moment and then recovered. "You mean the precious Archon? You think I'm taking orders from him?"

"No, not him. I mean your partner in the Hawkins Industries deal."

Before he could answer several things happened in quick succession. The phone rang. We all sat there looking at it dumbly for a moment. I got up to answer it, and there was the loud crash of an auto accident out in the street. Immediately there followed sounds of men yelling and scuffling. Steve went to the window to look out. The second Steve's back was turned, Chuck got to his feet, and carrying his chair with his hands still tied behind the chair-back, made a bull rush at him. I yelled. Steve half turned back, but it was too late. The force of Chuck's charge drove him against the wall. I felt like my feet were stuck in molasses. I took a step to help, but by that time Beck was out of his chair, knocking me to the floor. I managed to grab a leg, but he kicked me loose with the other. By the time I had gotten to my knees he had the gun and was at the window.

"Minutemen," he said. He looked at me. "You called Reynaud?"

I didn't answer. My hand was clenched to the spot on my jaw where his foot had connected. He stepped over to shove the gun in my face.

"Answer me," he screamed.

"Yes," I said.

I tried to look at him but all I could see was the black mouth of that pistol. It seemed enormous. There was a roaring in my ears again. I could see the hairs on his finger that rested on the trigger and the tensing of the muscles as he started to shoot me. I opened my mouth to scream, but nothing came out. There was a shout, but it wasn't me. I looked again and that awful mouth had disappeared. There was a loud bang, and I was shoved to the floor. I made a feeble grab at Beck's arm, but he pulled away from me, ran to the door and was gone.

"Richard," I heard someone yelling. "Richard, don't leave me here." Then Steve was pulling me to my feet and men in dark suits were filling the room. They seemed to part, and Bob Reynaud came in the door.

"Where is he?" he asked.

"Back stairs," said Steve.

Reynaud gestured, and three of his Minutemen ran out the door again. By this time, I had managed to get to the couch. My knees felt weak, and I didn't trust myself to stand. I looked up at Steve.

"Why didn't he shoot me?"

He shook his head.

"I think he was going to. Then one of those Minuteman appeared at the door and shouted. Beck turned and shot him. Then he just ran out the door."

Two other of the Minutemen had untied Chuck and were hustling him out the door. Reynaud was standing in the middle of the room glowering. He saw me looking at him.

"So, Gordon. Once again you half deliver on your promises."

If I was still shaky from my experience, his scornful tone cured me.

"What are you talking about?" I asked. "I just promised to tell you where he was. It's not my fault that you forgot to cover the back."

He sat down in the chair that Beck had occupied only minutes before.

"No great harm done," he said. "We'll get him. We've rolled up his little band. He's on his own now. I don't think he'll get far."

"What about his men?" I asked. "What will you do with them?"

He laughed. "What? Are you concerned about them now? Well don't be. They're due for a little retraining. The love and support of their friends will convince them of the error of following false prophets. In two weeks, they'll be my loving servants again."

"What about Beck?"

His eyes narrowed. "Well, we'll have to see about him, won't we?"

He got up to leave.

"What about the police?" I asked.

"What about them?"

"What will I tell them?"

"Don't tell them anything."

"But there's been a shooting. One of your men took a bullet."

"We'll take care of him. You just clean up this place. As far as you're concerned, there was a little disturbance in the street, but you didn't see anything. Don't worry, the police won't be too inquisitive." He started to leave.

"Wait," I said. "What about our deal?"

"Oh, that." He turned back. "I give you three days to deliver Brunell. After that I do my own deal with him. I think, after this, he'll be a lot more flexible, don't you?"

"But wait. I told you where to find Beck."

"That's true, but I didn't get him. And now you can't help me any more with him. My advice to you is to get Brunell on the team."

He turned and went out the door. The phone rang again. It was Harry. I told him to come in.

Chapter XV

Jerry died that night. He never really woke up to full consciousness again. Steve and Jane kept talking to him. Sometimes he would seem to respond. Other times they were taking any communication on faith. His breathing got more and more erratic. The end came at just about three in the morning. One moment he was there, the next he was not. The next couple of days were spent in dealing with the many details that a death entails, the death notice, the cremation arrangements, the death certificate, the memorial service and the endless telephoning. I told Harry that he would be safer back East as long as Beck was still around. Mary called him a number of times, trying to persuade him to come back East as well, but he wanted to stay until the service.

The third day of Reynaud's ultimatum was the day of the memorial service, and I had no more idea about how to deal with Wilfred Brunell than I had had three days before. Jane and I took a number of drives over the three-day period and, on one of them, she asked me what I was going to do. I could only shrug. Sometimes I thought I would just leave it alone. What was it that I had to fix? I didn't think Reynaud would do anything now to try and point the finger at Harry for Renfrow's shooting. Every day that went by would make backtracking more difficult. With a confession by someone else, even a retracted one, Bonnie Hirsch would have a breeze getting Harry off. And in the end, Harry would get his inheritance. Wilfred might block releasing the trust for a long time. But all Harry would have to do would be to stay away from the RTTR, and eventually some judge would agree that the terms were satisfied and release the shares to him. Meanwhile, Wilfred and Reynaud would agree on some disposition of the RTTR shares, but what did I care about that? Wilfred might wind up controlling the shares and the company for a time, but what was that to me? Eventually, the shares would get sold to the public again, Harry would collect his inheritance, and, if he was still interested, he could take his shot at running the company. He was young yet. What difference would a few years make?

As for Beck, I doubted that he would be much harm to anyone now. Reynaud had scooped up his soldiers, and he would never take over RTTR now. His best chance was to disappear for a long time.

So, I rationalized it, and it all made perfect sense. So why couldn't I shake the feeling of depression that I had? I had a feeling that someone was still out there ahead of me. I had a sense of a job unfinished, but I had no idea how to go about finishing it.

The day of the memorial service, the dawn showed up with one of those fronts that blow in off the Pacific all winter on the West Coast. Occasionally, these fronts have the bad manners to detour so far south that they drench Los Angeles on their way to dumping a load of snow in the mountains. These occasions are reminiscent of a major snowstorm back East. Cars skid on the slick roads; traffic congests to a standstill and roads close, not with snowdrifts, but with flooding and mudslides. We were a sorry little band as we set out for the church. Steve, Jane, Harry and I all crammed into my rental car with me driving. The church was an enormous cathedral on Wilshire. I let them all out at the front door and went hunting for a parking place. It took me ten minutes to find and just a few more to dash back to the church. I entered to find that our service had been stuck back in one of the little chapels on the side. Much better than being lost in the cavern of the main part of the church, I thought. There were about fifty people there, more or less soaked by the rain. Jerry's friends, both personal and professional. The service proceeded much as Jerry had planned in that little gathering we had had in his apartment. It had been only about ten days before, but it seemed like a lifetime. We were halfway through the minister's homily. He was telling Jerry's life, just as Jerry had told it to him. I happened to look around, and I caught the eye of a familiar face. Chuck. Chuck saw that I recognized him and gave me a big grin that left me cold. I turned back to the front of the church. Why on earth would Chuck be here? Whatever the reason, I knew it was not good news for us.

The service ended, and we went on to a little reception in the back. It turned out that the church had a charming little parish house behind the main cathedral with a little yard sheltered from the Los Angeles streets by a thick hedge and a high wall. Jane had planned to have the reception on the lawn, but the rain pushed everything inside. Most of the people from the service came for coffee and remembrances. We stood with our coffee cups and looked out on the rain pelting the grass outside. I scanned the crowd, but could see no sign of Chuck. Jane was greeting and embracing a succession of Jerry's friends. Harry was engrossed in a conversation with two officious looking men from some AIDS organization in a corner. I was beginning to feel suffocated with the smell of the damp, pressed bodies in the closed room. I went to find a phone. After the usual bit of negotiation, I got Reynaud on the line.

"Gordon," he said. "I hope you're calling to say you've concluded a deal with Brunell."

"Actually no . . . ."

"Well, I don't know why else I would . . . ." he started.

"Why is Chuck out and roaming about?" I interrupted.

"Why shouldn't he be? We don't keep our members prisoners, you know. Despite the propaganda of some misguided parents and deprogramming scam artists, our members are free to come and go as they like."

"So what's he doing at Jerry Hawkins' funeral?"

"Yes, I read about that. So sad. But what did Malcolm X say about Kennedy? Chickens coming home to roost, wasn't it? Fags like Jerry who engage in those unnatural practices might expect the consequences. You do believe in consequences, don't you, Gordon?"

"Where's Beck, Reynaud?"

"Unfortunately we have been unable to find him. No matter. He's no longer a threat to me. Or to you, I shouldn't think. I'm sure he's drowning his sorrows down in some gritty little tequila bar in Mexico."

"So if he is, what's Chuck doing here?"

"I'm sure I don't know. And now I'm bored with this conversation. Please call me again only if you have good news to impart about Brunell."

With that he hung up the phone. I stood there a moment looking dumbly at the receiver. I hung it back on the wall and returned to the reception. Steve noticed me coming in the door and came over.

"What's the matter?" he asked.

"Why?"

"I don't know. You look like there's a problem."

"There is. I saw Chuck at the service. I just called Reynaud, and he doesn't seem to give a damn."

"You think Chucky just walked off that ranch?"

"I don't think anyone leaves that ranch without Reynaud's say so."

"So is Chuck back in the good graces? Or, is he still working for Beck?"

"I don't know. Reynaud seems to have lost interest in our friend Richard."

"That seems a little out of character."

"Yes. Doesn't it?"

"So what do we do?" he asked.

"I think we need to get Harry out of here. He's the one they wanted before." I looked around but could not see him. My stomach tightened with apprehension. I found Jane in a little knot of people and went over.

"Have you seen Harry?" I asked.

"Not lately."

Just then there was a commotion on the other side of the room. Someone yelled, and then a woman screamed. I started over and there was Harry, with two men on his arms, pulling him towards the door. Both of them had black ski masks, but I recognized the one nearest me. Beck. I lowered my shoulder and went for him, hitting him in the midsection. It was like running my shoulder into a brick wall. I seemed to bounce, but I knocked him loose from Harry. I got up for another run. Beck was sitting on the floor. I took a step and then saw the gun in his hand. I froze. He got up slowly. Everyone in the room seemed to be frozen in shock.

"That's it," he said. "Everyone just step aside. Nice and easy." He motioned the other guy to take Harry. Just then, Steve crossed into my vision. He was holding a gun as well. Beck saw him just as I did and swung his gun in Steve's direction. It looked to me like it was moving in slow motion. I tried to yell and charge Beck at the same time. But no sound would come, and my feet seemed to be firmly anchored in the floor as his gun slowly traversed that long arc from me to Steve. There was a loud bang and then another. Suddenly, I was yelling and moving. I wrapped my arms around Beck, but he wasn't a brick wall anymore. He just felt heavy, and he slipped from my grasp. There was a spreading red stain on his chest. There was motion in the direction of the door so I kept moving. There was a roaring sound in my ears. I couldn't tell whether it was the people yelling around me or my own blood pounding in my head. Chuck was at the door when I hit him. He bounced back off the jamb, and we both fell backwards on the floor. He turned in my arms and got those steel hands around my throat. His favorite hold, I suppose. I began to feel weak as I struggled to get oxygen into my lungs. The last thing I remember was sirens in the distance.

I came to some time later on a couch off the room where the reception had been. Jane was sitting next to me wiping my head with a damp cloth. It was not until four hours later that we were able to get out of there. Steve had been taken to the hospital. He had been shot in the shoulder, but he was all right. Apparently he and Beck had shot at the same time. Steve had the better shot, or Beck hadn't had time to line up his gun. He was dead, shot square in the middle of the chest. Chuck was in police custody. Harry had pulled him off of me and sat on his chest until the police came. A very unpleasant Los Angeles detective interviewed me for over an hour. It was all very simple I had told him. Harry was an ex-RTTR member who wanted out. Richard and Chuck had been sent to kidnap him back to the ranch so that he could be re-indoctrinated into the fold. Yes, I had met Beck before. No, I had never seen the other guy. I speculated that Steve had picked the gun up off the floor in the scuffle. My real guess was that Steve had brought the gun left by Beck in the apartment, but the cop didn't need to know about that visit. And Steve didn't need the hassle of carrying an unlicensed gun. So the bad guys must have brought it. After a while, he left me alone. When Jane and I got out of there we went to see Steve. By the time we got there he was out of surgery and sitting up in the bed, wrapped in bandages. I suggested to him that he must have found the gun in the melee, and he assured me that I was correct. Then he dozed off, and we were out in the street again. The rain was still coming down. Harry had driven us, and he picked us up at the curb. Jane got in the passenger side, and I slid in the back.

"Where to?" he asked.

"I think it's time we headed east again," I said.

"There's nothing to keep me here," said Jane. "And Harry seems to be in constant jeopardy out here."

I sat back in the seat and looked at the back of Harry's head.

"Yes, he does," I said. "But I'm beginning to think that the real threat is back East. And if we're going to take care of it, that's where we have to go."

Jane turned and looked over the seat at me. "Don't tell me you've figured out what's going on?"

"I have to think about it a little bit, but maybe I'm beginning to."

We went back to Jerry's apartment to collect our things and headed from there directly to the airport. Usually, I can sleep on the red-eye, but on this flight I sat in my seat, wide-awake, trying to figure all the angles. By the time we landed I thought I had it.

* * *

We drove from Newark to North Beach. I suggested to Harry that it might be more prudent for him to stay at my house for the moment. If nothing else, I wanted him where I could keep track of him. Mary had moved back to the Wedding Cake. Harry called her up to come over to keep him company. Jane gave me a promising little kiss and told me she was going to catch up on her sleep. I got on the phone and called a reporter friend of mine at the Asbury Park Press. I managed to catch him at home. He thought he could find the picture I remembered, and agreed to fax it to me when he went in to the office. Then I headed over to find Rich. He wasn't at the station yet, so I took a chance to head down to the diner where he usually has breakfast. I got on Ocean Avenue south, passing Norman's house on the way. I slowed to a crawl to see if I could see anything. There was a car pulling out of the driveway. It was Mary on the way to Harry. She gave me a merry little wave. I looked into the driveway, expecting it to be empty of cars, but there was a gray car parked almost out of sight. I changed my mind and turned into the driveway. I pulled up beside it. A gray Jaguar with Pennsylvania plates. Just like Wilfred's car. I parked, blocking him in. I got out and walked up to the front door. The wind swirled around in the little courtyard. I wondered if I was making a mistake. I rang the bell. No one came, and I leaned on it. Finally, I heard some noise within and Florence opened the door a crack.

"What do you want?" she asked unpleasantly. I didn't blame her. It was still not quite eight in the morning. A little early for social calls. I smiled at her.

"I would like to see Mrs. Hawkins, please."

"She's not up yet. Come back in a couple of hours." She started to close the door, but coming back in a couple of hours was not what I had in mind. I kicked the door as hard as I could. The door sprang open, and Florence went down on the hardwood floor with a bump. I stepped in and closed the door behind me.

"Are you crazy?" she was yelling. "I'm going to call the police."

"Call them," I said. "In fact, that would be a good idea. I think you'll find Chief Skowronski at the Bayside Diner down in Lavalette. Why don't you just call him there to save time?"

"You are crazy."

"Maybe. In the meantime, get Lorraine out of bed and get her butt down to the living room."

I offered my hand to help her to her feet, but she waved me off. She got up and just stood there looking at me. I moved in so that my face was close to hers.

"Did you hear what I said?" She nodded without speaking. I think she thought I really was crazy. Maybe she was right.

"Then do it." I yelled and turned on my heel to walk over to the living room. Instead of waiting at the ocean end of the room to watch the ocean, I stayed at the driveway end where I could keep an eye on Wilfred's car. I waited about twenty minutes before Lorraine appeared.

"What is the meaning of this intrusion?" she asked from behind me. I turned to look. She had come in through a door at the other end of the room. She was wearing a white robe and looked quite regal. I started to say something when I caught some movement out of the corner of my eye. I turned back. There was Wilfred skulking around the side of the house towards his car. I turned back.

"You might as well ask Wilfred to come in," I said. "He's not going to be able to go anywhere until I move my car anyway."

Her shoulders slumped, and she sat down on one of the couches. She waved a hand.

"Why don't you go and tell him yourself," she said.

I left the room and went to the front door. Florence was in the foyer, glaring at me.

"Does Mr. Brunell come often?" I asked.

She didn't answer. I opened the door and looked out. Wilfred had discovered his predicament and had his hands on his hips. I suppose he was wondering if he could retreat back to the house and safely up to Lorraine's bedroom again. He started when he heard the door open.

"Wilf," I said cheerfully. "Why don't you come in out of the cold? We have a few things to talk about, don't you think?"

For a moment he thought he could brazen it out.

"If you would move your car, I was just leaving," he said. "I just dropped some papers off for Mrs. Hawkins' signature."

He saw from my expression that I wasn't buying it.

"I . . . ." he started again and stopped. I guess he was at a loss for words at long last.

"Don't embarrass yourself any further," I said. "Come on in."

His shoulders slumped the same way Lorraine's had, and he came in the house, preceding me into the living room. He immediately joined Lorraine on the couch, and they sat there facing me together, holding hands and looking for all the world like a pair of kids caught doing something naughty. I sat down opposite them and wondered how to use the momentary advantage that their mutual embarrassment gave to me.

"How long has this been going on?" I asked.

"About six months," said Wilfred. Lorraine wouldn't look at me, but stared out the window.

"Did Norman know?"

He shrugged. "I'm not sure. I think he must have guessed."

"So his death was pretty convenient, wasn't it?"

"Look," he said. A bit of the arrogant Wilfred Brunell I knew was beginning to come out. "I'm not going to say that I shed any tears for the passing of that son-of-a-bitch. But if you're implying that I had anything to do with it, you're nuts."

"Why nuts? We know it was Richard Beck who organized the job. He was working in security for Hawkins Industries at the time. You were their main counsel. Your office was in the same building. It would have been easy to arrange. You knew Ernie Fagin too, didn't you? In fact, I'll bet you put Ernie and Norman together, didn't you?"

He didn't answer, and I knew I had him.

"So I got all three of you, Ernie, Richard and you tied up in a neat ball. A neat little plan to take over Hawkins Industries."

"That's nonsense. You've got no proof of that."

"Well, we're working on it. Did you know that the day Ernie was shot, Rich Skowronski and I were following him? We had told him what we knew, and we followed him to see where he would go with it. We thought he would go to the Hawkins Industries Building and that's just what he did. I thought he was going to report to Beck, but he didn't, did he? He reported to you. And you decided you had to shut him up. He was dead before he could get back to his office."

"That's not true. He never came to see me."

"He went right up the Hawkins Industries bank of elevators. For a long time I thought that meant he was going to see Beck, but I forgot that, by that time, you had an office there as well, didn't you? Chairman of the Board. You're the one. I got you."

He sat a moment and thought. Then a slow smile came over his face. "You don't have shit," he said. "I remember the day Ernie died. I wasn't at Hawkins Industries. I wasn't even in the city. I was on a business trip to Atlanta. I've got records and a dozen witnesses to prove it."

I sat back in my chair to think about this new piece of information. Wilfred could still have set it all up by phone. But Fagin had been upstairs for over half an hour. My feeling was that he had met with someone. And if it wasn't Brunell, I was back to Beck.

I looked back at Wilfred. "Thank you."

He looked puzzled. "What do you mean by that?"

It was time to try out my alternative explanation. I looked at Lorraine. "Did you know, Lorraine, that Richard is dead?"

She looked at me, her eyes wide. For the first time, it looked like her composure had cracked. "What?"

"That's right. Shot dead in Los Angeles trying to abduct your stepson."

She was sitting up straight now, looking at me. Wilfred sensed something was going on.

"Lorraine?" he asked. "What is it?"

"Lorraine and Richard were lovers," I said. "Weren't you Lorraine?"

"Lorraine?" asked Wilfred again. "What's he talking about?"

"Not only lovers," I went on. "But partners. My guess is that Lorraine and Richard had a little plan to take all of Norman's fortune, didn't you Lorraine?"

"No," she said. "That's not it."

"Oh, but I think it is. You be the judge, Wilf. The divorce wasn't final. Lorraine would have had a right to take her widow's share no matter what the will said. One-third wouldn't that be?"

Wilfred just nodded.

"But that wasn't good enough, was it, Lorraine? You and Richard had a plan to take it all, didn't you?"

"No. That's not . . . ."

"Sure it is. If you could get rid of that troublesome stepson, it would all go to you under the will. Tell me, Wilfred." I was just guessing now. I had no idea what the provisions of the will were. But Wilfred did. "Had Norman changed his will?"

"No," he said. "He left the shares in the company in trust to Harry. We've already been over this."

"But what if Harry died too?"

He looked at me sharply. A little of the old Wilfred was coming back. I wondered what I was missing.

"Doesn't work, Gordon," he said.

"Why not?"

"For the money to go to Lorraine, the kid would have to have died within thirty days of the old man. Otherwise it's his and, on his death, it goes to his heirs. We're past thirty days now. Your theory doesn't hold water."

I sat back to think. "So the plan failed. Richard couldn't get at the kid to kill him in time. That doesn't change the fact that that there wasn't a plan. That doesn't change the fact that Lorraine and Richard conspired to kill her husband. She still gets one-third of the estate. When the divorce went through, what would she get? What would it have been Wilfred?"

He didn't answer me. He just looked at Lorraine. Now she looked at him, her eyes filled with tears.

"Wilfred." She took both of his hands in hers. I thought I was going to puke.

"Wilfred. I did have an affair with him. But it was over, I promise you. It was over when you and I started seeing one another."

"And you never even talked about killing Norman?" I cut in.

She looked at me, angry now. "Yes, damn you. We did. Or he did. He was obsessed by it. He kept pumping me for information, even after I had ended the affair. But I never thought he would go through with it. And I had no part in it."

"That's a little hard for me to believe, Lorraine," I said. "What would be the point of going through with killing Norman if he wasn't keeping company with you any more. That doesn't make any sense."

"I don't give a damn what sense it makes. It's the truth," she said.

I looked back at Wilfred.

"That brings it back to you, Wilf."

"What are you talking about?"

"One of you is lying. The only other possibility is that you both are. Beck killed Norman. And he didn't do it just for fun. He did it to benefit someone, and you two are my main candidates."

"I think we've heard about enough of this preposterous nonsense," said Wilfred. "I think it's time for you to leave."

I held up my hands. "No problem. I'm out of here. But I would suggest that neither of you go very far. I have an idea that the police will want to talk to you."

I left them on the couch. She was crying openly, and he was holding her hands and whispering in her ear. What a great little actress, I thought to myself. She was still my main suspect, but now I had to prove it. I smiled at Florence as she glared me out the door, and I hustled to my car. I wondered if I could still catch Rich at the diner. In ten minutes I was pulling into the parking lot. The wind had increased, and snow flurries were starting to appear out of the gunmetal sky.

I found Rich in a corner booth with a view of the bay eating scrambled eggs and bacon.

"You look like shit," he said. "Sit down and have a cup of coffee."

I slid into the booth opposite him.

"Found Beck yet?" I asked.

"No luck. He seems to have gone to ground."

I laughed. "Yes, I think that's literally true."

He took a bite of his egg and looked at me narrowly.

"Why don't you tell me about it?"

I started with California and brought him up to my interview with the two lovebirds. By this time, he had finished his breakfast, and we were both on second cups of coffee. He sipped at his and watched the wind swirl the falling snow outside the window.

"Well, smart guy," he said. "What do you suggest now? You've managed to tip off your main suspects and left them alone to get their stories straight."

I shrugged. "If they were in it together with Beck, they've had plenty of time to get their stories straight. If not, you just need to play one against the other. My guess is that they're both driven by greed more than love. One of them will rat the other out."

"Yeah," he said, gloomily. "What will happen is that the guilty one will rat out the innocent one. It will be a mess. What I need is a little leverage."

"Well, maybe I can provide that as well."

"Tell me, counselor. Don't hold it all in."

"Where's Jacobsen?"

"In jail down in Tom's River. He's not going anywhere."

"You remember he mentioned seeing a woman with Richard?"

"Yeah."

"Well, we know Lorraine was having an affair with him, but she says it was over. Suppose the woman was Lorraine. Wouldn't that tie her into this nicely?"

"It would indeed."

"Well, let's go. I got a reporter friend of mine faxing me a picture from the society page of Lorraine. Let's go show it to Rolf."

That got Rich moving. We stopped by my office to find that the fax had come in. The quality of a fax of a newspaper photo several years old is pretty lousy, but Lorraine and Norman were both easily recognizable. They were smiling at the camera at some long forgotten charity event, and he had his arm around her. I showed it to Rich.

"Duplicitous bitch," I said.

He looked at it closely.

"It'll do. Let's go."

He drove, and neither of us said anything on the twenty-minute drive to Tom's River. He had me wait in the reception area, such as it was, while he disappeared in the back to make the arrangements. It was another twenty minutes before he opened the door and beckoned me into the back. He led me up a flight of stairs and down a grimy hall to an interview room. Rolf was already there, sitting at a table looking belligerent.

"When am I getting out of here?" he demanded. "I told you all I know. I didn't do anything wrong."

Rich slid into the chair opposite him.

"Well, Rolf, some complications have come up. First we think you haven't told us the whole story."

"What do you mean?"

"You've done pretty good, Rolf," said Rich. "But before we clear this, I only have one thing more."

"What's that?" he asked suspiciously.

"You said when you met Beck, he had a woman with him. Do you think you could recognize her?"

"I don't know, maybe."

"Tell us where you met."

"It was at the Brielle Grille. We had already met before on the boat and agreed on the charter. I wanted the first installment in cash before

I did anything. He said to meet him at the bar that night. I went over, and he was drinking at the bar. We got one of those side booths and he gave me the envelope. I counted the money and it was all there."

"Where was the woman?" I asked.

"She wasn't there yet. When we were done, he told me to beat it. I was curious, so I waited for him out in the parking lot to see where he'd go. But he didn't come out. I slipped back in through the kitchen. He wasn't in the bar anymore. I was about to leave when I spotted him in one of the booths in the dining room. He was with this broad, and it was like they couldn't keep their hands off each other. I stayed and watched for a little, and then I left."

"So, do you think you could recognize the broad?" I asked.

"Yeah, probably. The light was dim, but I got a good look at her. She was right across the room."

"Is this her?" I pulled out the newspaper clipping and spread it in front of him. My throat felt tight. He looked at it quickly.

"Naa, that's not her."

I felt a wave of defeat spread through me.

"Are you sure? Take your time."

"I don't need to take my time. This ain't the one. Isn't this Hawkins with her? No she's too old to be . . . ."

Suddenly he picked up the clipping and looked at it more closely. "Wait a minute."

"What?" I asked, my throat tightening.

"That ain't her," he said. "But she's in the picture."

"What?" I asked again, stupidly.

"Yeah," he said putting the picture down and pointing with his forefinger. "This is her here in the back."

I looked and just a little behind Norman and Lorraine, there was another couple. The man was obscured, but the woman was Mary.

"Mary," I said. "Damn it. It's Mary."

"You mean little Norman's wife?" asked Rich.

"Yes, little Norman's treacherous, greedy little wife." I looked up at Rich in horror. "And she's with him now at my house back at North Beach."

"Let's go," said Rich. We bolted out the door, with Rolf shouting in our wake about getting him out of there. I found a phone to call. I got Jane on the line.

"Jane, where's Harry?"

"Peter," she said. "What's wrong?"

I realized I must have sounded panicked and slowed down.

"I need to speak to Harry."

"He's gone out."

I took a deep breath.

"Gone out where?"

"He and Mary have taken your boat to go fishing."

"Fishing?" I shouted. "There's a snowstorm out there. What idiot would want to go fishing?"

"Slow down. Mary just thought it would be fun. A little time for them to be alone now that he's no longer in danger. I thought it was a little weird. If they didn't want to do it with me in the house, what are motels for?"

"How long ago did they leave?"

"Pete, you're scaring me. What's the matter?"

"How long?" I shouted.

"Only about twenty minutes ago."

"OK, hang on there. We'll be there in about twenty minutes."

I hung up.

"Let's go," I said.

"They've gone out in a boat?" he asked as we ran out the door to get his car. "In this mess?"

"What better? Another unfortunate accident."

He started the car, and we took off down the road with his siren wailing. He called his office on the radio and asked them to request Coast Guard help from Manasquan.

"What boat did they take?" he asked me.

"The Grady-White. She was tied up at the house. They're probably around and through the inlet by now."

Rich conveyed the information to be relayed to the Coast Guard. The wind had risen some more and the snow was swirling heavily now. Visibility out on the ocean would be a matter of yards.

"So why are we hurrying?" he asked. "What are we going to do? Watch from the beach?"

"We're going out to find them."

"In what? I thought they took your boat."

"We've got Norman's lobster boat tied up at the dock as well. We'll take that."

"Oh great. I'm sure that thing will speed along at all of twelve knots. What's your boat do? Thirty? Forty? And how are we going to find them in this mess?"

"We find them with radar," I said. "Fortunately there won't be a lot of targets out there. And I don't think they'll go too far or too fast in the sea that will have built up. They won't be doing any thirty knots today."

He snorted. "They'll be going a lot faster than we will."

He was silent for about five minutes as we weaved through the traffic north on Ocean Avenue.

"How do you figure it?" he asked.

"Like anything else, it seems pretty easy once you've figured it out. And I should have figured it out a long time ago."

"So tell me."

"Norman left all of the shares in the company to his son. It was to be put in a trust pending Harry's separation from the RTTR, but eventually he would have gotten it. But the lawyers always put in a contingency. If the beneficiary pre-deceases, then plan B goes into effect. Plan B would have shoveled a lot more of the stock Lorraine's way. Probably all of the stock. But what usually happens is that there is a thirty-day provision. Wilfred reminded me of it today. If the beneficiary dies within thirty days, he's treated as if he predeceased. It's designed to cover a common accident where one of the victims lingers in the hospital."

"Yeah, I get the point. So for Lorraine to benefit, he's got to have died at the same time as the old man or shortly after him."

"Right. That's what I should have realized. If Lorraine was behind the plan, Harry goes into the water with the old man. They both wash up on the beach in a common accident. But with Mary, it's a different story. She's got to prove the old man is dead, but her loving husband has to survive for at least another thirty days. So Beck pulls Harry off the boat and then sets him up for the Renfrow shooting. For Richard it kills two birds. He gets to discredit Reynaud, and the kid is put on ice."

Rich looked at me. "So you think after the thirty days runs out, the kid has an accident in the shower in prison."

"You got it. But my deal with Reynaud messed all that up. Harry got out. But now the thirty days passed and the way's clear for Richard to just knock him off. With Harry dead, there'd be no excuse for Wilfred to hold the money in the anti-RTTR trust any more. And the money had clearly passed to the kid and then on to his loving wife."

I slammed my hand against the dashboard. "And it's dollars to donuts that Mary and Beck are the mystery buyer accumulating more shares. With RTTR money I bet. They get the shares they bought, the RTTR shares when Richard takes that over and all Harry's shares. They put the company up for auction and there's one great big payday at the end of the line."

"But now the plan gets screwed up again, right?" said Rich. "Harry comes home from the coast all full of himself with stories of how the great Richard Beck is dead and gone. And our dear Mary is now without a partner. Now she can't get at the RTTR shares. But the good news is she still can get Harry's, and she doesn't have to split it with anyone. All she has to do is arrange an accident for her husband."

"That's right, and I hope we're not too late."

By this time we were coming into North Beach. Rich wheeled his car into a side street and went flying the last two blocks. He pulled in front of my house, and we ran around the side. "Firefly" was there at the dock, engine running. Jane was at the wheel waving us to come on. I ran down the dock.

"I've got to get some foul weather gear and warm clothes," I yelled.

"All aboard," she yelled. "Come on."

"For Rich, too?"

"For Rich, too. Will you come on?" She revved up the engine to give emphasis to her words. I could see that the lines were all loose except for one springline. Rich jumped in the boat. I hesitated.

"You can't go."

"Get in the boat, damn it," she yelled. "You're wasting time."

I jumped in the cockpit, Rich let go the springline, and she backed the boat out of the slip, turned the bow and headed north towards the inlet. Rich and I shrugged into the clothes she had brought.

"How big of a lead do they have?" I asked.

"About forty minutes now."

Rich got on the radio and called the Coast Guard. They had already dispatched a forty-five footer from Manasquan. An eighty-foot cutter was inbound and would be in the area in an hour. They hadn't picked up any targets yet.

"Try to get him on the radio," I suggested.

Rich put it on channel 16 and started to call Harry. There was no answer, but he kept at it. I started our own radar. Visibility was so bad; we would need it just to get ourselves out to sea. We cleared the inlet before I got a target. It showed up about two miles southwest of the sea buoy. I gave Jane the bearing, and we headed towards it. Rich radioed the Coast Guard cutter. They had seen it as well and were on the way. It takes ten minutes to go two miles at twelve knots. The next ten minutes were probably the longest of my life. The snow started to taper off when we were half way there. By the time we were on the position, the visibility had improved to about one hundred yards. Rich saw the boat first. He shouted and pointed off the port bow. At first I could see nothing and then a ghostly shape appeared in the murk. Then it was her, dead in the water, rolling in the waves. There was one figure in the stern waving at us frantically. Just one figure, Mary. Jane drove the boat roughly alongside, going from full ahead to full astern in a roar.

I jumped into the boat and grabbed Mary by the arm.

"Where's Harry?" I demanded. She was crying and waving hysterically.

"He fell over the side." She grabbed me by the arm and pointed towards the water. "I tried to pull him in, but I couldn't. Then the boat just drifted away from him. I lost him in the snow. You've got to find him."

"How long ago?"

"I don't know. A couple of minutes."

"What's the matter with the boat?"

"I don't know. It just stopped."

"Did you go anywhere after he went over?"

"No. I just drifted. Can you find him?" The last was in the most pitiable, heart-rending tone of voice. I pulled her roughly to the rail.

"Get in with Rich."

I turned and went to see if I could start the engine. It cranked right over. I felt someone, and Jane was at my shoulder.

"Is there a chance?" she said.

"Not a chance in hell. I doubt he could last three minutes in this water."

"Sure he can. He's got on your wetsuit."

"What?"

"He said he had no interest in going out in the cold and wet no matter how much Mary pestered. I showed him your suit, and he was delighted. He figured Mary would get cold pretty quickly and demand they come back after about twenty minutes."

"She had a little more serious intent," I said. I fired up the engine, and waved to Rich to go east while we looked inshore. "Did she know he had it on?"

"No, that was the point. He'd be warm, and she'd want to break it off and come back in. He thought it was a great joke."

I looked around. There was nothing to be seen but gray sea and white out from the snow. The visibility was closing in again.

"It won't matter," I said. "We won't be able to find him anyway. Who knows how long ago she really dropped him or where she took the boat afterwards? I reached up and pushed a button on an instrument on the dash. It was a reflex action, and I thought nothing of it for an instant. Then I froze, staring at the instrument. It was a GPS navigational instrument. What I had done with my reflex action was plug in a waypoint that would permit me to return to this very spot if I needed to do that in the search pattern. Harry was no rookie as far as boats were concerned. If he was going offshore in bad visibility he might have left a waypoint at the sea buoy, or he might be as obsessive as I was. He might have left a trail of breadcrumbs all along his track. I went into the memory, and there it was. The last waypoint that had been plugged into the system was about a mile to the north. I shouted and shoved the throttle all the way forward.

"Hang on," I yelled. I got Rich on the radio with one hand while trying to avoid the largest of the seas with the other. Mostly, we just bounced from sea to sea with the prop out of the water as much as it was in. Rich acknowledged that he was following, but I had lost him in the swirls of snow. It only took us three or four minutes to find the spot. Then we started a slow search pattern downwind. How far could he have drifted? And how long had he been in the water now? Jane was up on the bow straining her eyes into the snow. The minutes ticked by. Five, and then ten. We never would have found him except that the snow let up and the visibility went up to over a hundred yards again. And there was something in the water. And then Jane was yelling and pointing. I called on the radio, and the Coast Guard cutter answered. The eighty-footer was just a mile away. I gunned the boat up next to him, and Jane grabbed him by the collar.

"Are we too late?" I asked breathlessly. I shut down the engine and came over to help her. He hung lifelessly from her grasp. I took a hold as well and, on the count of three, we dragged him right over the rail and into the boat. He lay in the boat looking as blue as I have ever seen anyone. But he was breathing.

"What do we do?" I asked Jane. "Get him out of that wetsuit? Or leave him in it?"

"Get him out and get blankets around him," she said.

By this time Rich had come up and gotten a line on us. And I could hear the whine of the big turbines that were driving the Coast Guard cutter. Someone was at my shoulder again, and I looked up expecting Jane. It was Mary. She was crying again. She knelt down to cradle Harry's head.

"Will he be all right?" she sobbed. "Tell me he'll be all right."

I smiled cynically. "It's good news, Mary. I think he'll be fine."

"Thank God," she said, and stroked his brow lovingly. Then there was a jolt, and the side of a cliff appeared right next to us. Before I could move, three sailors jumped aboard with a stretcher and a medical corpsman was elbowing me out of the way. He felt Harry and checked his pulse. Then he motioned to the others and, in a ballet of quiet competence, they strapped Harry onto the stretcher and swung him aboard. I stopped the corpsman.

"How will he be?"

He shrugged. "Too early to tell. The main thing is to get him warmed up. It's too windy to risk the helicopter, but we'll have him at the hospital inside of an hour." He looked down at my hand. "That is if you let me go."

"Wait," said Mary. "I have to go with him. He's my husband." She started towards the rope ladder that had been draped over the side of the cutter. She didn't get very far. Rich grabbed a wrist and snapped a handcuff on it. With a quick motion he grabbed the other hand behind her back and captured the other wrist.

"I think not," he said.

She turned on him in a fury.

"Have you lost your mind? I have to go with him."

Rich smiled. "Mary Hawkins," he said formally. "You are under arrest for the murder of Norman Hawkins, Sr. and the attempted murder of Norman Hawkins, Jr."

Mary took a step back in shock and surprise. As Rich went on to read Mary her rights, her eyes changed and an expression of hate came over her face. Just for an instant, but there it was. Together Rich and I deposited her back on the lobster boat.

With a whine revving to a scream the cutter left us and headed towards Manasquan. It got to full speed in the space of a few boat lengths and disappeared into a snow shower, its razor bow slicing the seas like a knife. Rich put Mary down below on the lobster boat. Without anyone holding them, the boats started to drift apart. He leaned over the rail and yelled at us.

"You guys OK?"

I looked at Jane, and she smiled at me. I waved at Rich and he waved back, turned to the wheel and turned the boat to Cranberry Inlet.

"So it's over," Jane said to me.

"No," I said. "It's just beginning." I felt exhausted, but it was a happy exhaustion. "Annie's still in the house."

She came up and put her arms around my neck. "Actually, she's not. When she heard Beck was dead she packed up her stuff and went back to Philadelphia."

I turned to the wheel and put the boat back on a plane to the inlet and home.

Epilogue

The next morning I woke up to the smell of bacon cooking. There was no one in the bed next to me, so I threw on some jeans and went down. Jane was in the kitchen. I went up to give her a kiss.

"Go sit down. I'm feeling very domestic."

"How's Harry?" We had called the night before, and they had said he was doing fine, but discouraged visitors. That had been all right with us.

"I talked to him. Rich has already been in to get a statement."

"Mary pushed him in?"

"That's what he said. She got him to look at some imagined problem with the propeller. He was leaning over the transom, and she just kicked him in the water, gunned the boat and left him there."

"That's some determined lady."

"Yeah, poor Harry. He never really had a chance with her, did he?"

There was a knock on the door. I went to answer it. I was expecting to see Rich. It wasn't Rich. It was Dave Stockard.

"Dave," I said. "You're back."

"Actually, I've been back for over a week, but we seem to keep missing each other."

"Ahh, well I've been traveling around a little."

"So I hear. Mind if I come in, and maybe you can tell me about it."

"Oh, sure. Come in and have some breakfast."

"Breakfast I've had, but a cup of coffee would be fine."

I introduced him to Jane, and we sat down at the table. I spent the next hour telling the story as it had unfolded since I had first consulted him over the phone.

"What are you going to do now?" he asked when I had finished.

I shrugged. "I don't know. I thought I could use the leverage of Lorraine's involvement to get a deal out of Wilfred. Since it turns out Lorraine wasn't involved, I'm not sure I can do anything. It's a stand-off."

"Maybe not. Wilfred called me last night. I think he's ready to deal."

"Why would he be ready to deal? I've got nothing to offer him."

"Well, he doesn't see it that way. It seems that he hasn't been exactly candid with you."

I sat up, suddenly interested. "Not candid, how?"

"Well, it seems that Norman and Lorraine's divorce and property settlements were all signed and sealed. The only thing was that the order hadn't come through from the court yet."

"But why would he try to mislead me about that? It only led to me to believe that Lorraine was behind the murder."

"He didn't know that the order had been signed until yesterday."

Jane laughed. "Don't tell me that he'd developed his relationship with Lorraine because he thought she would get one-third of the estate? And now she's not? What a letdown for the old bastard."

Dave smiled. "Let's not try too delve to deeply into his motivation. He says he plans to marry Lorraine as soon as he can."

"So, what wasn't he candid about?" I asked. "If he just found out about the court's order yesterday."

"What he's concerned about is that Norman did change his will."

"He did?"

"Yes, he left some of the company stock to Jane here."

"To me?" asked Jane, incredulously.

"Yes. It's only about three percent, but it's several million dollars."

"But it's shares that he can't control through the RTTR trust," I said. "So Wilf is getting a little nervous. Lorraine no longer has any shares he can count on, and the trust shares will be less than he thought."

"Yes."

"So what's his deal?"

"He'll agree to the deal with Reynaud, and he'll agree to release Harry's shares from the RTTR trust."

"What's in it for him?"

"He stays as Chairman for five years. Harry gets to be a board member, and Jane gets another seat. They'll continue the search for a CEO, but they won't pick one that's objectionable to the family."

"Why should we agree to that?" I said.

"I asked him the same thing. He asked me if I really thought Harry was in a position to take over a major public corporation. He thought no, but with his support, Harry might be able to do so in five to ten years."

I looked at Jane. She shrugged. "As a prospective shareholder of Hawkins Industries, I'd have to agree. Harry's just twenty-five and, face it, he's been a member of a cult for the past two years. What kind of preparation is that?"

Dave coughed. "Actually, Brunell said something very similar."

"I don't like it," I said. "Brunell gets just what he's been after the whole time."

"That may be true," said Dave. "But it's not as if he might not get it anyway. He's still too strong to take on in a proxy fight."

"He'd win it now," I said. "But he wouldn't have any five year guarantee. And I can break the trust in the meantime."

"He is a capable guy," said Dave. "You ought to consider the concept of having him with you rather than against you."

I looked at Jane. "What do you think?"

"I think we do the deal on one condition."

"What's that?"

She turned to Dave. "Pete goes on the board as well. Then we'll do it."

"What about Harry?" asked Dave.

"He'll agree," said Jane. "Will Wilfred go along with Pete on the board?"

Dave smiled. "He won't like it, but I think I can get him to agree. Good," he said, getting up. "I'll go take care of the details."

"One more thing," said Jane.

"What's that?" he asked.

"Pete's taking a vacation."

"He is?" asked Dave. "He just started work two months ago."

"I know. And he hasn't done too badly, has he? He's already brought in a major client."

"Hawkins Industries?"

"Exactly, I'm sure there's plenty of legal work to go around, and who's in a better position to pick it up?"

"I see. Would it be too much to ask where he's going?"

She was looking in my eyes as she answered. "Oh, he's going on a little boat trip. A certain lobster boat needs to be taken to Florida. And the prospective new owner needs some help taking it there."

I don't really remember, but I suppose that Dave let himself out.

The End